HOUGHTON MIFFLIN
COMPANY
2 PARK ST., BOSTON

take pleasure in presenting
you with this review copy
and ask that you please send
them two clippings of your
notice.

Price $3.75
Publication date

Mar. 5

The

KEAN LAND

and Other Stories

BY JACK SCHAEFER

The
KEAN LAND

and Other Stories

JACK SCHAEFER

HOUGHTON MIFFLIN COMPANY BOSTON

The Riverside Press Cambridge

1 9 5 9

To Jon
—*and about time*

Contents

Contents

The

KEAN LAND

and Other Stories

The Kean Land

*

It is a small city in western Colorado. The main business section is downstream about a mile and a half where the railroad
crosses the river. This is upstream where the suburban area
crowds along both banks pushing on up the valley. Here, on
the left bank, between the valley highway and the river, out
of place, incongruous in the midst of closely built homes and
street-corner stores and service stations and housing developments, is an oasis of clean uncluttered fields and woodlot, a
farm caught, surrounded, imprisoned by the expanding city
yet still complete, intact in its own quiet integrity. It has a
small barn and a low flat-roofed building that was once a
feeding shelter for cattle and a small house, half original log
cabin, half frame addition.

   On the porch of the addition sits an old man. He sits relaxed on an old rocker in heavy old work shoes and faded levis
and once-bright flannel shirt. His huge old frame, once power-
fully muscled, is now lean and gaunt with age but his old eyes
glow with an ageless vitality. He is talking to a younger man,
to a writer of tales of the American West that was and is no
more.

So JEFF MARTIN put you onto me. I haven't seen Jeff
in eight-ten years since he moved away but a friend of
Jeff's is a friend of mine and you can drive a nail on that.
Maybe I'd better apologize for speaking so sour when you

pulled in here. I thought you were another of those billy-
be-damned real estate sharpers. Three of them already
this week. They keep raising the ante. Can't seem to
pound into their heads price doesn't mean a thing, I'm
just plain not selling.

Sure, they'd like to get hold of this piece. One hundred
sixty acres good land. What would they do with it? Slap
together a couple hundred maybe more of those silly modern shacks they call ranchhouses a real rancher wouldn't
live in and make a lot of money which seems to be the most
important thing anybody can do nowadays. That's progress. So they say. They've been putting the squeeze on
me these last years, specially since this last boom started.
Raised my taxes, twice. Zoned the section so I had to get
rid of the cows. The horses too so I have to use a tractor.
But I raise some garden stuff and take hay off the fields
and with what I've got in the bank I make out. No one
but me to worry over anyway. The kids are all grown.
Getting kids of their own. Scattered from here to breakfast and all doing all right. They don't feel about this
place the way I do and no reason they should but all the
same they say stick to it, dad, if that's what you want and
try a little buckshot on those real estate boys and if you
need any bail money just holler. I promised Lettie, that
was my wife, I wouldn't sell, I'd keep it like this to the
finish and there wasn't any need for that promising because I'd always felt the way she did anyway. So I'm keeping it. When I'm laid under, the land grabbers can bid
themselves silly over it and there'll be a nice chunk of
cash out of it to be split among the kids and I won't be
around to see what happens to the place . . .

So Jeff told you there's a story in me, in my hanging on
here. Well, yes, yes there is. About this place, yes. About

how I came to be living here, in this house, the old part
there first of course. But the real story goes way back and
was over and done before I moved out here. I don't figure
in it much. I was just around and saw it happen and didn't
do much of anything that mattered myself except once
when I unlocked the jail door down in town and maybe
if I'd known what that meant I wouldn't have done it.

I haven't talked to anybody about what happened back
then since Lettie died, that'll be four years this fall. Nobody to talk to. The kind of folks crowding in around
here now aren't interested in the old days. Too busy making money or trying to and tearing up and down that highway there in cars that aren't ever full paid for because of
always being turned in on new ones and worrying about
meeting installments on all the billy-be-damned gadgets
people think they have to have nowadays cluttering their
houses and getting in the way of decent living. They think
me a cracked crotchety old fool. Much as say so. Maybe I
am — from their side of the fence. I'll say this much, in
this country a man's still got the right to be cracked and
crotchety if he wants to. But try to tell folks like that how
it all was and why I'm keeping this farm and they just
plain wouldn't get it.

Maybe you would. Seems Jeff Martin thinks you would.
But I'm warning you, it isn't pretty. The right and wrong
of it's hard for some to see straight. If you do anything
with it you can fix the words up some, unravel them out
where I get tangled. But don't you go doctoring what
happened any. The trouble with you writing men is you
like to have things go along neat and fitting in together
the way they don't in real living. Trouble is you like to
have things too fancy, twist them around so they work out
slick in the end the way plenty times they just plain don't.

I won't pretty this any. I'll give it to you straight the only way I can which is telling about me and what I saw happen . . .

I grew up back east in Nebraska, back in the flat country. My folks had a farm there and I was their only kid. Something happened to my mother when I was born and she couldn't have any more. That didn't slow her down in other ways though. The land was good being a piece my father had to buy because by time he came along there all the public land was gone and he went a heavy mortgage to get it but it was kind of far from the nearest settlement so we were to ourselves a lot. About all I can remember clear when I was a boy other than working twelve-fourteen hours a day when school wasn't on and I'd be hiking the miles to it is those two, my father and my mother, fighting, arguing. Over just about anything any time but mostly over me. I was good size from the start and my father figured since I was all he'd have he'd get all the work he could out of me. He believed in work anyway, always said it was the best medicine for any human ailment. Mother figured the opposite. I was all she'd have and so she was bound determined to make something of me and her idea of something was an educated man. Less work and more learning was her stand. The two of them hammered away at each other all the time, thinking up arguments and throwing them at each other. They'd get so hot over it I'd be out working with my father and see him throw down whatever was in hand and go stomping into the house and I'd know he'd thought up a new argument and was hurrying to try it on her. I was near full grown before I understood that was how they liked it, how they kept some spice and tang in a hard life. My father had a big voice and

when he got going he could shout her down but all the
same I noticed it was my mother usually had her way.
She had her way the year I hitched rides over into Illinois
with a bank draft in my pocket and to Galesburg and en-
rolled in Knox College.

I can't say I enjoyed that year though it started me reading some as I've done off and on ever since and I expect
I learned plenty. Had to or be dropped from classes and
my mother wouldn't like that. But I was big and clumsy
and fresh off the farm with only spotty schooling behind
me and I didn't fit in with the others. Didn't specially
want to. I never was what you'd call social-minded. More
I saw of the students others looked up to because they
had a little money and more I listened to some of the silly
guff handed out by la-de-da teachers in their town clothes
and their party manners, the more I kept thinking about
my father back there on the farm who'd never had a full
decent suit in his life and had to read following the words
with a finger and spelling them out and did two men's
work every day and got peeved at himself because he
couldn't do more and still found time to go stomping into
the house and show my mother what he thought of her
by arguing and shouting her down and ending up doing
what she wanted after all. I was about ready to quit anyway, near the end of that year, when the letter came from
a neighbor there was cholera back home.

I took a train far as I could and hired a horse the rest of
the way but even so I was too late. They were both gone
when I got there. Already buried because people around
were frantic over the cholera and got rid of bodies fast as
they could. That was when I found out the two of them
had pushed the mortgage on the farm up to the limit to
get me that bank draft. The sharper who held the paper

had already stepped in and foreclosed. I checked and found he'd done it the day they were buried. Maybe I could have stirred trouble but I was too hit to give a damn. I was seventeen-eighteen at the time. I had some money left from that draft. And I had a note from my father he'd given that neighbor for me the last day. It was just a misspelt scrawl in the squiggly squarish printing which was the only way he could write. I've still got it tucked away somewhere. I didn't pay much attention to it right off but it turned out the best thing he could have left me. *dere son — bruther scott wil help — in collerado*

As I say, I didn't pay much attention to that at first except to tuck it away in my purse as a keepsake. I wasn't interested in asking anybody for any help or chasing down any relative let alone an uncle I hadn't ever seen but only heard about some the few times my father had talked about his folks that he'd split with when he sided with the union in the Civil War. I just wanted to be let alone and to hell with the whole stinking world so I drifted off by my lonesome and down through Kansas and knocked around the panhandle and over into New Mexico.

I had my full growth already in those days and looked older than I was. People took me for a grown man so I tried acting like one and began drinking more than I could hold right and bucking smalltime faro games. Didn't take long before I was flat broke. I kicked around picking up odd jobs, cadging handouts between, never staying long any one place, then I got into freighting, heavy hauling out of Santa Fe with the ox teams. I could do that. One thing I had in those days was muscle. Not much sense but plenty muscle. I'd sign on for a trip out and back and when we'd pull in again and be paid I'd quit and loaf around till the money went and go back and sign on again. Freighters in those days were a tough crew. A man who couldn't hold his quart a day and bust a barrel with one wallop of his fist didn't have a chance with them. They'd work up a fight and take a saloon apart just for the fun of it. Me, I'd hold back some because I wanted to make my pay-money last a while between jobs but then I'd get to feeling low again and I'd join in the drinking and likely the fighting too and wake up next morning in a back lot with a busted head or in jail for busting someone else's head.

It was one of those times, in the Santa Fe jail I mean, that I got to thinking. There I was coming twenty-two and not doing so well by myself any way you figured. I wasn't taking either my father's or my mother's side in that endless arguing they used to do. I was working, yes, off and on. But I wasn't working the way my father had, steady and slugging it through and aiming at some goal which for him had been paying off the mortgage and owning his land outright for once and building up his farm and though he never got there it was always there ahead of him and he was aiming at it. I wasn't aiming at anything. There wasn't even anything I felt like aiming at except maybe thumbing my nose at existence in general. And I sure wasn't learning much the way my mother had wanted me to — that is, not the kind of things she had in mind. Thinking of those two reminded me of that note. I didn't really fit where I was like I hadn't at Knox and I didn't have any notion where I would. That note was a hunch and I might as well play it. Soon as I could pull out I headed up here into Colorado looking for my uncle Scott.

I didn't know much about him except he was a few years younger than my father and like my father had headed west after the Civil War broke up the family back in the Kentucky hills. Not much on size, my father said once, and not much use with a plow but all the same a gol-damned good fighting man when the trouble came even if he did join the rebs and had to be licked. Seeing that they'd been on opposite sides in the war and kept going different ways after and neither one was a letter-writing man, how my father had managed to keep any track of him is something I never have figured out.

I didn't even know where he was in the state or if he was still around but it didn't take long to find out. I headed up Taos way and over the line, following the Grande upstream asking questions. Right away at Del Norte I hit a man who'd heard of him and sent me on towards this Mesa country. I kept on, asking my ques-tions, and when I got up this way I was surprised to find how well known he was. I was surprised another way too. I'd say I was looking for Scott Hammon and people would stare at me quick and sharp and check me over before they'd talk. After a while I figured what they were doing. They were checking did I pack a gun. I didn't and when they saw that they'd loosen some. But they wouldn't say much, just send me on to the next place heading here.

That's how it was when I reached this valley. There wasn't much here then, just a little settlement that was hardly even a real town yet, just a stopping-off place where a couple stage lines crossed and some stores and a few saloons and a blacksmith shop had sprung up to take care of people from the ranches scattered about and those who had come into the state in the mining-boom days and prospected around and got sense enough to quit that dream-chasing and settled here because it was nice coun-try. No, there wasn't much here then — except the things that made it nice country. I hadn't realized how much I'd been missing the feel of good growing earth under my feet down in the dry sandy areas till I got up here where the valleys were wide and green and had trees that were trees not twisty prickly little runts. It wasn't flat and dull like over east in the part of Nebraska I'd known. Lift your head any time and you'd see the mountains ranging off into the distance telling you to stand tall with rock in your spine the way they did. It was my kind of country. It's still the same kind but it isn't the same any more. Look out there and the mountains are still all around, still standing tall with real rock thrusting through. But about everywhere in between, like here in this valley, there's the mess and clutter and meanness and littleness and frittering around that somehow blots out most of the decent when too many people get crowding together. But that's a side trail, not what I started to tell you . . .

As I say, I finally came drifting up here. I dropped off the stage I'd hooked a ride on about where the bank building is now down there in the center. It was along mid morning. First person I saw was a gent wearing a storekeeper's apron leaning against a hitching rail soaking up sun. I asked my question and he took his time looking me over and pointed at a two-story building across the road and sitting back about a hundred feet. It was fairly wide with a single doorway in the middle and a platform running clear across the front that could have been called a porch only it didn't have a roof. I went over and up on the platform. The door was open and I looked in. A hall ran straight back through and around the stairway leading up and to another door at the back. I stepped into the hall and there was a doorway on each

side of me. I picked the one on the right and looked in
and saw a big room, the length of the building back, fixed
up for a meeting place and makeshift courtroom. No one
was there. I turned around to try the other doorway and
saw a sign tacked up over it: Sheriff Office. The door was
ajar and I pushed it further and saw a small room with an
old desk and a couple chairs and another door, standing
open, leading to whatever was behind. This room too
was empty and I was wondering whether to push in further when I heard my father's voice coming through that
open inner doorway. It was my father's voice, the same
flat tone with the lingering trace of Kentucky drawl, only
it wasn't because it was a bit sharper, had more of an edge.
"Sobered up, eh? Prove it. Walk that chalk line."

I stepped quiet over to that inner doorway and looked
through and there he was. He was standing about eight
feet in with his back to me and just like that as I saw him
first is still how I remember him best and I knew him at
once and why people were careful talking about him because there was a big handle-worn forty-five hanging in
an oiled old holster at his side and he was just as my father had said, not much on size, but the bare sight of him,
just the back of him, standing there straight with a kind
of military erectness and a plain completeness within himself told with no mistake he was a goldamned good fighting man in any kind of trouble no matter what side he
might be taking.

It was a fair-sized room he was in, the rest of that side
of the building behind the little office. The back half of
it was rigged for a jail with bars across and a partition in
the middle making two cells. He was facing the one on
the left and in there was a scrubby mean-looking man
concentrating in a sort of silly mad earnestness on putting

one foot after the other along a chalk line on the floor. This one was facing towards me. When his head came up he saw me and in the instant my uncle Scott was aware and was around, checking me over. He didn't know who I was or anything about me but in that one look he knew I was just a big young one and harmless. "Have a chair," he said. "Be with you in a minute." Somehow doing what he said seemed a good notion and I backed off and sat on a chair by the front window and I heard a lock rattling in the inner room and then the mean-looking man came in and stood scowling and my uncle followed and went to the old desk and pulled open a drawer. He took a gun out of it and walked over and dropped it in the man's holster and stepped back and stood still with his hands hanging limp and easy at his sides. "You did some blowing last night," he said. "About what you'd do when you sobered and had your gun again. Well, you're sober and you've got it."

The man stood rigid all over like he was frozen and couldn't move. His throat worked some and he got his voice out. "Quit it, Hammon. That was just the whiskey talking."

"Well, then," my uncle Scott said. "I can't think of a single reason why you ought to stay around this town any more. Can you?"

The man took a deep breath. "No," he said.

"Right," my uncle Scott said. "Your horse is out back. It's a good day for traveling."

The man turned and faded through the outer door and my uncle went over and sat down behind the desk and looked at me. "Well, bub, what's on your mind?"

I gulped some and didn't know how to begin. "I'm Ben," I said. "Ben Hammon."

He just kept looking at me in that steady way of his. "John's boy?"

"Yes," I said.

He studied me some more. His voice was careful, not showing anything. "How is John doing these days?"

"He's dead," I said.

My uncle Scott's eyes shifted and he was looking past me, out the window. "When?"

"Four years ago. He and mother. Cholera."

My uncle Scott looked out that window what seemed a long time. Then he was looking at me again. "What are you doing here?" I fumbled in my mind and couldn't figure how to say what I wanted to say so I reached in my shirt pocket where I had it now and took out that note. I leaned over and put it on the old desk in front of him and sat back and sudden I was about ready to bust out bawling because he reached the way my father would have done and held that wrinkled old note with one hand and pushed the forefinger of the other along it, spelling out the words. "You took your time coming here," he said without looking up and there wasn't any real answer to that and we just sat there, me on my chair by the window and him behind that old desk looking down at that note and then he raised his head and about hit me with the words. "What're you after now? Money?"

That did it. That cut me loose. "Goldamn it, no!" I said. "I been taking care of myself! I'm looking for a place where maybe I belong! That's sure not here!" I was starting out of that chair towards the door when he stopped me short. "Sit down." It was about the same as if he'd caught me with a rope and put me back on that chair. He reached that note over and watched me put it in my pocket. "Your father," he said, "was a big noisy stubborn stiff-minded jackass. Like maybe you are too. He went his way and I went mine. But when we were kids and I was a scrawny little runt he whopped every big lout that tried picking on me. Maybe this is where you belong and maybe it aint. We'll just find out. I've got quarters upstairs and there's room enough for you too. You go get — "

"Wait a minute," I said. I didn't want to say this because I didn't know how he would take it but I had to say it. I stood up and looked right at him. "Maybe you," I said, "maybe you were kind of stubborn and stiff-minded too." And somehow that was the right thing for me to say and the little wrinkles around his eyes showed plainer. "Good lord, boy," he said. "Of course I was. Still am. I'm a Hammon same as your father was. Waited till he was dying before he turned to me. Likely I'd have done the same. But he knew damn well he could, didn't he? You go get your things and move in."

"Well, sir," I started in to say.

"None of that," he said. "The name's Scott."

"Well, now, Scott," I said. "Everything I've got is on me right now."

He looked at me sharp and the little wrinkles around his eyes showed even plainer. "Been taking mighty good care of yourself, haven't you? That wipes out any moving problem anyhow." He pushed up from behind the desk. "Come along. I'll introduce you around."

That's what he did, took me out and to every place near, the stores and the saloons and the blacksmith and the harness shops and the few houses close in, introducing me to everybody, nothing fancy, just telling who I was and I was visiting a while and if I liked it maybe I'd find something to do and stay around. What struck me first was how easy and friendly people were with me, how they took me as someone to be easy and friendly with and no questions asked except those meant to make me feel the same. Then I figured why. It wasn't anything about me, it was the fact I was being introduced by a man named Scott Hammon and he was backing me and that was enough for them and not because there was a big forty-five hanging in a worn old holster at his side that showed it had been used plenty but just plain he was Scott Hammon and they liked him and were proud having him as a neighbor and as their sheriff who kept things quiet in their little town so folks could be easy and friendly with each other.

I learned all about that the next days, some from him but most from other people. He'd worn a badge in one place and another for quite a while up in the mining country and made himself a name calming some rough camps. He was fast with a gun, people said. Not as fast as some of the real experts were supposed to be and he'd been winged a few times, but once he had his gun out he was so billy-be-damned thorough with it that after a while he was known around and even the best would think twice or maybe three times before forcing him to a draw. He never backed away from a showdown but he didn't go about pushing things to that either if he could avoid it. His way, when he could, when he had to arrest somebody and knew he couldn't do it peaceful, was to try to get in close and jump the play quick and lay the barrel of his gun along the side of the man's skull with power behind it and tote him off unconscious. More than one man, thinking it over after, had thanked him for doing it that way. And right too because a sore head's better than being dead any time.

Then he sort of slowed down. Not really, just in how he looked at things. Maybe that was because he got married, a woman who'd come into the mountains for her health, lung trouble, and he had a fair taste of being peaceful with her before they found she'd come too late. They settled here because it was nice country and a quiet place and he worked at the stage station and took care of her till she died and then he quit his job and sat around all day staring off at the mountains and the town people knew a good thing when they had it and got together and asked him wouldn't he take care of them now as their sheriff. He got up and took that old gunbelt off the nail where it'd been hanging and buckled it around his waist again and he only had to use it a few times on troublemakers passing through, nothing serious, before word was around who was sheriff here and it was sensible to look for trouble other places and after that the town was even quieter.

Don't take me wrong. Not what you'd call quiet nowadays. In the old days even in a little place like this was there was always some horseplay or even brawling going on now and then and on paydays some cowboys coming in to yip and pepper the landscape just for the hell of it and get rid of their money on any sort of damfoolishness. Like the time two of the outfits that were always trying to get ahead of each other worked up a jackass and bear fight. The one was raising mules as a sideline and had a tough old jack that'd shown itself boss of their range by about killing a big stallion twice its size and they got to blowing it could whip anything and the other outfit said a bear would eat it for breakfast and some of them rode out hunting and had themselves a time getting their ropes on a bear, a big black not a grizzly because they knew they couldn't handle one of those, and brought it in. They figured to turn them both loose in the stage corral and see what'd happen. Bets were heavy and everybody around was backing one or the other. Me, I was for the jack, maybe because I'd been a farm boy, but the billy-be-damned critters wouldn't fight. Not each other I mean. They took a look at each other and lit out in opposite directions and the bear went over the rails and scattered the crowd and away and when my uncle Scott could stop laughing he had a job straightening out the bet money all around. But that's a side trail again. The point I'm after is that things happened around here now and then. People who did hard and lonesome work out in the open as plenty people did then had to blow off steam. My uncle Scott didn't mind that, knew it was just normal. He'd interfere only when somebody really stepped out over the line. All the same, alongside Santa Fe where I'd been it did seem sort of quiet.

"Scott," I said. "After all you've done and places you've been, doesn't it seem a mite dull here to a man like you?"

"Dull?" he said. "It aint ever dull with life going on all round you — life how it ought to be lived. People living decent and being neighborly. Letting each other be and do what they want long as they don't step on any toes too hard. Not so damn many of them they can't know each other and don't have room to breathe right. Town growing slow the way a town ought with new people coming in now and then with a chance to get to be known and shake down and be part of the place. Trying to get ahead, yes, but not to make a pile fast and at somebody else's expense. I've had a bellyful of the boom places. Things here the way they are suit me."

They suited me too. As I say, it was my kind of country. Inside a week I felt like maybe I belonged. I was bunking with Scott upstairs and taking meals with him at Mrs. Morrison's, wife of that storekeeper sent me to him the first day, and already I had a couple jobs to pay my keep. In the mornings I'd go down the road and help the blacksmith with any heavy work he had. A short thick one he was, built about like a barrel and named Rufe, Rufe Martin, who'd really have been talking if he spoke as many as twenty words in a whole morning. Yep, he was Jeff's father only Jeff wasn't more than three-four then, just a little kid playing around with his mother always chasing after him for fear he'd get burnt in the shop. In the afternoons I'd be helping my uncle Scott with his paperwork. That is, I'd be doing it because if it was up to him it wouldn't be done. It was only about the second day I found him at his desk scowling at a letter he was spelling out with one finger. I took it and read it off to him and it was from a commissioner over at the county seat about seventy miles off squawking because they weren't getting any records from him and not even any answer to their letters and sometime they were going to get a mite peeved about all that. When he saw I could wrangle words enough to make sense he just plain got up from the desk and told me to wade in. I pulled open the drawers and there was the goldamndest accumulation of stuff you ever saw. He'd been shoving everything into those drawers for years.

"Records?" he said. "All the records I need are right here in my head. I jail a man for stirring trouble, why I jail him and that's that. I aint going to hold it against him after long as he behaves himself. Any lawing we've had, well, Morrison's a justice of the peace and he takes care of that and what he's decided is all in there somewhere. People hear it at the time and they've got mem-

ories, haven't they? Any real serious business goes over
to the county seat anyway so what're they hollering about?
If it's records they want and you feel up to it, why give
them what you can." So I waded in and I chucked out
everything more than four years old and started straightening out the rest best I could. He'd sit by the window
watching people go by outside and talking with those that
came in to pass the time of day and answering my questions when I couldn't make out something. It was kind
of pleasant in there doing that. But all the same I'd get
to studying him and feeling low. I'd found him and he was
all I had and he was something for anybody to have but still
I'd get to feeling lonesome. He was so goldamned complete
and sufficient in himself, the way his life and that stubborn
stiff-mindedness had made him, it seemed to me nobody
could ever get close to him. Then one day, maybe two
weeks after I'd arrived, he took me by surprise. "Ben," he
said. "Can you handle a plow like your father could?"

"No," I said. "He could just about plain push the thing
through the ground himself. I have to have horses helping."

"I'm thinking of horses," he said. "Old Brent Kean's
broke his leg. You haven't met him and you'll enjoy that.
If his garden plowing aint done soon the season'll get past
him."

We went out back and he saddled his tough little gray
and I put one on the big bay he'd said would be mine for
fixing up his paperwork and he brought me up the trail
that's now that highway out there and to this place.

First thing I saw here was a fenced pasture, that first
field down there, with half a dozen cows, steers that is, and
a couple riding horses in it. Then I saw the house here,
the log part that was all there was then, and beyond on

there, past where the barn is now, two women plowing a good-sized plot. Trying to plow. They'd run a few furrows and those were the billy-be-damndest things you ever saw. Zigzagged all over. The team pulling was willing enough but it was a big plow and those women couldn't handle it. One had the reins and was guiding the horses. The other was holding to the plow and fighting it and losing the fight every few seconds when the handles bucked and pitched her around. My uncle Scott tickled his gray faster and swung over in by them. "Now you two quit that foolishness," he said and they stopped and turned to look at us.

The one holding the reins was a big woman, tall and big-boned, getting along in years with kind of wispy gray hair. Right then she was about the tiredest person I ever saw. It was worth seeing how her face lit up when she saw my uncle Scott. She dropped the reins and put her hands on her hips. "I was telling Brent only this morning," she said, "if anybody found time to get out this way today it'd be that little rooster Scott Hammon." She was sure glad to see us.

The other one wasn't. Or she didn't show it any. She was big too, about the same build, only a lot younger and still slender the way a girl is that's going to be a real chunk of woman someday but hasn't got her man yet and started having a family. She was a sight right then. She had a lot of hair, dark it was then, that'd been fastened in two long braids wound up on her head and they'd started falling down and unraveling and her face was all sweaty and streaked from rubbing a muddy hand across it and she was mad. Told me later she'd never been so mad before. Mad at that plow. Mad at her father for being so goldamned silly as to go off hunting again at his age and after mountain goat too and fall and break a leg and have to crawl nine mile dragging it and be toted home. Mad at us for catching her looking like that. Mad at anything and everything she could think of right then. "You're so smirking smart, Mister Scott Hammon," she said. "You tell me how we're going to plant the garden without plowing this ground!"

"Well, now," Scott said. "That's an easy one. That ground'll be plowed. I've brought you here the best damned plower in seventeen counties and a few more acres besides. My nephew here, Ben Hammon, he's been loafing around in towns so long he's just a-aching to get hold of a plow again." And do you know, he was right. The smell of that fresh-turned earth and the sight of those work horses standing there as such horses do which are the kind I've always known best anyway, patient and waiting and ready to dig in when told, and that big old plow sticking up cockeyed out of the ground like it was daring me could I make it behave made me want to jump down and roll up my sleeves and get started. I'm not saying I was feeling like being a farmer again. That's plowing till you're sick of the sight of the billy-be-damned thing and planting and cultivating and fussing with stock and never enough time for everything that's got to be done and keep going only because it's all just plain got to be done and you started it and come hell or highwater you're going to finish it and hardly anybody with all their labor-saving machinery nowadays knows what that means any more. I was only feeling right then like a spot of plowing would stretch a few kinks out of me. But my uncle Scott was talking.

"Ben," he said. "I want you to meet Sarah Kean here who patched me up the first time I stumbled into this valley chasing a road agent from up Leadville way and he saw me first and put a bullet in me. For thirty years maybe more she's been doing the impossible which is making old Brent so happy and contented he behaves almost like a human being. That short-fused piece of dynamite there is their daughter Lettie. Taking after her father today. Hard to believe this minute but I've seen her scrubbed and neat enough to catch a man's eye." She wanted to say something and it would have been a scorcher from how she looked but he cut across her quick. "Come along to the house. Ben'll want to meet Brent before he does your choring."

We trailed to the cabin here and in, that is Scott and Sarah Kean and me because that Lettie girl faded out of sight somewhere around it, and we hadn't more than started in the doorway when a big voice that could have stood right alongside my father's was booming at us. It was coming from a man sitting by the side window that gave on up the valley on a chair that'd been padded with a couple old buffalo robes. He had one leg stretched out in splints on a little nail keg. He was sitting straight upright on the chair and he looked like a half-closed jackknife because he was long and thin, not what thin is nowadays which is spindly and brittle but thin the way a tough old timber wolf is which means lean and taut-stretched all over and made out of gristle and rawhide and not a snitch of extra weight or fat anywhere. He had big features, sharp, what you could see of them pushing out from a shock of gray hair and thick eyebrows and a beard that hadn't known a razor for years only scissors to snip it around the edges.

"Get out of my cabin, you low-bellied rattlesnake," he was booming, throwing the words smack at my uncle Scott and making a cup rattle over on the shelf by the stove. "Where'd you get the notion I'd want to see a strutting mangy little coyote like you a time like this? Couple of months and you don't get out here at all! Soon as I get laid up you come sniffing around to start crowing over me! Think I couldn't hear you powwowing out there? Do my plowing! Make me beholden to you! My rifle was in reach I'd — "

"Shut up!" my uncle Scott shouted and the cup on the shelf rattled some more and I didn't know he had that much voice. And Sarah Kean didn't pay any mind to the shouting at all except to kind of smile a little to herself and she went to the stove and began doing things with the coffeepot. "Shut up!" my uncle Scott shouted again. "I'll break that leg clean off you and whang you one with it!"

"All right, Scott, all right," this old Brent said in a surprising mild voice and that was kind of comical because the idea of Scott tangling barehanded with him, crippled and banged up as he was, would've been like a snapping little terrier tackling a lean old grizzly. "Ben," Scott said, swinging to me, "I didn't mention outside it was this moth-eaten old wreck here brought me in to be patched that time. Found me up in the hills that he knows like they were his backyard. He's been around these mountains so long that he's mostly animal but now and then a bit of human shows through."

Old Brent wasn't paying any mind to him. He was looking me over. "Big one, aint he," he said to Scott. Then to me: "See that chest over there, boy. Let's see you hyst it one." I went over and it wasn't so big but it was solid and must have had heavy stuff in it because when I took hold it felt like it was nailed down. I heard a chuckle from old Brent and I was peeved then so I squatted and wrapped my arms around it and rocked it up a little and braced it with my shoulders and got my hands under and I straightened up with it and just to show that old jackknife on the chair I heaved it on up clear over my head and held it there a couple seconds and let it down, straining hard to set it down without any bumping. "Fair," old Brent said. "Middling fair. Now why aren't you out plowing?"

I could feel the mad start in me at that and I might have done some shouting too but I noticed my uncle Scott was watching me like he was wondering which way I'd jump and Sarah Kean was pretending to be busy with her coffeepot but was really doing the same and I took hold of myself and saw that old Brent's eyes in that big sharp bristly old face didn't have a trace of meanness and something that had been tied up tight in me for a long time sort of slipped loose and I found I could do it right. "Well, now, you broken-down old misfit," I said to Brent. "Don't you go swilling all the coffee because I'll be wanting some after. I'm going out and give that ground the first real plowing it's ever had so it'll be glad you busted that leg and couldn't get to messing it up again."

That's what I did. I went out and looked that ground over. I could make out the plot lines because it'd been worked other years, but it'd been done the wrong way. It's always been plowed crosswise, down the slight valley slope towards the river, and that meant when there was rain, water could go running down the furrow marks and off taking soil and in seedtime maybe some seed with it. I swung the team and the plow around and started slicing my furrows lengthwise. I felt fine stepping along with that big plow and the horses did too because they knew right away as horses can that they had a man behind them knew what he was doing. I'd run four-five furrows and was at the near end near the cabin and swinging around to start another when I saw that Lettie girl watching me. I could tell what she had been doing because her face was scrubbed and her hair was fixed up again and she had a ribbon holding the braids in place. I went on down the line with her watching and just to show her I let one hand drop and held the plow firm with only the other on the one handle and went strutting along. I swung and came back and she'd moved closer. "You're going the wrong direction," she said. "Oh, sure," I said. "All wrong. You're such an expert you'd know." And I went on down another furrow.

I came back and she wasn't saying a word and that should have warned me because when Lettie wasn't saying anything that always meant she was getting ready to do something and when I was swinging to start away again she picked up a stone and threw it and hit one of the horses and the horse jumped and started thrashing about some and then they were both jumping and the plow yanked over and near threw me and I had to do some hollering and wrangling with the reins to calm things down. I was stopped there and peeved and when she started in with something about maybe slow-witted as I was maybe now I'd listen I was mad and though I didn't know it then it must have been the kind of mad my father was when he argued with my mother because it wasn't really an angry mad and I just stomped over and picked her up big as she was under one arm and went stomping into the cabin here and plopped her on a chair. I looked around at the rest of them. "I'm plowing that ground the way it ought to be plowed," I said. "Anybody else tries interfering with me I'll take this whole billy-be-damned place apart." I stomped out and as I was going out the door-way I heard old Brent's voice. "Go to it, boy. But she's a neat armful, aint she?" I went out and I ripped into that plowing and did the whole plot without stopping and that was one of the times it was just plain good being alive.

There was a healthy supper waiting when I finished and we sat around talking after, that is Scott and old Brent talking with Sarah Kean chiming in some and me listening. Lettie ignored me rest of that time like I didn't even exist but she knew goldamned well I was there just as I did she was too. Then it was Brent doing most of the talking with Scott only drawing him on. He was a talker, that Brent, when he got going though there weren't many he'd do that for. I learned about him then and later when Scott and I came out so I could work the ground with an old spiked-log harrow for the women to do the planting and after that when I took to coming out some on my own.

He'd come from England, Brent had, from up in the Northumberland hill country somewhere. He wasn't much more than ten-eleven when his folks brought him to this country and he'd been here so long and out in this part that everything English had long since worn off. Except, sometimes, when he'd be real deep interested in what he was telling, he might slip into speaking in a clipped precise kind of way and pick his words neat and you'd realize that back in those early years, likely back in England, he'd had some good schooling and the few old calfbound books he had on a shelf weren't falling apart just because they were old. He had a couple Walter Scott, I remember, he swore by. He had a rifle too hang-ing on the wall over those books, a Winchester repeater, last of a series of rifles he'd had beginning with a muzzle-loading Kentucky long. A few books and a rifle, those summed a lot of old Brent.

His folks had settled in Tennessee but already, back in the 40's it must have been, that was too tame for him. When he was about sixteen he headed west driving team with some emigrant outfit and never saw his folks again though sometimes when he had a good season he sent them money and he heard from them off and on till they died. He was close to seventy when I knew him and he was a walking history of a big piece of this whole part of the country. He'd hunted and trapped all through these mountains. He'd been with Captain Stansbury's outfit that made the first survey of the Salt Lake country over in Utah. He scouted some for the Army and did some guiding through the mountain passes and sometimes when he needed a stake he supplied meat to the mining camps. He'd known Indians back when they were still Indians, the Kiowas and the Comanches and the Utes and the rest, even some of the Cheyennes, and he'd fought them and he'd lived with them some and likely had a squaw a few years as plenty men did in those days because he was a lot of man and still was when I knew him.

When he was getting along in his forties he thought of settling down, what he'd call settling down, and looked around for a woman to sort of anchor him. He saw Sarah, Blanchard was her family name, walking long-legged behind an emigrant wagon herding the cows and spare mules. The outfit belonged to her sister and the sister's husband and she was tagging along because there wasn't anything for her back where they came from, Missouri I think it was, and lucky for them too because she was doing most of the work. She was no youngster herself then, not one to take an ordinary man's eye not being

pretty or soft-looking or special feminine at first notice.
She was big and toughened by a lot of hard work and had
a tongue and wouldn't take real sass from anyone. Well,
Brent saw her and went along with the outfit a few days
bringing in some meat to help out. Then he went straight
to her and said he'd been looking her over and maybe
she just might be enough woman for him and she said
right back she'd looked him over and it could be maybe
he was enough man for her and he said she'd have to understand he wasn't one to give a woman fancy geegaws or
sweat his guts out trying to make a lot of money and he'd
expect her to trail with him and no squawking and live
how he wanted to live which was simple and being satisfied with a place to stay and enough to eat and nobody
bossing around and she said that suited her only any children would have to learn their lettering and he said he
could handle that and why in hell wasn't she getting her
things together.

They settled here when there wasn't even the beginning of a town. Just built their cabin here where there
was water and grass and timber and plenty game around.
He made a living hunting and trapping. After a while
when more people had come in and the game was thinning they collected some cows and a few horses and he
fenced in pasture and he'd cut hay for winter feed and
they began depending more on their garden and even
selling some off it as well as some stock now and again and
they made out and were living as they wanted to live.
Everybody around knew them but I can't say as everyone
liked them because old Brent could be cantankerous as
an old brier bush and mighty short and sharp with people
he thought fools and he thought most were but even those
he rubbed the wrong way maybe wouldn't have had him

different because he was like a natural part of the country that just bumped out and annoyed them but belonged here.

They'd had one boy, Brent they called him too, but croup took him at about five. They buried him in a little clearing you can't see from here but's behind those trees over on the riverbank. Sarah being well along they didn't think they'd have another so were surprised when a couple years later Lettie came along. They raised her right, real and straight-grained and this-is-me and you-can-be-you like themselves, and Brent gave her schooling and she thought there couldn't be a match for the two of them anywhere and in some ways she was right. Old Brent in particular. She thought anything he did just plain oughtn't be done any other way, like that plowing.

As I say, we sat around after supper and Brent got to talking. He was telling how he and Sarah covered a lot of territory and did a lot of looking before they picked this valley and figured it would be home. There were still a few Indians through this section then, mostly Utes. First people in some of the other valleys had trouble with them but he and Sarah never did. That's because he was straight with them and treated them like people which they were. He scouted first off and found some living on up the valley and came back and got an extra rifle he had then and told Sarah to come along and like always she did. She was worried so he explained they were just going visiting and that wasn't to be worried over because the last thing decent Indians ever would do was hurt any-body came calling in friendship and was a guest in their camp. He was right as he knew he would be because he knew Indians. He lugged a deer along and they all, that is Brent and Sarah and those Utes, had a feast day and they slept in the local chief's lodge and next day they had a council. He knew some of their words and was fair at sign-talk and he put across that he liked their country and wanted to live down the valley here and he wasn't one to go around killing game just for the fun of it but only what he needed and the door of his cabin would always be open to any of them passing by and wanting a meal and to show his heart was in the right place he was making the chief a present of that extra rifle. Those Utes powwowed a while, taking their time the way Indians did, and likely it helped their seeing Sarah hobnobbing with the squaws and trying to do something for a kid that was ailing. At last they told him, best as he could figure it, they'd learned not to put much faith in anything white men said but they liked the way he'd come straight to them for a talk. Since he came as a friend they wouldn't let him get ahead of them in that kind of decent doing. He came in peace and they wouldn't be the ones to change that. From that day forward, they said, he and his woman would be safe in their country. They'd pass the word around and as long as what he'd told them stayed true no one of their tribe would raise a hand against him.

"And not one of them ever did," old Brent told us. "Even along in '79 when they were being pushed out and those up north along the White River started real trouble and killed Agent Meeker who was a blundering fool with Indians anyway and troops were called out and the trouble spread down into these parts too, we never had any. Some cabins were burned not far from here. Some stock was run off and a man killed just over the next ridge. Other people were scurrying down river to the nearest fort. Sarah and me, we stayed here with the door open like always and they didn't bother us. They'd said they wouldn't, so they didn't. I'd trust most Indians I've known more than I would most white men I've known. We'd got well acquainted with some of them. They'd stop by and keep Sarah hopping to fill their stomachs and do that three or four times running till I'd think they were making too much of a good thing of it only I'd remember they'd share their own last bite if we went calling, then one morning I'd find a nice skin or two on the doorstep and I'd know where that came from. It seemed a shame to me when they were all shoved over onto a reservation in Utah. This was their country first. Sarah and me always felt we got this place from them, like they gave it to us."

"Brent," my uncle Scott said. "You're the best man with a rifle I ever met but you're a double-barreled jackass in other ways. Talking about Indians like they were people when everybody knows they're just thieving skunks who had the all-fired gall to get first hold on land that really belonged to white men who just hadn't got around to discovering it yet. Talking about getting your place here from them. That kind of title won't hold in any court. I'll bet you haven't even filed on this piece."

"Filed?" Brent said. "You mean recorded my claim? I've been recording my claim to this piece of land by living on it for twenty-seven years. Everybody around knows it's mine. Besides, this country up in here hasn't been opened to homesteading yet."

"It's been opened," Scott said. "Last month. The whole county except for some mineral lands. Word came through a couple weeks back. There's a land office been set up at the county seat. We're not crowded up this way and not likely to be. Too far from markets. All the same I'm passing word to thickheaded old squatters like you to get over there and make things legal."

"Legal!" old Brent shouted. He banged a hand down on the splints on his leg and that made him wince and touched him off even more. "That's what happens when too damn many people get to crowding in! Everything's got to be legal! Everybody told what they can do, what they can't do! A bunch of fools way off in Washington who aint ever seen this country, don't know a thing about it, get to making a lot of silly rules and you think that gives a runty little packrat like you wearing a badge a right to go bossing around —"

"Shut up!" Scott shouted. "I aint a federal marshal! Federal rules can go hang for all of me! I'm only sheriff of this district and I make most of my own rules anyway! I aint ever tried bossing you! Far as me and the rest around here go this is your land! But you aint going to live forever! You'll be wanting to leave it to Lettie here and that —"

"Lettie," Brent said in that surprising mild voice again. "You're sighting straight I'm leaving it to her. That's what Sarah and me want. This was Ute land once. Now it's Kean land." He stared at Scott some and then he kind of sighed. "All right, Scott. Soon as this leg's in shape I'll go over and file my claim."

There. Maybe by now you begin to have some notion what this is all about. I've been wandering on wordy about myself and my uncle Scott and those three Keans and the little settlement we had here so maybe you'll understand how it was, how I felt about it all, knocking around and getting nowhere then finding this kind of country and people like that. But it didn't last long. Not the way it was then. Old Brent didn't get a chance to wait till his leg healed. Maybe, considering all angles, it wouldn't have made much difference if he had. He'd still have bumped against the law. But it was only about two months later when he was just starting to get about limping with a crutch he'd made that he was smack in the midst of real trouble.

It was the railroad changed things. The railroad people pulled a smart one. They were building into this end of the state and they were peeved at the way speculators jumped in ahead of them to grab off likely station sites and try to get fancy prices so they let on they were heading for a pass about ninety miles south and sudden they shifted and it turned out the line was coming past here, would cross the river right by our town. First we knew of it their advance men were here, snapping up the space they wanted and staking their land grant route. Then grading crews were coming our way and camping near and a bridge outfit hit town and there was activity all over the place though it would be a while before the rails themselves reached here.

The town was booming, almost overnight. People crowded in, all kinds. Tents and shacks went up, jammed together, pushing out around. Couple of weeks after it started there were seven saloons, some just in big tents, all going full blast and trying to outdo each other with brass bands and dance girls and such. The racket never quit all night long and most of them had gambling tables too. Town lots went shooting up in price and land sharks were trading in them right and left and people were slamming stakes into the ground wherever they thought they could make a claim stick and even land that wouldn't have been rated worth taking a while before was being grabbed on the chance it would bring a price soon.

I figured it was exciting at first then I saw how it was

going and was plain disgusted. What had been a nice little town was getting to be a sprawling mess of ugliness and clutter and noise. I'll admit some of the people crowding in were decent enough, just looking for a new place to settle and live. But most of them were after quick easy money and didn't care much how they got it and didn't give a hoot for the town because they'd be moving on to the next rail stop soon as the same thing started there.

My uncle Scott, he was disgusted from the first day. When the rush was going strong he talked some of turning in his badge and heading into the hills for peace and quiet but others like Morrison and even Rufe Martin who pushed himself into talking a bit asked him not to. "All right," he said. "I aint ever backed away from anything and I'm too old to start now. A land boom aint as bad as a mining camp anyway. The people aint as tough, just cheaper and meaner. It'll quiet down when the rails are in and the crews move on. Meantime I'm going to make me some rules and ram them down the throats of these tinhorn sharpers." So he did and had me letter them on a chunk of cardboard and tack it up outside the office, just a few simple things like curfew on the saloons at midnight, no gunplay or be run out of town for keeps, and settle all gambling debts personal without squawking about crooks to the sheriff.

He swore me in as a deputy and told me to take care of the office because he was damned if he would with people in and out all the time asking this and that and making silly complaints. "Have to get it through their heads this town aint organized much yet," he said, "so they'll have to take things as is. Treat them decent long as they behave decent. Anybody makes too much fuss, throw him out.

He gets nasty, throw him in the jail instead. I'll do the outside work." Which was what he did. He patrolled the town, not a regular beat or anything like that, just ambling around and somehow managing to be where most was happening anytime and it was right interesting to see how things would quiet down when he came along. Only real trouble he had those first weeks was over that curfew and that wasn't much. The new operators complained he was hurting business and interfering with their rights as free citizens of the state. "Likely I am," he'd say, "but if you're intending to stay around here and become part of the place, why, in about six months it'll be election time and the town'll be getting really organized and you can throw your votes around and try to elect another sheriff. Meantime I'm sitting on the lid. Would you like to make something of it?" He'd stand there ready for any move with that big old forty-five in plain view in its holster and they'd look him over and remember what they'd heard about him and subside grumbling.

There was one though named Ballard, Tim Ballard, who had a jaw and lived up to it. He didn't complain. He just kept his place open so after warning him once a few minutes after midnight and waiting a while after, Scott ambled up to the doorway and unleashed that old forty-five and shot out the four lanterns with four shots and ducked away out of the doorway and called out there was still one bullet in his gun and more in his cartridge belt did anyone inside want to argue. They didn't and that was that. But Ballard sent a letter off to the county seat protesting what he called such high-handed proceedings and got one back from some official there saying that if he could figure a safe way to make that little gamecock Scott Hammon change his style of doing why let them

over there know because they never could and why not
just quit beefing and do what they did which was let him
go his way because the results seemed to be good. Ballard
came into the office and showed Scott and me that letter.
"You win, Hammon," he said. "Blamed if I don't think
I'll put up a building instead of that tent I'm using and
settle down here. I didn't know there were men like you
and a place like this left anywhere around any more."
He turned out to be a good man, that Ballard, though
there weren't many his caliber came in with the land rush.
But that's a side trail again. Point I'm making is that if
we'd had just an ordinary land boom, hitting a peak during the rail building then shaking down after, we'd likely
have made out all right. Sure, there were arguments over
land titles starting and a few lawyers from the county seat
were in town drumming up business and there'd have
been some small-scale land-grabbing and feuding over
that, but things wouldn't have got out of hand. It was
the big-scale grabbing, managed from outside, that caused
the real trouble.

The first settlers in the territory, same as almost anywhere, had the best land. That was natural, they'd had
first pick. Some had hurried over when the land office
was opened and registered their claims. But some hadn't
got around to that yet for one reason or another and even
some of those who had didn't have clear titles anyway.
The old homestead and pre-emption laws had a lot of
tricky angles like the one that tripped plenty people, the
little paragraph that said a person could make only one
entry, that if he'd ever made one on public land and gave
that claim up and moved on he couldn't make another.
Many a man who'd kept drifting west as one territory
after another was opened up, trying first one then an-

other, just changed his name and filed again but there was always the chance he'd be found out. So some of the big land companies that'd been getting rich picking off public land through political pull and all kinds of slick schemes figured an easy way to get hold of good land cheap was to hire men to jump claims of early settlers who hadn't filed yet or whose titles weren't clear. That way they'd be getting some of the best pieces and even some already pretty well developed. They were operating outside the law, using the law for their purpose while breaking it themselves, because it was plain on the point that homesteads were for people intending to live on them and make homes on them and who weren't acting as agents for anybody else. But a man who grabbed a claim and went along and met the legal requirements and got his patent then sudden changed his mind about living on it any longer and sold out cheap to one of those companies was acting within his rights, wasn't he? How could you prove he was really hired to do that from the beginning, specially when any proving would have to be done in courts that were under the thumbs of those companies anyway? They'd grabbed off plenty in other parts of the state and maybe other states and learned all the tricks, those companies had, and then one of them moved in on our town.

Its agents had checked the area careful and had everything planned and organized. That was plain the day the first batch of its hired claim jumpers hit town and the man in charge of them came into the office. He was one of those smooth-seeming characters that make the hair on the back of your neck rise, all smooth and easy on the outside, well dressed and even some fussy about clothes and a glib talker and underneath as shrewd and mean as they come. Scott was in the office between rounds resting and this gent introduced himself as Herbert Goss, a lawyer he said he was, and got right to business.

"A group of new citizens of your admirable community," he said, "as a matter of fact so new that they have only arrived here today, have asked me to act as their representative, their counsel so to speak. As an attorney I can assure you that their papers are in order, that they have duly recorded their claims at the land office and intend to take up residence upon them and begin improving them in accord with the law. Unfortunately some lawless squatters happen to be living on some of those claims. That is why I am here to see you."

"Even up in here," Scott said. Then he didn't say another word. He just looked at this Goss and nobody knew him would have been comfortable under that look.

"Mr. Hammon," this Goss said. "I was speaking to you. I said I am acting as representative for a group — "

"You mean," Scott said. "You mean you've brought a bunch of claim jumpers to this town and they're working for you and you're working for some gypping land company."

"Oh, come now," this Goss said. "A man as smart as you seem to be knows how these things are. Suppose you happened to be right. How could you ever prove it? And why should you ever want to? Everything that shows in this is absolutely legal and airtight. We don't want any trouble. All we want is to have these squatters, these trespassers, moved off with a minimum of difficulty. I have made arrangements for a deputy marshal to be sent here but he will not arrive for some days and we are in a hurry. Every day lost means a day longer on meeting the residence requirements, you know. A local sheriff who cooperated in this might find it to his profit. Others elsewhere have. I've brought along a list of the places and the squatters and if you — "

"Shut up," Scott said. He didn't shout it. He just said it but it stopped the smooth words coming from this Goss like a knife had sliced them off. "Shut up. And get out."

This Goss didn't seem to be bothered much. Maybe he'd expected that and had only been going through the motions. He sighed like he was sorry he wasn't understood right and started to leave and my uncle Scott stopped him. "Wait. Let me see that list." Goss pulled it from a pocket and laid it on the desk and Scott took it and began pushing a forefinger along it spelling out the names. Part way down he stopped reading and his head dropped lower and his eyes closed and he sat there like that for a moment then he raised his head. "I'll handle that one," he said.

"Why?" Goss said, quick and sharp. "Why just one?"

"Because the name's Brent Kean," Scott said. "You go out there and with half a dozen deputy marshals too and he'll kill you. Maybe that'd be a good thing. But not for him."

So Scott and I were saddling the horses again and coming out the trail that was getting to be a road and past the new shacks going up here and there and to this place. There wasn't any sense delaying, he said, because if anything was to be done for old Brent it would have to be strict legal, the way the company was pretending to be, and the first move was to get Brent off the place and forestall any fighting. We came out the trail and it was early summer and the grass was growing good and in that plot I'd plowed and harrowed the plants were beginning to show in green healthy rows. Lettie was out there with a hoe and came over to greet us and Sarah must have seen us coming because the coffeepot was on when we stepped inside and Brent was sitting on his chair by the side window with his hurt leg out straight, not saying anything, just waiting, because he saw Scott's face as we came in. I noticed something then, that these two, my uncle Scott and old Brent Kean, when they had something serious to talk about, they didn't do any shouting, they didn't do any name-calling. They spoke soft, almost gentle, and direct to the point and they had silences between speakings and they said about as much to each other with their eyes as with their words.

Scott didn't wait for the coffee or any small talk. He started right in and told what was happening. And Brent sat still, not a muscle moving, only his weathered old cheeks above the beard seemed to stretch tighter and his eyes seemed to sink back in deeper.

"So that's that," Scott said. "It's a man named Malley has filed on this quarter section. Hunt around outside and in some corner there'll be a stake with his name on it. I don't need to see it to know it's there. Put in some night on the quiet and with a witness too. This outfit is thorough. But this land business is tricky and there's a lot of angles. You three pack some things now and move down into town for a while so there can't be any trespassing or obstructing the law charges. Fred Morrison has room enough. He's had some law training too and lately he's been deep in these land rules. He'll figure a way for you to bust this case open and get a title."

Sarah and Lettie were tight-faced but quiet. They knew who was head of that family and had the say-so in the tight spots. And old Brent turned his head slow and looked out the window. After a while he turned it back slow and looked at Scott. "Suppose I don't feel like trusting to any law doings," he said. "Suppose I don't feel like moving. Now or any time."

"Then I'll have to do what I aint ever tried with you before," Scott said. "I'll have to do some bossing around. I'm here as an officer of the law."

Old Brent's eyes flicked over to the rifle hanging above the shelf of old books and flicked back.

"Brent," Scott said. "There's things we both know. Even if you didn't have a game leg I could put a couple slugs in you before you even reached that rifle. You're just damned tough enough to drill me too before you went under. So we'd both be done. We'd both be out of a world that sometimes like now don't exactly seem worth living in. But there's Sarah and Lettie to think about."

"You'd use your gun," Brent said, very soft. "On me?"

"I've figured this," Scott said. "I've set a course. I'll hold to it."

Brent turned his head slow and looked out the window. He turned it back again and looked at Sarah. "Brent," she said. "I've been beside you in anything you felt like doing for about thirty years. I'm not changing now." He nodded his head a little, slow, and shifted it again and looked at Scott. "I aint afraid of your gun," he said.

"I know," Scott said.

"Then that's enough," Brent said. He took a deep breath and sat up a little straighter and he looked at me. His big old voice came booming at me in a shout. "Well, boy! You overgrown lunkhead! Why aren't you out harnessing the team?" I jumped and started out and I could hear him booming away inside. "Sarah! Lettie! Gather some clothes together! We'll try town living for a time!"

I slapped on the harness and hitched the team to

Brent's big wagon but I wasn't along on the trip in because Scott sent me to herd the stock that was in the fenced
pasture over to the MacPherson place, a couple miles over
there where the sharp slope starts up and there's one of
those big fancy shopping centers nowadays. Mac was
another early settler, that is he'd been around maybe ten
years, but he'd hopped over to the county seat and done
his filing in time and he was straight as a string and nobody would be trying to move in on him. He was more
than willing to take the stock in with his and keep it for
Brent and he was plenty peeved when I told him what was
going on. "You tell the old rattlesnake," he said when I
was leaving, "that if it gets to where we have to run those
butting-in jumpers clean out of the county, me and my
shotgun'll be ready."

It took a while, herding that stock over and swinging
back into town. When I got there the Keans were already
settled in with the Morrisons who had a fair-sized house
behind the store. I found Scott and Brent in our office.
Fred Morrison was with them. They had the door locked
and I had to bang to get in. Scott and Brent must have
been giving Morrison all the details because he was just
starting in to figure the angles, sort of thinking out loud,
when I arrived. The boom was bringing him big business at his store and he'd had to take on clerks and he was
dealing in town lots too and he wasn't against the money
coming his way. But all the same he was one of the oldtimers and he didn't like this claim-jumping any more
than MacPherson did. "That was the right move," he was
saying, "to get off the place first thing. Now there can't
be any loose charges floating around to confuse matters.
No one can say we aren't trying to obey the law. Without
digging further, there is one thing sure. We can bring

suit and Brent here can collect full value for his cabin and any improvements like fencing and such. He was not trespassing when he put them up. The place had not been taken yet."

"Forget that," Brent said. "It's the land that counts."

"All right, all right," Morrison went on. "I was just talking. But there's a provision in the homestead law or one of the revisions, I forget which but it's been upheld, that when public land is opened original settlers who have been living there some length of time before the opening have three months leeway for their filing. Three months protection that means. Well, it's been a bit more than three months since this area was opened — "

"Three months and a day," Scott said. "I told you this outfit's thorough."

"All right, all right," Morrison went on. "But as I get it from you two it has been less than that since Brent here knew about the opening. From his point of view the protection is still there. Not from the law's necessarily but from his. It has not been three months since he was, in a sense, officially notified. And his busted leg adds another factor. He couldn't very well get over for his filing with a bum leg and the land office is strict about people appearing in person. We can work up a case that could sound right good. We might even win with it in land court. Given a fair shake that is. But my guess is it wouldn't come to that. We make it sound good in advance and we let word around that plenty about claim-jumping trickery is coming out in the trial and we'll worry this Malley so much — really the company but they wouldn't come out in the open, they would only act through him — that he'll just fade out and abandon the claim."

Morrison rubbed his hands together the way he did

when he thought he'd swung a bargain or made a point. He turned straight to Brent. "All right, all right, Brent. I suppose you have your papers in order."

"Papers?" Brent said. "What papers?"

"Your citizenship papers," Morrison said. "You were born in England, weren't you?"

Brent just stared at him and Morrison shook his head. "Man, man," he said. "Don't you know public lands are open only to citizens or people who have started the process of being naturalized by appearing in court and filing a declaration of their intentions?"

"Citizenship," old Brent said. He wasn't shouting. His voice was soft and sort of deep and it was bitter. "My parents brought me to this country because this was where they wanted to live. Sixty years I've lived in this country and I've done my share for it. I've worked for it and I've fought for it and nobody ever threw citizenship up at me. Stansbury didn't say anything about it when he signed me on as a guide when he surveyed Salt Lake. Nobody mentioned it when they came running for me and glad to get me for the Colorado Volunteers in the Indian troubles in '64. I've led emigrant trains through these mountains. I've taken mapping crews into places they didn't know existed till I showed them. I've made one whole damn big stretch of this country mine the way hardly anybody else has or ever will because I know every rock and river in it and I've dropped my sweat and spittle on every square mile of it. Now when all I want is a little piece of it to live on and leave my daughter and that's been mine anyway for twenty-seven years, you tell me that just because some fool Congressmen way off in Washington — "

"Whoa, now," my uncle Scott said. "Didn't your father get naturalized?"

"Certainly he did," Brent said. "He told me so in a letter once."

"Then that's it," Scott said. "That covers you."

"Maybe," Morrison said. "Maybe. That depends on when. If Brent here was still a minor, yes. If he was past twenty-one, he was on his own and it wouldn't cover. All right, all right, Brent. Were you?"

"How in hell would I know?" Brent said. "That was close to fifty years back. Maybe I was, maybe I wasn't. And don't ask me have I got that letter. All such truck went when we were burned out along about the second year Sarah and me settled here. Some of those Utes helped us rebuild. Said we were fools to want a wood lodge but they helped. I told you they gave us our place. That's title enough for me. All your legal foofarawing only frazzles things till there's no real right or wrong left only what you can get some side-squinting judge to say. Men can get along together if they want and there aint too much law mixed in. You just tell that Malley he can have a piece of my land if he's set on it and he'll live decent and stay out of my hair. I don't need the whole quarter section. I'll just go back out and if anybody else comes around claiming, well, I've got my rifle. I've trusted to it and not to any finagling with laws most of my life now and it's — "

"Man, man," Morrison said. "This isn't back in the wild days. This is eighteen hundred and ninety-six. Do you want me to help you or don't you?"

"Yes," Scott said, cutting in quick. "Yes he does."

"All right," Morrison said. "All right and all right again. I'll start suit for you, Brent, to have this Malley's filing set aside. The land court is so jammed with cases piled up from back along the rail line that it will be a while before yours can come up and that will give us time to handle this citizenship business. You write to where your parents lived, Kentucky wasn't it — "

"Tennessee," Brent said.

"Tennessee, then," Morrison went on. "Tennessee. Address it Clerk of the Circuit Court in the county where they lived. Find out the right date, then we'll know. Meantime, on the chance, you be ready to hobble over to the county seat soon as the court, state court, is in session, federal court is too far off and state will do, and file your own citizenship intentions. We'll be on solid ground then either way when your case comes up."

That was all could be done right then and it meant waiting, which is bad enough anytime. I don't know whether Morrison really thought Brent could win his case or just figured to ease him along by doing something while he got used to the idea that he'd have to lose his land, lose this particular piece anyway, and meantime he'd be getting his citizenship straightened out so he could file somewhere else later if he wanted. Anyway Morrison never said, not to Scott or to me, not then or even later when what came out of it was all over. He just went ahead and wrote the case up, his brief he called it, and went over to the county seat and had some trouble because the company was getting strong in politics there but he managed to wangle it onto the docket. Soon as he came back and said it was started Scott went looking for Goss and told him he'd better warn his man Malley to be mighty careful what he did if anything at the place out here. "Don't let him try living in the cabin," Scott said, "or I won't be able to answer for what Kean might do. Myself either. This case is just started."

"Just started?" Goss said. "It's already finished. Your

legal shenanigans don't mean a thing. Just a nuisance.
The law is behind us — beg pardon, behind Malley, since
you are so sensitive on such things. The trouble with you
and Kean is that you're both old-fashioned, your time is
past and you're just a pair of relics walking around. A
man as smart as you seem to be ought to realize that."

"There's better things than being smart," Scott said.
"I'm old-fashioned, yes. Old-fashioned enough to wish
you had guts enough to carry a gun and spirit enough to
be crowded into trying to use it." But Goss just laughed,
a mean little scratchy laugh he had. "That's what I mean,"
he said. "Direct action. That's your way. So old-fashioned you ought to be under glass in a museum. Manipulating the law is a lot better than manipulating a gun.
Safer. More profitable. Now a man as smart as — " But
Scott didn't let him finish, just swung away, and what he'd
said had some effect because when I rode out checking
for him I saw that Malley wasn't touching the cabin, was
living in a tent he'd put up.

Meantime the boom went on booming. It spread out
around because with the railroad through here shipping
to market would be easy. Several more batches of claim
jumpers and paid settlers came in, though the racket did
let up some because the grading crews were moving on
and only the bridge outfit was still in town. A temporary
branch of the land office was set up in town here. Legal
squabbles over town lots and building sites got to be so
frequent that two days a week a judge came over from the
county seat to handle cases right here too. That deputy
marshal arrived and he wasn't any help at all. Maybe he
was getting paid by the federal government but he was
really working for Goss.

There was plenty tension in the air. The company was

having things its way but most of the oldtimers around
and even some of the newcomers, the decent ones, didn't
hold with this wholesale land-grabbing. Some of the people whose claims were jumped just faded away, ran out
without putting up an argument, likely those who knew
they couldn't get a clear title anyway. Some yelled and
made a fuss and had to be pushed out and there were a
few near-fights but Goss always had a half-dozen husky
men with him when he went about notifying and after a
few days that deputy marshal too. My uncle Scott took to
sitting in the office a lot staring at the floor and muttering
soft under his breath because it was all legal, on the surface anyway, and there wasn't a thing he could do except
what he was doing which was refusing to have any part
in it. Only once did he mix in and that was the time one
man got so mad when Goss and his crew came to push him
out that he ducked back into his shack and grabbed a gun
and let fire a couple shots and lucky he missed and he
slammed the door and barred it.

Those claim jumpers milled around outside and more
of them were gathering and they were talking wild about
stringing him up and likely that deputy marshal would
have just stood aside and looked the other way but somebody got word to Scott and he went larruping out there.
He made Goss and that marshal promise there wouldn't
be any charges if he got the man out peaceful and he went
up to the door and called out who he was and the man let
him in and what he said in there was his business but in a
few minutes he and the man came out. Those claim jumpers, they were an edgy bunch and mean-natured anyway
or they wouldn't have been in such doings, started crowding around and talking ugly and Goss and that marshal
turned their backs and went walking away and Scott got

mad. He let the lid blow off and what was boiling in him
come up. He cussed that crew the way likely they'd never
heard before and he wound up shouting at them to go
ahead start something, start something, start something.
They knew he was plain itching to unleash that old forty-
five of his and they backed off and he took the man and
his few things into town and stuck with him till he was on
the stage away.

Some of the people who'd been pushed out found places
to stay in town and hung around, maybe waiting to see how
old Brent would come out because they knew he was fighting the company in a law suit and if he won they might
be able to do something too. That didn't make for a peaceful feeling because the men of these families were apt to
be bumping into some of the claim jumpers any time and
there'd be arguments. They'd have liked to look on Brent
as sort of a leader and sit around talking with him working
up their mad but he wouldn't do that. He was in town
but you'd hardly ever see him. He stayed most of the day
in the room at Morrison's he and Sarah were using, reading in his old books or pretending to and staring at the
wall like he could see right through it off into the distance
and maybe he could, off into a distance that wasn't only
in miles but in time too. He was one of the last of the old-
time mountain men and a special breed of them at that
and he had the patience they had to have, the kind that
could hold them quiet under cover, for days if necessary,
outwaiting danger on their trail. He'd made up his mind
when Scott called him that he'd try this legal and like those
Ute friends of his when he said he'd do something he'd
do it. Only at night, late, when there wasn't much going
on, he'd step out, hobbling on his crutch at first then later
without it, only limping some, and cover miles in a circuit

around avoiding houses and such and back and to that room again.

Sarah helped Mrs. Morrison all she'd let her and stayed in most of the time too. Lettie was working in the store. Sometimes in the evening she'd walk out with me but then again sometimes when I'd go for her there'd be some other young one ahead of me and we'd fuss around trying to outsit each other and I'd get mad and stomp away. Being with her wasn't what you'd call too pleasant then anyway. She took this claim-jumping hard and had to be always worrying it. She seemed to think Scott and me were somehow a part of it because we had to do with the law and it was the law that was hurting old Brent.

"That's federal law," I'd tell her. "It's only local law we have anything to do with. Can't you see it's Scott who's doing all he can and who's kept your father from getting into real trouble he couldn't ever get out of? The most he can lose now is just his land and he can always get another piece somewhere." "And can't you see," she'd tell me, "that it's not just land, it's that piece of land? If he can't have it, he won't want to go on living." "Shucks," I'd say. "He's the toughest old rooster I ever saw. He could start all over again right now and beat out any of us young ones." "But why should he have to?" she'd say and tear into me and the only way I could shut her up was ask her what in all the billy-be-damned possibles did she think we could do.

It was one of those times I made a fool move. We'd been walking and the dark had come down, only a trace of light left, and we were coming back through the trees behind Morrison's house. She'd stopped and was glaring at me and I got to thinking of those girls around Santa Fe, how you didn't talk much to them, just took, and I reached out thinking I'd kiss her and show her a thing or two. I took hold of her and she came in willing enough, her head down like she was being shy about it, and she was in close and sudden her head snapped up, hard, slamming against my chin with a jolt that knocked me loose and back a step. She was gone towards the house and I was about ready to follow and maybe get really rough when I heard a chuckle off to the side. I turned and old Brent was limping up.

"Goldamn it!" I said. "What're you doing? Keeping tabs on us?"

"Simmer down, boy," he said. "I just happened to be heading out. Lettie don't worry me any. You're lucky she didn't give you a knee. Come along, stretch your legs some." He started off looking around at me and there wasn't much else to do so I tagged. Limp and all, he sure could move fast without seeming to hurry, quiet and easy like a long-legged shadow slipping along. "Now you take Lettie," he said. "She aint one of these coy things likes to tease the men. Sarah and me, we've raised her right. When she finds her man, why he won't have to coax around and try nipping a hug. If he aint got sense enough to put it straight, she will." We went on some and I found myself trying to move the way he did, not clomping on my heels, but putting my feet down flat and letting my weight glide forward easy onto them. "See that shack over there," he said. "Past those trees. I remember shooting a bear there once. Big black. And fat. Enough grease to last us for cooking and on biscuits a couple months. Well, there's some things about what folks call progress that're all right. Like butter. Bear grease's good. Butter's better. All the same a man likes to remember he's used bear grease and brought it in himself." We went on like that, quiet most of the time with him remembering now and again, then I saw he'd taken me without any seeking landmarks on a circuit around and we were coming back to Morrison's from the other side. "Don't go rushing her, boy," he said. "This is a rough stretch for her right now." He stopped and looked off into the dark. "For me and Sarah too." I had a sudden feeling he was ashamed of saying that and he swung abrupt away and towards the house.

I went to our building and up the stairs. Scott was asleep on his cot and I made noise sitting on mine so he'd wake. "Goldamn it, Scott," I said. "Isn't there anything we can do, you can do anyway, about this jumping business?" He rustled a little and I could begin to make him out lying there and staring up. "You think I aint been beating my brains out?" he said. "I'm doing all I can see straight which is not helping it along any myself and seeing that arguments don't get growing into people getting hurt."

"That's not much," I said. "Why, the way some people are feeling, even some like MacPherson, why with you and Brent leading we could all get together and run those sharpers clean out of here."

"What'd that do?" he said. "Except blow up trouble and plenty people hurt on both sides, maybe killed. We'd be breaking the law then, not a leg left to stand on. They've got the government behind them. Don't forget we're wrong too. We let things slide. Brent's wrong. Didn't file in time. I'm wrong. Didn't make him. But maybe it'll work out. The law aint so bad. It's broad, got to be, covering so much. When you get down to cases there's got to be leeway. Maybe we can make the court see that. If a man can't have some faith in the law, how's he going to live?"

"But what if it doesn't work out?" I said. "What'll you do then?"

He lay there quiet, staring up. "I don't know," he said after a while. "I plain don't know."

That was the worst of it. There wasn't anything we could do, except wait till the case would come up and hope the judge would be decent enough to realize sometimes the strict letter of the law isn't as important as the spirit behind it. Morrison was working up every scrap of evidence he thought could help, things like details on Brent's guiding for the government and his military service, which wasn't in the regular army only in the state volunteers, but might have some effect because the law favored old soldiers in regard to public lands.

But that case never came up. Something interfered. Sarah took sick.

As we found out, it wasn't a new sickness. It was what she called a misery that'd been in her family for generations and had bothered her some, not too much, off and on the last years. My guess is some kind of internal cancer and the doctor, we had one in town then, thought so though they didn't know much about that in those days. My guess is too it hadn't bothered her much before because she was happy out here with old Brent and had so goldamned much to do taking care of him and Lettie and working around the place and enjoying it all that her system just plain wouldn't let that misery take good hold. Soon as they moved into town and she didn't have much to do, not what she'd call much, and had the land worry hanging over her and had to see old Brent staring at the wall day after day, she just plain let down and quit fighting it without knowing that was what she was doing. It took hold of her hard one day and after that she was in pain most of the time and in a few days she had to stay in bed. She began dropping away fast. She was unconscious a lot of the time which was a blessing because the pain wasn't letting up any now and Brent or Lettie and usual both together stayed with her constant and one evening she roused up and pushed herself up in the bed and spoke in what seemed her normal voice again.

"Lettie," she said. "Don't you tell your father what I said this morning. I didn't really mean it." She looked at old Brent. "You ornery old scrawny hoptoad," she said. "You've been man enough for me since the first time I ever set eyes on you." She sort of fell back on the bed and when they hurried close she was unconscious again and a couple hours later she was gone.

We buried her the next afternoon in the big lot that'd been set aside for the town cemetery which is about the only thing down there near the center that's still the same as it used to be. Crowded around now with buildings though and so jammed full of graves you can't even walk easy in it. That's progress. Not even room enough any more for the dead to rest right let alone for the living to live right. But as I say, we buried her next day and Scott had to take charge because old Brent seemed kind of numbed. It was surprising how fast word got around and how many people came in. I don't know whether Scott had anything to do with this or I ought to give Goss some credit, but he kept out of sight and kept his jumpers out of the way too, even those who spent a lot of time hanging around, and the town had a respectful quiet feeling during the funeral time. But what worried me was the way Brent behaved. He moved along not paying attention to anyone, not even answering when spoke to. He hadn't had much sleep for days and none at all the night before. The skin of his cheeks above the beard was stretched tight, too tight, and his eyes were sunk way back. He wasn't really numbed. He was aware. He was mighty aware. You could see that in the old eyes deep in their sockets. He was just going through with this funeral and he wasn't going to let anyone break in on his thinking and what he was thinking you couldn't tell.

Lettie was beside him and she was about the same. Her face was set and she wouldn't listen to anyone so after a while people gave up trying to sympathize with her. When I tried to take her hand and walk along with her she shook me off and looked at me like she didn't know me and didn't want to. But when it was over and Scott told her to get Brent back to Morrison's and make him rest, she nodded and did what he said. And not more than two hours later, when everything else around town was still kind of hushed and quiet, she was running head-long across the street and to our building and into our office shouting at Scott. "I can't find him!" she kept shout-ing over and over like she couldn't stop and Scott jumped and grabbed her and shook her and slapped her hard and she stopped with a jerk. He pushed her down on a chair and squatted in front of her. "All right, girl," he said. "Slow and easy. What's happened?"

She'd got old Brent back to the room at Morrison's and he went readily enough. Soon as they were inside he started: "What was it Sarah told you?" He kept after her and at last she told him. He quieted down right away like he was satisfied. When she said he ought to rest he lay right down and she thought he went to sleep and she sat in a chair and was so worn she slipped off too. She woke sudden and looked at the bed and he wasn't there. That startled her and then something scared her and she ran through the house and out around looking for him and then all she could think of was running to Scott.

"Easy now," Scott said. "What was it Sarah told you and you told him?"

"That she wished — " Lettie said. "That she always wished she'd be buried out home beside her boy."

Scott stood up. His voice was soft, almost a whisper. "And what scared you was that you saw his rifle was gone too."

"Yes," she said.

There. Maybe now this story begins to take some shape for you. Old Brent Kean with long memories in his mind and a rifle in his hand. That's the story. The real story. He took hold of it and it was his and clear through to the finish and that was a week later it was his.

We didn't know at first. Scott suspected and he told me to look out for Lettie and was out back slapping a bridle on his gray and he didn't bother with a saddle and went larruping bareback up the trail but the first of it was already over and those claim jumpers were gathering when he got out here. They were talking ugly and splitting into groups and starting to scour the country around. Scott didn't pay much mind to them, just to find out what he could. Then he rustled a wagon and brought the three men in, one dead, one dying, and the third, Malley himself, in bad shape. He left them with the doctor and came back to the office. From what he'd seen and heard and what we learned later the whole thing was plain enough.

Old Brent slipped out of Morrison's and headed up the trail, not on it but to one side holding to cover. He still limped some but a limp wouldn't slow him much and he moved along fast. When he reached the place out here Malley and two other men were busy cutting hay off the meadow there. His hay. Malley was driving a mower and the other two were stacking. Brent stepped out and went across the field to them. Malley saw him coming and stopped the mower and the other two did too and came over by Malley and they were all three bunched together watching him. He came up close. "Get off my land," he said. He was speaking very soft and that should have warned them but they just laughed and told him to run along quit bothering them. "Get off my land," he said again, "or I'll kill the three of you." But they just laughed again and slapped the guns they had at their hips and said if an old coot like him wanted trouble why they'd give it to him. He turned around and walked to the edge of the field, to the fence along the side of the pasture, and climbed over and turned again and rested the barrel of his rifle on the top rail. He squinted along the barrel and made his whole body relax the way he knew how so no muscle would be tense and make the gun quiver and he sighted and started firing. His first bullet took Malley through the right shoulder, low enough to rip through part of the lung, and knocked Malley off the mower seat, hurt bad but not so bad he couldn't crawl quick behind the machine. Brent grunted to himself for being so sloppy with his shooting and fired again at one of the others who was clawing at his gun and this bullet hit this one exact center in the left breast and he was dead before he even collapsed to the ground. The third man had his gun out and was ducking and dodging and sending his own bullets Brent's way but Brent sighted slow and careful and picked him off with a bullet through the belly before he'd gone far. Brent could see Malley's feet sticking out from behind the mower and he watched and there was no sign of movement. Then he heard shouting a distance off and saw some people running from the next place up and across the trail and he climbed back over the fence and headed off into the woods and faded away.

Scott hadn't much more than finished telling Lettie and me what he knew when that Goss was running into the office. He was so excited and mad he wasn't smooth-talking. He was shouting. "You're the sheriff!" he shouted at Scott. "Why aren't you out with the posses after that murderer?"

"Posses?" Scott said. His voice was tired which was how he seemed to be too. He was acting like he was just pushing himself along doing what had to be done for no other reason than just plain that it had to be done. "You call those fool mobs posses? They're wasting their time."

"You just going to sit there," Goss shouted, "and let him get away?"

"I'm going to sit here," Scott said. "But I'll tell you something. Anybody brings him in it'll be me. In my own way. And you and your damned hired men'll stay out of it."

Goss caught himself then and pulled down into something of his usual style. "All right," he said. "But with you acting like this I won't be responsible for what they do when they get hold of him."

"You're not so strict law-abiding, are you," Scott said, "when it pinches you some. Now get out." Goss did and Lettie was staring after him, wide-eyed, and she turned to Scott. "Why, he means they'll — they'll — "

"Lettie," Scott said. "Brent's off up in the hills that're like his own backyard. They won't get even a sniff of him. I know I couldn't if I tried and I'm fair good myself. They won't get him."

"But even so," she said, "we've got to do something. He can't just keep on hiding and running away."

"Lettie," Scott said again. "I'll take care of him. All that anybody can now. You think a minute. You know him even better'n I do. He's never run away from anything in his life. What will he do now?"

She stared at Scott and after a minute she nodded her head slow and I couldn't follow them. "What do you mean?" I said.

"You'll see in the morning," Scott said. He took Lettie across the street to leave her with Mrs. Morrison and we had a hectic evening with the town buzzing and men riding in and out and reporting all kind of rumors. Brent was supposed to be heading off here and there and about everywhere at once. That deputy marshal was running in circles and giving orders then changing them and no one was paying much attention to him anyway. The man Brent had hit in the belly died about ten o'clock and that stirred new buzzing and more groups were forming and riding out and people like Morrison and Rufe Martin kept coming in the office wanting to know why Scott wasn't out at least to try to keep things under control if they did catch up with Brent and he just kept telling them in that tired voice to go away let him alone.

When the sun showed early in the morning the town seemed near deserted. "Come along," Scott said and we saddled and rode up the trail. It was all quiet and peaceful with the hunting way off now. The cabin here was still and silent as if nothing had ever happened. We rode right up to it. The door was closed. Scott lifted the latch and we went in and on a chair by the one front window with his rifle across his knees was old Brent. "I been waiting for you, Scott," he said.

"Yes," Scott said. "Yes. I know." He pulled over another chair and sat down slow and tired on it and hitched it around a little and the two of them sat there side by side looking out the window.

"Brent," Scott said. "A man has fool thoughts sometimes. I been thinking we could barricade the door and each take a window. You and me. We could put lead in a lot of them before they got us. You and me. There'd be some satisfaction in that." They kept on looking out that window then Scott said: "But we can't."

"No," Brent said. "We can't. I've been sitting here thinking. I lay out a while last night the way I used to in a place I know up in the hills. That's good for a man. Bigness all around and the sky wide and clean above. But you can't turn time back. I was wrong. I'd do it again but I was wrong. Men like that don't really count any more. They're only doing what they're paid to do and there's always that kind around. Always." He looked down at the rifle and ran a hand along the barrel. "Maybe I've just lived too long," he said.

The two of them sat there still and quiet looking out that window. "Brent," Scott said. "I been thinking too we ought to say to hell with the whole kit and caboodle of them and what they're doing to this country and head up north where it's still big and clean. You and me, Brent." And after a minute he said again: "But we can't."

"No," Brent said again. "We can't. A man's got to follow the trail he's started. Now mine's led to your jail." He stood up and he looked around at me and then he near tore me apart inside because what he did was call up for me something of that old gleam in his eyes and he sent that big old voice booming at me. "Well, boy! You overgrown lunkhead! Why aren't you down in town looking after Lettie?"

That was it. That was what he always did to me. He

slammed at me with that big booming voice that might make some people mad and with words that might seem mean and cantankerous and what he was really doing was reaching out and taking me right into his own world with him and seeing me as another whole human being and saying stand up there boy and be yourself and if you can stand up to me there'll be a pair of us.

"I'm not in town," I said, "because somebody has to take care of an old crook-leg like you. I rode a horse out here. You'll be needing it to go in with Scott and I'll be hiking."

That was how we went, Brent on my horse and Scott on his riding ahead and me walking along behind. I watched them pulling on away from me towards town, the two of them riding together, not saying anything because they didn't need to, just riding along together side by side.

Things happened fast after that, or anyway they seemed to though it was really five-six days. Brent stayed in our jail, not because Scott wanted him there or had the least little trace of a thought he'd try to slip away but because that was the safest place. Scott himself rigged a cot in the office and took to sleeping there instead of upstairs and he was mighty particular who he'd let come into the office to see him. It was lucky the searching hadn't been organized, just haphazard bunches of men out hunting around hit or miss, because that meant they came straggling in one bunch at a time, tired and disgusted, and when they'd hear what had happened they'd blow some about what they would have done if, then they'd drift off for food and sleep so there wasn't many of them close around at any one time. Goss was hammering on the office door every few hours wanting to know was Scott going to help or hinder the law, was he notifying the proper authorities so a trial could get started. He was worried, Goss was. He wanted to see Brent at the end of a rope and fast. He didn't want what Brent had done to get contagious, have other people taking guns and trying to chase his jumpers off land that had been theirs. I expect that was the only thing Scott and that Goss ever agreed on, that the trial ought to be over and done quick as possible. Scott knew Brent and knew that was all Brent wanted now and that staying in jail was hard on a man like him.

Scott sent Morrison over to the county seat right away to make arrangements. He wanted to get Brent out of our town where feeling ran high and over there where he thought the trial would be anyway. But Morrison came back and three other men with him. They turned out to be a new judge and an assistant clerk of court and a lawyer who'd been sworn in to act as prosecutor. "They're so jammed over there," Morrison said, "that it would be months maybe longer before this case could get in. The best they can do and they about insist on it is spare these men a few days so the trial can be held right here. It's irregular but it's legal enough." Scott was disappointed but after he thought it over he even perked some. "Maybe it's for the best," he said. "There's still a bit of the old-time spirit left around here."

He was right. You could almost feel it in the air around town. The most talk, the most noise, was made by the claim jumpers and those who sided with them, who figured the old days were gone and maybe a good thing too because they were poky and not much money around so let's go along and make things boom and make money too because that's the most important duty a person has and anybody who gets in the way ought to be shoved aside and we can't have old soreheads going about shooting people anyway. But here and there were those who'd lived here longer and known what it was like once and who looked on old Brent as one of them, something that had belonged to them in a special peculiar way like an old landmark and the big rocky quietness of the mountains around, and even if they didn't mind the town getting bigger and more bustling they still didn't hold with having a bunch of newcomers pushing people out and taking over and beginning to run things. Arguments were plenty along the main street and in the saloons. That makeshift courtroom across the hall from the office was packed to the limit when the trial started about the fourth day.

I'll say this, the judge was fair. He didn't like the assignment much but he was fair and he knew his law and he had a sharp dry I'm-in-charge-here manner of speaking that helped keep reasonable good order. Picking a jury took all morning. Morrison was acting for Brent who just plain wouldn't hear to hiring a special lawyer. "I don't want any legal trickery or finagling," he said. "All I want is an old friend and an honest man and Fred here's both." Morrison and that prosecutor had some wrangles over jurymen but when it was finished Morrison had what he was after. He had five of the old settlers on that jury.

After noon recess Scott and I brought Brent in and the real business started. It took longer than was needed, most of the afternoon, because that prosecutor insisted on calling as witnesses just about everybody who'd hurried to the place here soon after the shooting. He even wanted to have Malley carted in on a stretcher to testify, but the doctor was firm against that. Malley was still in bad shape, touch and go with that ripped lung, and the doc wouldn't let him be moved. The prosecutor didn't know old Brent or he'd have known all that wasn't needed, there wouldn't be any contesting the facts or twisting what happened. There'd be straight truth-telling and no dodging and no whining. And that's what he got when Brent took the stand.

Brent had been sitting there while the rest went on, Scott on one side him me on the other, sitting still and quiet as an old rock, looking across the room, over the heads of the jury facing him, right through the opposite wall and off into the distance. When he was called he stepped up on the little platform and sat on the chair there and when that prosecutor started on him he bent his head forward a little and focused straight on him. He answered the first questions polite enough. Then he saw how that prosecutor was winding around and he was a bit peeved. "Son," he said. "What you're after or should be is to show what happened. Your way'll take all day. Shut your yap and I'll tell you." The prosecutor began bur-bling something and the judge cut in, sharp and dry, with the comment that might be a good notion. So Brent told what had happened out here, straightforward, sim-ple, and it tied in with what some of the witnesses said Malley'd said when they got to him. Listening to Brent you knew, everybody knew, that was exact how it was.

The real wrangling came when Morrison took over. He couldn't explain away what Brent had done but he could aim at showing why. He kept Brent on the stand quite a while, bringing out the background of the whole business and digging into the claim-jumping and just about every question he'd ask, that prosecutor would be on his feet shouting objections and there'd be cracking back and forth whether it was pertinent or not and the judge would have to rule and mutterings and remarks were breaking out all through the room. It was Brent shut it off. "Quit

fussing, Fred," he said. "You mean well but you'll only
tangle things more. Everybody on that jury knows all
that, knows why I did it, or they're more stupid than they
look." Most of the jury sat up straighter, staring at him,
and the room quieted and he went right on. "Let's get
this over with. I killed those two men. It was just my
sloppy shooting didn't make it Malley too. The only question now is does that jury think I had reason enough.
Likely not. They don't look like much to me."

The judge was staring at him, eyes narrowed, like he'd
never bumped against Brent's kind before. The whole
room was quiet and in the quiet there was a sudden sound,
a sobbing catch of breath. It was Lettie, on one of the
back rows of seats between Mrs. Morrison and Mrs. Martin, fighting hard not to cry. And old Brent looked out at
her. "Lettie," he said. "None of that. Aint I always told
you how a man should be? When he decides to do something, why do it and face up to what it means." Brent
turned towards the table that was the judge's bench.
"Judge," he said. "You been acting square, according to
your rules. Can't you hurry this thing along?" He stood
up, stretching tall, and he stepped down from the stand
and came and sat between Scott and me and nobody made
a move to stop him.

The judge hurried it but he didn't have to do much
urging. That prosecutor kept his remarks to the jury
brief and to the point. He figured it was a cinch now,
that Brent had clinched it himself by admitting everything right out and then ruffling the jury. Morrison was
just as short. He knew by now that what would happen
would happen regardless of what he said and if he'd done
anything it was when the jury was being picked. Then
the judge gave his instructions, brief too, and he sent the

jury upstairs to our living quarters to do their deliberating
and the waiting began.

We could hear them moving around some up there and
now and again we'd hear voices, not clear enough to make
out words, just enough so we'd know they were arguing.
It got to be suppertime and most people drifted off to eat
and some came back and wandered around, inside and
out, waiting. The judge and those other two officials went
out and came back and Scott and I took turns. Old Brent
was back in the jail and ate there. Lettie brought him
food as she always did, going past Scott and me like we
didn't exist, in and out without a word, and we left her
alone in there with him as we always did too.

About nine o'clock the foreman came down. He was
red-faced, peeved. They were having a time, he said, and
that prosecutor snorted at that and the foreman went on,
couldn't they knock off for the night and go at it again in
the morning. But the judge said no, his time was running
out, he'd keep them up there till they reached a verdict.
He couldn't stop them flopping where they could and nap-
ping some and he'd have food sent up but that was all.

We worried through that night and no verdict. The
judge said call him if and he and the other two went and
got some sleep somewhere. Scott and I made out in the
office. All the next morning and the same. The whole
town was waiting. People were milling up and down the
main street, talking and arguing and wandering around.
The saloons did mighty good business. Goss and his special crew were camping in the courtroom, trying to or pretending to play poker in one corner and getting madder
by the minute, and most of his paid settlers were around
town somewhere. The judge was getting impatient. He'd
planned to leave by the evening stage. He sat at his table-

bench playing solitaire and near wore out his cards. And old Brent sat sometimes on the chair in his part of the jail and lay sometimes on the bunk, still and quiet as an old rock, staring right through everything around him off into the distance.

"Goldamn it, Scott," I said. "Why aren't you in there talking to him? He seems so all alone."

"No," Scott said. "He's off where I can't follow. He's been farther and done more than I ever did. He's best alone now."

So the waiting went on. Along late afternoon the whole jury came stomping down the stairs. They looked like they'd been having a time all right. They were all red-faced and they wouldn't look much at each other. The foreman didn't even wait for the judge to get in a peep. "We're quitting!" he said. "We had it seven to five for a hanging at the start and we got it down to nine to three and we're stuck and we're quitting!"

The judge looked them over, disgusted, and took hold. "All right," he said. "We ought to have the prisoner in here and make this formal but I won't bother. I'm discharging you as a hung jury. I'm declaring a retrial. Date to be set soon. You'll get your duty money in a few days. Now clear out, I have a stage to catch." It happened so fast word hadn't got outside yet and not many people were in the room. Those jurymen straggled out. Other people followed them, hurrying to spread the news, and that left only Goss and his crew. They'd dropped their cards and were standing in a bunch looking mean, specially Goss. His law-manipulating wasn't going according to schedule. And the judge showed then maybe he knew more about what was behind all this than I'd figured before. "That means you too, Mr. Goss," he said. "I'm clearing this courtroom." And there wasn't a thing Goss could do, not then, except go out and his crew with him.

The rest of us, that's Scott and me and the judge and those other two officials, went into the office so they could fix up their records. I ducked back to the jail part and told Brent and all he did was raise up a little on the bunk and say: "So it aint over yet. They didn't look like much. Couldn't even make up their minds." He lay back again and I hurried out because I wanted to get across the street and tell Lettie. I had to plow through people milling around in the street because the word was spreading fast. I pushed right into the house and she had the room door closed where she was and I hammered on it and shouted something about the jury and then I shouted didn't she hear me. Sudden she yanked the door open and she really looked bad, all worn and tired and red-eyed. "They couldn't agree," I said, "so the judge discharged them." Her face lit up like a match when you strike it. "Does that mean they'll let him go?" she said. "No," I had to say. "It means there'll be another trial." Her face got hard and she glared at me. "You and your law," she said. "You're just playing with him. Dragging it out. Making it worse." She slammed the door shut and all I could do was go back to the office.

The judge was just leaving, the other two with him. "Don't get me wrong," he was saying to Scott. "I was dragooned into this job so I'm doing it. I don't care a hoot whether he hangs or not, except how, though he does have a lot of pepper in him and we don't seem to have too much of that nowadays. It's for a jury to say. But I'll do what I can. I'll see about a transfer right away and let you know." They left, heading for the stage station, and Scott closed and bolted the front door of the building after them and came back into the office and settled on a chair by the front window.

"Ben," he said. "I aint your father and I aint built right to be, maybe not even a fair substitute. I don't know how to put things. But you're getting a strong taste of it. The way it is sometimes. The law I mean. Being a sheriff aint always making people behave decent and strutting some with a badge and getting a name. It's being the middle sometimes with the right and wrong of things all mixed and all you can do is set a course that seems right to you and hold to it. There's that Goss that's first cousin to a rattlesnake and I wouldn't trust with a nickel walking around free as air. There's Brent that I'd trust my life to anytime anywhere in the jail waiting for another trial that can mean his neck. You could pull out of this, Ben. A young one like you with everything still ahead. Maybe that's one thing would make sense."

I looked at him sitting there, not much on size but all the same with that clear and almost lonesome completeness within himself a goldamned good fighting man and I don't mean just fighting with a gun or muscle but fighting straight and steady and maybe bullheaded and stubborn but still straight and steady through all the doings big and little and decent and mean alike of all the days of living and I thought of old Brent back there following the trail he'd started and Scott sitting here holding to the course he'd set and I saw that pulling out wouldn't make any sense, not for me, and that maybe one of the few things that do make sense is sticking to what you've come to believe in no matter what and seeing some purpose in living other than just getting through the days pleasant as possible and even if I didn't have any yet nobody could stop me going on looking.

"No," I said. "I'm not pulling out. But not because I

like what I've seen of the law much. Likely for a lot of
reasons. Maybe one's because my father whopped people
that tried picking on you once and I know why he
did."

He looked at me. "Thank you, Ben," he said, simple
and quiet. "That pays for a lot. I guess you're a Hammon
all right. Now get upstairs and clean things some. Likely
they made a mess."

They had. They'd made a real clutter. It took me a
while cleaning up and when I went down again Scott was
still by the window. "I don't like it," he said. "Trial's
over and they know how it came out and the new one can't
be for a while but the crowd aint thinning out any. Not
much anyway. They're staying away from this building
and that's good. But they're hanging around."

"You want me to go out and circulate around some?" I
said.

"No," he said. "Neither one of us is leaving here.
Maybe I'm just jumpy but we'll sit tight."

I watched out the window with him and he was right.
Too many people were out there. They were staying
away from the open space in front of the building but we
could see them going up and down the street, wandering
around and talking in bunches and drifting on down towards the saloons and out again and around, and too many
of them were men that'd come into our territory taking
orders from Goss. But they were staying away from our
building. They'd look over towards it and a couple times
I saw some pointing but that was all.

We sat by the window and the sun was low, throwing
long shadows outside, ready to drop behind the mountains to the west, and then Lettie was coming across the
street with her tray of food. I unbolted the front door for
her and bolted it again. She marched into the office, not

looking at either of us and maybe the reason she wouldn't
and wouldn't speak was she was afraid she'd break down
but you couldn't be sure, not the hard way her face was set,
and she put a plate with a couple fat sandwiches on Scott's
desk. "Nice of you, Lettie," Scott said. "That's Mrs. Morrison," she said and went right on with her tray into the
back room and pulled the door closed after her. We ate
the sandwiches and after a while she came out, still not
looking at us, and headed for the outside door. "Lettie,"
Scott said and she kept on. "Lettie," he said again, sharp,
almost mean, and she stopped. "Quit acting a fool," he
said. "Soon as you get back you tell Fred Morrison to
move about some and come here the back way and tell
me what's doing." She just nodded and I unbolted the
door for her and she went on and across the street.

It wasn't much later when Morrison rapped on the door
at the rear end of the hall. I was waiting for him and let
him in. That door had a good bolt too and I fastened it
soon as he was in. He was uneasy and worried, but not too
much. He started talking right there in the hall. "Well,
Scott," he said. "Well. I'm glad you sent word. I was so
busy catching up accounts at the store I wasn't aware. But
I don't think you'll have trouble. There is considerable
talking. Yes, yes. What you would expect. The law is
too slow. It is not certain. Perhaps something should be
done. With the usual cuss words and foul language for
trimmings. But no one is steamed up enough to touch
things off. There has been one ruckus. One of those jury
holdouts was fool enough to stay around and just a while
ago several of the others jumped him and he took a beating before he got away. That was tough on him but maybe
it was a good thing. It's something new to talk about and
it blew off some of the steam."

"Goss," Scott said. "What's he doing?"

"Yes," Morrison went. "Yes. That is the real trouble spot if there is one. He is buying drinks. He is buying all they will take for those talking against Brent. I don't know what he is saying because he kept his mouth shut when I was by. I am not so certain he would really like to get something started, though he was mad enough earlier. It isn't as if Brent were acquitted."

"Maybe," Scott said. "But he was after a hanging and he hasn't got it. He aint absolute positive now he will. And he knows his jumpers aint going to be feeling safe till he does."

"Well, yes," Morrison said. "Well, yes, perhaps. But just a delay is not enough to push things. He is not getting anywhere. He is only getting them drunk. In a short while now they will barely be able — "

Morrison stopped. He jumped a little. I guess we all did. There was another rapping at the rear door. Scott's old forty-five was in his hand. I don't know how but sudden it was there. He motioned me to go unbolt the door. I did and the person outside pushed in. It was Tim Ballard, that saloon man Scott tangled with when the boom first started. He nodded around. "Hammon," he said. "I thought you ought to know. Malley's just died."

There was silence in that hallway and faint, far off from down the street outside, we could hear some yelling and that faded out and the only sound was the soft slither of metal on leather as Scott slipped his gun back in its holster.

"A man came legging into my place with the news," Ballard said. "I saw how the boys were taking it. Then Goss came in talking big and he looked too blamed pleased to suit me. So I came here."

Morrison sighed. He looked older all at once and kind of sad. "So I was wrong," he said.

"Hammon," Ballard said. "You cut down my profit with your damn curfew. You busted four lamps for which nobody's paid me a cent yet. I don't know why that puts anything up to me but somehow it does. My bartender can take care of the place. If you don't mind I'll stay here a while with you and see what happens." He reached a hand into the side pocket of the jacket he had on and pulled it part way out, enough to show he had a gun there. "I'm not too good," he said. "But I've used this a little in my time."

The back door was opening again. It was Morrison, going out. That shook me. I hadn't figured him that way. I hurried and bolted the door after him. "Stay there," Scott said. "Watch that door. You never can tell." And he and Ballard went into the office where they could watch out the window.

I stayed there by the back door and faint I could hear the yelling again and the quick dusk of this mountain country dropped and it was dim and growing dark in that hall. Then I heard, not a rapping, just a scratching on the door. "Who's there?" I said. On the instant I could hear Scott and Ballard coming into the hall behind me. "Morrison," a voice said outside, low and not much more than a pushing whisper, but it was his voice and I opened the door and he came in and he had an old shotgun in his hands and right behind him was the thick barrel-shape of Rufe Martin. "Bolt that door," he said and I did. "Scott," he said, "Lettie is safe at the house. I told the wife to keep her there no matter what. Rufe and I thought perhaps we could slip Brent out. But they are posting men around."

A cold shiver hit me, thinking of us cooped up in that building with men around watching to keep us there for whatever would happen, and then it was gone because my uncle Scott was speaking. "Going to play it rough," he said. He didn't say that at all worried. There was even an edge of eagerness on his voice like he was glad how things were because maybe at last he'd have a chance to cut loose. "They don't know what rough is," he said. "They'll find out."

He took us into the office stumbling some in the growing dark and he lit a lamp and set it on the floor in a corner behind the desk so the light was just spread out dim through the room and enough into the hall so we could make out to move around. He went to the old cupboard in the opposite corner and unlocked the padlock on it and took out a rifle and loaded it and handed it to Martin and another for me. "No shooting," he said, "unless they rush us. I've bluffed out these things before."

That was when he heard the yelling again, louder, coming closer, fading out again only now in front of us, across the way. Out the window we could see them, dark shapes across the open space and in the street, a whole crowd of them, more than a hundred I'd say because somehow people who aren't really in on a mob still go straggling along sort of fascinated and blood-hungry and eager to watch and maybe are even stampeded into taking part. There was one bunch, about fifteen of them, close together and pushing out some and they were the ones to watch and a half dozen of them came cautious across the street and the open space and up on the porch. "Hammon," someone shouted. "We want to talk to you."

"Go ahead, talk," Scott shouted.

"Where we can see you," the voice shouted.

"Talk is it?" Scott whispered to us. "That's a good sign. They aint screwed to the point." He stood up from where he was crouching by the window. "I'm going out," he said. "In the doorway. Got to show them I aint afraid of the whole caboodle. Let them see too we're ready for them." He posted us in the hall backing him where the dim light from the office would show on us. "Stand back from that door," he shouted. "I'm coming out." He unbolted the door and the second the bolt was slipped they pushed from the outside, swinging the door in and shoving him back, and two of them crowded into the doorway and in the same instant Scott's old forty-five was in his hand bearing on them and they saw us all facing them with guns ready and they froze where they were. "Talk fast," Scott said.

"What the hell?" someone said. "That's Ballard."

"The blacksmith too," another one said.

They were some surprised. They fidgeted around but they didn't back off.

"Thought you wanted to talk," Scott said.

"Hammon," a voice out on the porch said and it belonged to Goss. "I'm not speaking for myself. I'm just speaking for these men here who — "

"Quit that, Goss," another voice said. "You're in this too. All we want, Hammon, is for you to clear out. You chuck in your badge and clear out and you'll be all right. We aint waiting for any elections. We're taking over."

"A bunch of drunks like you?" Scott said. "I ought to lock you all up but I aint got the time. You thought there was only two of us here. There's five good guns waiting if you start anything. You won't. Now clear that doorway."

"This is a public building, aint it?" someone shouted. "We got as much right here as anybody."

"Say something," Scott whispered to Morrison and that Morrison, quick on the talking trigger, began spouting something about being a justice of the peace and as such ordering them to disperse and go home think things over. But I didn't hear much because Scott was whispering to me. "Any gunplay now the whole town'll bust loose. Can you clear that doorway?" And sudden I felt good. I'd been trailing along thinking I was about useless because even with a rifle in my hands I couldn't do much being as I never was good with guns. I was just a big overgrown lunkhead. But I had size. I had muscle. I reached over in the dim light and leaned that rifle against the wall. I put my head down some and sudden I drove forward and I curved out both arms to take in those two in the doorway and I carried them right off their feet and on out through and smacked them and myself into those outside and I heaved the way I'd spent years heaving on big old plow handles when I was growing and the whole bunch of them went sprawling this side and that and some even off the porch and I ducked back in fast and Scott slammed and bolted the door.

"All right, Rufe," he said. "You and Ballard take the courtroom windows, front and side. "Fred, you take the back door. I'll take the office window. Ben, you be ready for wherever you're needed. Keep an eye on the front door but that's likely safe. Anybody comes close'd be in crossfire from the windows." The others scattered to their places and he crouched by the office window and raised it open a bit. "Every door and window's guarded," he called out. "Better call it a day and go home."

Those who'd been at the door had scurried back to the street, maybe thinking a bullet or two'd come after them, likely mad as hornets. There'd been some satisfying crunching when I hit. Across the way there was a lot of racket, people talking and shouting and milling around. More of them seemed to be out there even than before but they were staying away from in front of the building.

"Too much light in here," Scott said. "Makes me an inviting target at that window. But we got to have a little." He took the lamp from the corner and opened the door to the back room to set the lamp on the floor inside and to one side so only a little light would come through the doorway. That lit up the blank-walled big inner room and back in the jail part we could see old Brent. He was sitting on the edge of the bunk watching us. As the light hit his deep old eyes you could tell that he knew, that he knew everything. His keen old ears had been hearing things through those single-partition walls and he knew. "Scott," he said and it was sort of funny, him telling us who'd been out front in it. "Scott. There's bad weather brewing. A real storm."

"Nothing we can't handle," Scott said. "Don't you worry."

"I aint worrying," Brent said. "Not about that." And Scott swung around, hurrying again to his window, and Brent caught me with a little flip of his head. I went closer and he beckoned me right up to the bars. "Boy," he said. "Where's Lettie?"

"Over at Morrison's," I said.

"Good," he said. "This aint for her. Her time's ahead. I've had mine. This is me alone again the way it ought to be with Sarah gone. The way it was before I knew her, when it was mostly just me and the bigness of this country around and now and again — "

"Shucks, Brent," I said. "You're not alone. There's — "

He stopped me with a hand up. "Think I don't know?"

he said. "It's a crazy fool world, boy. There's a lot of men out there working themselves up and plenty will get their fool head shot off if they start something and this whole section'll get split apart worse than it is already and there'll be bush-whacking and dry-gulching and fighting around for a long time. There's that damned little coyote Scott who'll maybe get his fool head shot off too though that'll take doing. There's you, boy. And those others. That Ballard now. Who'd have thought it of him? And it's all over what'll only be a pile of old bones at the end and soon enough anyway. That's me. It ought to make me feel important. It don't."

"Brent," I said. "It's not just you."

"Don't try to blow it up, boy," he said. "Right here and now it's me." There was a new burst of yelling outside and he looked past me towards the front. "Go see what's happening," he said.

I hurried to the office and crouched down by the window with Scott. They'd started a fire in the street, down a little ways, and were piling wood on it. A wagon came up and the man driving swung it sidewise near the fire and stopped the horses and another man climbed up on the seat and stood up there and started talking. We couldn't hear him but we could hear shouts rising off and on and we could see pretty well in the firelight. "I'll be damned," Scott said. "They've got a body in that wagon. Must be Malley's. And that's Goss talking."

The crowd was thick around the wagon and Goss up on the seat was having to raise his voice to be heard but even so we couldn't make him out because the men swarming around were raising what reached us as just a mixed angry yelling. Then one voice climbed above the others: "Burn 'em out!"

Scott pressed closer to the window and something pulled me around to look into the back room. Brent was up, standing close against the barred door to his part of the jail. He was beckoning to me. I slipped away and Scott was so intent he didn't notice me go. "Well, boy?" Brent said. "They're planning to burn us out," I said. He looked at me and that look held me there, still and waiting, and then he said, soft, very soft: "All right, boy. Unlock this door."

I've wondered countless times why I did it. Maybe I figured that if they were going to try set fire to the place it wasn't right for him to be penned in there. But I don't remember any figuring. I only remember doing it. I think it was just plain because old Brent Kean told me to. I think it was simple as that. I leaned the rifle I was carrying against the side bars and I reached in my pocket for the big flat key that was the same as the one in Scott's pocket too and I unlocked the door.

He pulled the door open and came through. He moved swift and easy as a big lean old cat despite his limp. He reached with one hand and set it for a tiny tick of time on my shoulder as he passed me and with the other hand he scooped up that rifle. He stood there in the open a few seconds checking the load with quick experienced old fingers then he was moving towards the office and as I say, that's the story, the real story, old Brent Kean with long memories in his mind and a rifle in his hand.

He slipped into the office, quiet, and the rifle held at his hip was bearing on Scott and the first Scott knew he was there was when he said: "Hold it, Scott. Don't move." And Scott froze still, crouched down by the window, only his head moving so he could look around and up, and Scott's eyes flicked over at me following Brent into the inner doorway and narrowed some and back to Brent. "I'd use this gun," Brent said. "On you. All I want is one minute. One minute for myself before you do anything at all."

Scott looked up at him. It seemed to me Scott just plain wanted to cry, wanted to put his head down and bawl. "I aint afraid of your gun," he said and then his voice broke and the words came shaking. "Or any man's. Or anything they think of trying."

"I know that," Brent said and they looked at each other and then Scott's voice was steady again. "Then that's enough," he said. "Have it your way." And old Brent turned and was out in the hall and we heard him unbolting the front door and we heard Morrison's voice from the rear end of the hall saying something in surprise and the front door opened and Brent was out on the porch.

I jumped to the window by Scott and we both peered out. He loomed up there on the outer porch edge, lean and tall in the faint far edge of the light from the fire out in the street. Then they saw him. The yells climbing told they knew who it was. He stepped down and out some into the open space and he raised that rifle and fired once, twice, and the first answering shot was an echo of his third and more guns were blazing from out in the street and he staggered and dropped to his knees and collapsed slow sideways and lay still.

The silence that shut down outside was sudden and complete then there was the sound of running feet and all of us in the building were out on the porch and those men in the street were scattering, scurrying off into the darkness, and the wagon went clattering off fast, and its sound faded and there was only a fire out there lighting the emptiness. We looked down at the body of old Brent, limp and still on the ground. "The damned old wolf," Tim Ballard said. "He wanted to go down fighting."

"No," Scott said.

I stared at him because I didn't get it at first.

"He could pick off a running deer at three hundred yards," Scott said. "There was a whole crowd out there. Maybe a hundred twenty feet. Look sharp. You see anybody hit lying out there?"

We looked. There was only an empty street and a fire lighting some of it and sending flickering shadows along it.

"Fred," Scott said. "You go over to Lettie. Rest of you take him inside." And Scott stepped down off the porch and started away. I hurried after him. "Where you going?" I said.

"Goss," he said. He went right on. He went right past Brent's body without stopping. I hesitated then I followed and I picked up the rifle lying beside Brent's body as I passed. All kind of wild notions were pounding in my head and I was fed up with the whole goldamned world and I kept thinking that even if I couldn't do much with that rifle as a gun I could do plenty damage with it as a club. But I should have known. He was Scott Hammon. He couldn't be anything else. He made his own rules and he held to them.

We stopped at the first saloon and looked in. There were quite a few men in there but not as many as I thought there'd be. They were crowded by the bar and they were being unusual quiet. They saw Scott in the doorway and looked at each other and away and fidgeted around. But Goss wasn't there. It was in the fourth place that we found him. We went in and Scott went up and took his stand about ten feet from him and the population in that saloon dwindled mighty quick.

"Now, Hammon," Goss said. "Don't you go — "

"Shut up," Scott said. He didn't take his eyes off Goss and he spoke kind of slow and cold. "A man smart as I seem to be knows what happened can't be pinned on anybody. Technically Kean was breaking jail. Impossible to prove whose bullet got him anyway. But there's one piece of my old-fashioned law I can still make stick. I'm running you out of town. Disturbing the peace. Inciting to riot. I'm giving you one hour to get out. I find you here then or any time after I'll shoot you on sight."

Goss got out. We never saw him again.

Of course the company just sent in another man but he was wary, he only stopped by every so often to check and he didn't push things. Claim-jumping in our section slowed down. No more jumpers were sent in and some of those first ones quit and left though most of them finally got title and collected before they left too. The company did all right, got most of what it was after as such outfits about always do.

We buried old Brent the next morning, next to Sarah in the town cemetery. There was one thing funny about that. Lettie didn't show at all. "Staying in her room," Fred Morrison said. "She doesn't want to see anybody." But she was a Kean, Lettie was. She had old Brent's blood in her and Sarah's too and she could take hold.

It was early afternoon the same day and we were sitting in the office, Scott and me. He was by the window and he wasn't saying much, not even about my unlocking the jail door. He never once said a thing to me about that, not once even in the years after which weren't too many for him though the kids did get to know him some when they were little before the big blizzard and he was out helping open the way to snowed in families and froze a foot, the one that didn't have good circulation because he'd been winged in that leg once, and gangrene set in and took him in just a couple days. I figure knowing him even that little helped the kids turn out right.

But as I say, he was by the window and I was by the desk, about as low as I ever was. Even with Scott sitting there, a Hammon like me and not really so complete and firm within himself that once in a while he wouldn't break down and let me know it, even with that I felt like I didn't belong anywhere at all, not even around here. I wasn't going to stick around that office any more, not after what had happened. It had the smell of law about it even though maybe only Scott's kind of law and I'd had enough of any kind. I didn't have anything to be doing, to be aiming at, and couldn't even begin to think of anything. And then I got to thinking about when I was plowing that patch out there and how it was, doing what I really could do right and Lettie watching me and making me mad, the kind of singing-inside mad my father must have had when he was arguing with my mother, and that made me even lower because what I'd done had finished that. And Scott said: "There's a wagon outside."

I looked out and there was Brent's big old wagon with his team hitched to it and it was stopping out front and Lettie was up on the seat driving.

All I could do was stare and Scott said: "Get on out there."

"I can't," I said. "Not after what I did."

"Aint you learned anything yet?" he said. "There's people and there's people. That's Lettie Kean out there. Brent Kean's girl. Now you jump."

I went out because there was something I had to tell her and I didn't want to but I had to do it. She sat there looking down at me and she was in pretty bad shape. She couldn't keep the tears out of her eyes and some would slip over and run down and she'd been wiping at them with a hand dusty from the reins and that'd left dirt streaks.

"Lettie," I said. "I'm the one let him out."

She looked at me and her eyes didn't waver any. "He wanted you to, didn't he?" she said.

"Yes," I said.

She looked at me and she nodded her head a little and then it hit me, her being there on that wagon.

"Where are you going?" I said.

"I'm going home," she said. "He wanted it to be Kean land. He wanted a Kean to be living on the place. Malley's dead and no relatives and the claim's open. I'm a citizen. I was born here and I'm past twenty-one. I've been at the land office and I've filed on it."

"Lettie," I said. "You can't do that. A woman can't handle a farm all alone."

"I thought," she said, "I thought maybe I wouldn't have to do it alone." And then she fixed me for life. She raised her voice, not a real shout, just an echo of a big old voice we both had known. "You overgrown lunkhead," she said. "Why aren't you climbing up on this wagon?"

I stepped up on the near front wheel hub and to the seat and sat beside her. I reached and took the reins from her and we drove on out home here.

Stalemate

*

A STORY? Me? Expect there's plenty packed away in
this head of mine. But my yap's been closed on them so
long likely they're a mite mildewed. I been sitting here
by the fire listening to you young ones tell yours. Been
noticing how you blow considerable air into them. How
the hunting you say you've done gets dangerouser and
dangerouser. How the critters you say you've killed get
bigger and bigger. That's plumb natural. Storytelling
runs that way. Next story's always got to top the one afore
or it aint worth the telling. All the same such talk puts me
in mind of a man I used to know.

This was back down the years a good piece. Charlie
Forespell was still around then, had a nice spread a couple
miles out that level stretch west of town. Ranch buildings
about where the railroad yard is now. Open country it
was then with the fence lines just beginning to sneak in
around the edges. Old Charlie'd been one of those hated
even the thought of a fence but he'd learned a thing or
two back in the winter of '86. He'd been near wiped out
like the other cattlemen in these parts. Cattle on the open
range couldn't take it that winter. Couldn't stand out
the storms. Couldn't get through the snow to the dried
bunch grass. Starved. Froze. Come spring maybe one in

ten was still staggering around. Old Charlie never forgot that. Winters seemed to ease some after but Charlie never forgot. He ran some fence of his own. Built himself a winter feedlot, big one, must have been more'n a hundred acres. Kept his best stuff in there through the bad months. Couple of his boys would bring a wagon along the near fence every morning and fork the hay over.

This time I'm telling about the winter wasn't bad, not much snow and warmish spells. One morning the boys on the hay wagon came running to the house to get old Charlie and took him out to the feedlot and through the fence and showed him something on the ground inside. It was one of his best steers, a four-year-old, lying there with its neck broke and big chunks of the belly and haunch meat gone. Didn't need even an oldtimer like Charlie to know what'd happened. The tracks were plain. It was a grizzly'd done that trick, a granddaddy grizzly from the signs, big and knowing, that'd slipped down out of the mountains and right to that feedlot not much more'n a quarter mile from the barns and bunkhouse and over the fence and to dinner. Didn't stampede the rest of the steers or set them to bawling. Just nipped off that one over in a corner to windward. Surprised it, that steer, bedded down and it piled up and started running and this bear was alongside in about three jumps and smacked it on the head with one paw flip and broke its neck.

Charlie was plenty peeved. If this big old bear was having a restless winter because of the warmish spells and couldn't sleep through and took to roaming some and couldn't find ready meals and had to knock over one of his cheap-grade range steers, why Charlie wouldn't have minded too much. That was part of the cattle game in those days. Course he'd have had his boys packing rifles when they were out and on the prod for anything in fur, but he wouldn't have taken it so personal and peevish. This blamed bear hadn't bothered with any of the scrub stuff roaming loose. It'd come straight to headquarters and picked one of his prize stock.

Charlie whistled in all hands and they saddled and took out on the trail. Tracking was easy because there was snow in patches and this bear hadn't tried to skirt them, had gone straight ahead like it didn't care what followed, leaving its sign big and bold. Charlie and the boys found where it'd snugged down for a nap and had roused and started on not too far ahead now. They rode hard and they rode long and they climbed into rough country and wore out the horses and then the tracks just faded. Seemed like this bear'd figured to give them a workout and final decided to shake them and did. They beat the brush some but not too thorough where it was thick because they'd seen the size of those tracks. They rode home about dark, tired and disgusted and jumping at shadows.

Well, now, that was only the beginning. Four nights later this bear was back. Nipped off another steer in the far corner of the feedlot and made a meal and departed. This time Charlie sent a couple of hands out with supplies on a packhorse to stick to the trail and scour the country where it led. Three days and they were back, ready to draw their time rather'n do any more of that kind of work. The blamed bear'd been running them out of their saddles and about out of their boots too. Seemed to them like it knew what they were doing and wanted to wear them down. They'd find tracks and follow and these'd take them over country that'd worry a mountain goat into places they'd have to go on foot worrying about the critter jumping them any minute. They'd lose the

tracks and spend hours searching around and be about
wore down to quitting and there'd be more tracks, fresh-
made like just done for their benefit and the whole thing'd
start all over again. Nights they were certain sure the
critter was somewhere close, maybe arguing with itself
whether to try a new kind of meat, and that didn't encour-
age sound sleeping. Two days and two nights and the
closest they came to catching sight of this bear was spot-
ting a little snarl of silver-tip hair on a bramble bush.
Third morning they found a nice set of tracks new-made
close by and figured to try once more. They followed a
quarter mile, maybe a mite more, when they heard a
racket back by their camp. Scurried there, rifles ready,
and this bear'd been and gone. The packhorse'd snapped
his picket rope and likely was halfway to the Missouri already and their camp stuff was smashed and scattered over
half an acre. They looked around careful but they knew
they'd never get a sight down on a critter that smart.
Started talking together and in a matter of minutes talked
themselves into heading for the ranch. Old Charlie cussed
those two some but not too much. He'd seen some of those
tracks himself and had a taste how this bear could operate.
He simmered down enough to lay out a schedule of night
work, two men a night to be patrolling the feedlot from
dark to sunup.

That was one way to do it. Keep the steers safe, that is,
not get this bear. Likely it slipped close and figured what
was doing because long as there was night guarding things
were quiet. But there was a catch. Man who's been out
all night in the shivery, moving to cover territory and
keep warm, aint in shape or mind to do much the next
day. Charlie had to let his night men lay off days and
being as he was close-handed already that meant getting

behind on regular work. About a week and he stopped the night guarding to catch up and this bear was back for another meal off another steer.

Charlie was more'n peeved now. Went around muttering to himself and swearing he'd have this bear's hide for a rug so he could tromp on it. Tried everything he could think up. Hid traps along the fence lines and caught only a lonesome old coyote and one of his own horses that got out of the corral and went wandering. Horse had to be shot after what the trap did to a leg. That didn't improve Charlie's feeling much of anything. He left the latest steer carcass lying in the feedlot dosed heavy with poison figuring this bear might try a second helping the way most of them will but the critter knew about such or just plain didn't like its meat cold and nipped off a fresh supply. He got Cal Whipman out from town who had a pack of dogs he boasted about and they spent a long day on the trail and pulled in late and lame without once sighting this bear but the dogs must of because two of them never came home at all and the rest dragged in, tails on the ground and acting like they wouldn't tackle even a rabbit any more.

Charlie began taking all this mighty personal. Seemed to him like this bear had a grouch against him alone. A couple of other ranchers were within riding distance, easy range for a bear like this one, but they didn't lose any stock. Course Charlie could of looked at that as another proof he raised the best beef around but he was raising that beef for cash-money not bear food. He took to prowling at night himself, night after night, old as he was, wearing himself ragged what with the cold and the lack of sleep until final, at the doc's say so, the boys had to put him to bed and tie him down.

Next morning they came in to tell him another steer
was nipped, seventh it was since the whole business began,
and old Charlie was licked. He'd had a stiff neck always
and he'd taken care of things himself or with his own outfit never asking for help but this blamed bear had him
licked. He lay on the bed and chewed his old mustache.
"Unwind this rope," he said, "and don't fret over me cutting any capers. I aint playing it young any more." So the
boys unwound him off the mattress and he had himself
heaved on a horse and rode into town to see Cal Graham
who used to put out a little weekly sheet between more
pressing duties tending his bar. "Five hundred dollars,"
old Charlie said. "Spread that big in your paper. I'm
paying five hundred good American dollars to the man
that brings me the hide of that grizzle-hair that's raiding
my place."

Well, now, that stirred quite a fluttering. Charlie had to
clamp hard on his own hands or they'd have been out most
of the time whacking the brush and he wouldn't have got
any work done. People packing rifles were thicker'n bugs
in a bun for a while up in the hills where this bear hid out.
Plenty ammunition was wasted by jackasses blazing away
into thickets on the off chance of flushing the critter. Only
thing accomplished that way was when one fool firing
into a big patch winged another who was around the other
side preparing to do the same. A few others claimed they
sighted this bear with each swearing it was bigger'n the
one afore but talk like that don't cost much. Likely this
bear, being what it was, knew the first day what was doing
and passed the light hours off somewhere high up where
it could see the fun, slipping down during the dark to
leave more tracks and keep the pot boiling. Anyways
nothing real much happened and after a time people be-

gan thinking they didn't need five hundred dollars that bad or if they did maybe they'd find easier ways of getting same. Course soon as they'd all been gone a day or two this bear ambled down to headquarters again and nipped another steer. But old Charlie was clean beat by then. "Guess I'll have to figure it something like taxes," he said and took to moping in the house.

That was when this man came along. Came jogging along late one afternoon on a mean-looking knotty buckskin shy an ear leading a scrub-haired packhorse weighted with his gear. Stepped right to the ranchhouse and in the door. Saw Charlie doing his moping in a rocker. "Still offering five hundred?" this man said. "Yes," Charlie said. "Get it out of the bank," this man said. "I'll be coming for it soon." He turned and went right out again and stripped down his animals and shooed them into the corral and headed for the bunkhouse where the boys were slicking some for supper. Went straight in, blankets under one arm, rifle hooked with the other. Tossed the blanket on an empty bunk and set the rifle careful against the wall and it was a .303 Savage and a mighty powerful and efficient-looking weapon. "Howdy and greetings and all such palaver," he said while the boys were reading his sign and seeing it meant he was one of them, half horse and half human and gristle all through. "Have a good look," he said and gave out his name and smacked himself on the chest. "I'm the one," he said. "I been hearing how you lost souls let yourselves get buffaloed by a bear. Me, I eat bears for breakfast when there aint anything more substantial to work on. I'm the one going to get that hide just so you bangtails won't be afraid to go out in the dark."

That was a bad jump-off but the boys knew the name he'd given and they figured it was worth a fair bit of brag.

He wasn't so old, this man, not more'n in his middle thirties then, but he was a hang-over from the old days when
a man could make a living with a rifle and traps collecting
bounty on wolves and a bear or two and once in a long
moon a mountain cat. He was good and no mistake because he was still making a living at it though the critters
were getting scarce and scary and a man had to follow
them into country where the odds came close to even.
The boys didn't bristle too much. They let him brag and
he talked through supper doing the impossible which was
eating more'n his share with his tongue still wagging and
he kept on talking back at the bunkhouse spinning his
tales with each one getting taller and the critters bigger
and his talk was so plumb full of the little one-letter word
"I" and the little two-letter word "me" that final somebody had to call him. It was Long Bullard did the job.

"Lookahere," Long said. "You been blowing about
doing this and doing that and killing this-here whale that
wore panther skin and that-there elephant that had bear
fur and I'm atelling you that's mostly wind. To hear you
tell a man'd think you chewed or clawed those critters personal to death all by your lonesome. I'm atelling you it
aint you, it aint the skin and bones and maybe some
stringy muscle and a thimble of brains that's you asquat-
ting on a bunk there, that did all that. I'm atelling you,"
Long Bullard said pointing at the .303 Savage against the
wall, "it's that gun did it. A passel of mighty smart men
who could put more brains into a sneeze'n you could into
ten years living did a lot of inventing over a lot of years
to make that gun which you couldn't make in a whole hat-
ful of lifetimes. Those men made you bullets that'll carry
straight and pack the kick of a thundering old he-buffalo
and then you take those bullets and put them in that gun

and go point same at a critter and squeeze the trigger and keep squeezing if there's need and that gun does the killing and you go strutting around saying you did it. You helped some and that's all. Take that gun away, you'd be as harmless to those critters and special to this bear that's bothering us as a squeaking little field mouse."

This man sat there on the bunk with his lower jaw sprung. He wasn't as stupid as Long said. He'd just never thought along such lines afore. But his temper was up and he didn't take to being dressed down that way. "You think," he said, "you think I couldn't get this bear's got you bluffed without a gun?" "Think?" Long Bullard said. "I know." "You'll know different," this man said, "when I bring in the hide. Find a bullet hole in it and you can kick me from here to Christmas."

Well, now, that was a fool way to talk. But this man said it and the boys heard him say it and he was stuck with it. He pulled out early next morning, him and that knotty buckskin and his old packhorse with what of his gear he figured he'd need. Went straight up into the hills where this bear had its private range. Lonesome country that was, lonesome and rough, the kind that can make a man feel mighty single and small if he lets himself get low in his mind. First time this man came on some of the tracks he stopped and studied them and he whistled soft under his breath and maybe a first bit of real worry began to creep into him. But he didn't make camp, not then, not there. He knew bears. Not just the blacks and the cinnamons but the big gray-tips too. Matter of fact, some folks back then said he was part critter himself and that was why he could still get skins. Anyways, he didn't spend much time fussing around about tracks. He just took to studying the country higher up. Began to figure what he'd do was he an old maverick he-bear boss of the whole range with an itch for privacy when tired of having fun. Picked the likely territory, up where the rock ledges climbed and the slide-rock gave bad footing, and went towards it, close but not too close, and had to go afoot leading the horse part of the way and found a level piece with good windbreaks and some graze free of snow and made camp.

Early next morning he was out of blankets and had breakfast and was scouting the ground. Found a rubbing tree with some tufts of hair clinging to the bark and knew he was right. Found another tree with gashes in the bark way up, high as he could reach standing on tippytoe, and stepped back and measured the distance from the dirt up to those jaw marks with his eye and maybe a bit more of the worry crawled inside him but all the same he left that .303 Savage where it was, wrapped in a piece of old canvas at his camp, and went about his business packing only an ax and his side Colt which he'd have felt undressed without anyways. He spent all that day combing the slopes for a mile each way, picking his places. Spent all the next day placing and hiding his traps, heavy steel ones that'd caught him many a critter. Baited for those traps with some jerked beef he'd brought along. Went back to camp hungry and hopeful. Come morning he found this bear'd made the circuit, sprung the traps one way or another, taken the beef, left a few calling cards as a kind of insult, and moved on.

That was when this man began to have real respect for this bear and the worry began to take on some real size in him. Three days he'd been on this bear's range and likely it'd known he was there from the first hour or two and maybe'd been keeping tally on him and he hadn't so much as seen a bush move the whole time. Course he hadn't been trying to spot the critter the way he would of if he'd been packing that Savage and looking for a shot. But all the same the only way he knew this bear was there was from the feel of it in the air which he could tell, being as people said half critter himself in those days, and from what it'd done to his traps. A bear like this one could be mighty tricky if it had a hankering for his hide like he had for its hide. Only thing that kept the worry from getting too big and sending him scurrying for the Savage was that he was about certain it had plenty of respect for him too. It stayed out of sight and didn't come near his camp and was careful not to leave tracks for him to follow.

Well, now, that got to be quite a game up there in those rocky hills. Between times this bear slipped down to the ranch again and nipped another steer but this man didn't know that then. He was busy hatching his schemes. Seemed to him like the critter thought about him the same way Long Bullard did and he was bound determined to have its hide and without a bullet hole too. Got so, by instinct more'n anything else, he felt he knew more about this bear without ever seeing it than he'd ever known about another critter. Knew where its trails were, the regulars it used when not scouring for food, always on the hard rock and slides and ledges where no tracks'd show. Got so he thought he knew how it felt day to day according to the weather and why some days there was more hair on the rubbing trees and others there was new gashes on the biting tree. He put all he'd ever learned about such things into trying to get it without gunning. Tried every kind of trap he'd ever rigged before or ever heard tell of and some he thought of new. Tried rope traps and spring tree traps. Spent two days rigging a heavy deadfall, triggered neat. Spent four days building a stout box trap. He was wasting time and just providing little between-meal snacks for this bear and after a time he knew that and wouldn't let the knowing sink in. Three weeks he'd been up there and he didn't have anything left for bait and nothing for his own food but some flour and raisins and he was using old coffee grounds third and fourth rounds. Day came he squatted an hour or two staring at that piece of canvas with that .303 Savage in it with anger a bitterness in his belly and getting bigger and he took that gun and slapped shells into it and started out. Covered miles, combing the likely places. Thought once he saw it, shadowy and moving away through a thicket, and poured lead through that bush and found himself yelling while the echoes died but when he pushed in watching careful there was nothing. Maybe this bear'd been there, maybe not. But when he headed for camp just afore dark he met the buckskin wandering with a snapped picket rope and near the camp itself he found the old packhorse down with a twisted neck and the claw marks plain in the torn hide.

Anyone wants to can figure that any way suits him. This man figured it his way. Maybe you'll say he was sliding off to one side in his mind. Anyways he looked at the carcass of that old packhorse and he began thinking. Wasn't much used to thinking in those days and it took him time. "The critter knows," he said smack out loud like someone could hear him. "I broke the rules. I didn't play it square." He looked at the carcass of that old packhorse and did some more thinking. "Here's bait," he said smack out loud again. "I'll try it another last time."

Not much sleep for him that night. He was going over the country in his head, picking his spot. In the morning he saddled the buckskin and put a rope on what was left of the packhorse and dragged the carcass to the place. This was a kind of pocket like a good-sized hiding place at the bottom of a rock cliff that rose straight up behind some thirty foot or more. He brought his steel traps there and hid them careful all around. Course he didn't have the littlest notion of catching this bear with those. Idea was to fool this bear into thinking he did. He was about certain it'd come see what he'd been doing, locate those traps, spring them one way or another or just plain work around them, and maybe then make a meal. Soon as the traps were hid right he took a wide circuit up and around and came out on the cliff top. This was just the way he wanted it which was why he'd picked the spot, sloping down to the edge and the straight drop below. Direct above the packhorse carcass he set his key rock. Piled others behind it and fanning out some, big ones, big as he could lug, each set careful and leaning on the one ahead, till he had a heap there that'd crush anything in its way if it ever got moving. Only thing holding it was that key rock and if that was pried loose the whole heap'd start plunging down and over the cliff edge. Got himself a stout pole and trimmed it and wedged one end in behind that key rock. He'd trigger that trap himself. He'd be up there and when the right time came he'd heave on that pole and those rocks'd cut loose.

Well, now, this man had himself a trap, a big one, maybe about the biggest any lone man ever made, baited with other traps and some horsemeat that'd begun to get a mite ripe around the edges under that afternoon sun the way some bears like their meals. He scurried to camp and made his own meal with the flour and raisins and old coffee, hurrying to use the last of the light, and by full dark he was back on his cliff top, stretched out flat by the outer end of his lever pole where he could just lift his head and stretch his neck a bit to peer over the edge. It being nighttime didn't bother him much. Never gets so dark up in the hills under the starlight except where trees're thick that a man can't make out shapes and any movings and there was a late moon coming to help and anyways this man had half-critter eyes in those days. Snugged himself down comfortable as he could on the rock and waited.

Moon came on schedule and sometimes the wind sighed mournful overhead and the dwindling cold of winter's last days soaked into him and he lay there waiting. Passed the time tightening and loosening the muscles of one leg then the other then his arms then his back then his belly to keep the circulation good without him moving around on that cliff top and the moon climbed mighty high and nothing happened. Found his mind wandering and thinking of this bear like it was a person that could get mad and take to hunting him like he was hunting it and was afraid and shook that off. Lay quiet there and got drowsy and maybe closed his eyes a time or two and sudden was awake, every last little twitch of him, with sweat starting on his skin spite of the cold. He just plain knew, that critter instinct was telling him, this bear was near. He stretched his neck, peered out, studied the whole ground far as he could see below. Nothing moved, not anything anywhere, and the only sound was the wind passing with a sigh and his nerve ends shook him with little jerks. Pressed himself hard against the rock and the shaking went away and the prickling on his skin faded and he knew, certain as before, this bear was gone, had been somewhere below and was gone. He lay quiet, arguing with himself whether to wait longer, and sudden the knowing had him again, strong and shaking, and his breath dragged unwilling in his throat and he rolled over and up to sitting position in one motion and his muscles froze stiff and rigid because it was there, not more'n fifteen feet away, there on the cliff top facing him. It was big, up against the skyline from where he was low sitting, bigger'n any bear he'd ever seen, bigger'n any critter in any of the stretching tales he'd ever told. He could see the moonlight faint on the silver tips of its winter coat and gleaming low on the long claws of those forepaws that could snap the neck of a grown steer with a single stroke. He could see the bulk of it, shaggy with the long hair of winter, blocking out half the whole sky, and all the power and strength of the whole wide wild of the mountain in it. And there he was squatted low on the rock with the cliff edge right behind him and that .303 Savage far away at his camp and only his side Colt handy which wouldn't be more'n a kid's popgun to this bear and he couldn't use anyway because if he moved to pull it this bear could be on him afore he even cleared the holster.

There they were, this bear standing still watching this man and this man sitting still watching this bear, and time just plain stopped being at all and there wasn't anything only the dark stillness of fifteen feet of space between them. This man wasn't afraid, not any more after the first shock of seeing. He was past being afraid. He felt empty and like he'd been pushed past some limit inside his own mind. Felt there was nothing he could do or not do that would change things at all. Felt this bear had him and the whole world right where a crunch of big jaws or a flick of a forepaw could wipe everything away into a nothingness and he watched it standing there big and still and it made him feel small and smaller and not just in size. He saw a thin vapor float up in the cold from its muzzle and heard his own breath, held back till now, empty from his own lungs and he saw it move, not hurrying, steady, turning and swinging and drifting, quiet as it'd come, out of sight back over and beyond and below the skyline.

Well, now, this man eased down till he was lying flat

again, on his back now. Lay there staring up, not thinking
because he didn't need to be thinking. He knew right
down in the marrow of his bones what he had to do. He
just lay there staring up and not even noticing the cold till
the first streaks of light showed off to the east. He pushed
up then, stiff and creaking some in the joints. Pulled his
trigger pole out from behind the key rock and tossed it
aside. Climbed around and down and hunted out his
traps from around the carcass of that packhorse and slung
them together so he could carry them. Went straight to
his camp and dumped them and ate some of the raisins
and crammed the rest in his pocket. Picked up that .303
Savage and checked to see the magazine was full and
started off again.

He went back the way he'd come and circled wide
around where he'd fixed that biggest trap of all and
climbed on up and up the next hogback ridge rising
maybe two hundred yards beyond and found a perch, a
flat ledge wide enough to lie on and settled down there
flat on his belly with the Savage beside him. Across and
down he could see the cliff top where he'd spent the night
and below in the kind of pocket place the packhorse carcass and all the pathways up to and around for quite a
stretch. He lay quiet again, not watching sharp yet because now in this hunting he was all critter only with his
man's mind there and in charge and he knew this bear'd
be holed somewheres sleeping and likely wouldn't show
for a while. Knew too it'd be hungry not having much
food, this being the bad time of year, and likely would
wake with a gnawing belly and get to remembering that
horsemeat ripening there that hadn't been touched yet.
Was so certain he'd figured it right and the sun was so
warm on his back that he drowsed some himself and then
the sun was sliding below the peaks behind him and the

shadow chill was on him and he was full awake and watching.

Moving an arm cautious, he eased some raisins out of his pocket and to his mouth and chewed slow and steady. Moving the same, he eased the Savage closer alongside so he could check the sights for the distance. Maybe he smiled a bit to himself under the whisker grizzle of three weeks without shaving because he knew what he could do with that gun at even two or three times the distance. He lay quiet and sudden he had that prickling on his skin and it was there, out and down by the packhorse carcass, and he hadn't even seen it come and it was there, nosing into the pocket place and testing where the traps had been. It was small across the two hundred yards slanting down and he felt a little jolt of disappointment and then he saw the bulk of it against the measuring size of the old packhorse and he saw it lower its head and take hold of the packhorse carcass and lift this till only the legs were dragging and back off carrying that eight hundred and maybe more pounds of dead weight like a cat with a little gopher and he knew he was looking at the great granddaddy of all the grizzle-hairs that ever lived. He saw it take the carcass twenty feet out from under that cliff trap and drop it and raise its head to test the wind in all directions and lower its head to feed and then inch by inch he began to ease that .303 Savage forward.

Cautious, by slow stages, this man got the gun in position, stock snug against his right shoulder, barrel out and resting in his left hand with the left elbow braced on the rock and the forearm straight up and down. Measuring careful in his mind, he drew his lines crossed for the spot that'd drive the bullet direct forward from behind and a bit under the big shoulder to the heart. The sights steadied on the crossing spot and he drew a deep breath as he always did and let it half out and held it so the barrel wouldn't waver from any tiny movement of his chest and shoulder and his right forefinger tightened on the trigger like for the final squeezing only it didn't squeeze and he let the rest of that held breath out in what could of been a chuckle only it was mighty grim and he stood up and started off without once looking back.

Well, now, that's what this man did. Made a wide swing around and went to his camp and saddled the buckskin and draped his gear over it best he could. Headed straight for old Charlie's ranch. Took considerable joshing from the boys for coming in empty-handed and minus a horse without saying much in return. Gathered the rest of his stuff and went into town and sold all his hunting gear. Got himself a job horse-wrangling at a ranch further out on the flat and I expect that's about all there is to tell.

Oh, you're wondering about the bear? Well, now, I don't rightly know. Spring was coming which always brings plenty natural bear food of one kind and another and old Charlie's steers weren't bothered any more so likely this bear felt he didn't need prime beef or else just moved on deeper and higher into the hills. Couple of line riders bumped into a bear along in summer, a grizzly too, not far from where this one'd been playing its games, and had themselves a time afore they killed it. Claimed it was the one but Charlie wasn't paying by then and anyways it wasn't. Good-sized skin all right. But not big enough.

And what's that? How do I know so damn much about what this man did and what this man felt up there alone in the hills? Well, he didn't tell me. Didn't need to. You just figure that out for yourself. I'm through talking for one night.

Nate Bartlett's Store

SOUTH LICKS was a nice town in those days. It couldn't compete with the boom cattle-towns along the railroads, not in bustle and noise and general human devilment, so it didn't even try. It made out fair enough as supply and market center for a rising number of homesteads and small ranches round about and picked up extra business feeding folks passing through on the stageline. It was a nice town, not wide open and roaring like some but all the same not fussy about folks having their fun as they saw fit, and it had Nate Bartlett's store.

Nate was New England Yankee stock seasoned by a lot of grown-up years out in the new States and territories where there was plenty of room for the spirit in a man to stretch and grow some and that was a combination hard to beat. He'd turned his hand to many a thing in his time and he'd made his pile, staked a claim on a rich ledge and sold out to a mining syndicate for a fine price, and he'd looked around and settled on South Licks as the place to do what he'd always wanted to do and that was run a store. All those years he'd remembered the one his grandfather had back east when he was a kid and he'd remembered the tangy smells and the neighborly feel and he'd never got over the notion that running a good store right was a pleasant way for a man to spend his slow-down days. He put up a solid frame building fronting on the main street with living quarters for himself at the rear. He stocked that building with anything and everything he could think of in the general merchandise line. He sent away to have a sign made and he hung that sign on a pole sticking out from the roof of the building and that was some sign.

NATHANIEL P. BARTLETT
Dealer in
E V E R Y T H I N G
Wholesale & Retail   Satisfaction Guaranteed
"If we haven't got it we'll get it."

A sign like that was certain to make comment and liven a town's temper. It wasn't long before the South Licksians were proud of Nate and his store. They noticed it had special tangy smells and a special neighborly feel and they enjoyed themselves testing Nate's service. They'd stroll in chuckling and ask for some odd thing or other. More than likely Nate'd have it somewheres in his stock. Even if he didn't he'd never bat an eye but just remark he was fresh out of that particular item and would have it ready in a day or two. Smack after closing he'd be over at the stage office confabbing with the telegraph operator there and right enough, in a matter of days, he'd have that item ready and at a fair price, the straight cost plus his usual per-centage. Like the time Al Foster who ran the Good Licks Restaurant came in and asked for a pair of red-white-and-blue suspenders. Nate looked up from the mail-order catalogue he was scanning for more things to put on his shelves. He never even cracked a smile. "Any particular design?" he said. "Why, certain," Al Foster said. "Red straps, white hooks, blue cross-hatches." Nate tapped his forehead thoughtful like he was studying over what he had. "Seems to me I had some like that," he said, "but I'm fresh out as of now. Come around next week." And right enough, when Al was passing the store one day next week, Nate hailed him from the door and Nate had those suspenders, just as ordered. He'd sent to the factory and had them made special. Al was so tickled with them and the talk they stirred he was down a while with pneumonia in the fall waiting too long to start wearing a coat over them.

It was about two-three months after Nate arrived in South Licks and opened his store that Kemp Ackley first saw that sign.

Kemp was a Texan-born-and-raised who'd been away from his home state long enough to have the usual brag and horny layer rubbed off exposing the real man underneath and that was a hard combination to beat too. He was somewheres in his early thirties, a hard-riding, hard-working, hard-playing man who'd filled his pockets one night bucking a faro game and right away put the cash into good cows and started building himself a herd. He had a ranch about eight miles out of South Licks, the biggest spread in those parts. He worked the place himself, along with four-five riders who could keep pace with him at whatever he might be doing whether that was working or playing or just plain yipping at the moon. The scale he operated, he didn't try to market through South Licks. Roundup time he'd cut out his beef stuff and drive cross-country to one of the railroad towns. He'd collect his money there but he wouldn't spend it there even though he and his riders'd be ripe for a pay-off spree. He had local pride, Kemp Ackley had. He figured that South Licks was his town. He figured that if he and those who sided him were going to take any town apart and fill the evening air with the clink of glasses and the clatter of chips and the melody of song and gunshots, why then South Licks ought to be so favored. He'd head up there from the railroad and coming near he'd collect dry-throated gents from the smaller ranches along the way till there was quite a crowd of them raising dust on the road and they'd come whooping into South Licks with him to help him spend a fair share of the beef money and whatever they could scrape out of their own pockets.

This time Kemp came whooping along in the lead and when he swung into Main Street the first thing he saw was that sign hanging bright and brave overhead. He pulled his horse back on its rump and the others did the same and he looked that sign over. "Well, now," he said. "Here's something new to add to the merriment of men and nations and such. Aint that a pretty target!" He pulled a gun and spun it fancy on a finger through the trigger guard and clamped his hand on the butt and was raising his arm to fire when out of the corner of one eye he caught sight of old Nate standing in the store door. Nate was leaning easy against one doorjamb and he was holding a double-barreled shotgun hip-high with both hammers cocked and both barrels bearing on Kemp. "I wouldn't do that was I you," Nate said.

Kemp stayed still, just as he was. "Is that thing loaded?" he said.

"I wouldn't take a chance on it was I you," Nate said. "I heard you coming the whole last mile."

"Well, then," Kemp said. "I expect you're right. You've got two mighty powerful arguments there." Kemp let his arm down slow, careful where his gun pointed, and slid that gun back into its holster. "Shucks," he said. "You ought to know popping signs is all part of the game. Likely you've peppered a few in your own time."

"Likely I have," Nate said. "But I've learned different too in my time. I'm learning you different right now."

"Well, now," Kemp said, "it kind of looks like you are at that." Something about that old rooster of a Nate leaning there quiet and easy and maybe deadly too seemed to tickle him. "Boys," he said. "This is one sign we leave strict alone." He slapped spurs to his horse and led the way on along the street to swing in by Ed Lafferty's Licks-That-Thirst saloon.

It was six-seven-maybe-eight drinks later, near the time Kemp and his crew'd be heading to feed at Al Foster's place and get up strength for a full evening's fun, that Kemp got to realizing he couldn't keep that sign out of his head. "Cocky old bird," he said to himself. " 'Dealer in EVERYTHING.' Puts that in capitals too. I expect we ought to give him a whirl." He downed the last in his glass and called out, "Come along, boys. We've got to find out does everything mean anything." Nate was tidying up his store for closing when the crowd came in. He set his broom aside and took his usual spot behind his main counter.

"No hard feelings on what was previous," Kemp said. "I was just wondering do you really stand by that sign outside?"

"Certain as sunrise," Nate said. "Each and every word."

Kemp chuckled low in his throat and tipped a wink around at his crew. "Well, then," he said, "me and the boys here have a hankering for some genuine one-dollar-per-each seegars."

Nate tapped his forehead thoughtful. "I'm fresh out of any at that precise figure," he said, "but maybe these might do." He rummaged under his counter and came up with a fancy box and slit the seal and lifted the lid and inside were fat cigars each wrapped separate and that lid said in curlycue letters they were super-extra-panatelas-de-luxe costing one dollar and twenty-five cents per each.

"I'm a flop-eared jack rabbit," somebody in the crowd said. "He's topped you, Kemp. You'll have to pay."

Kemp paid. He had to shuck his roll plenty to spread those cigars all around but he paid. He didn't mind that much. What he minded was being capped so neat by Nate. He lit his cigar and looked around and tipped another wink at his crew. "Well, now," he said, "you met me on that and I've paid. But now me and the boys are thinking it would be nice to top off eating this evening with some of that stuff they call cavvy-yar."

"Are you certain you want some of that?" Nate said. "That's powerful stuff for simple stomachs." There was a twinkle deep in Nate's eyes but he was speaking slow and hesitating like he was worried some.

"Certain I'm certain," Kemp said. "I want all you've got — if you've got any."

Nate turned and went to pushing things aside on his shelves and pulled out a flattish wooden box and pried off the top. Inside were twenty-four flattish round cans. "That'll be seventy-two dollars," he said.

"Yippee for Nate!" someone shouted. That was Al Foster standing in the doorway and snapping his red-white-and-blue suspenders. "He'll match you every time, Kemp my boy. You'd better quit."

"Quit?" Kemp Ackley said. "I'm just beginning." He stood there scratching the slight stubble along one side his chin. He leveled a finger at Nate like it was a gun. "I'm telling you what I want now," he said. "I'm wanting me a pair of those fancy striped pants dudes wear back

east when they go strutting up the avenue showing off
for the ladies. I'm wanting me a forked-tail coat to go with
those pants. And some pearl-buttoned spats and a — a
— "

"Top hat?" Nate said.

"Certain a top hat," Kemp said. "And a gold-headed
cane and — "

"And I'm telling you," Nate said in a voice that showed
he'd been a lot of things in his time and had stood on his
own two feet wherever he was. "I'm telling you I've got
all those items right here in my stock and more of the trimmings than you'd ever think of. And I'm telling you I'm
not going to sell them to you. Fun's fun. But you don't
need those things and you'd look like a misplaced jackass
in them and it's closing time for this store anyway. And
now," Nate said with the twinkle in his eyes shining plain,
"I'm telling you too, son, there's a few aspects of your so-
called disposition that remind me of the kind of fool I
was at about your age. If you'll let me pay the tariff on
food for the crowd, by which I mean up to and including
that caviar, and then soak in some liquid refreshment to
sort of catch up, why then I'll show you how we used to
outhowl the coyotes on payday when I was a cowhand
down on the Cimarron."

South Licks rocked some on its foundations those evening hours. There were folks used to date things before
and after by that night. But the chief thing to be dated
from it was the game played by those two, Nathaniel P.
Bartlett and Kemp Ackley. Just about everybody else
knew better than to keep betting against Nate about that
sign but Kemp couldn't quit. Every time he came to town
he'd try again. It got so he'd be out with his riders working his cattle and sudden he'd swing his horse and head

for town and they'd know he'd hit another notion. He'd step into the store and say, "Still standing by that sign?" and Nate'd say, "Certain as sunrise," and Kemp'd spring his new one and sometimes Nate'd have it already and sometimes Nate wouldn't but he'd take the order without batting an eye and come through on it surprising quick. One time it was a genuine imported Swiss cuckoo clock. Nate located one in Chicago and had it out by special express and a pony rider in five days. Another time it was a live monkey with coconuts for feeding. Nate spent plenty of telegrams over that but all the same he had one there in a cage with a crate of coconuts too in a day over three weeks. Kemp was about sure he had Nate stopped the time he stepped in and said he wanted an engine, a locomotive like they used on the railroad. Nate just looked at him and said, "Eight-wheeler or ten-wheeler?" and Kemp had to say something and said, "Ten-wheeler, of course!" and Nate said he was fresh out of that particular kind but he'd have one soon and in five weeks there it was, standing solid on all ten wheels back of the store. He'd bought it from the railroad by offering more than they'd paid themselves and had it taken apart and carted up to South Licks in freight wagons and put together again. Kemp had to put his ranch in hock to meet the bill that time. He managed to sell the thing back to the railroad at a fair figure but even so he was hit with quite a loss plus the cartage.

That should have slowed Kemp down. It only made him more determined. He thought and thought and took to moping around in his bachelor ranchhouse thinking. He knew he'd have to get something mighty tricky and special and at last he had it. The more he thought about it and from fresh angles the more tickled he was. He

slapped his thighs and laughed smack out loud. He saddled up and rode into town. He looked at that sign and
read it over again and laughed some more. He stepped
into the store and grinned at Nate. He waved a hand back
out towards the sign.

"Everything?" he said.

"Everything," Nate said.

"Well, then," Kemp said, fighting to hold back the
chuckles. "I'm here to order me a wife."

For a full moment, maybe two, old Nate really was
stopped. He stared at Kemp and his mouth dropped open
a little. Then that twinkle started deep in his eyes but his
face stayed solemn. He waggled his head sorrowful and
started to talk. "I've been here and I've been there," he
said, "and I've been about everywhere in between. I've
seen strange things and some stranger yet only a fool'd
believe. But I never thought to see the day a white man
of the male sex and cattle-handling persuasion would regard a woman of the female sex, a wife-to-be of his board
and bosom, as a merchandisable item to be talked of as
such across a storekeeper's counter. True, I've heard tell
that in biblical times . . ." Nate kept on talking and
Kemp kept on grinning, certain he had Nate licked at
last and Nate was just stalling to avoid admitting he was
licked.

". . . and I've bumped into an Indian tribe or two,"
Nate said, "that some folks might claim put a price tag
on a squaw. But you aint an Indian and I expect it aint a
squaw you have in mind." Kemp shook his head, still
fighting the chuckles, and sudden Nate reached a pencil
and order pad and popped quick words: "Any particular
specifications?"

Kemp was startled some. He hadn't thought much past

just putting his joke. Then he chuckled out loud. Old Nate was trying to run a bluff on him. "Why, sure," he said. "I like me a woman that has good meat on her bones. Nice curves in the right places, up and down. Face that won't stampede a steer and — and — "

"Reddish hair?" Nate said.

"Why, yes, if you say so," Kemp said, near to busting inside at the way his joke was growing. "I'm kind of partial to reddish hair. And I like me a woman old enough to know better but — "

"Know better'n what?" Nate said.

"Better'n to marry a maverick like me," Kemp said, "but still young and giddy enough to take a chance." He couldn't hold the laughing in any more and he let it out in bursts between his words. "Oh, I know — you're fresh out — that particular item — but if I'll come around — next week — next month maybe — next lifetime'd be more like it. Shucks, you're licked — backed right off the board — just too ornery to say so." Kemp was staggering around, slapping his arms and weak with the laughing. He plain had to share his joke with others who'd appreciate it the way his boys would and he staggered out the door and climbed aboard his horse and went skittering towards his ranch.

For quite a stretch, maybe four-five miles, that was about the most enjoyable ride Kemp Ackley'd ever had. He was rolling in the saddle, figuring to get his boys and swing back for some real celebrating, tasting already how he'd tell his tale, about Nate's jaw dropping and Nate's long-winded stalling and Nate's trying to run a bluff and how he'd called it. Then sudden, for some reason, the whole business didn't seem so funny to him. He began remembering. He remembered things like one-dollar-

and-a-quarter cigars and a cuckoo clock and a monkey and a locomotive. He yanked his horse around and headed larruping back to town. He pulled to a stop in front of the store. The door was closed tight and padlocked. He saw Al Foster coming along the sidewalk.

"Nate?" Al Foster said, snapping his red-white-and-blue suspenders in a way that seemed mighty suggestive to Kemp. "Nate's closed down for a few days. Caught the afternoon stage out of town."

There was a lot of talk around South Licks all the next weeks. People knew Nate had gone off to get something Kemp had ordered and since he'd gone off personal they figured it must be a tough one and they began laying bets would he get it. At the same time there was a lot of silence out at Kemp Ackley's ranch. Kemp sat around in his ranchhouse chewing his fingernails. Every now and then he'd stand up and try to kick himself clear across the room. He sent one of his riders into town each day in turn to loaf about and keep an eye open for Nate's coming back. He got so he shivered like he had the ague just at the sight of the day's rider coming home along the road. He thought some of selling out, maybe just leaving without bothering to sell out, fading away into the hills so he wouldn't have to face the town, but he'd never dodged off yet on a bet or a debt and he knew he'd have to play this through. Then it was late one afternoon and the one of his boys they called Skimpy because he couldn't raise much hair was fogging home in a hurry. Kemp made it to the porch and wilted there waiting.

"Nate's back," Skimpy said.

Kemp groaned. "Alone?" he said.

"Not exactly," Skimpy said. "There's something with him."

"Something?" Kemp said. "Is it alive?"

"Seems like," Skimpy said. "Leastways it was moving under its own power."

Kemp groaned again. "Female?" he said.

"More'n likely," Skimpy said. "But I couldn't be sure. Nate had it wearing his long coat and his hat with a veil down hiding the evidence."

Kemp was getting expert with all his practice and he managed to kick himself clear across the porch.

"My oh me oh my," Skimpy said, grinning wide. "That's some fancy acrobatics. But you'd best save your strength. Nate says he believes in prompt closing of important deals so he'll be open this evening waiting for you."

Kemp Ackley came into South Licks that evening like he was coming to an execution for which he was slated principal performer. He kept thinking of the happy free-roaming days likely he was leaving behind. He kept seeing horrible visions in the air around him of the frightening things unfeeling folk might regard as marriageable critters of the female sex. His boys had the good sense to tag back a bit where their grins and undertone joshing were out of range. In town, he climbed off his horse and looked up at that sign shining in the light from the store window and he shuddered all over. It didn't help his spirit any when he went inside and found near all the inhabitants of South Licks perched at vantage points on counters and boxes about. He looked around, mighty fearful. There wasn't a woman in sight he didn't already know as the nailed-down wife of some South Licks man. He saw Nate sitting quiet and easy on the usual high stool behind the main counter. He sighed.

"All right," he said. "I'm here."

"So you are," Nate said. Nate's face was solemn as ever but that twinkle was showing deep in his eyes. "Seems to me though," Nate said, "you're a mite pale as a man ought not be on a happy occasion such as this. Now before I produce the merchandise you saw fit to order through me and my store I want to tell you that so as to be able to produce same I've had to talk myself into a sore throat two weeks running and prognosticate things about you as an upstanding gentleman and citizen of this community that your own mother'd blush to believe. Be all that on my own head, but you came blowing in here with what you maybe thought was a good joke but nothing about this store of mine is a joke to me and I took what you said straight and I'm making good on it. I've got the merchandise and to be certain the service along with same is right I've had myself made a justice of the peace so as I can do the ceremony myself."

Nate stepped back to the door that led to his living quarters and opened it. "South Licks in general and Mister Ackley in particular," he said, "I'm making you acquainted with my ward and niece, Miss Barbara Bartlett, late of St. Louis and points east." And out through the doorway, stepping dainty as primed in advance by old Nate, with color high in her cheeks and the lamplight shining on reddish hair, came as fresh and shapely and hearty-looking a young woman as any South Licksian'd ever seen. There were clucklings from the other women present and foot-shufflings and a few whistles from the men. Kemp Ackley stepped back like someone had hit him. He reached up hesitating and took off his hat and a sort of sick grin spread over his face. He pulled himself together and stiffened some. "Howdy, ma'am," he said.

"Whoa, now," Nate said. "I intend to do this proper."

He motioned Kemp to come closer and all the while this Barbara niece stood still as a statue with a twinkle like old Nate's deep in her own eyes. "I aint forgot those specifications," Nate said. "I aint going to have you claiming misrepresentation any time later. You said good meat on her bones. Any objections to the meat on these bones? Step up and feel it if you've a mind to."

Kemp jumped back like someone had kicked him. "Oh, no," he said, quick. "Looks all right from here where I am."

"Nice curves too," Nate said, "and in the right places. So you specified. Find anything wrong with these curves?"

"Now, lookahere, Nate," Kemp said. "You've got no call to — "

"My oh me oh my," someone said in the background and it was Skimpy, grinning wide again. "If you're scared out, Kemp, step aside and I'll take over."

"And give yourself a real good look," Nate went right on. "Do you have any lingering suspicion that face might stampede a steer?"

"Shucks," Kemp said. "Aint you through riding me yet? How'd you expect me to have any objections anyway with the woman herself standing right there listening? There aint any need for all this talk. I'm caught on my own fool play and — "

"Humph," this Barbara niece said. "So he feels caught, does he? Well, this specifying business goes two ways." She stepped out and around Kemp while he stood stock-still like he was fastened to the floor, only swiveling at the waist to keep an eye on her. "Uncle Nate," she said. "You claimed he was handsome. Well, maybe he is in a coarse, unwashed sort of way. You said he has a good ranch and is the kind of man could give a good home. I can't say I see much evidence of that in his present appearance looking like a sick calf that's afraid someone'll say boo."

Kemp jerked up straight. His color was high now too. He was getting his hell-raising legs back under him the way they hadn't been ever since Nate left town.

"Sick is it," he said, "and a calf? You just try saying boo and I'll — "

"Boo!" this Barbara niece said.

Kemp tossed his hat to one side and started for her and old Nate jumped between them. "Whoa, now," he said. "Don't you two go messing up this deal just because one's stiff-necked and the other's got reddish hair. This is a business proposition and for and as of now it's to be regarded as such. It's considerable irregular because in this case the merchandise can talk back so it's only fair it be a two-way deal. Barbara," old Nate said, "seeing him now and remembering the things I've told you, are you still willing?"

"Humph," this Barbara niece said. "Marrying a man who seems to think a wife is something you can pick up at a store like a barrel of flour is likely a poor risk." She was looking at Kemp mighty intent and speculative and seemed to enjoy watching him squirm. "But seeing as how the honor of our family seems to have got involved through that sign of yours, Uncle Nate, why maybe I can take a chance." "Well, then, Kemp," Nate said. "Here's your merchandise as per order. How do you stand?"

"What's the price?" Kemp said. He was looking at this Barbara niece just as intent and speculative as she was at him and he seemed to enjoy watching her wince at that question of his.

"No price," Nate said. "Except your present freedom as a bachelor."

"All right," Kemp said. He wasn't going to let himself be outdone by any woman. "Seeing as how my own honor's got involved here too, why I'll just pay that price."

It was on that basis those two let old Nate marry them. It was on the same basis those two behaved, free and easy with everybody else except each other, all through the evening at Al Foster's restaurant where the South Licksians cleared away the tables for a noisy dancing jamboree. It was on the same basis they departed for the ranch about sunup in a buckboard from the livery stable with this Barbara niece sitting way over on one side of the seat and Kemp sitting way over on the other side and her trunk behind them in the wagon and Kemp's boys riding well out of earshot range.

Old Nate stood under his sign and watched them go. "Maybe I've pushed it too far this time," he said to himself, "but it still seems like a good notion to me. Once they're alone together they'll work it out. If I was either one I'd want me another one just about like the other."

But Nate had his doubts when he went out to call two days later and found those two acting like a brace of gamecocks walking around wary and ready to start clashing spurs over any little thing. Neither one could say much at all without the other snapping to twist it into something mean. Nate didn't stay long because he was too uncomfortable. Any way he looked at it, he knew he was really responsible for bringing them together and maybe, because of the way he'd handled it at the store, for setting them to striking sparks. He felt he ought to do something but he couldn't figure what.

Nate's doubts didn't improve with the rumors that began reaching town the following days. Kemp was said to be staying in the bunkhouse with his boys. This Barbara niece was said to be holed up in the ranchhouse. Nate was worried plenty when he heard that. He was just tidying things to go on out there and see what he might be able to do when this Barbara niece came walking in the store door. She was mussed and dusty and right ready to cry any minute. She'd waited till Kemp and his boys were off somewheres out of sight and she'd wangled a horse out of the corral and made it to town.

"Uncle Nate," she said. "I'd hate to have that long-legged excuse for a husband you wished on me think I'd run away from anything but it can't go on like this."

Nate was mighty sorry for her but he remembered she was good Bartlett stock and he figured he could be brief and blunt.

"So maybe you'd like to get free of him, eh?" he said.

"Well, I don't know," she said and she was so close to crying that a couple of tears leaked out and started down through the dust on her cheeks. "Out there bossing around that ranch which is where a man like him belongs I can see maybe he's some of those things you said he is. But he isn't a real man. He's just a big chunk of wood. He's got about as much sentiment in him as one of those big steers of his. Every time he gets near me he can't seem to get past thinking of all that silly specification business and how he was caught and just had to marry me."

"I wonder now do you give him much chance to — " Nate started to say and had to stop quick because he saw something outside. He managed to push this Barbara niece into his living quarters and close the door and be back at his main counter when Kemp Ackley came in, walking slow and sorrowful and looking back at that sign outside.

"Nate," Kemp said. "When I think of that wife you

pushed off on me holed up in the ranchhouse and me slipping off in the other direction and circling around to come here so she won't know what I'm doing, well, Nate, I feel plumb bad. Things can't go on like this. You take that sign of yours now. You still stand by it?"

"Certain I do," Nate said, stiffening some.

"Well, it says something I never paid much notice before," Kemp said. "It says 'Satisfaction Guaranteed.' "

"So-o-o," Nate said. "So you aint satisfied with this last transaction." He felt a mite sorry for this Kemp too but he remembered Kemp was stock he'd thought could match the Bartlett and he figured he could be brief and blunt this time too.

"You want to turn the merchandise back?" he said.

"Don't be so allfired hasty," Kemp said. "I aint exactly complaining about the merchandise as such. It meets those specifications right enough and now I've seen it close maybe some we didn't even mention. But it acts most of the time something like a snapping turtle that tolerates living in the same country with me only because of that silly family-honor business. I aint so cocky as I used to be. I'm not demanding a thing. I'm just wondering is there any way you could go about guaranteeing some of that satisfaction."

Nate looked at Kemp a long minute or two. Then that twinkle began to show in his eye. "Kemp," he said. "If you acquired a windmill or a hay cutter or some such piece of machinery from me, there'd be instructions how to operate same and keep it operating along with it. You'd pay smart attention to those instructions, wouldn't you?"

"Of course I would." Kemp said. "That's simple sense."

"Precisely and exact," Nate said. "Well, you acquired a

wife from me. There was some instructions supposed to go along with her that I forgot to give you. Wait a spell and I'll see can I remember what they were." And old Nate took a piece of paper and his old quill pen. He chewed the top end of the pen a while and then he dipped it in ink and started scratching with it. He finished and reached the paper across the counter to Kemp.

INSTRUCTIONS
to keep a wife happy
and derive satisfaction from same

Rule 1. Tell her you love her.
Rule 2. Tell her how pretty she is.
Rule 3. Think up three new ways each day
         for following rule 1.
Rule 4. Think up three new ways each day
         for following rule 2.
Rule 5. Mean what you say each time.

"And now," Nate said. "You just keep that paper out of sight but not out of mind. And start following those rules right away." He took Kemp by the arm and back to the door of his living quarters and pushed Kemp through and closed the door again. He stood there listening a moment and then he nodded his head. He returned to his main counter and perched himself on a stool behind it and began looking through catalogues for new things he might put on his shelves. He raised his head and looked out the window at that sign and the twinkle in his eyes was blazing bright. It wouldn't be too long now before he'd be having some grandnieces and grandnephews and they'd be in and out of his store and maybe in later years they'd remember the tangy smells and the neighborly feel of the place.

The Old Man

*

JERRY LINTON was ten the year the old man came to live with them in the still-new house his parents had built the year before. He knew the old man was coming, knew it the day the letter came and his mother read it with her lips folding in to a tight line and put it up on the mantelpiece and in the evening he sat cross-legged in his flannel nightshirt on the floor of the dark upstairs hall behind the top newel post of the still shiny front stairs and heard his parents discussing it downstairs in the parlor. He could even hear the faint rustling of paper as his father refolded the letter.

"Frozen his feet," said his father, dry-voiced and precise, nailing down the essential fact in invariable precise manner. "Well, something was bound to happen to the old fool sometime. I suppose this means we'll have to take him in."

"Trapped," said his mother. "That's how it makes me feel. Just plain trapped. If we don't, you know what they'll all say. We have the room. We're about the only ones can afford it right now. But if we do — well, you know what he is."

"Yes," his father said. "I know. But he's your kin and that's that."

So that was that as it always was when his father spoke and Jerry Linton knew the old man was coming, the not even imaginable old man who lived alone off up somewhere in the far mountains, whom he had never seen and never dared ask questions about because his parents and all the relatives, the few times the old man was ever mentioned, looked at each other as if even thinking about him was a mistake and hurried on to talk of almost anything else. But Jerry Linton did not know what to expect and the excitement in him that he kept hidden because his mother did not believe in noise and disturbance about the house reached a high pitch that Saturday morning as he and his mother stood on the front porch and watched his father, coming back from the station, drive their new Ford with its gleaming brass oil lamps into their alleyway and stop it and get out of it all alone and come towards them and shrug his shoulders in an exasperated way and say: "He wouldn't come in the machine. I've got him coming in a carriage from the livery stable."

Then the carriage came and stopped out front and the driver swung down and opened the door and Jerry Linton was disappointed at first because what climbed out, slow and awkward, backing out and down and leaning against the side of the carriage to turn around, was just an ordinary old man, thin and stooped in wrinkled and dirty clothes. The driver took him by one arm to help him up the front walk and he snapped out something in a sharp peevish old voice and shook the driver's hand from his arm and turned back again to reach inside the carriage and lift out a battered old carpetbag with something long strapped to one side and sticking out at both ends. He held the bag with one hand and leaned away from it to balance the weight and hobbled up the walk, taking slow short steps and easing down carefully on each foot in turn as if it hurt him to step on it. He hobbled up the walk without a look back at the carriage pulling away and he was a very old man with skin drawn tight over high cheek-bones and a scraggly gray tobacco-stained mustache hanging down over his mouth and bright old eyes deep sunk below heavy brows. He stopped by the porch steps and set the old carpetbag down and what was strapped along its side was an old heavy-barreled rifle. He straightened and peered up at the three of them on the porch, at Jerry Linton and his mother and father.

"Made it," he said. "Bet ye thought I wouldn't. Mebbe hoped so. Aint nothin' wrong with me 'cept these gol-damned feet." He poked his head forward a bit at Jerry's mother. "Mary, aint ye? Young Tom's girl."

"That's right, Grandpa Jonas," said Jerry's mother in her careful company-manners voice. "It's so nice seeing you again. It'll be so nice having you with us."

"Will it now?" said the old man and he peered straight up at her and there was a short embarrassing silence and Jerry's mother broke it by turning to him. "Gerald. This is Jonas Brandt, your great-grandfather."

The old man turned his head a little and his bright old eyes peered at Jerry. "Looks like his father," the old man said and leaned and picked up the carpetbag and hobbled up the steps. "Where'll ye be puttin' me?"

But Jerry's mother had noticed the rifle. Her voice was normal again, with an extra little thin cutting edge. "Grandpa Jonas. We might as well get some things straight. One is I won't have any firearms in my house."

The old man stood still, caught, motionless, frozen in the midst of easing forward from one sore old foot to the other, penned between Jerry Linton on one side and

Jerry's mother and father on the other. He looked at Jerry's mother and she looked right back at him and he lowered his head and looked down at the porch floor. "Aint no hurt in it," he said. "It's broke. Won't work no more." He turned his head sideways towards Jerry Linton and put up his free hand as if to rub his cheek but the hand was there just to hide his face from the other side and far back in Jerry Linton's consciousness a slight tremor of shock and a kind of savage joy shook him because the old man was winking at him, the heavy old brow coming down and the high skin-stretched cheekbone seeming to rise to meet it until the bright old eye was lost between them, and then his father was making it that's that again by saying: "Well, then, Mary, there's no real harm in it. Just so he keeps it where the boy can't get at it."

So the old man was living with them and at first it was difficult because Jerry's parents didn't know what to do with him, what he could or would do to pass the long hours of just being alive. That was really Jerry's mother's problem alone most of the time, except on Sunday, because every other day in the week his father left the house right after breakfast exactly at half past seven to go to work at the bank and was away all day until the clock on the mantelpiece was striking six and he was opening the front door and coming in to hang his hat and coat in the front hall closet. But the old man solved that problem himself. At the supper table, after only a few days, he suddenly put down his knife, which he always held in his right hand all through the meal while he used his fork with his left hand, and poked his old head forward a bit diagonally across the table corner at Jerry's father and said: "Ye payin' that coalman much a anythin'?" He meant the man who stopped by three times a day to tend the big round furnace in the basement that sent hot air up through tin ducts and out through square registers into all the first and second floor rooms.

Jerry's father started a little in surprise. He pursed his lips together in a small frown because he disapproved of discussing financial matters at the table. "I'm paying him enough," he said. "Probably more than the job is worth."

"Get rid a him," said the old man.

"Now, Grandpa Jonas — " began Jerry's mother.

"These goldamned feet aint that bad," said the old man. He picked up his knife again in his right hand and let the fork drop from his left hand and reached with it and took a slice of bread from the dish in the center of the table and began mopping at the gravy on his plate. Jerry's mother watched him shove the dripping bread through his drooping old mustache into his mouth and take half of the slice in one bite and chew it briefly and shove the rest of the slice in. She turned her head and saw Jerry staring in fascination as the old man pushed out his tongue and pulled it back in through the mustache hairs with a tiny sucking noise to get the traces of gravy there. She looked straight across the table at Jerry's father and raised her eyebrows and sighed.

"Bein' fancy aint never made food taste better," said the old man and reached for another slice of bread and bent his head over his plate to concentrate on the last of the gravy and an almost imperceptible little shivery tingle ran down Jerry Linton's spine because he saw, just as the old head bent down, the glint, the unholy fleeting sparkle in the old eyes under the heavy brows.

So tending the furnace kept the old man busy much of the time. He was always up at the first light of dawn and this filled the early morning for him, hobbling his slow way down to the basement, shaking out the night's ashes, shoveling in the coal and fussing with the dampers until the fire was burning right for the kind of weather outside. After breakfast there was the job of taking the ashes and clinkers out to the growing pile behind the garage that would be hauled away in late spring. Then there was only an hour or two to sit smoking one of his stubby old pipes, in good weather when the sun was bright on the front porch steps, in bad weather in the parlor by the front window looking out on the street, before it was lunchtime and the furnace to be tended again and only a few hours more of sitting and smoking before it was suppertime and the furnace to be tended yet again. And when the warm weather really arrived there would be the other chores the coalman had done, cutting the grass of the neat rectangle around the house which was the yard, trimming the hedge along the side opposite the alleyway, cleaning out the basement and getting rid of accumulated trash. For an old man with frozen feet these things could consume many hours.

That left the evenings and at first these were particularly difficult because Jerry's parents tried to be polite and include the old man in at least some of whatever talk there was and he just couldn't or wouldn't fit into their kind of talk and almost always said things that seemed to irritate or embarrass them. But the old man solved that problem too. There was the evening they were all in the parlor, Jerry's mother with her sewing in her platform rocker under the overhead electric light and Jerry's father with his newspaper in his easy chair by the red-tasseled electric lamp and Jerry with his arithmetic homework on the high-backed sofa and the old man with his pipe on the straight ladder-back chair by the front window, and Jerry's mother looked up from her sewing and said in her half-joking voice that meant she was trying to make a point without any fuss about it: "Grandpa Jonas, don't you think it would be nice if you trimmed your mustache more often?"

The old man looked at her what seemed a long time. He looked at Jerry's father who was being very quiet behind the paper. He turned his head to look out the window where one of the town's carbon arc lights on its high pole cast a wide yellow circle along the street. "Mebbe so," he said and Jerry's mother took up her sewing again with a triumphant little half-smile curving her lips. And suddenly the old man turned his head back again and said right out into the middle of the room, his old voice cracking some: "Don't ye folks ever do anythin' diff'rent? Allus the same doin's the same time. Like a bunch a goldamned clocks."

Jerry's mother stopped sewing. She stared at the old man and two spots of color began to show on her cheeks. Jerry's father lowered the paper and looked over it at first one of them then the other. "Regularity," he said. "That's the secret of success." But for once Jerry's mother paid no attention to his father. She had her hands folded in her lap over the sewing and she stared at the old man. Her voice was prim and sharp. "Grandpa Jonas. We are decent, respectable people. The least you can do is try to understand that. You, of all people, trying to tell us how to live."

The old man pushed up from his chair and balanced himself on his sore old feet. "Wasn't tryin' to tell ye a goldamned thing," he said. "Was just wonderin' why." He hobbled across the room and into the front hall and they could hear him making his slow way upstairs.

And the very next day his deafness began to develop. It came on fast and within a few days he couldn't hear a thing that was said to him unless a person was close and shouted. That was peculiar because the way his eyes moved and the look in them changed off and on when there was talking going on around him made it seem as if he knew who was speaking and maybe even what was being said. But he kept quiet and when anyone spoke directly to him he poked his old head forward and cupped one hand by an ear and the remark or question had to be repeated in a loud voice before he would understand it.

So his being deaf made the evenings easier because there wasn't much sense in trying to talk to a person who couldn't hear. It wasn't long before none of them ever said much of anything at all to him except to shout things absolutely necessary. It wasn't long before his evening routine was settled too. After supper he hobbled down to the basement and took a time tending the furnace for the night and hobbled back up and sat by the parlor window and waited for Jerry's father to finish reading the paper. When the reading was done and the paper refolded and placed on the parlor table, he pushed up from his chair and hobbled over and took it and hobbled out into the hall and on up the stairs to his own room.

All the first weeks he was something new and strange to Jerry Linton and the boy couldn't help staring at him and watching him. Jerry's mother worried about that and had one of her talks with him about it. "Gerald," she said, "you're still a child and children are very impressionable. I don't want you ever to forget that you are a Linton and I intend you to grow up to be a gentleman like your father." That was a word his mother used often in these talks. Sometimes it seemed that she thought there was nothing worse than not being a gentleman. But this time she was not talking about how a gentleman behaved and what a gentleman did or did not do. She was talking about the old man. "Jonas Brandt," she said — she usually spoke of him not as if he were her grandfather, Jerry's great-grandfather, but someone removed who had no real connection with them — "well, Jonas Brandt is, well, he is just not a very nice person. That may not be altogether his fault because he didn't have a very good upbringing and, well, he just couldn't be after what he did. I don't want you watching him all the time and maybe learning bad habits — "

"But, Mother, what was it that was so bad that he did?"

"Gerald. It's not nice to interrupt. Jonas Brandt just wouldn't ever settle down and take care of his family the way a decent man would. Expecting a woman and with children to go off into wild country and not live decent when there was nice work he could do at home. He was always going off by himself and doing what he wanted and not even thinking of them and getting just cruder and coarser all the time. And then he — well, I'm sorry, Gerald, but you're not old enough yet to know about that. You just have to take my word about him. After all, I'm your mother. He has to stay with us because there's no place else for him to go and after all he is related. The least you can do for my sake is just not pay much attention to him at all."

And after the first weeks that was not hard to do. The newness of the old man was gone. He was there, but he was less and less there in actual seeing and noticing, somehow quietly slipping or being pushed ever further into the background of household affairs. He never ate with them when they had company and used the dining room and Jerry's mother had out a linen tablecloth and linen napkins in honor of people from the bank or members of her Book and Thimble Club. He took to using the back stairs all the time, the narrow enclosed flight of steps that led from the rear of the upstairs hall down to the kitchen. He was no longer sleeping in the other back bedroom across the hall from Jerry's room. When Aunt Ella came to stay a few days he moved up into the little finished room in the attic so she could have his room and after she left he stayed on up there where he didn't have to bother so much about Jerry's mother wanting things neat and tidy even though being there meant another flight of narrow steps to climb.

He was no longer on the front porch steps when Jerry came home from school, just before lunch and again in midafternoon. Jerry's mother worried about him sitting there, what people would think, seeing him dirty and disreputable sitting there, drawing on his bubbly old pipe and spitting sideways into the shrubbery. She bought him a nice new suit that first Easter, one with matching coat and pants and vest, and he grumbled some and at last began to wear it but within a week it seemed as wrinkled and dirty as his old clothes had been. She must have said something then because he shifted around to the back steps and, later, to a bench he built behind the garage.

He was no longer even in the parlor, even in bad weather, except the brief silent time each evening when he waited for the paper. There was the rainy afternoon Jerry's mother was upset because Jerry had tracked mud into the front hall and the old man was sitting by the parlor window with his pipe in his hand and his old head cocked a bit to one side as if he could really hear what she was saying to Jerry and she caught a glimpse of him and swung around and marched into the parlor and said in a sharp voice: "Grandpa Jonas. Do you have to smoke that horrible pipe in my house? It's ruining my curtains." She didn't wait to see if he heard her. She swung around again and marched out to get a broom and dustpan and sweep up the drying mud. But the old man must have heard because after a few minutes he pushed up and hobbled off and down into the basement and after that, in bad weather when he couldn't be on his bench behind the garage, he stayed down there, sitting and smoking on an old kitchen chair with an old cushion pad on it in the recess between the coalbin and the basement stairs where a window up behind him just above the ground level gave some light.

So he was just there, something familiar now and receding ever further into the taken-for-granted background of daily living. Jerry Linton hardly ever even thought or wondered about him any more. Every morning, for some reason, lying in his bed in the second-story back room, the boy would suddenly be awake and the first light of dawn would be creeping in his window and he would hear, overhead, slow hobbling footsteps, quiet and muffled, that would fade away then be heard again coming down the narrow attic stairway and going past his door and fading out again down the back stairway to the kitchen. But even then he would not think of the old man, not as another living person separate and discernible apart from all the ordinary almost unquestioned everyday surroundings. The hobbling steps were simply another sound out of the familiar round that measured existence and they simply meant there would be time for more sleep and somehow the best sleep before his mother would be calling to him to get dressed and come down to breakfast.

Jerry Linton was two weeks past his fourteenth birthday when the man from the historical society came to call. He came on a Saturday afternoon in a dust-covered green Maxwell that he had driven all the way from the state capital. Jerry answered the door because he was in the stage of being taught how a gentleman greeted strangers and he did very well, inviting the man in and showing him into the parlor before running to get his mother.

The man sat in the platform rocker facing Jerry and his mother on the high-backed sofa. He introduced himself as a Mr. Finley, as the secretary of the state historical society, and said he was assembling information for an article he was writing for the society's quarterly publication. Jerry's mother sat up straighter with a proud little smile on her face and then suddenly she looked as astonished as Jerry felt because Mr. Finley was saying that he wanted to talk to a Jonas Brandt.

Jonas Brandt?

Why certainly. Of course, what was happening nowadays in the state, the tremendous strides forward of economic and social progress, was what was really important. But still it was interesting to get down facts about the past and the time to do that was now while some of the oldtime settlers and pioneers were still alive. Of course, their memories were not always to be trusted but the scholarly approach, checking this against that, sifting out the probable truth, often yielded excellent results.

Mr. Finley was somewhat self-important as he explained his work. Jerry's mother listened and seemed a bit worried as she listened and she gave a soft little sigh of relief when Mr. Finley said his article was about the Sioux outbreak of 1862, about one aspect of it, one incident, that had been generally overlooked in the wealth of material available. He had his article well in hand. In fact, he was quite satisfied with it. But his scholar's conscience told him he should check his facts with every source and, after all, he liked traveling about and so where was Jonas Brandt?

He was out on his bench behind the garage but Jerry's mother did not tell that. She simply excused herself and went out to get him and in a few minutes he had hobbled in after her and was sitting, of all places, in the big easy chair by the red-tasseled lamp. He sat on the edge of it, hunched forward in his wrinkled and dirty clothes, his old hands on his old knees, peering at Mr. Finley from under his heavy old brows.

"Mr. Brandt — " began Mr. Finley.

"You'll have to speak up," said Jerry's mother. "He doesn't hear very well."

"Mr. Brandt — " began Mr. Finley again in almost a shout.

"What ye shoutin' fer?" said the old man.

"Well," said Jerry's mother quickly. "This must be one of his good days."

"Mr. Brandt," began Mr. Finley again. He spoke slowly, separating the words, almost as if he were speaking to a child. "In August of 1862 you were living in a little crossroads settlement about ten miles from the town of New Ulm."

"Nope," said the old man. "Just passin' through. Freightin'."

Mr. Finley cleared his throat. "In any event, you were there when the Santee Sioux under Little Crow went on the warpath and began massacring defenseless women and children."

"Men too," said the old man. "Fightin' men." His old eyes were beginning to brighten.

"Well, yes," said Mr. Finley. "In any event, you were one of the party, all the people there, who set out to slip through those massacring Indians and get to Fort Ridgely."

"Yep," said the old man.

"Thirteen of you, including the children."

"Sixteen," said the old man.

"Very good, Mr. Brandt. I was just testing your memory. And who was in charge?"

"Feller named Schultz. Marty Schultz."

"Splendid, Mr. Brandt. And this Martin Schultz was an excellent leader, was he not? Took charge and — "

"Nope. Seven kinds a fool. Didn't know much. About Injuns anyway."

"Now, Mr. Brandt." Mr. Finley seemed somewhat irritated. "Let's not permit personal feelings or perhaps even jealousy creep in here. The facts prove otherwise. There were only five of you men and the rest were women and children and Martin Schultz was in charge and you were three days getting to the fort with just about no food at all and unable to make a fire with murdering Indians all about — and yet you all got through safely. Now, didn't you?"

"Yep."

"And on the last day you wouldn't have. You were hiding in a ravine and an Indian way off on a hilltop sighted you and if he had got word to the rest of his band or been able to signal them you would all have been slaughtered. But he didn't because — "

"Ye're goldamned right he didn't!"

Mr. Finley was excited now. He jumped up from the platform rocker and began pacing back and forth in front of it. "There you are, Mrs. Linton. That is my article. With full details added of course. I got it first from Martin Schultz himself. And two of the women are still living. They check it on most points. Can you see it? Of course you can. What a climax. That murdering Indian off on the hilltop and sixteen innocent white people hiding in that ravine. And Martin Schultz takes his rifle and steadies it on a rock and takes his aim. It was all of nine hundred yards, Schultz claims, but of course that's exaggerated. Those old guns you know. But it was quite a distance anyway. And sixteen lives dependent on that one shot. And Martin Schultz knows that and maybe offers up a little prayer and — "

"Quit yappin'," said the old man. "Marty allus was one to hog it. Never made that shot." The old man raised his old hands and slapped them down on his old knees. "I did."

Mr. Finley stopped pacing. He raised one hand and looked down at it and turned it over and studied his neat fingernails. He cleared his throat. "Yes, yes, of course, Mr. Brandt. After all these years and thinking about it so much, perhaps it seems — "

"It was better'n a thousand yards too!"

Mr. Finley looked at Jerry's mother and raised his eyebrows and shrugged his shoulders. He cleared his throat again and followed this with a little cough and turned towards the old man. "Well, thank you, Mr. Brandt. You have been most helpful. At least I'm sure you meant to be. Perhaps sometime I will want to consult you about some of your other — "

The old man was not even trying to hear him. The old man was pushing up from the easy chair and hobbling towards the hall. "Thought ye wanted facts," he said and disappeared towards the back of the house.

So Jerry's mother was out in the front hall with Mr. Finley by the front door and she was saying apologetic things to him and Mr. Finley was saying polite things to reassure her and alone in the parlor, tense upright on the high-backed sofa, was Jerry Linton, shaking, shaking far down inside with a kind of savage joy and a desire for knowing, knowing, knowing —

"Mother. What was that other thing he did?"

"Oh, Gerald. I don't want you thinking about such things. We're civilized now. I don't see why, even if it is history, people have to go raking up all those horrible old things and making people remember them. People ought just try to forget things ever weren't as decent and quiet as they are now. I wish that Mr. Finley, even if he is a gentleman — "

"Mother. What did he do?"

"Well . . . I suppose you do have to know sometime, Gerald. He, well, after his wife died — worried her into her grave, I'm sure that's what happened — he took up with, well, with an Indian woman. And he, well, he never even married her. There. I've told you. Now I want you to just put it out of your mind and not go around thinking about it . . ."

Out of mind?

So Jerry Linton had to wait until his mother was busy again picking up and tidying about upstairs then go find the old man. He was not out behind the garage. He was in the basement, on his old chair in the recess by the coalbin. Jerry Linton, stretching and gangling into his fifteenth year, almost as tall already as his father, stood on the basement steps near the bottom and saw the old man sitting there sucking on a bubbly old pipe and was afraid, afraid of this suddenly strange-again old man, thinner and more stooped than when he first came, with old eyes dulled now, somehow even in his dwindling meager smallness looming tremendous and blotting out the whole neat horizon of accepted living.

Jerry Linton could barely get the word out. "Grandpa."

It was really one of the old man's good days. He did not turn his head but he heard. "Eh, boy?"

"Did you . . . did you really shoot that Indian?"

Long seconds of waiting then the old man's head turned

slowly towards Jerry and nodded. "With that rifle a mine. That's a Sharps, boy."

"They . . . they don't believe you."

"That don't mean nothin'. How'd they know? Thing is, I know."

It was peculiar. Grown folks couldn't talk to the old man. But a boy could. Jerry Linton sat down on the second step from the bottom. His chin fitted into the notch between his knees poking up with his arms around his legs holding them together and by twisting his head just a bit he could look at the old man.

"That Indian woman . . . Why didn't you ever marry her?"

"Yer mother's been talkin'." The old man chuckled. "Fact is, I did. Injun style. Good enough fer her so good enough fer me. Stuck with me till she finished." He chuckled again. "Tell ye somethin', boy. She was more woman 'n the first one . . ."

And after that Saturdays were special because in the mornings when Jerry's mother was uptown doing her household shopping and picking out the groceries that would be delivered in the afternoon he was with the old man, in the basement or out behind the garage, and there was no end to the questions that kept coming.

"Grandpa. Did you ever shoot a buffalo?"

"Buffler, boy? That's fer sure. Partner'n me worked hides two-three years. Toted in more'n 'leven hundred once. Worked out a Bismarck up in Dakoty . . ."

That was the way it was, simply the plain unslicked statements somehow more real and exciting because of their very matter-of-fact plainness, to be expanded in imagination and given meaning in the thinking over afterwards.

"But why won't you ever ride in the car?"

"Goldamned machine. Legs or a hoss's the way to get around. What good'd that thing be fer rough goin'? Up in the mount'ns? Aint worth a buffler chip off a road. Me, I aint never stuck to roads . . ."

"Did you ever see Jesse James?"

"Nope. Didn't miss much nuther. Saw Boone Helm once. Knife man, he was. Killed a lot a people. Folks got together an' used a rope up in Montanny. Used to see the place freightin' into Virginny City . . ."

"But, Grandpa, weren't you ever scared? Indians and wild animals and things like that?"

"Why, fer sure, boy. Lots a times. Bein' scared's all right. Backin' away aint. I'd start shiverin' an' I'd say, Jonas, ye goldamned mule, ye got yerself into this here fix an' so what comes ye can just take — an' after that it wouldn't be so goldamned bad . . ."

So Jerry Linton, in a sense, was living two lives, one neat and orderly, cushioned by security and the polite courtesies of respectability, bounded by school and family meals and the rules and almost unvarying routine of his parents' household, the other unruly and exciting, pushing haphazard into the long echoing past of an old man who had never stuck to roads, pushing in imagination outward into the open spaces of new land and of wild land and of land not yet tamed but only being tamed where distance pulled at the mind and danger could be a frequent companion and a man could look along the barrel of a Sharps rifle and aim true. After a while the two lives began to merge in almost unnoticed small ways, unnoticed even by Jerry Linton himself. But one day in history class a picture of Andrew Jackson came alive on the page and he suddenly knew that the names in the book were not just names but people and not people apart and different but ordinary everyday-seeming people who ate meals and dressed and undressed and sometimes were tired and sick and just went ahead and did things and lived and in time grew thin and stooped and old.

Walking to school he saw the other houses in their neat rectangles of yards, the squared corners of the streets laid out in regular blocks, and he knew that almost everywhere out beyond the town were the neat sectioned farms with their neat cultivated fields and pastures, almost everything here and out there neat and decent and respectable. It was not always like that. Indians once roamed even this tamed land at will. And buffalo. Men had made it the way it was, men like his father, steady and dependable, careful with figures, planning ahead. And suddenly he knew, knew in real knowing not just as an idea taught in class, that other men had come first, men who didn't stick to roads and who knew Indians and fought them and sometimes even lived with them and could bring in eleven hundred buffalo hides in a single season. The wind drifting in from the west was not just the wind any more. Maybe that blowing against his cheek came from way off, beyond this Minnesota, from beyond the far Black Hills near the Devil's Tower where the old man had killed a mountain lion once or even from on up in the real mountains themselves where Boone Helm lay buried with a rope-broken neck.

In small ways. Even in games. When he was in grammar school he never played much with the older boys, except sometimes with the two younger ones who lived next door. The older boys stayed around after school and played on the grounds and on the athletic field beside the big building. His mother wanted him to come straight home, to play around the house and yard. She couldn't see why boys always liked to play such rough games anyway. There were so many ways they could be hurt, like the boy in the next block who broke an arm playing football. Now Jerry was in high school, even just the first year, it was different. His mother had one of her talks with him and told him he could stay around after school two or three days a week if he really wanted to because she was sure she could trust him not to be wild and rough like some of the boys. He stayed around and it was early fall and they were playing football and at first, for quite a few days, he just stood and watched. He wanted to play too but he couldn't help thinking about getting hurt. And one day he pushed in with the others and he was let be on one side just to fill in and then he was out on the field more frightened than he had ever been before and ready to run away. And suddenly he was telling himself without thinking how or why that he'd gotten himself into this fix so he'd just have to take what came and in a kind of savage joy almost as if he hoped to be hurt so he could show he could take it he plunged into the game and it wasn't so bad after all. In a little while it was even fun, to be running and yelling and bumping into other boys trying to block them and gasping for breath with the blood in him pounding strong.

It was spring and Jerry Linton was past the halfway mark of his fifteenth year when his mother came home one Saturday morning from her household shopping and called and called to him and at last he answered from behind the garage and then he forgot and she had to call him again.

"Gerald," she said. "I do wish you would come when I call. Now carry these parcels upstairs. The least you can do is help with all the running up and down stairs that has to be done in this house." And when he had put the parcels in the upstairs hall and was back down and starting out the kitchen door she stopped him. "Gerald. It seems to me you're spending entirely too much time with Jonas Brandt. It's beginning to show in your talk. And you're becoming entirely too loud and noisy lately."

Jerry Linton stood in the doorway shifting from one foot to the other and his mother said: "Sit down, Gerald. I want to have a talk with you. I don't see how it can do you any good to have a man like Jonas Brandt filling your head with wild notions and horrible old stories that very likely aren't the least bit true anyway. I'm sure most of the time he's just trying to justify himself and make you think that after all he really was something. You know how old people are, getting things mixed up and getting to think maybe things are true that really weren't true at all. I'm sure you remember what happened when that Mr. Finley — "

"Oh-h-h, mother. He really did shoot that Indian!"

So Jerry Linton had spoken back to his mother and spoken sharply too and his father had to have a talk with him, dry-voiced and precise, reasoning it out. "Jerry. I know you didn't mean to upset your mother but you did and that's that. I know when we're through here you will go and tell her you are sorry. What you have to realize is that she is right. No doubt there is some truth in the things your great-grandfather has been telling you. But he is nearly ninety years old and they happened a long time ago. Most people's memories, especially old people's, are very faulty as we keep finding out at the bank. Trying to straighten out wills and property deeds and things like that. Your great-grandfather has not given much evidence in his life that he has much sense of responsibility. And, after all, what happened so long ago is not nearly as important to a growing boy as what is happening right now.

This is a practical world we live in these days and it is run on business principles. What you should be doing is tending to your lessons and learning how best to get along in it."

So Jerry Linton told his mother he was sorry. But his parents saw the stubborn look on his face and worried about it and only a few days later his father brought home a copy of the historical society's quarterly and showed him Mr. Finley's article.

There it was, in the cold clear neat precise not-to-be-questioned authority of printed words, the whole story, very well told and with impressive footnotes, of sixteen people fleeing for their lives under the leadership of a Martin Schultz and evading the bloody-handed Sioux for three days and on the third day sighted by an Indian scout who never got word back to his band because of the cool courage and unerring marksmanship of Martin Schultz. The only mention of Jonas Brandt was in a footnote: *The fifth man was a freighter named Jonas Brandt, who joined the group for added safety in reaching the fort.*

So his parents were right. There were no more Saturday mornings behind the garage for Jerry Linton. He was too busy playing with the other boys. It wouldn't be exciting listening to the old man anyway. Jerry Linton saw him in sensible perspective now and realized that for quite a while his memory had been getting bad after all. He contradicted himself sometimes and when he tried to pin down a date he kept getting mixed up. He was just an old relic out of another time who didn't fit in the modern practical world.

Jerry Linton was fifteen, in his sophomore year at high school, when he woke one spring morning in his second floor bedroom soon after the first light of dawn with a strange feeling that something was wrong. He found himself listening and not sure for what. Then he knew. There were no slow hobbling footsteps overhead. He lay quiet wondering about that and after a while slipped back into sleep and when his mother called him and he dressed and went downstairs there was a slight chill in the house and his father was in the basement rattling and banging at the furnace. While they were eating breakfast the doctor came and Jerry's father went off with him upstairs. In a few moments they were back down, the doctor bustling and good-natured, rubbing his hands together and saying: "Nothing to get too much upset about, Mrs. Linton. He's a bit feverish but that's to be expected. He's had some kind of a light stroke. A remarkably tough old constitution, I'd say. Wouldn't surprise me to see him up and about again in a few days."

But it was not a few days. It was the very next day, early in the morning with the first light of dawn. Jerry Linton woke and heard slow hobbling steps overhead, quiet and muffled, that faded away and then were heard again coming down the narrow attic stairway and going past his door and fading out again down the back stairway to the kitchen. A kind of warm feeling drifted through him and he slipped back into sleep and suddenly he was awake again. Wide awake. The footsteps were returning past his door and on up the attic steps, not slow and hobbling, but quicker, lighter, hurrying. Jerry Linton lay still and listened and they came down the attic stairs again and were going past his door again. He eased quietly out of bed and tiptoed to the door and opened it a crack. The old man was just disappearing into the back stairway and he was carrying his old rifle.

Jerry Linton couldn't move at first. He was still, motionless, with his face pressed close against the door crack.

Then he opened the door and went, soft and quick, along the hall towards the front of the house and stopped by the closed door of his parents' bedroom. He stared at the door almost a full minute. And suddenly he turned and hurried back to his own room and dressed as fast as he could and pulled on a sweater and went out and down the back stairs.

The old man wasn't in the basement. He wasn't on the back porch or anywhere in sight in the yard. He was behind the garage and he was standing straight, hardly stooped at all, with the heavy old rifle firm in one hand, and his old eyes were brighter, brighter than they had ever been, when he looked at Jerry coming around the corner of the garage.

"Time ye were out a blankets," he said. "There's things doin'." He looked at Jerry in a strange way, not the way he ever had before, in a strange and straight and piercing way almost as if Jerry were someone else who should have been out of blankets before this. "What's got into ye, Jed?" he said. "Can't ye sniff it? Injun smell." He pointed with his free hand off across the vacant lot behind theirs and the fields beyond to the slight rise that hid the town dump. In the growing light of dawn Jerry saw it, a last thin wisp of smoke floating upward and dissolving away. "That's just a fire over in — " he started to say but the old man was poking his old head at him and saying in a fierce whisper: "Tell me I don't know Injun sign! Some-un's got to do some scoutin' or they'll be on us afore we know it!"

The old man started off, striding fast, across the vacant lot, and Jerry Linton wavered and turned to hurry back to the house and stopped. Slowly he turned around again and saw the old man striding away, head forward and intent, striding fast on old feet that must hurt him but he didn't seem to notice that, striding ahead with his heavy old rifle in his right hand, and far down in Jerry Linton a tingling started and shook him and would not stop and he was running to catch up.

The old man flicked one sideways glance at him as he came alongside. "Right, Jed," the old man said. "Two's got more chance 'n one."

They were across the vacant lot and they struck straight across the fields beyond, climbing fences as they came to them. Once a dog ran up barking at their heels and the old man swung around and down and snarled something at it that didn't seem to be words and it stopped barking and put its tail between its legs and dropped behind and away. They went over the rise that hid the dump and on past the dump itself where some fire still smoldered which the old man didn't even notice and he stopped and raised his left hand to shield his eyes against the sun just beginning to show over the horizon and peered all around, studying the countryside. "They'll come snakin' down that draw," he said and struck off again towards the only rough land, the only untamed-to-farming land, anywhere around, towards the far base of the huge wide slow-sloping hill that rose west of town with its near slope torn and eroded by an ancient dry boulder-strewn stream bed. They reached the base of the hill and Jerry Linton's legs were tiring from the pace but he couldn't have stopped if he had wanted to. It was impossible how the old man kept going on his old frozen feet, striding forward, head swinging from side to side, old eyes bright and intent under their heavy brows. He struck straight up along the upper left side of the dry stream bed that widened upward like a vast shallow funnel and Jerry Linton followed and followed and his legs were aching and the old man stopped. "Can't figger it," he said. "Sioux aint been liftin' hair lately." He started on and they were near the top of the hill and Jerry Linton's legs were aching and suddenly the old man clapped him on the shoulder so hard he went forward on his knees. "Down," said the old man in a fierce whisper, dropping to the ground and scrambling over behind a boulder. "Over here."

So there they were, Jerry Linton and the old man, behind a boulder on the edge of a wide gully, really just a wide stretch of rough eroded hillside, and far off down the slope and across the level, like a neat picture in the midst of neat surrounding farms, was the neat town with its square-blocked streets where decent and respectable people were still sleeping with maybe some of them already beginning to stir in their neat houses. And the old man raised and peered over the boulder, intent old eyes studying the wide gully. "Take a peek, Jed," he said. "See 'im? Ahind that rock looks like a keg. Straight across an' down some."

Jerry Linton, aching and scratched but with a tingling inside that wouldn't stop, peered over the boulder too and at last he saw the rock that looked like a keg, way off across and up the other side of the wide gully. But it was only a rock and that was all.

"Got it," said the old man. "Pawnee. Sneakin' devils they are. Paint up like that." And then Jerry Linton, squeezing his eyes to sharp focus, saw showing above the rock in a small patch an outcropping of red sandstone in the ground beyond, bright and shimmering a little in the early morning sun.

"Likely a passel a bucks over the ridge," said the old man. He turned towards Jerry. His old voice was an urgent hoarse whisper. "Git amovin', Jed, an' rouse the folks. I'll slow 'm here while ye get help."

It was the tingling in Jerry Linton that pushed him up and started him a few steps away. Then he felt foolish and he stopped and looked around. The old man was beside the boulder, flat on his stomach, and he was shoving the old rifle forward and muttering to himself. He put a finger in his mouth and licked it and stuck it up to test the air. "Wind about ten mile," he muttered. "Figger the drop across there maybe thirty feet." His left arm was out, resting on its elbow, and his left hand held and steadied the heavy old rifle barrel and the stock was snuggled up against his right shoulder and he squinted through the strange old double sights and suddenly the old Sharps roared like a Fourth of July cannon and the recoil smacked shaking through the old man's body. He rolled over and behind the boulder again and sat up with the rifle still in his hands and yanked down on the trigger guard and the breech opened and he clawed in a pocket and took out a funny old linen cartridge and started reloading and his fingers fumbled and dropped it and the old gun fell too, down and across his legs, and his whole body seemed to stiffen into a kind of rigidness. Slowly his old head came up and his eyes, dulling rapidly, looked around and stopped on Jerry Linton.

"What ye doin' up here, boy?" he said and his whole body sagged out of the rigidness into a kind of limpness and relaxed back against the boulder and slipped down sidewise to the ground.

Jerry Linton knew. He had never seen this before but he knew. He looked down at the crumpled still body a long time. He looked up and across the wide gully where a patch of red sandstone showed above a keg-shaped rock.

Slowly he started down the rough eroded near side of the gully and then he was walking faster and then he was running, down and across the center dip and up the other side and then slowing, almost afraid to look.

There was the rock. There behind it, farther behind than it seemed from the other side, was the patch of red sandstone. And there, near the top of the patch where it would show over the rock, close to the edge but there, was the fresh, chipped, the shining gouge in the stone.

Jerry Linton stood with his back to the patch of sandstone. He started again across the gully, taking long steps, stretching them to what he judged the right length. Down and across and up. One thousand and twenty-seven. Taking into account the slope down and up that was still close enough.

Jerry Linton picked up the old rifle and looked at it. There was not a spot of rust on the metal. The old stock was sound. "Yes," he said. "Yes. I'm a Linton. But I'm a Brandt too." He said it to the body of an old man who had given him what no one else could, what no one could ever take away from him because always, simply by closing his eyes, he would be able to see, across a thousand yards of untamed land, a patch of red chipped sandstone.

He turned and went down the slope towards the town to get his father, who, in his own precise way, steady and dependable, would make arrangements to take care of what was left of the old man.

In Harmony

*

T HE HORSE rose in the air, spine arched, and switched ends and came down stiff-legged. Monte Walsh, easy in the saddle, took the jolt with a grunt and raked the wet flanks with his spurs. The horse doubled its forelegs under and rocked down on its side and Monte stepped out of the saddle going down. "That won't get you nowheres," he said. The horse bent its head backwards and rolled the white of an eye at him. It lunged to its feet and Monte stepped into the saddle coming up. The horse stood, head hanging, legs braced.

"Watch 'im," said Chet Rollins from his perch on the gate of the small circular corral. "He aint done yet."

"Who's riding this thing?" said Monte. "Think I was weaned just — "

The horse exploded, coming off the ground with legs spread-eagled, and hit again running and streaked straight for the corral fence. Monte wrapped the reins around his hands and yanked its head around to the left till the nose almost hit the straining shoulder and it swung in an arc, stumbling, fighting its own forward weight for footing. It lined out again straight for the opposite curve of the corral. "Go ahead break your fool neck," said Monte. He loosened his toes in the stirrups, ready to leave the hurricane deck. The horse saw the rails ahead and faltered and swung this time on its own and raced around the inside curve. Monte took off his hat and slapped it in hearty rhythm against the heaving withers. "Yow-eee!" he yelled. "Run, you bat-brain! Catch your own tail and eat it!"

The horse stopped. Its head drooped. It was a statue of disgust and dejection, motionless except for heaving ribs and a slight quivering of the legs. Monte swung down and walked around by the drooping head. "Well, now," he said. "You behaved medium to good considering—" He leaped backwards. The horse's head was up and a forehoof slashed the air half an inch in front of his shirt. He leaped in close and grabbed an ear in each hand and hung his weight on the horse's head, pulling it down.

"Playful, aint he?" said Chet Rollins on the corral gate. He jumped down and ambled forward through the settling dust and loosened the double rigging and pulled the breaking saddle off the horse. He ambled back and set the saddle on the top rail and opened the gate leading into the big main corral. Monte let go the ears and took hold of the headband of the bridle and in one sweeping motion stripped the bridle down and off the horse's head and jumped aside. In a swirl of dust the horse sliced through the open gateway.

Monte Walsh and Chet Rollins sat on the top rail of the fence, backs to the circular corral. In amiable silence they watched the half-broken horses in the big corral move with restless twitchings and roll off the sweaty itch of the day's working. Monte inspected his blunt battered fingers. He pulled a jackknife out of a pants pocket and opened it and began cleaning dust from under his fingernails. "Action," he murmured. "That's what I need. A little action."

Chet Rollins turned his head slow and looked at him. Monte closed the knife and slipped it back in the pocket. He pushed his hat up his forehead. "Shucks," he said. "That's just a job."

Chet Rollins fished a stubby pipe out of one shirt pocket and a small tobacco pouch out of the other. He took a long time filling the bowl to final satisfaction. He sighed. "It's only been two weeks since — "

"That long?" said Monte. "That's a mighty long time." He reached an arm and lifted the pouch from Chet's pocket and fished a paper from one of his own shirt pockets and rolled a cigarette. He leaned over and tucked the pouch where it belonged and lit his cigarette from Chet's match over the pipe. He settled back on the rail and watched the two streamers of smoke that emerged from his nose. "At my age anyway," he said.

Chet Rollins sighed again. He drew in a lungful of smoke and took the pipe from his mouth and blew a series of lazy drifting rings and reached to poke a finger through the last one. Beside him Monte shifted rump on the rail and turned a bit towards him.

"No," said Chet. "I aint got a cent."

The hot glaze of midafternoon shimmered over the two corrals and on out over the far plain. Off to the right the cook came out of the cookhouse carrying an empty bucket and disappeared into the supply shed and emerged with the bucket full of potatoes and disappeared again into the cookhouse. Monte Walsh flipped his cigarette butt into the dust and pushed out from the rail and landed light with one boot covering the butt. He strolled to the side fence and vaulted it and angled to the bunkhouse. Inside he began a thorough search, unhurried, competent, pulling out the pockets of the clothes hanging on wooden pegs along the front wall, peeling back blankets and feeling under the lumpy straw-filled mattresses in the bunks along the side walls. Several dollar bills and some change began to accumulate in his left pants pocket.

"There'll be a little ruckus," said Chet Rollins in the doorway. "When the boys get in."

"Shucks," said Monte. "They always ante in an emergency." He started on the clothes hanging along the rear wall. A quarter hit the floor and rolled. He bent to retrieve it. "This is an emergency," he said. He pushed past Chet in the doorway and strolled towards the fenced enclosure behind the barn, collecting his saddle and bridle and a rope from the barn on the way. The experienced cowponies in the enclosure eyed him with wary suspicion and drifted to the far side. He dropped his gear by the fence and slipped through the rails. He carried the rope coiled in his left hand and shook out a loop with the right. He looked the horses over and picked a short-coupled pinto and with sure instinct the pinto knew and drifted further away among the others. He strolled forward with the loop trailing on the ground beside him and the horses drifted to one side and he angled that way and they bunched in the corner, the pinto far back among them. He strolled closer and they broke, scattering to left and right to race past him, and the pinto feinted fast to one side and wheeled to plunge to the other and around, snorting, head high, hoofs pounding, and his right hand flipped forward and the rope snaked out and the loop opened and dropped over the pinto's head. It reared back, testing the rope and his hold. Its forefeet dropped to the ground and it stood, patient and resigned, watching him approach.

Ten minutes later, jogging along at a steady pace across

the plain, he heard hoofbeats behind him. Chet Rollins
on a chunky gray came alongside and pulled to the same
pace. They jogged along in a companionable silence.

"Poorest outfit I ever was with," said Monte Walsh.
"Only seven dollars and seventeen cents."

The unorganized town of Harmony slept in the afternoon glaze. Curtains were pulled or flour bags hung at the
windows of the few houses to shut out the sun. The doors
of the livery stable and the blacksmith shop and the stage
station were closed for the same sensible reason. The
wide porch of the combination hotel and office building
served the same purpose. A blanket hung down over the
one wide window of the barbershop. An innovation, an
awning, shaded the front of the general store. Even three
of the four saloons had the solid doors behind the swinging
doors closed. Down the brief length of the main, the only
recognizable, street not a twitch of movement disturbed
the silence. Two freight wagons stood motionless in the
street dust, their ox teams lying down under the yokes.
Across the way an old farm wagon sagged over its axles,
its team still and wooden, too dulled even to flick tails at
flies. Harmony reigned in Harmony. And over the last
rise of the rolling plain that stretched to the horizon all
around and on down to the main street jogged a short-coupled pinto and a chunky gray.

"Well, lookathere," said Monte Walsh. "One new shack
and a frill on the store."

The two knowing cowponies swung together to the tie
rail in front of the one open saloon. Monte and Chet Rollins dismounted and eased cinches and stepped up across
the plank sidewalk and went inside. The bartender,
perched on a stool behind the bar and hunched forward

on his elbows reading a newspaper, looked up and saw them coming. He reached under the bar and set out two small glasses and a plain labelless bottle half filled with a dark deadly liquid and returned to his paper.

"Not that stuff," said Monte. "We can pay."

The bartender turned his head to look up sideways. He waited. Monte fished in his left pants pocket and pulled out one of the dollar bills and laid it on the bar. The bartender swiveled on the stool and reached with both hands, one to take the dollar, the other to take a bottle with a bright label off the shelf behind him. He set the bottle out by the two glasses and in the same motion restored the first bottle to its place beneath the bar. He settled again on his elbows over the paper. "That'll cover four," he said.

Monte Walsh and Chet Rollins drained the first pair and leaned with backs against the bar surveying the interior of the saloon. An old man in too-large clothes that looked even older sat slouched on a chair near the front staring dull-eyed out the one side window at the blank wall of the next building. Farther back the two freighters from the wagons outside slept with long puffing snores by a streak-topped table. One was upright, head back, mouth open. The other was slumped forward on the table, head cradled in his arms by an empty bottle.

"Mighty lively," murmured Monte Walsh.

The bartender slapped his hands down on his newspaper and pushed up straighter. "What d'you expect?" he said. "A brass band and dancing girls? Won't be payday for any outfit around for a week or more." He settled again to his paper.

Monte Walsh and Chet Rollins drained the second pair. Monte stooped down and peered towards the back of the saloon. At this level he could see, behind a round table in a corner, stretched out on three chairs in a line, the long thin form of a man lying asleep with a hat over his face. Monte strolled back and fingered the top chips in a box on the round table. He picked up the deck of cards beside the box and riffled them with little snapping sounds. The figure on the chair stirred and a voice issued from under the hat. "What've you got?"

Monte tried to sound joyful. "Six dollars," he said.

"That aint even drinking money," said the voice.

Monte strolled towards the front. Chet Rollins was inspecting what looked like a framed picture on the wall but there was no picture in the frame. Between the board back and the glass many nails in zigzag patterns stuck out from the wood, their tips almost touching the glass. Along the top were slits in the frame. Along the bottom, behind the glass, was a row of little compartments. The one in the middle offered, in gilt letters, the golden legend: $10. Two others, spaced out on each side, proclaimed $5. The others were blank. Pasted to the back boards in an upper corner, plain through the glass, was a diagram showing a coin being inserted in one of the slits and tracing with a dotted line its course bouncing from nail to nail and dropping into the $10 compartment.

"Aint that cute?" said Chet Rollins. "Those blamed nails're so close together over the winners nothing could get through if it tried."

The bartender slapped his hands down on his newspaper. His voice was aggrieved. "Man so stupid he can't figure that out," he said, "deserves to lose his money." He settled to his paper again.

Footsteps sounded on the plank sidewalk outside. Two pair of polished boots showed beneath the swinging doors and two top hats above them passing by. Monte Walsh and Chet Rollins stood by the bar and looked at each other. Monte reached for the bottle but the bartender's hand was there first. The bartender went on reading, his hand holding the bottle. Monte fished in his pocket and extracted another dollar bill. The bartender's hand left the bottle and took the bill.

"Wonder who's dead?" murmured Monte. The bartender turned his head and looked up. "Funeral aint it?" said Monte.

"No," said the bartender and returned to his reading.

Monte Walsh and Chet Rollins drained the third pair. Monte strolled over to the old man by the window. He was beginning to bounce a bit off his toes as he walked. "Hello, Johnny," he said. The old man's head lifted and swung towards him. Monte leaned closer. "Buffalo," he said.

The old man straightened on the chair. His eyes brightened. "Where?" He jumped up and looked around and his eyes focused on Monte. "Aw-w-w, you," he said. "Cows. That's all you know. You aint never seen 'em. Thick as flies they was, right around here." He waved an arm in a wild gesture and his voice began to climb. "Skinnin' was what I did. Any jack kin shoot a gun. You gotta know to skin." He moved out into the open and began to flourish an imaginary knife. "Cut it around the neck. Up by the horns. Slice it down the belly. Clear to the tail. Slit it down the legs. Peg it through the nose. Hook on the team and start — "

"Not now, Johnny," said Monte Walsh. He was headed for the door and the sound of hoofs and creaking wheels outside. The old man subsided, shaking his head, and returned to his chair.

Outside on the sidewalk Monte Walsh and Chet Rollins

watched the stagecoach swing in by the hotel down the street. They saw two men climb out and recognized them despite their dressed-up appearance as the proprietor of the general store and one of Harmony's three land-claim lawyers. They saw these two stand aside, very respectful, while a third man climbed out, very neat and respectable in a matching suit and tall hat. They saw the three be greeted on the hotel porch by the two who had passed the saloon and all of them disappear inside. They looked at each other and returned to the bar in a companionable silence.

Monte filled their two glasses again. The old man was off his chair and coming close. "Lemme tell you," said the old man. "Sixty-seven in one day. That's what I did. It was out — "

"Some other time, Johnny," said Monte. He leaned over the bar and reached under and found another small glass and filled it from the bottle and handed it to the old man. "Make it last," he said and the old man retired to his chair hugging the glass to his out-size old shirt front.

The bartender took the bottle and set it back on the shelf behind him. "Oughta count that," he said and returned to his reading.

Monte Walsh and Chet Rollins raised their fourth pair and looked at each other over the glasses. "Preacher?" suggested Chet.

"No," said Monte. "Wrong kind of collar. Railroad man maybe."

The bartender groaned. He folded his paper and set it aside. He picked a cloth from under the bar and began to wipe already dry glasses with mechanical gestures. "It's a judge," he said. "Kind of a judge. Justice of the peace. Sent out by the county to civilize you heathen."

Monte studied his glass, shifting it to catch the light

from the door through the whiskey. "Anything interesting for him to judge today?"

"No," said the bartender. "Aint been a payday lately."

Monte studied the glass some more. "You mean," he said, "you get a judge here today and there aint a thing for him to judge about?"

The bartender shrugged shoulders and eyebrows at the same time. He made a point of turning about and retiring with his cloth to the other end of the bar.

"My oh my," murmured Monte Walsh. "What'll he think of the place?"

Chet Rollins sighed. He drained his drink and picked up the paper and edged away from Monte and unfolded the paper and inspected the front page.

"What kind of a judge d'you think he is?" said Monte. "Five-dollar kind?"

Chet Rollins folded the newspaper slow and careful and put it down. He pointed at the nail-studded contraption on the wall and held out a hand, palm flat. Monte fished in his left pants pocket and pulled out a nickel and laid it on the palm. Chet ambled over and dropped it through one of the slits. It joggled from nail to nail and bounced into a blank compartment. Chet ambled back. "See?" he said.

Monte Walsh paid no attention. He was cradling his drink in his right hand and rocking slow and soft on his boot soles and staring upward dreamy-eyed. "Looked like a five-dollar judge to me," he said.

Chet Rollins sighed again. "I ain't listening," he said. "I ain't even here." He ambled to the opposite side of the saloon and set a chair by the wall and sat on it, tilting it against the wall and settling his feet on one of the rungs.

Monte Walsh reached his left hand into his left pants

pocket and took it out and counted what was in it. He put the hand back in the pocket and took it out empty. He drained his drink and set the glass down with a little flourish. He strolled out into the middle of the floor and reached up and pushed his hat off his forehead. "Yow-eee!" he yelled. "I'm ahowling!"

The old man turned on his chair and regarded Monte with a vacant stare and turned back to his glass and the window. Chet Rollins sat still and studied his boot tips with a pained expression on his face. The two freighters stirred a little and went on snoring. The man lying on the three chairs at the rear jackknifed up to sitting position and surveyed the room and retrieved his hat and lay down again. The bartender groaned again and tossed his cloth aside and leaned on his arms on the bar to watch developments.

Monte pushed his hat farther back and scratched by one ear. He strolled over by the freighters, bouncing off his toes with each step, and fingered the high crown of the hat of the one slumped over the table. With gentle touch he tested the space between the top of the crown and the head beneath. He strolled back to the middle of the open space and pulled his gun and fired and the hat lifted off the freighter's head and flapped to the floor with a neat hole through the crown. The two freighters jerked on their chairs, struggling out of sleep, and their eyes focused on Monte. They saw him dropping his gun into its holster. They saw him stand, rocking on his boot soles, grinning at them. "Yow-eee!" he yelled. "I'm really ahowling!"

They looked at each other. One fished a coin out of a shirt pocket. "Tails," he said and flipped it spinning and caught it and slapped it on his other wrist. A slow smile spread over his face. He tucked the coin back into the pocket and started to rise. "Shucks," said Monte, rocking forward. "I mean both of you." He took hold of their table and tipped it onto them and they went sprawling and came up off the floor in a roaring rush.

The bartender reached under the bar and took hold of a heavy bung starter and walked down the length of the bar and around the front end. "That aint polite," said Chet Rollins. He was quiet on his tilted chair but his gun was out of its holster and held in his right hand on his lap. "All right," said the bartender, "but it's a lot quicker." He laid the bung starter on the bar. He threw back his shoulders and drew in a deep breath and plunged forward into the whirling melee in the middle of the floor.

"Yow-eee!" yelled Monte Walsh, slammed into the bar to the tune of rattling glass and bouncing off and using the momentum to drive a shoulder into the bartender's mid-riff. "Three's more like it!"

Justice Coleman rocked with slight little testing sways in the swivel chair that adorned the office that had been his for almost an hour. He liked the chair. It fitted his rear proportions and did not squeak with the rockings. Encouraged, he leaned back in it until it rested against the edge of the rolltop desk behind him. He folded his hands in his lap and looked straight ahead to inspect the battered stocky figure of Monte Walsh. "Disturbing the peace, eh?" he said in a careful judicial tone. He turned his head a bit to the right to inspect the battered figures of the two freighters and the bartender. "There would appear to be ample evidence," he said and turned his head to the left towards the row of townsmen along the wall for appreciation of his remark and obtained it. He looked straight forward again at Monte Walsh. "Well, young man. I expect you are expert at explanations."

"Shucks, no," said Monte. "Things were so damned peaceful seemed to make sense disturbing 'em."

Justice Coleman unfolded his hands and folded them again with fingers reversed. "So you proceeded to disturb them," he said. "Logical. From your point of view. But alas, not legal. So it becomes my duty to disturb you."

"Go right ahead, judge," said Monte and shoved his left hand into his left pants pocket.

"I intend to," said Justice Coleman. "That will be ten dollars — " He stopped. He straightened in the swivel chair and pushed it with his feet against the floor as far back as possible butting against the rolltop desk. Monte Walsh was halfway to him, hands out to grab, before intercepted by one of the freighters in a flying dive, followed close by the bartender and the other freighter. Justice Coleman tucked his feet out of the way under the swivel chair and watched a repetition of the original disturbance. He began to be worried. Reinforcements sprang from along the wall. He sighed in relief. He pushed his feet out again and settled into a more comfortable position and looked down at Monte Walsh flat on the floor with a man sitting on each leg and arm. " — or ten days," he said.

The last light of the sun low to the horizon shone through the one high window in the rear wall of Harmony's new shack. The bright patch it cast on the front wall was marred by four perpendicular shadow lines made by four iron bars set into the window frame. There was no glass in the window. An outside shutter had been swung back and hooked to the outside wall. The door to the shack stood open. A grillwork of iron bars filled the doorway, hung on heavy outside hinges at one side and fastened with a heavy padlock on the other. A plump graying pear-shaped man in old dungarees and a plaid shirt stood by the grillwork peering through at Monte Walsh inside on the edge of the cot along one wall.

Monte lay back on the cot and put his hands up behind his head and regarded the ceiling. "Shucks," he said. "How was I to know they'd got a jail too?"

"Don't go getting snooty," said the pear-shaped man. "It ain't just for you."

Monte continued to regard the ceiling. "Now me," he murmured, "I'd be plumb ashamed to be running a jail."

"It's a job," said the pear-shaped man. He turned away and disappeared from view. Monte waited a moment. He came to his feet in one motion and made a quick circuit of the shack. It was firm and solid. He stopped by the grillwork door. Near the bottom, between two cross strips, a segment of bar had been removed leaving an opening about ten inches square. "Have to be a circus freak," he said, "to wiggle through that." He put the one chair in the shack under the one window and stood on it and looked out. A hundred yards away Chet Rollins sat easy and casual on the chunky gray holding a lead rope fastened to the bridle of the short-coupled pinto. He saw Monte's face between the bars and waved his free hand in cheery salute and took hold of his reins and swung the horses away. Monte watched him jogging into the distance. "Why that low-bellied snake," he said. "Leaving me here." He returned to the cot and lay back again and regarded the ceiling.

The bright patch on the front wall faded and the diffused light of dusk crept through the shack leaving darkening shadows in the corners. Monte heard slight sounds by the doorway and turned his head. A plate heaped with beef stew was coming through the small square opening near the bottom and being set on the floor just inside.

"Wondered what that was for," he murmured. A large tin cup of coffee followed the plate. He sat upright on the cot. The hand holding the cup was small and feminine. He came to his feet, light and quick, and was over by the doorway. Outside a neat figure, plump and pleasing, was rising upright from a stooping position. It filled out an old gingham dress with satisfying completeness and the head above the dress was young and healthy with a broad glowing good-natured face and a quantity of darkish hair pulled back and tied behind with a small ribbon.

"My oh my," said Monte Walsh. "Where'd you come from?"

She stepped back a pace and looked him over. "You don't seem so much," she said. "I thought you'd be horrible. Beating up three men . . . Oh. From that house next door. That's where we live. We've been here five weeks already."

"No," said Monte. "All that time and I've missed you?"

"You wouldn't see me," she said. "Not the places you'd go. Just put those dishes outside when you're through." She started away.

"Hey," said Monte. "You married to him?"

She stopped and swung at the waist to turn her head back towards him. "I can't see as that's any of your affair. But it's no. He's my father."

"Lovely," said Monte. "Just plain lovely."

She turned around to face him, hands on hips. "Listen, mister cowboy. This is business. See? You mean a dollar a day to us on the feeding and that's fifty cents profit if you don't eat too much."

"Shucks," said Monte. "I'll just nibble a little." He was talking to her back as she departed. He squatted on the floor and sniffed the stew. He cleaned the plate and finished the coffee. He set the dishes outside through the square hole and retired to the cot and the ceiling. The dusk deepened into darkness and a thin sliver moon emerged in the sky. He heard soft sounds at the window and rolled his head to look. In the faint light of the moon he made out fingers tying a rope to one of the bars. He came to his feet, quick and light, and stepped up on the chair by the window. The round stubbled face of Chet Rollins beamed at him through the bars. "Nice evening," said Chet. He was standing on his saddle on the back of the chunky gray. The short-coupled pinto, ground-reined, waited patiently thirty feet away. Chet's face sank from sight as he dropped down into the saddle.

"Hey," whispered Monte. "Don't — "

"Nothing to it," came Chet's voice from below the window. The gray moved out from the rear wall and the rope stretched taut between the bar and the saddle horn. Chet tickled the gray with his spurs and it plowed forward, head low and straining, and the window frame, complete with its bars, ripped out of the wall and bounced to the ground.

"Why that double-crossing jackass," murmured Monte. He watched Chet Rollins swing to the ground and amble over to the fallen window frame and start unfastening the rope. He heard running footsteps coming from the house next door towards the doorway of the shack. He jumped off the chair and stepped over by the grillwork door. The pear-shaped man appeared in a nightshirt, a shotgun in his hands, his eyes wide and popping as he tried to see into the dark interior. "What's going on in there?" he said.

"Nothing much," said Monte. "I tripped over the damn bucket."

"Well, quit it," said the pear-shaped man. "I need my

sleep." He bent down and took up the plate and cup and departed towards the house. Monte retired to the cot and lay back and closed his eyes.

"What're you doing in there?" said Chet Rollins from the window opening. "Packing a trunk?"

"Go fly a kite," suggested Monte.

Chet Rollins shifted his feet to a firmer position on the saddle and leaned on the edge of the window opening. "That judge can't boss outside of town," he said. He waited. There was no response. He sighed. "Who's the girl this time? How'd you meet her stuck in there?" He waited again. He sighed again and pushed out from the window edge and dropped down into the saddle.

Monte opened his eyes and raised his head, listening. He heard soft hoofbeats, muffled in the dust, fade away. He settled his head back down and wriggled into a more comfortable position on the cot. "Three times a day for ten days," he murmured and was asleep.

The thin sliver moon arched downward and dipped below the horizon and the first faint glimmerings of the light before dawn crept into the shack. There were small scraping noises in the neighborhood of the window opening. Monte Walsh stirred and wriggled on the cot and sudden was still, eyes wide open. He had company. He rolled his head and saw Chet Rollins a few feet away, flanked on one side by Dally Johnson and on the other by Powder Kent.

"I could yell," said Monte.

"We could ram a gag down your throat," said Chet.

"Coming peaceable?" said Dally. "Or do we have to truss you like a dressed chicken?"

"Better had," said Powder. "One of those dollars was mine."

"Did you think," said Chet Rollins, leading the way to the window, "I was going to finish topping those broncs all by my lonesome?"

The unorganized town of Harmony was wide awake in the afternoon glaze. Curtains were pulled at some of the houses to shut out more than the sun. The street doors of the livery stable and the blacksmith shop were wide open. New signs offering new bargains were tacked on the front of the general store under the awning. Cowponies in rows stood patiently twitching tails along the tie rails. Down the brief length of the main street floated the sound of voices and chinking glass emanating from all four saloons. The temporary harmony of the beginnings of serious drinking reigned in Harmony. And out beyond the last close rise of the rolling plain, skirting around it and staying below the skyline, jogged a short-coupled pinto.

"Got to be cagey about this," murmured Monte Walsh.

He circled and came in behind the livery stable and swung down and rapped on the rear door. He rapped again and it opened and disclosed a short hunchbacked man holding a pitchfork. The man stepped aside as Monte led the pinto in. "Keep this thing for me and my gear," said Monte. "Likely some days before I'll be needing 'em."

"Sure thing, Monte," said the man. "Grain 'im any?"

"Shucks, no," said Monte. "Don't go giving that thing fancy notions." He started back out the door and stopped. "You ain't seen me," he said. "I aint in town."

"Sure thing," said the man, staring at him. "If you say so."

Monte strolled on out the door and along the rear of the stable. Part of a month's pay burdened his left pants pocket. He ducked across the alley between the stable and the barbershop and rapped on the rear door of the shop. It opened part way and the upper portion of a thin little man in old checkered trousers and a once white shirt peered around it.

"Anyone in there?" said Monte.

"Not right now," said the barber. "Only me."

"That's plenty," said Monte. He pushed in past the little man and settled himself in the one barber chair. Twenty-five minutes later, shaved, hair cut and shampooed, he strolled out the way he had come and back across the alley and on past the livery stable to the rear kitchen door of the combination hotel and office building. He went in and tossed a greeting at the combination cook and waiter who was pounding chunks of beef with a hammer and strolled on through and around and along a hallway to an open doorway with a board nailed above it marked SHERIFF. He leaned against the doorframe and regarded the broad back of a big curlyheaded man sitting at a desk by a window busy shuffling papers and tucking them away in pigeonholes.

"Howdy, Mack," said Monte. "Heard they gave you a badge."

The big man turned his head and saw Monte. "I aint proud. Somebody had to take it," he said and returned to his papers.

"Well," said Monte. "I'm here."

The big man did not look up. "So you are," he said. "Looks like you anyway."

"Mighty quiet," said Monte. "Ain't you after me?"

The big man shifted his chair around and put a hand on each knee and looked up. "What is it you've been doing now?"

"Nothing much," said Monte. "Finished up a job and got straight with the boys. But I got ten days to do."

The crinkles around the big man's eyes deepened and he leaned back in the chair and put both hands up behind his head, elbows wide. "Aint anybody told you?" he said. "Judge inquired around the next day. Figured why you did it and killed the charge. He aint through laughing at it yet." The big man hitched his chair around and returned to his papers.

"Shucks," murmured Monte. "That ain't fair. I was counting on those days." He studied his blunt battered fingers and pulled a match out of a pocket and began cleaning dirt from under a fingernail. He flipped the match at the big man's broad back and strolled out along the hallway and out the front door of the building and along the street to the small house beside the jail. He took off his hat and held it in his left hand and rapped with his right on the front door. He waited and rapped again. The door opened and he regarded a neat figure, plump and pleasing, which filled out an old brown skirt and a faded frilled shirtwaist with satisfying completeness.

"It's you," she said and started to close the door and caught it and held it open a little way and peered around it. "Why aren't you over at one of those saloons?"

"Shucks, ma'am," said Monte. "They're all right when there aint anything better to do. There's a nice little buggy over at the livery stable. I thought you and me'd take a ride."

"After what you did!" she said and started to close the door again. Monte's left boot was in the way. "Well now, ma'am," he said. "I know I did kind of run out on you back there a bit."

She pushed on the door. The boot was still in the way. "On me?" she said. "Well I never! It took Father half a day to fix that window!"

Monte transferred the hat to his right hand and fished in his left pants pocket and pulled out a five-dollar bill. "Kind of like to make that right," he said. "Fifty cents profit for ten days. That's what you'd've made on me. Here it is."

"Why — why — you —" With quick movement she pulled the door farther open and slammed it back against the boot and Monte tottered hopping on his right foot and she closed the door with a vigorous snap. It opened again a few inches, almost on the rebound, and her voice came through. "And don't you ever try to come near me again!" The door closed with a definite click.

"Now aint that a girl," murmured Monte Walsh, trying to feel his left toes through the boot leather. They seemed to be intact. He put his hat on and pulled it down and limped across the street and sat on the edge of the plank sidewalk in front of the general store and studied the house across the way. "Can't let any of the boys beat me to her," he murmured. "Got to have the inside track." He looked up the street. Something had been added. Two freight wagons now stood at one side, their ox teams chewing cuds in placid endurance. A slow grin spread over Monte's face. He uncoiled to his feet and limped up the street. A small jingle sounded from his left pants pocket. He slapped his left hand over it. "Got to unload that," he murmured. "Might get in the way."

He limped into the saloon opposite the freight wagons. Lined along the bar were Chet Rollins and Dally Johnson and the rest of the Lazy Y crew. At a table by the wall sat two freighters with a half-empty bottle between them. There was a neat hole through the crown of one of their hats.

Monte limped to the bar. He pushed in between Chet

Rollins and Powder Kent. He looked sideways at Chet and Chet looked at him and grinned a sheepish grin.

"Have trouble shaking the sheriff?" said Powder Kent.

"Check your hardware," said Dally Johnson down the line. "There's a jailbird loose in here."

"Shucks," said Monte. "Some of you might have told me." He beckoned to the bartender. He fished in his left pants pocket and laid a fistful of crumpled bills and change on the bar. "Keep your damn count," he said. "But they're all on me long as that lasts."

"Well whatta you know," said Dally Johnson, reaching quick for a bottle. "He's celebratin'."

"Addled," said Powder Kent. "But in a mighty encouraging way."

Chet Rollins said nothing. He sighed. He picked up his glass and added another drink to those already behind his belt. His eyes began to brighten. Color was climbing up his cheeks. "Job's done," he said. "Nothing really pressing." He started to turn towards Monte.

"No," said Monte. "You aint here. Remember?" He pulled a bottle towards him and leaned over the bar and reached under and found a glass. He drained one, two, three, four. He set the glass down with a little flourish and stood rocking on his boot soles, letting the whiskey settle some. "Feel about right," he murmured and strolled out into the middle of the floor. He took off his hat and sent it skimming and it smacked into the bottle on the table between the two freighters and the bottle fell gurgling into the lap of one of them.

"Yow-eee!" yelled Monte Walsh. "I'm ahowling!"

Trail Crew

*

THE TRAIL HERD was bedded on a wide flat finger of plain stretching between long low hills. To the east, out of the hills, the plain spread vast and open into limitless distances. To the west, between the hills, it dropped imperceptibly across the miles to the lower level of an ancient long-dried lake bed.

Large and luminous in the clean depth of sky an incredible number of stars looked down on the wide land and on the dark speckling blotch of the bedded herd and on Monte Walsh riding slowly around the rim serene in saddle atop a sturdy short-coupled dun.

"Keep amoving," murmured Monte. "Want me to fall asleep astraddle your knobby backbone?"

The dun swiveled an ear back towards him and ambled on. It felt him slumping lower into the saddle and slowed to a stop, head drooping. Monte pulled himself awake. "Keep agitating those legs," he said, "or I'll give you a leathering. Personal." The dun sighed and raised its head and ambled on.

Monte stretched erect in saddle and looked around. Off to the left he could see the compact blotch of the cavvy in its rope corral and the dirty-gray blob of the chuck-wagon canvas and the small individual dark blobs on the ground that were others of the trail crew sweetly sleeping. Faintly he could make out the glimmer of the remains of the cookfire.

Off to the right, across the big speckling blotch of the herd, he could see the slow-moving small blur that was Chet Rollins atop a chunky gray. A soft breeze stirred and Chet's voice drifted to him, a melancholy tuneless monotone.

> Now, all you young maidens, where'er you reside,
> Beware of the cowboy who swings the rawhide.
> He'll court you and pet you and leave you and go
> In the spring up the trail on his bucking bronco . . .

"I've heard frawgs could croak better," murmured Monte. His attention was caught by movement nearby in the herd. The old barren cow, point leader of each day's drive, was heaving to her feet. He stopped the dun with a touch on the reins and watched. Head high and swinging, slow, the old cow tested the air. Slowly she turned until she was facing back over the herd, back down the long finger of plain between the hills.

"Got the worries, old girl?" said Monte. He turned his head to look in the same direction. Clean and cloudless with its myriad stars the sky arched into distance to meet the far horizon. "Nothing back there but sky and a thousand miles of grass," he said. He tilted his head to look up. "My oh my," he murmured. "Time has been footprinting along." He swung the dun and started back along the rim of the herd.

Towards him out of the dimness of dark, easy and comfortable atop gently jogging gray, came Chet Rollins, round stubby pipe poking out of round stubbly face. The two cowponies stopped, nose to nose.

"Quite a man," said Monte. "That braying of yours gave old Gertrude the itch."

Chet extracted a match from a pocket of his open jacket, scratched it on blunt fingernail and applied it to the pipe. Monte nudged the dun forward, reached and pushed Chet's jacket farther open and plucked a small pouch from Chet's shirt pocket. Out of his own shirt pocket came a small paper. Deftly he hollowed this between fingers and poured a portion of tobacco along the tiny trough. In the one easy moving one hand tucked the pouch back in Chet's shirt pocket and the other rolled the cigarette. He raised this to his lips and licked along the paper edge.

"One of these days," said Chet Rollins, "I'll quit buying tobacco."

"No," said Monte, aggrieved. "I aint ready to quit smoking." Out of one of his own jacket pockets came a match and flared briefly. "Shucks," he said. "Always carry my own papers and matches, don't I?"

The cowponies drowsed, heads dropping. Monte dragged deep on the cigarette and watched the smoke float from his nose in two tiny streams. "Wonder what's keeping the boys," he said. "The dipper up there's been dipping." He drew again on the cigarette, inspected its shortened length and stubbed it out on stirrup leather. "I'm a growing boy," he said. "Need my sleep."

"Don't be so damned previous," said Chet, amiable, conversational. "They're coming now."

Monte swung the dun to face the night camp. Two dim blurs had left it and were moving towards them. These came closer and were Dally Johnson astride a squat bay and Powder Kent astride a leggy roan.

"Anything doing?" said Powder.

"My oh my, yes," said Monte. "Busy every minute. We had to fight off two jack rabbits and a horned toad."

"Old Gertrude's uneasy," said Chet. "Better keep an eye on her."

In companionable silence Monte and Chet jogged to camp, dismounted, eased cinches and picketed their horses by the others kept ready, saddled, for night duty. Together they pulled blankets from the bed wagon beside the bigger chuck wagon and unrolled these on soft spots earlier picked and claimed. Monte straightened and looked towards the remains of the cookfire. On the tripod over it hung a battered coffeepot.

"Monte," said Chet, low-toned, casual. "Why not forget the coffee tonight. You'll sleep better."

"Shucks," said Monte, starting away. "Gabriel tooting wouldn't keep me from sleeping."

Chet sighed and collapsed down on his blanket. He raised on one elbow, watching.

Over by the chuck wagon Monte pushed a hand under the canvas and pulled it out holding a tin cup. "Good old cookie," he murmured, moving towards the embered fire. "Always leaves me some in the pot." Leaning down, he tipped the battered pot until a dark liquid gurgled into the cup. Squatting back on his heels, he poked a finger into the liquid and yanked it out fast and shook it vigorously. He bent his head and blew into the cup and sloshed the liquid around in it. He tried the finger again. "Just right," he murmured and raised the cup and tilted back his head for a long drink.

"Ow-w-w-w!" yelled Monte Walsh, uncoiling upward like a tight spring suddenly released, spluttering, spitting. Frantic in haste he plunged towards the chuck wagon and tripped over the wagon tongue and went sprawling. Still frantic in haste he scrabbled to the water pail hanging by the wide tail gate and grabbed the dipper. Water dribbled down his shirt as he gulped and spat, gulped and spat.

He stood by the chuck wagon, dipper in hand, and looked around. Not far away, up on one elbow, Chet Rollins regarded him with solemn interest. Elsewhere about lay five other figures, under blankets, quiet, apparently serene in sleep. He reached and let the dipper drop with a clatter into the pail. He waited. No sound, no movement marred the quiet. "Some bat-brained baboon — " he said and stopped. There was a quivering under one pulled-over blanket, a strange small moaning sound. The blanket flipped back disclosing the lean whipcord length of Petey Williams, shaking, knees doubling up.

"Lordy!" gasped Petey. "Oh lordy lordy lordy lordy lordy! Maybe that'll learn you not to come thumpin' in every night clitterin' an' clatterin' an' wakin' us up."

"Why you — " said Monte, starting forward.

"Easy, Monte," came the voice of trail boss Hat Henderson. "Or we'll all take a hand."

Monte stopped, rocking on his toes.

"Not me, Monte boy," came a voice from the chuck wagon. "Anybody like my coffee an' says so like you do kin have all he wants any time."

Monte looked around, calculating the odds. The slender shape of fourteen-year-old Juan Rodriguez, brought along to wrangle the cavvy, did not count. But the wide sloping shoulders of Hat Henderson, sitting up on his blanket, were enormous in the dim starlight. The black-mustached face of Dobe Chavez, sitting up too a few feet away, could have been wearing a hopeful grin. The big barrel body of Sunfish Perkins bulged huge under his blanket.

"Shucks," said Monte. "If that damned pepper hadn't made me feel right puny I'd scramble the whole bat-brained bunch of you." Injured dignity emanating from him, he stalked to his blanket, took off his hat, lay down, set the hat over his face and pulled the blanket over him.

Silence settled on the camp.

"Holy hell!" said Monte Walsh, lifting the hat off his face and setting it aside. "How'n I going to sleep without my coffee?"

"Quit it," came a voice. "Or we'll put you to sleep permanent."

Silence settled again. Monte lay still looking at the myriad stars overhead. He raised a bit and spat to one side. He lay still again. A small quivering began to shake his midriff. "My oh my oh my," he murmured. "Bet I looked like a new-branded calf diving for that water." He began counting stars. At seven he was asleep.

The boot toe against his ribs were hurried, not gentle. Monte Walsh plunged awake in the dark grabbing. The thick-muscled leg of Hat Henderson pulled away from him.

"Snap it, Monte," said Hat. "Everybody out. There's a storm coming."

Monte pushed to his feet. High overhead the stars shone, large and luminous in clean depth of cloudless sky. The air was still, soft and still.

"Shucks," said Monte to the retreating back of Hat Henderson. "What's the fuss? Regular spooning weather."

"Not for long," said Chet Rollins, gathering up his and Monte's blankets and stepping to toss them in the bed wagon. "Take a look yonder."

Monte turned to look down the long finger of plain between the hills. Dark and ominous, piling in heavy layers, a great bank of clouds blotted the far horizon. As he looked, lightning played high over them and laced through them and the low mutter of thunder rolled in the dim blankness of distance.

"What do you know," murmured Monte. "Old Gertrude sure has a nose." In the one swoop of moving he picked up his hat, jammed it on his head, and was running towards the short-coupled dun.

He heaved on the cinch, tightening, and behind him heard Chet Rollins gently cursing at the same chore. Other voices floated on the still air, cheerfully complaining, wryly joshing. Over them rose the voice of Hat Henderson, responsibility spurring him, he who was a cold bolt of concentrated action in the midst of an emergency, now as always wailing and worrying in the anticipation of it. "Jeeeeesus, boys! We gotta hold 'em! Those fool cows get araring and arunning out into that open it'll take a week to gather 'em again! Those we can find!"

The cinch slipped in Monte's hands. He grabbed a fresh hold and heaved. The dun, disliking the prospect, sidled away and blew out its sides, eating air. "Go ahead, be smart," said Monte, making it grunt with a knee hard in its distended ribs. "I'll twist a couple of your ears off. Personal."

"Frettin' again, Monte," said a voice above him close by the dun's rump. Petey Williams grinned down from the back of a hammerheaded sorrel. "Mebbe you oughta stay an' help cookie lash down the wagons. Feelin' puny the way you do." The sorrel responded to spurs and took off fast.

"I'll puny him," murmured Monte. "Maybe biscuits.

Petey's a hawg on biscuits." He stepped into stirrup and swung up to join Chet out to the herd.

The night air hung motionless, still, too still, clinging and oppressive. Silent now, waiting, wearing slickers now, untied from behind saddles, the trail crew of the Slash Y, eight men on eight homely runty tough little cowponies, rode circle around fifteen hundred four and five-year-old longhorn steers and an old barren cow. And out of the southwest, the long back trail they had traveled hundreds of miles from the wide *vegas* of New Mexico, the great bank of clouds, huge, indifferent, funneled forward between the hills.

Whisperings of wind ran through the bunch grass. The cattle were up, shifting restlessly with rattlings of horns as they pushed against each other. Arching high above, the topmost layer of clouds, driven from behind, rolled forward, blotting out the stars. The first drops of rain, large and irregular, fell with tiny splattings on the dry ground. Suddenly, as if scenting the herd, wind leaped in rushing gusts and a wall of rain, swirling, torrential, swept over.

The wind beat in rushing gusts and the rain poured in heavy sheets and the cattle shifted and swayed in frightened mass, trying to work downwind before the storm, individuals and small bunches making frantic dashes to break away. Around them, battered, drenched, sighting by sound and instinct and intermittent flashes of lightning, swinging superb with every twist and wrench of saddles, rode the trail crew of the Slash Y, yielding ground downwind but holding the circle, tough little cowponies as alert, as dedicated, as desperate as the men, squat hard-muscled rumps quivering as they leaped, dashed, pounded to head the runaways, push them, shoulder them, bully them back into the herd.

Abruptly the cloudburst passed. The rain dropped to a steady downpour and this slowly thinned and the air was alive, crackling with electricity. Fireballs hung on tossing horns and little lightnings streaked along the ground. The rain died away and the mutter of thunder dwindled.

"Looks like we make it!" The voice of Hat Henderson lifted out of the dark. "Close up an' quiet 'em down!"

From elsewhere out of the dark rose the voice of Chet Rollins in hoarse tuneless somehow soothing monotone.

> I love not Colorado where the faro table grows,
> And down the desperado the rippling bourbon flows.
>   Oh-h-h-h-h-h,
> I love not Colorado where the card sharp fleeces fools,
> And a girlie-girl won't give a man—

Lightning in one great flare of flame ripped the dark and a steer reared bellowing, outlined in fire, and thunder broke like a cannon shot. Out of the void of blackness following the flash came the heavy rising roar of the herd in motion, a dark tide of panic-stricken animals pouring downwind in relentless onrush.

Above the muffling roar, the cracking of hoofs, the rattling of horns, climbed the shrill yell of Hat Henderson. "Jeeeesus! Ride, you mavericks! Ride!" And Hat and seven other men rode.

Out in front, Dobe Chavez and Powder Kent, caught in the onrush, engulfed by it, surrounded by frenzied running steers, jostled, hit, battered, their horses fighting to hold their feet, ears flat, heads slugging in desperate effort, plunging forward, kicking in stride, taking advantage of every break to work out towards the side. On the left flank Petey Williams and Monte Walsh and Dally Johnson and Hat Henderson, strung out, racing headlong into the dark, ripping off slickers at full gallop, striving towards the head of the herd. On the right flank, Sunfish Perkins and Chet Rollins, dropping back to dash around the rear of the stragglers and drive forward after the others on the left.

"Puny is it?" yelled Monte Walsh, yanking the dun past the tail of Petey Williams' sorrel to join him in smashing in towards the lead steers, flailing at them with his slicker. A horn tip raked across his thigh, ripping through cloth, drawing blood, and he did not know it. The slicker flapped in shreds. Pounding alongside a big steer, he flung the slicker remnants in its face. He pulled his gun and began firing into the ground in front of the foremost steers.

Other guns were out and sounding, flaring in the dark, a barrage angled out across the rushing forefront of the strung-out stampede. The leaders swerved, swinging to the right, the others blindly following. They hit the first slopings towards the hills and slowed some on the climb and, under pressure, swung still more. More, and the herd was running in an arc, a wide U-shaped course. Still more, and the leaders were swinging back into their own tracks, catching up with the stragglers, and the rough flattened circle was closed. The cattle milled around it, gradually slowing in weariness, letting themselves be crowded inward, slowing more to a shuffling walk, slowing at last to a stop, sides heaving, tongues hanging.

Gray and forlorn under overhanging clouds, dawn crept over the great open plain that was miles closer now and slipped down the wide finger between the hills. In the dim half-light the chuck wagon with trailing bed wagon, lurching behind their four-mule span from where the camp had been, stopped a quarter of a mile away. In a few moments the first flickering of a fire showed, fed on wood carried and kept dry under the canvas. From back down the finger of plain a weaving blotch of dark shapes approached, the cavvy coming up.

In the gray growing light the trail crew of the Slash Y left positions around the herd and gathered together, men with eyes bleared and bloodshot, clothes torn and mud-spattered, horses bloody and sweat-streaked, legs quivering, worn close to exhaustion and still standing to whatever more might be asked of them.

"Those bonehead cows aint going anywhere," said Hat Henderson. "Not now for a while anyways. I reckon we can go in and get us something hot."

"Hey, look," said Sunfish Perkins. "There's the horses coming. The kid must a held them."

"Of a certainty, señor," said Dobe Chavez, grinning. "He is of my people. A boy in the years. A man with the horses."

"Damn lucky for us," said Hat Henderson. "We got us a day ahead. I saw a couple bunches break into the draws over there. Must be strays all through these hills."

Silent again, the trail crew of the Slash Y started towards the chuck wagon, horses wearily plodding.

"Coffee," said Monte Walsh. "Aint that a lovely smell? If Petey tries messing with — "

"Petey," said Chet Rollins. "I ain't seeing him around."

"Jeeeesus!" said Hat Henderson, rising in stirrups to look about. "Has that fool gone an' — " He stopped speaking and sank down into saddle, shoulders sagging. He spoke again, voice heavy. "All right, boys. Spread out an' look sharp."

Quiet, separated each in his own searching silence, seven men rode back over the wide trampled ground reaching towards the hills beyond. There was daylight now, veiled with stringy gray mists under the overhanging clouds. It was the voice of Powder Kent that called. The others gathered with him on the flat bench a short way up the sloping where a colony of prairie dogs had riddled the sandy soil. They looked down at the sprawled shape, the lean twisted whipcord length of Petey Williams, rain-washed face upturned, strangely white and empty, head awry at grotesque angle. Thirty feet away the sorrel, crumpled on the ground, both forelegs broken, raised its head and whinnied softly at them.

Hat Henderson shifted weight in saddle, turning to see who was closest to the sorrel. His voice was small, tired. "All right, Monte. Shoot the horse."

Monte Walsh stared at the still, twisted shape. He forced his head to turn a bit and stared at the sorrel. The muscles along his jaw ridged and the tendons in his neck stood out taut. "Goddamn it!" he said. "I broke that horse. Taught him his manners."

Fury flared in Hat Henderson, shaking him, shaking his voice. "You soft-brained bitching bastard! I said shoot that horse!"

Monte swung to face the other man, tense in saddle, body muscles tightening towards the blessed relief of motion, action. A shot sounded and, caught, he turned and saw the sorrel's head dropping, the whole body going limp, and turned more and saw Chet Rollins slipping gun back into holster. The muscles along Monte's jaw twitched. A small humorless smile showed on his lips. His head moved in a slight nod, saying what he could not say in words, what he could not even comprehend in words. *Thanks, Chet. That's how it is. You've rode with Petey too. You helped me break that horse. I blow a lot and I strut a plenty and maybe I can ride a horse or two you can't and take on two to your one in any kind of brawl. But dig down to bedrock you're the better man.*

Slowly, wearily, Hat Henderson dismounted. He moved close by Monte and reached and slapped Monte's leg. He did not look up. "Petey and me run together a long while," he said. "Kind of like you and Chet." He strode forward and scooped up the already stiffening body and came back to his horse and heaved it over his saddle. He took the reins and started leading the horse towards the new camp.

Silent, staring at the ground, the others followed. It was Monte Walsh who carried Petey's saddle in front of him over the tired shoulders of the dun. It was Dobe Chavez who turned back and leaned down in weary but still graceful sweep from the back of his tired bay to pick from the ground the muddied felt that had been Petey Williams' hat.

The fire was little more than a smoking smolder, fighting the heavy moist air. The trail crew of the Slash Y hunkered on heels close by it, scooping food from tin plates. Hat Henderson laid his, emptied, on the ground beside him. "Got to bring in those strays," he said. "That rubs out today. Three days maybe on to the Springs an' that's only a stage stop. I reckon we got to do it here." He straightened. "Dobe. Sunfish. Get a couple fresh horses and out to those cows. We'll holler when we're ready." He strode to the bed wagon and pulled out two shovels.

The mists had lifted some and rain fell in a thin drizzle. Chet Rollins and Monte Walsh worked on the deepening grave. The cook, limping on old game leg, rigged a canvas shelter for his fire. Young Juan watched in mournful useless silence. Hat Henderson and Dally Johnson and Powder Kent leaned over the stiffened body of Petey Williams. They wrapped it carefully in a blanket. Around this they rolled a trimmed-down tarpaulin. Around this they stretched two bridle reins and tied them.

"Jeeeesus!" said Hat, stretching up from the task. "Aint there anything we can use for a cross?"

The fire burned better under its canvas shelter. Coffee was hot in tin cups. Hat Henderson looked up from his. Out of the drizzle young Juan was approaching, riding bareback on his little roan. He was dragging something on a rope after him, the weathered broken cast-off endgate of an emigrant wagon.

"You're all right, kid," said Hat Henderson. "Dally. Get an iron and stick it in the fire. We'll rig a marker out a that."

The two best boards were fastened together with horseshoe nails to form a crude cross. Dally Johnson knelt on another board, running iron in hand, burning letters into wood. The others watched, silent, intent.

Dally looked up. "Maybe," he said. "Maybe this ought to say Peter."

"Petey," said Hat Henderson, quick, sharp. "That's what he was all the time I knew him. That's what he'd a wanted to be."

Dally reached and laid the end of the iron in the fire. "When was he born?" he said.

Silence. "Damned if I know," said Hat Henderson. "About my age but I never did know exact. We got to leave that go."

Dally took the iron and bent over the cross. "What's to-day?" he said.

Silence again. "It's April anyways," said Chet Rollins. "That's close enough."

Dally finished and rose to his feet. They all stared down at the crude cross. Near the top of what would be the up-right, the Slash Y brand. Under this, on the wider cross-piece, the simple legend.

PETEY WILLIAMS
died on trail
April 1887

"All right, Dally," said Hat Henderson. "I reckon we're ready. Kid, skip on out and fetch Dobe and Sunfish."

"Goddamn it!" said Monte Walsh, kicking viciously at a clod from the freshly dug grave. "That's a hell of a measly marker for a man like Petey!"

Small and alone in the big land they stood around the grave, seven riders and an old man and a boy. Using lar-iats slipped under, they lowered the rolled tarpaulin into the grave. They stood in an uneasy silence.

"Jeeeesus!" said Hat Henderson. "Aint there anybody knows a few of the words?" The silence held again. "Maybe just as well," he said. "Petey never was much on churches."

"He was a damn good man with a rope," said Sunfish Perkins. "Maybe that'll count some."

"Petey never cussed much," said Powder Kent. "Only when he was mad an' that don't mean nothing."

"He was almighty good company," said Chet Rollins. "Always keeping things lively."

"The long-legged loon was one up on me," said Monte Walsh. "That coffee sure fixed me plenty."

The silence held again. Hat Henderson broke it. "Petey wouldn't want us moping around like a bunch a mangy coyotes," he said. "We got work to do. Cookie. An' you, kid. You can fill this hole. All right, boys. Fresh horses all around. We got to comb these hills."

The herd had grazed part of the day and watered at pools collected in old buffalo wallows. It was bedded again close to where the last night's storm-driven run had ended. In the deepening dusk clouds still hung overhead, blotting out most of the stars emerging in the high clean depth of sky above. The three dark shapes close by the bedded herd were Monte Walsh on a rat-tailed skittish roan and Chet Rollins on a thick-necked black and Hat Henderson on a big rangy bay.

"Hate to stick you two with it," said Hat. "You're bushed as the rest of us. But it's your watch. Looks nasty but maybe it won't do more'n rain a bit. I'll try an' keep an eye open. Anything happens we'll all come afanning."

Monte Walsh and Chet Rollins watched him jog away towards the camp. "Creeping catfish," said Monte, wriggling inside shirt and jacket. "Feels like I'll never get dry again. Been raining off and on all day."

Chet fumbled in a jacket pocket and found his pipe, in shirt pocket, and extracted the small pouch. He began to shake tobacco into the pipe.

"A hell of a life," said Monte. "Wearing out your backside in a saddle all day, all night, chousing cows that belong to somebody else. If you aint cooking in the sun you're feeling like a cold sponge. A hell of a life."

"Yeah," said Chet. "Aint it." He found a match,

scratched it on blunt fingernail and applied it to the pipe.

"Forty and found and break your fool neck," said Monte. He forced the roan to sidle closer to the black and reached and extracted the pouch from Chet's shirt pocket. He fished in his own and extracted a wad of wet gummy small papers. He stared down at these in his hand and in disgust threw them on the ground.

"You'll get to a pipe yet," said Chet, taking the pouch.

"What in hell did we ever come on this damn junket for anyway?" said Monte. "We could of stayed at the ranch. There's that new bunch of three-year-olds to be broke."

"Hat was short-handed," said Chet. He extracted another match, scratched it and tried again on the pipe. "Shorter now," he said.

"Petey," said Monte. "You ever think he didn't even know who he was working for? Who we're working for. Not even a man. Just a goddamned syn-di-cate. A bunch of soft-bellied money-grubbers back east somewhere."

"Yeah," said Chet. "That's right, aint it? But Petey wasn't thinking of that. Petey was just doing what he signed on to do." Chet swung the black and started off around the herd.

"A hell of a life," murmured Monte, starting in the opposite direction. "Seems like I aint slept in a week. Maybe two." The roan shied at a low bush, swinging its rat-tail and skittering sideways. "Quit that," said Monte, clamping down on the reins. "I aint in no mind for games. Just to sit here trying to forget I got wet pants on."

The clouds gathered overhead, moving silently, closing all gaps. Monte Walsh pulled out of a doze in the saddle. Sudden wind rushed in violent gusts down the finger of plain towards the open. He looked around. The cattle were up, beginning to push against each other. Back a bit around the curve of the herd a blur of dark was Chet Rollins on the black, sweeping to head a batch of runaways. Another batch broke loose. Monte wheeled the roan, spinning on hunched hind legs, and lit out after them. He had them back. He snatched a quick look towards the camp. All he could make out was the flicker of the low fire, licking up under the lash of the wind. It was blotted for an instant as a figure ran past it.

The wind increased in violence and whipped rain with it. The herd shifted and swayed with rattling of horns. Two men on a rat-tailed roan and a thick-necked black dashed back and forth, holding the frightened steers against the hills rising beyond. Over by the camp a sharp crack sounded, and another, and others following. The canvas top of the chuck wagon had ripped loose on one side and flapped up in the gusts like a huge whip snapping.

"Good God amighty!" said Monte, hearing the heavy rising roar of the herd in motion. "Here we go again!" A dark shape rushed past him, Chet Rollins bent low on the black, scudding fast for the head of the rushing herd.

Monte Walsh dug spurs in. The roan leaped into full gallop. "Yowee!" yelled Monte, leaning forward to shout in one of its ears. "You let that fat-faced baboon beat me to the point I'll rip your hide off! Personal!"

Out from the camp in ragged sequence pounded other dark shapes, angling to join them. The trail crew of the Slash Y, seven men on seven tough little cowponies, raced headlong into the rain-drenched dark.

The Fifth Man

*

Is NOT all matter composed of atoms, themselves of whirling mites of energy, and some simple in organization, as hydrogen, and others complex, as uranium, with all shadings from simple to complex between? Do not these atoms, restless as in gases, more serene as in solids, impinge upon one another, touch and meet and often mingle, all through any cluster of matter, star or planet or moon or meteorite, out to the edges where what is discoverable, verifiable, merges into the mystery of space? And does not a movement, a convulsion, among these atoms anywhere send impulse radiating outward, producing effects according to the character of the ever adjoining atoms? What was it Carlyle said? "It is a mathematical fact that the casting of this pebble from my hand alters the centre of gravity of the Universe."

Just so perhaps with people, individual atoms of humanity, ranging from simple to complex, restless to serene, impinging upon one another in the cluster called society, civilization. What one, or a group of ones does, sends impulse radiating out, communicating atom to atom, person to person, in the wondrous involved web of existence. And who can know how many atoms it reaches before it fades into the mystery of surrounding space?

That is a kind of nonsense, of course. You do not understand what I am saying. Who among us ever truly understands another, what another says or does, in full impact of meaning? I do not understand it myself. I simply see glimmers of a possible pattern, impulse communicating person to person, and am trying to pin down a manifestation of it in these words. A story perhaps, yet not really a story, simply an account and a wondering.

Various people in the little southwestern town told me he was crazy. He lived some twenty miles out, in a lonely arid region, at a long-ago-abandoned stage stop. Squatted rather, because he did not own the place, did not need to. No one else wanted it, had wanted it for the thirty years or more since the new road had by-passed it by many miles. He ran a few bony cows and now and again butchered one and jerked the meat in the sun in the old almost forgotten manner and raised a few beans and chiles and other things and at long intervals appeared in town, walking in moccasins of his own make, to count out a few coins for a few necessities.

Yes, they said, old Cal Kinney was crazy, in a harmless sort of way. Crazy to be living out there alone with nothing but horned toads and coyotes and a sidewinder or two and a few bony cows for company. Crazy in the way he didn't talk or, when he did talk, didn't make sense. But he never bothered anybody so why should anybody bother him? And he did keep the tiny spring out there cleaned and flowing its small trickle which was sometimes a good thing when some fool took to wandering that dry region without an extra canteen.

You never know exactly what you will turn up in a case like that, not in this Southwest where time is an almost tangible dimension of all things and the past is part of the present and the dust your toe stirs in the emptiness of apparent nowhere may have crumbled from Spanish adobe puddled before the Pilgrims set sail or from Indian masonry worked a thousand years before Columbus. Sometimes a tale of treasure, a legend of buried gold or silver, and a secretive man poring over an ancient map always obtained at third or fourth or fifth hand in some mysterious way and digging, digging, digging, here and there and everywhere as his taut obsessed mind extracts new interpretations from his ancient map.

There was no tinge of treasure this time. Not a whisper of legend in the region. I packed some supplies with the sleeping bag in my car and drove out.

Maybe a truck or two had been over that old stage route within the last ten-twenty years. You couldn't tell. But the old trace was plain enough, passable if you didn't mind scraping cactus, dragging bottom once in a while, taking small arroyos with a rush through the sand. I knew I was there when I saw the cottonwood, the only tree other than a few scrubby junipers in the twenty miles, big, big as a barrel at the base, but more than half dead, broken off jagged among the top branches, kind of a half-skeleton of a tree. It must have had a tremendous root system to suck moisture out of that dry basin. Maybe, back along the years, the spring about a hundred yards up the side slope at the base of a rough outcropping of red rock had trickled on down here and given it a start. Maybe the water was once even piped down, because the stage station had been close beside that tree. The building, probably just a stable for change of horses or mules, was gone, not even a weathered board left, but the lines of the stone foundation still showed.

I left the car by the tree and walked up the slow slope. The spring seeped out of the rock at the base through clean sand and trickled into a small catch basin inside a three-sided pen out from the rock made of old boards, probably from the onetime stable. A small wooden sluice led the overflow outside the pen into an old tin bathtub sunk into sand for a water trough. Off to the right, out a bit from the abrupt rock behind, was the garden, enclosed by a fence that must have been made of every odd piece of anything accumulated around the place in the active years, chunks of old pipe and beams for posts, snarls of rusty barbed wire, a stretch of mangled chicken wire, several old doors propped lengthwise, glassless window frames, a crooked old bedspring, even an old stove. Inside that parody of a fence the garden itself was neat and practical, leveled, laid out in humped rows separated by little irrigation ditches. A length of one-inch old pipe poked out the side embankment of the catch basin, through that fence, ending in a small faucet at the lead ditch along the end of that garden.

Over beyond the garden was the cabin, shack, hut, whatever you might want to call it. A haphazard squarish crazy-quilt thing, covered around with odd-sized old boards fastened this way and that and some places two and three over each other to close off cracks. My guess was it was the tender's cabin, once well built, that had weathered weak and started to collapse then been patched up again. I walked over. The door was open and I looked in. The walls and roof were as makeshift as that fence, but they were tight enough. The interior was as neat and practical as that garden. Two windows, one with glass panes intact, the other covered with chicken wire and with a hinged wooden shutter that could be closed over it. A homemade wooden cot with several old blankets spread, a table, a chair, a bench along one wall, a couple of long shelves, supplies on one, a few books and some old dishes and a kerosene lamp on the other. In the back corner a small old woodstove with two boxes beside it, one filled with dry cow chips, the other with pieces of dry juniper.

I stepped back out of the doorway and looked around. There were two small sheds beyond that cabin, low, solid, doors closed and fastened with rusty clasp hatches. Toolshed, I figured, and storehouse. Angled back a ways behind them was another small square structure. Outhouse. I looked on around. Not a movement anywhere. There was a biggish box upturned like a bench along the shady side of one of the sheds. I sat there studying the whole layout.

A clinky sound started, faint at first then clearer. A gaunt old cow with a tarnished dull-clappered bell on a leather thong around her neck came stepping slow, stiff-legged, down from where the outcropping of red rock shaded off into sandy slopeside. Two others followed. A half-grown calf, late, tagged them, coming with a little scrambling rush, then slowing into place in the plodding procession. They moved straight to the old bathtub.

I remember I was sitting on that upturned box wondering how he ever managed to get a cow bred in that empty arid loneliness when I realized I was looking at him. He was down by that tree, suddenly there out of nowhere, standing quiet, motionless, as if he had always been there, staring at my car. He was about as ordinary-seeming a man as I ever saw, except that perhaps ordinary men don't often live to be as old, age showing in the shape and sagging outline even at that distance and yet with it a kind of indestructible ageless spry endurance. He wore the moccasins I had heard about, faded shrunk levis with a piece of rope for a belt, a faded patched denim shirt, a frayed-edge battered Mexican-style straw hat. I've seen men dressed about like that by the dozen all through the out-of-the-way little settlements of the Southwest. In a way he was just a natural part of the country.

All the same I remember thinking there was some little thing wrong, not quite right. He was clean-shaven. Usually, in these cases, there are whiskers, maybe a sign, a gesture, of independence, maybe just that a man living out alone doesn't see much sense in shaving, in doing more than a bit of trimming now and again. He was clean-shaven.

He turned and came up the slope towards the cabin. He was spry enough in those moccasins all right, not hurrying, but moving along as if he were quite aware of what he was doing every moment and quite capable of doing it. I didn't see him look at me but he knew I was there and I knew he knew. He went into the cabin.

I sat quiet. The beginning is the most important time in these things. You try to shove in, push yourself forward, and like as not you run head-on into stubbornness, irritation, maybe rejection. So you sit quiet and let the situation drift and the other man make any move.

He appeared in the doorway, stepped out, sat down on the big chunk of red rock that was the doorstep. He stared down-slope at my car. He seemed more interested in that car than in me, that my being there or not being there barely brushed against an indifference in him.

I sat quiet. At last he turned his head and looked at me.

"I'm writing a story," I said, "that takes place in country like this. I thought maybe you wouldn't mind my staying around a few days."

He looked back again at the car. I was about ready to

give up hope of an answer when he spoke. "We don't mind," he said.

I sat quiet, studying on that. Did he mean himself and those old cows?

He stood up. "You'll have to move that vehicle," he said. "He might not like it there." He disappeared into the cabin.

I sat quiet, listening to sounds from inside of the old stove being rattled. I had the tingle. There was something around. I could wait. I could let it drift. I went down to the car, started it, drove it up past the two sheds, began to pull out a few things for my own camp.

Two days and I knew that the days didn't matter. It was the nights.

He was regular in his habits, punctual as a still-sound old clock. He slept late in the morning, or at least he lay in there on that cot until late. He had to, I expect, because he didn't sleep much during the night. And he could be comfortable until along towards forenoon before sun beating on the flimsy roof would heat up that cabin because the sun rose behind the rock outcropping and had to be well up before it could find the cabin in the rock shadow. He fixed himself a good breakfast, in quantity anyway, because he didn't bother with a midday meal. The rest of the morning he puttered around, checking over his entire layout, fiddling with anything that seemed to him to need fixing or cleaning or setting straight. Along in early afternoon he set out somewhere and was gone about three hours. He didn't go like a man going any particular place with any particular purpose. He just walked off. He took nothing with him. He brought nothing back. He was just passing time.

When he came back he fussed around his garden. He

didn't that first late afternoon because my being there, my car being there, threw him off stride some. After that he was in routine again. He alternated his work on that garden, weeding and a little cultivating one afternoon, watering the next. Then he retired to the cabin and took his time with his evening meal and afterwards, in the deepening dusk, lit his old lamp and settled beside it with one of his old books. The day was done, passed. There wasn't a clock in that cabin and he had no watch, but he had clocked off the hours as if he had a timepiece tucked away in his head.

As I say, two days and I had that straight. I was getting hold of the nights too.

That first night, along about full dark, when I was deciding whether to sleep on or inside my sleeping bag, I heard him moving in the cabin. He blew out the lamp and came to the doorway and stepped out and sat down on the doorstep. The moon, nearly rounded, was beginning to show over the rock outcropping behind but he was in the shadow of both rock and cabin and I couldn't make out what he was doing. I watched and listened. Not a movement, not a sound. He was just sitting there. At last I drifted into sleep. I woke up suddenly a few hours later by my watch and he was still there. The moon was high now and I could see him plain. He was just sitting there, staring down towards that old tree. I drifted into sleep again and when I woke up several hours later, maybe waked by sense of the movement, he was stretching up and going into the cabin.

The next night, after the first full day of watching him, I was certain he would be right on schedule. He wasn't. The lamp went on burning and he went on reading. I lay quiet and time passed and the lamp was blown out and he came to the doorway and sat on the doorstep. I looked at my watch. Something past nine, about an hour later than the night before. I lay awake quite a while before I had an answer that could fit.

The next night, after two full days of watching, I knew I was right. He would blow out the lamp and take position on the doorstep soon after ten. He did. The moon, almost completely rounded now, was beginning to show over the rock behind, sending its soft shimmer down-slope towards that tree.

All this time he paid about as much attention to me as to those old cows which wasn't any more that you could notice than a look morning and evening to see if they were still alive and around. His indifference seemed to be complete. He gave the impression that there could have been dozens of me, all kinds of people, cluttering the immediate neighborhood and he would still have been alone, going his way, following his routine, wrapped inviolable in his own existence. I couldn't figure how I might get in to him or get him to come out to me.

It was late afternoon of the second full day that I caught a glimmer. People are people. A man is a man. There is always some residue of recognition of the existence of others, of another, an instinctive perhaps unthinking reaching out. It is the ineradicable call of kind. He was at the end of his garden by the pipe from the catch basin and had just opened the small faucet to let water run into the lead ditch. He saw me sitting on the upturned box by one of the sheds. He saw me look at him. He raised a hand to focus my attention. He turned away and straddled over a low part of that parody of a fence and stepped up by one of the posts of the pen around the catch basin and reached and lifted off a nail something I had not noticed before. An old tin dipper. He held this up. He

hung it again on the nail and straddled back over the garden fence and went on with his watering.

I studied on that. He was not only aware of my presence but aware enough to notice what I did. And he did
not resent me. He might even feel some small tinge of
companionship because I was there. He had seen me going on my frequent jaunts to that catch basin for a drink
of the water trickling fresh and cool out of the rock. He
had seen me carrying my tin cup over and carrying it back
again to my camp.

In the morning I made my own move. I remembered
something I had seen that first day when I checked the
cabin. On the supply shelf a small bucket half filled with
used coffee grounds. There is only one reason anyone
saves used coffee grounds. To use them again. I waited
until sounds from inside the cabin told me he was starting
the day and until he had come out with his big bucket and
started towards the spring for his morning supply of fresh
water. I slipped into the cabin. I set on the table a fresh
unopened one-pound can of coffee and slipped out again
and sat on the upturned box by one of the sheds.

He came back, leaning to the weight of the bucket, apparently not even noticing me, and went inside. I waited.
The can of coffee came out the doorway, turning over and
over in the air, and hit in the dirt and rolled a short way
down-slope. I waited. He stood in the doorway, not looking at me, staring down at the can in the dirt. Time
passed. He walked down and picked up the can and returned to the cabin and went in. More time passed. He
stood in the doorway. He looked directly at me. "There's
two cups on the table," he said.

That was a beginning. I sat on the bench inside drinking coffee and he sat on the chair eating his morning meal. Crazy? Not in any way you could notice. Individual, eccentric, opinionated, yes. If you said something that failed to interest him, to touch him, he simply ignored you. It hadn't been said. If he felt like being silent, he was silent. If he felt like talking, he talked, and in a steady unhurried flow that gave the impression nothing less than a sudden cataclysm could stop it. I touched off one of those flowings when I reached and pulled the book lying on the table a bit closer so I could see the title. It was an old geology text. He started talking and for the next ten to fifteen minutes without a break gave me a lecture on the geologic history of the Southwest in general and of that specific area in particular. He talked about that outcropping of red rock behind the cabin as if it had life of its own, placing its birth, its formation, in such and such an age, tracing its long burial under the sediments of inland seas, its rise again with shiftings of the earth's crust and exposure after millennia of erosion.

He stopped, looking at me as if I might be some sort of geologic specimen myself. "If you're prospecting around here for some kind of mineral strike," he said, "you're a fool."

I took a chance. "The only strike I'm after," I said, "is the kind you can put into words. In a story."

He pushed up from his chair. I watched him gather the few dishes and rinse them in his bucket. I wasn't there any more. He walked past me and out of the cabin and started on his morning round.

Early afternoon and I made another move. I waited where the rock faded off into sandy hillside and along he came, on schedule, for his afternoon walk. I swung into stride beside him. He didn't stop or slow or pay any at-

tention to me. Then suddenly he did stop. He looked at
me. As far as I could make out any expression on that ordinary old clean-shaven face, he was amused. "Do you
think," he said, "I've got a lost mine or anything like that
hidden in these hills? Or if I did, I'd lead you to it?"

"No," I said. "I think you're just passing time."

He nodded a bit, at least I thought he did, and he
started on and I went with him. One of those subtle in-
explainable shiftings had taken place. I was not just walking alongside him. I was going with him.

He took me quite a few miles. There was plenty of spry
vigor left in his old legs. We went wandering, what would
have looked like wandering to anyone watching, but I
could make out traces of trail, probably worn by successive
pairs of his own-make moccasins. He had something of a
routine out there too. In and about, following the low
levels, working on a wide circuit into hills that were not
really hills but the remaining twisted fingers of what had
once been the general land level now standing strange and
misshapen between sharply eroded arroyos and minia-
ture canyons. The Southwest has many of those stripped
eroded badlands where color and barrenness and the bare
bones of earth breed beauty and a haunting sense of pene-
tration towards the source of ultimate secrets. He had his
own private preserve, not his and yet his because there
was nothing tangible of commercial value there to bring
people and the blight of settlement and exploitation.

He slowed once to point out some pieces of what I
thought were a peculiar rock. "Petrified wood," he said.
"Triassic." And he was off on another lecture, not so
much a lecture this time as a speculation whether the region had once, millions of years ago, been truly tropical,
under heavy rainfall, or simply well supplied with water
in the low places by long run-off from other areas. He

slowed again to point out a jack rabbit scudding around a turn in the arroyo ahead. And he was off again, this time on a monologue about jack rabbits as the perfect adaptation of life to conditions in that particular region in this particular geologic age.

I was with him, yes, but I was stopped. I didn't dare push much, try to lead his talk, because the few times I tried I simply hadn't spoken. All I could get was his brand of scientific information and I knew enough myself to recognize that his brand was that of a man who reads some in the scant outdated books he has and applies that to what he sees wandering around.

His circuit brought us back on schedule, about the time the old cows and the calf came in for water. He puttered at his garden and I stood watching, certain that if I tried anything I would merely touch off a lecture on plants and the arid-adaptability of the pinto beans that comprised about half that garden. At last I went over and sat on that upturned box. At last he came towards the cabin and went in. I thought of getting a few things from my car and suggesting we share supper but decided no. He wasn't deliberately forgetting me and my can of coffee, deliberately pushing me aside. He was isolated in his own existence again. The shadows were sliding towards night.

And that night he broke his routine. Not a break really but a fulfillment. It only seemed like a break to me at the time.

I was ready, watching, quiet on my sleeping bag, at the right time. A little past eleven. That timepiece in his head clicked or nudged or prodded or whatever it did and he blew out the lamp and came to the doorway and sat on the doorstep. The moon, nicely rounded, was rising clear with only a thin tracery of light clouds floating across the sky. He was in the rock and cabin shadow but I knew what he was doing. He was sitting there staring down towards that old tree.

I remember thinking that maybe I didn't have a time-piece in my own head but I did have an awareness now that could tell me what he would be doing any hour out of the twenty-four. I had his routine fixed, filled in. What was needed was what was behind it, what went on in that old head when he sat on that doorstep. I drifted into sleep wondering what move to make the next day and time passed and I was awake and aware that something had changed.

The moon was high now and the doorstep was plain in the soft light. He wasn't there. I pushed to my feet, careful, quiet, and eased along by the first shed. He was out in the open, moving down towards that old tree. He moved slowly, cautiously, like a man stalking something either very shy or very dangerous. I looked on ahead of him. There was nothing to be seen, nothing anywhere about. That is a point I want to make very clear. There was nothing in sight. Absolutely nothing. Only that gaunt old half-skeleton of a tree standing still and silent on down the slope.

He began to move faster, hurrying. Then he was running. Suddenly he stopped, close by the tree, peering up through the gaunt branches then all around the immediate area. His head drooped and he stood still, as still as the tree itself, and it seemed to me that as he stood there, un-moving, he shrank some, the old outline of him growing older. At last he turned and came up towards the cabin, slow, tired, just a little old man lost and alone in his own private existence. I had the plain impression that I could have stepped out into the open and he could have looked full at me without seeing me. He went slowly into the cabin and I heard his old cot creak a bit as he lay down on it.

In the morning, as far as anyone watching the two of us could have told, nothing had changed, the night had not been. He was the same as before, right in his routine, moving through it with that same seeming indestructible spry vigor. I was part of it now, taken in on the basis of the previous day. I sat on the bench inside and drank coffee while he ate his morning meal and I listened to another lecture, this one on the probable history of an Indian pueblo whose mounded remains he said were still partially decipherable back in the hills. In the afternoon we went off on his circuit again and I listened to a monologue on some fossils from the Pliocene and another on the silliness of the fable of prairie dogs and prairie owls and rattlesnakes living in the same burrows.

It was the day before repeated. But I could sense the difference. There was a tension in him, a tiny beat of anxiety or apprehension under that ordinary old enduring time-passing exterior. And he was reaching out a bit more towards me, was willing to let a little more information slip out. I learned that he was Missouri-bred and had once attended some small jerkwater college planning to be a preacher and had originally come west for his health. I learned too that it was only seven years since he had come into the region and patched up that old cabin and squatted there. I was disappointed at that. It didn't fit into my thinking. I had been figuring that he had been there from way back in the stage days. I was fool enough for a while to feel that maybe I was wasting my time.

It was that feeling which made me try to push him. We

had just come back to the place. "That story you're writing," he said. "Are you making it all up?"

"Yes," I said. "Not because I want to but because I have to. This is the kind of place where things should have happened. But apparently nothing ever did." Then I pushed direct. "Or did it?" I said.

He looked straight at me. I could see it. Something. Something hidden in that old mind behind that ordinary old face. He turned away and went to his watering as if I no longer existed. But I knew. He was about ready to talk. All I had to do was wait and let the situation drift some more. What I didn't know was how soon and how completely it would break for me.

If I were reading this, not writing it, I'd say it was too pat, too neat, too tailored to old-fashioned tale traditions. Midnight, in such tales, is the witching hour, the hovering hesitant pause between one full day and the next when anything that is eerie, weird, mystic, is supposed to come to a climax. That is nonsense, of course. Midnight is only a man-marked moment, a notch in the twenty-four hour convention man has established for his own parceling out of the passage of time. And it is not a universal moment; it varies by approximately an hour every thousand miles around the girdle of the globe. To the universe in which man is an infinitesimal flicker, midnight has no significance beyond that of any other moment through the period of dark that itself is only the turning of a portion of the earth's surface away from the sun.

Why cannot fact plagiarize fiction? The fact in this case was the result of an orderly sequence of events. His nightly vigil was determined by the moon. The moon, in its current phase, was rising approximately an hour later each night. A little past eight the first night I was there. Then nine . . . ten . . . eleven. Now twelve. Midnight. A moon beginning to be flattened a bit on the edge now, into the waning.

If you have been patient and have followed me this far, you have the setting, the situation, in mind. A lonely spot in a lonely arid land where once were brief little spurts of once-familiar activity when stages arrived and teams were changed, the place and its type of activity now long since by-passed and all but forgotten in the forward push of what is called progress. An old man living there, existing through routined days aimed at the nights. And myself, edging in, meddling, prying, and justifying my meddling and prying as a search for story material, for more understanding of the endlessly varied ways in which we humans, we midges infesting, in Cabell's phrase, the epidermis of one of the lesser planets, confront the inevitable dilemma of living.

Midnight. Midnight in that particular time-belt, attested to by my watch and by the moon rising behind that outcropping of ancient rock. He blew out his lamp and came to the doorway and sat on the doorstep. I lay quiet on my sleeping bag and that awareness nudged and I pushed up and eased along by the first shed. He was out in the open, in the moonlight, beyond the rock-and-cabin shadow, moving down towards that old tree. There was no need to look on ahead of him but I did. Nothing was there. Absolutely nothing.

He moved faster, hurrying. Then he was running. His old voice rose, quivering through the almost still air, urgent. "Johnny!" he called. "Wait! Wait!" He stumbled and fell forward, almost at the base of the tree. I saw one old hand, clenched, beat on the ground and then he was still.

I moved into the open, down towards him. As I came

near, he rolled over and hunched up to sitting position. He looked at me but I don't think he saw me. He tried to stand up and made it and started towards the cabin, limping on his right foot. I moved in close and put out an arm to steady him and he relaxed his old weight some against me, aware of me, I'd say, in his muscles but not yet in his mind. Together we went to the cabin and in and I helped him slump down on the edge of his cot and I stepped over and sat on the bench along the opposite wall. There was enough soft light from the moon through the windows for me to make him out there on the cot edge.

We were quiet, both of us. But I could feel it. He knew I was there. He was grateful that someone was there with sense enough to be quiet and just be there.

I heard him draw in a deep breath and let it out slowly. "Something did happen here," he said.

"Yes," I said. "There were people here. So something had to happen."

"Not many," he said. "Just two. Usually one and sometimes two. And one night more."

I waited. At last he told me, not like one of his lectures, but slow, careful, completely objective, simply stating the facts.

There was a man named Johnny Yeager, a breed, a half-Cherokee, who drifted into the Southwest out of the Indian Territory as a freighter with his own small outfit. He was a quiet capable man with no itch to make money, just to live and enjoy life in his own way. When he worked, he worked hard, picking up jobs with his mules and two wagons freighting supplies to some of the more isolated Army posts. Between trips, when he had money in his pocket and could pay his way with no need for more, he liked to go on pack trips into the lonely distances or loaf around some place where he had a friend or two and soak up southwestern sun. He spent considerable time, off and on, at the stage station by the old cottonwood, then a flourishing tree and landmark. He knew the station tender, the agent as the company obligingly let the tender call himself, and the two of them got along well together. Johnny Yeager would hang around the station, making it his headquarters for long rides round about, pitching in with a will to help with change of horses when a stage came through. He was a good man with anything on hoofs. He liked to sleep in the open. He liked best to sleep on the flat roof of the stable where he said the sky seemed spread out best for him and the air moved friendly all around him.

There was a man too named Mills, another freighter, but down on his luck, or maybe it was his irritableness that was his bad luck, losing him business until he lost his outfit too. Johnny Yeager took him on as a driver on one of his trips. Johnny already had a second driver at the time but Mills pestered him for a job and Johnny took him on. Out along the lonely way Mills began making trouble. He had his own ideas about handling mules. He didn't like taking orders from an Indian, even a half-Indian. Maybe he was brooding over his bad luck too. Somewhere along the trail he worked himself into a rage and pulled his belt gun and began shooting at Johnny. That was a mistake for him with a man like Johnny, who jumped in by the second wagon, yanked the rifle there from under the lash rope and drilled Mills through the forehead. The other driver had seen it all and at the inquest he testified straight and Johnny was exonerated.

But there was another man too named Mills, a brother,

and he came up from his place further south. He talked around that white men ought to be ashamed letting a goddamned thieving Indian get away with murder. One night he and three other men rode out and around into the badlands and staked their horses and slipped down to the station. The first the agent knew anything was happening was when they were in the cabin and one of them woke him with a gun barrel in his ribs and said: "Where's Yeager?" The agent was fuddled with sleep and all he could focus on at the moment was that gun barrel in his ribs. "Sleeping on top the stable," he said.

They made the agent get up and go with them, soft, silent, slipping down by the stable. One of them held a gun jammed against his back every step. They hugged in close against the stable wall, under the jutting roof. "All right," this Mills whispered. "Call him down. Try to warn him any and you're done."

The agent didn't have a chance. That gun barrel was hard against his back. He tried to make his voice sound natural. "Johnny," he called.

They could hear the man on the roof rousing some, probably sitting up. "Johnny," the agent said. "Come on down here a minute."

Johnny came to the roof edge and sat down, legs hanging over, and pushed out and as he landed the other three of them jumped him. They all rolled over scrambling and then they had him and they jerked him to his feet still struggling and he saw the agent standing there with another man behind and he stopped struggling and stared at the agent and looked away and let those three take him, not struggling any more, down the slope towards the tree. Two of them had him tight by the arms and the third went into the stable and came out with a rope. Down by the tree they fixed a noose and put it around his neck and were ready to throw the other end over the first big limb about eleven or twelve feet up and that was when Johnny spoke.

"I'm not afraid to die," he said. "I'll show you how a man does it." He pulled loose from the two holding him, who let him go but stood and watched close, and he stepped to the trunk of the tree and climbed up by the rough bark and a few old branch stubs with the rope dragging from his neck and hitched himself out on that big limb. He passed the rope end around it and pulled it taut from his neck and knotted it. "Just remember this," he said. "I know you. Each one of you. If there's such a thing as a spirit staying here on earth, I'll do it. I'll make life a hell for each of you as long as you live." And he pushed out from the tree limb, dropping straight to the sharp snapping jerk of the rope.

The agent did what he could. He took Johnny's body into town and arranged for decent burial. He knew that Johnny had a sister in the Indian Territory and he sold out Johnny's outfit and sent her the money. He went to the sheriff and tried to have warrants sworn out. The sheriff made a few gestures at investigating but the four men alibied each other and rang in testimony from accommodating friends and the inquest verdict was death at the hands of persons unknown. The agent made a nuisance of himself trying to stir some action until people were telling him to shut up and why make a fuss over the killing of an Indian anyway. He quit his job and drifted away.

We sat in that patched-together old cabin and he was quiet again. I waited. I knew what he would say, what he would have to say. I expect you do too.

He stirred on the cot edge and raised his head a bit higher. "I was that agent," he said.

I waited. I knew that all he had told me was only the beginning, the background, that he was over the hump now.

"My mistake," he said, "was telling them he was on that roof. The moment I did that it was all inevitable. It had to be."

I waited. "Johnny wouldn't have made that mistake," he said. "Johnny would have been all awake at once and aware. He would have handled it somehow. He doesn't know how it happened, but even if he did, he wouldn't blame me. He knows I slept hard in those days and took a time to come really awake. He knows I don't think fast. He knows I'm not a brave man. He knew all that from the beginning and still he was my friend."

I waited. He was started on this and he would do it in his own way.

"People think I'm crazy," he said. "Maybe I am. Or maybe they're the ones who're crazy. I don't know and I don't care about that. I just know what I know. It took me a long time to believe it and to have it straight in my mind."

He put his thin old arms behind him and leaned back on them on the cot. "That Mills," he said. "The brother. He was first. Only three years later. He was on a prospecting trip. In the Sacramento Mountains. His packhorse came in without him. A search party found him, what was left of him, at the bottom of a forty-foot cliff. There hadn't been any rain and the tracks were still there. He'd camped several hundred feet away, on the upper level. Sometime, probably in the night, he'd roused and started running. Why would a man do that unless he was running after something or away from something? But there wasn't another track except those of the pack-horse where it'd been tied and finally broke loose and wandered home. He was running, in the dark, and he went over. . . .

"Then the one named Skinner. Five years later. He knew something about pharmacy and he'd started a drug-store along with a trading post in town. He began having headaches, mostly at night, that wouldn't let him sleep well. He'd been a big man and he got thinner and thinner and more stooped and worried-looking. He took to dosing himself with all kinds of pills and powders for those headaches. One night, so his wife told, he got up and stumbled around and went into the store to fix himself something and he took hold of the wrong bottle or can or other kind of container. Suicide, some people said. Accident was the official verdict . . .

"All right. That was two. Coincidence, you might say. The fact is, that's what I did say to myself when I heard about it. Or tried to say . . .

"Then there was Cramer. He had a saloon in town but he sold that and moved on. I heard about him once in a while. I don't know what he was before but he was a rest-less man now, always trying it some new place, always moving on. He'd settle some place and seem to be doing well, then he'd start drinking and getting careless with money, and then one day he'd just sell out whatever he had for any price and move on. Nine more years it was and I hadn't heard anything about him for a long time and I was handy-man for a couple of geologists studying strata over in the Caballo Mountains and I was gathering wood for the cook-fire and a magazine some hunter or somebody had left up there caught my eye. There wasn't any breeze blowing that I could feel and yet some of the pages were fluttering so I couldn't miss it. I picked it up and turned a few pages and there he was. Cramer. In a picture with some other men. I checked what it said under the picture and the name was right. There was an article too. It didn't have much about him but it had enough. He'd been up in Montana for a few years guiding hunting parties. The party he was with this time got caught in an early blizzard. It couldn't have been too bad because the rest of the party, who didn't even know the country, pulled out all right. But Cramer got separated from them somehow and never showed again. They found him later, froze stiff, nearly buried in snow where he'd hunched down between some rocks like he'd been hiding from something . . .

"All right. That was three. By that time I knew I had to know about Nordyke. I couldn't find any trace of him. He'd run a kind of overnight and eating place in town but sometime back he'd sold out and just disappeared. I'd work a while and get some money together and then move on trying to find him or something about him. I'd tell myself that was silly but all the same I knew, I just felt, I'd get track of him. It was just a matter of time. About five, close to six years it was and I noticed I was moving north and east. Every time I'd have a new stake and start out again a kind of hunch would set the direction for me. I was up in Nebraska, eastern Nebraska, in a little town there, and I'd checked for the name and I was about broke again and I was sitting on a bench in a little park like a plaza there and a piece of newspaper kept blowing around and finally caught in a bush right beside me. I took hold of it. The edges were all ragged and it was only a little piece but there was one article complete. Some politician was demanding an investigation of certain institutions.

He claimed they were poorly run. He referred to what he called the Nordyke case . . .

"All right. I had the name. It was a Lincoln paper. I went to Lincoln and to the public library and looked through back issues of that paper. I found it. All of it or anyway enough. It had happened a few weeks before. This Nordyke, and the first name and initial were right, had been committed to an insane asylum on evidence given by his wife and relatives. He'd been subject to bad nightmares for quite a while and they got worse and he took to sleeping or trying to sleep in a room alone with the door and windows locked and then he even boarded up those windows and then he began having fits in the day-time too. He'd hide somewhere around the house and jump anyone who happened to come near and start shouting for someone to bring a rope. So he was committed to that asylum. They had to take him in a strait-jacket. He wasn't there two days before he got hold of a sheet and tore it into strips and knotted those together and hung himself . . ."

We sat quiet again. I waited.

"All right," he said. "I knew what I had to do. I had to tell him. I wandered around kind of aimless for a while, just working some and waiting, before I understood he wouldn't come to me. Not in any way I could know him. So I came here."

He was silent. He was silent so long I had to speak. "And he was here," I said.

"Of course he was here," he said. "Where else would he be? It isn't finished. There wasn't just four men he saw that night. There was five. But he was always straight and he was my friend and he won't bother me. I have to tell him. And he won't let me. He stays away from me. He shuts me out the way he did that night when he just looked at me once and that was all. The only time I can even try to catch him is when he comes and sits for a while on the branch of that tree. I think he has to do that. It's a kind of ritual he has to go through. And he only does it when everything is just right, the way it was, in a summer month when the moon is about full."

It was so dark in the cabin I could barely make him out now. He was just a shape in the dimness. But I could hear him ease out breath in a sigh. "It'll be about another month now," he said, "before I can try again."

He was silent. I had to push a bit. "Do you really see him?" I said.

"I'm not positive," he said. "Sometimes I do and then again I'm not sure. That's unimportant. I know when he's there. I can feel it, the same as it was that night, that exact moment when he was up on that tree branch. But when I go down there he fades away. He just goes. He shuts me out . . ."

He stopped. He was not just silent. He had stopped. He thought he had told it all and perhaps he had. All the pieces were plain and I could fit them together. But I wanted to be certain. "What is it," I said, "that you have to tell him?"

I could sense him peering at me in the dimness, a bit exasperated, a bit sorry for my stupidity. "I have to tell him," he said, "that they had a gun in my back."

I lay outside on my sleeping bag in the thin grayness before dawn, aware of him inside that old patchwork cabin stretched on his old cot, and I could see the whole thing complete. Nothing more would happen for another swing of the moon in its ancient cycle and what would happen then would be only a repetition of what had happened. There was nothing to hold me now and I had already spent more time than I really had available on this side trip. I would be leaving in a few hours.

I could see it all complete. I thought I could see something of a pattern in it, of the way things happen to and by us midges infesting the epidermis of a lesser planet. For a beginning there was a movement, a convulsion, involving two individual atoms of humanity, a Johnny Yeager and a man named Mills. Not really a beginning, as no movement is ever a beginning only a becoming in an infinite webbed process, because that movement was the result of all those before that had made those two atoms what they were and to behave as they did. But a beginning at least in the sense of a happening isolated, selected, as a starting point. That movement, that impulse, radiating outward, was communicated to the brother, the second Mills, and through him to three more men, Skinner and Cramer and Nordyke, and the reaction of those four took in another, the agent, Cal Kinney, then a youngish man, now an old man lying in there on that cot. The initial movement and its result, the shooting of the first Mills and the hanging of Yeager, were long since over, done, finished as discernible movements. But the impulse, reinforced, had remained in the minds of four men and a fifth. It held, certainly the evidence suggested that it held, as a strong influence through the years and the lives of those four. It was still strong in the mind of the fifth, influencing him, determining his very existence.

I fell asleep in the satisfaction that sometimes comes when, in the very process of drifting into sleep, you feel that you have really grasped something, have caught hold of something vital that will expand into something valuable when you get to work on it.

And in the late morning light, when I was stowing my things in the car, I didn't think about it because I knew from experience that such notions, such graspings, are elusive and rarely stand practical examination in the wide-awake daytime arena. You have to let them simmer and season in the background of your mind that the psychologists are exploring nowadays and then come forward when they have taken on shape and substance.

He was up and puttering on his morning round, apparently indifferent to me again. He acted as if he had told me nothing, as if the night had not been. Perhaps he regretted telling me; he made no move to share coffee with me. Or perhaps he had seen me packing and had just not bothered. He was crazy, yes, in a harmless way. But I wanted to shake his old hand. He had given me what I had come to find and I wanted to give him something in return.

I went over and stepped in front of him. He stopped and looked at me. I put out my right hand. He put out his and I could feel that spry enduring vigor in the brief clasp. "Could he read?" I said.

He hesitated. I could see the recognition and the reluctant acceptance of a sharing in his old eyes. "Of course he could read," he said.

"He won't wait for you," I said. "You can't tell him. But you can write a note and fasten it to that tree."

He stared at me. At last he nodded a bit. At least I think he nodded. I turned and went to my car. He was still staring after me as I drove away.

So there it is, the account. There remains only the wondering. That remains because of what I did not realize at

the time, that the impulse launched by the initial movement, the killing of a man named Mills by a Johnny
Yeager, was still radiating outward, still producing effects
according to the character of the adjoining atoms.

I say that because it had been communicated to me and
it had produced an effect according to the composition of
the individual atom that bears my name . . .

I couldn't write that story. It simmered and seasoned
in the background of my mind and never came forward in
shape and substance. At last I thought I knew why. I did
not have it all. It was not finished. There had been and
there still was a fifth man.

Eventually I was back in the little southwestern town.
I heard what might seem to be a finish. About a month
after I left that first time he appeared in town and found
a buyer for his old cows and the calf and went out with the
buyer and helped bring in the stock and he brought along
the few personal things he had and settled in an abandoned shack on the edge of town. He wasn't crazy any
more, not in any way that showed. He wasn't anything,
except perhaps a nuisance, just another old character who
wandered around doing nothing except drink himself into
a kind of silly grinning stupor and talk endlessly about the
old days with anyone he could get to listen and, when his
money gave out, cadge drinks and enough food to stay
alive from people in the local cafés and, when the propri-
etors finally kept him out, panhandle tourists for whatever he could inveigle out of them. It was only about six
months later that he went stumbling after a quarter some
tourist gave him that fell out of his hand and rolled into
the road and he tripped over his own feet and fell right
in front of a fast-moving big interstate bus.

So the story of Johnny Yeager and a man named Mills
and four more men and a fifth was finished, is finished.

But the impulse launched by that movement, that happening isolated, selected, as a starting point, is not finished. It goes on, still radiating outward. It exists in me, in my mind, as a wondering. I reacted to it, I interfered, I nudged old Cal Kinney with the notion that led to his finish. I know, as surely as if I had been there, that about a month after I left, a piece of paper or cardboard or maybe a board was tacked or fastened somehow to that old tree and old Cal Kinney blew out his lamp and got up from his book and went out and sat on the doorstep of that old patchwork cabin. And I know, as surely as if he had told me, that as he watched that tree in the moonlight his old mind solved for itself the problem it had created for itself. Whatever my motive, the result, I can see now, was as inevitable as the result of his mistake, his telling that Johnny Yeager was sleeping on the stable roof.

There was an old man living alone yet not alone at an old abandoned stage station out in the arid hauntingly beautiful badlands of this southwest where time is an almost tangible dimension of all things and the past is part of the present and life has worked through the dust of millennia. He was crazy, yes, if you see any meaning in that word. But he was a distinct independent individual, a character complete within himself, a whole man, an atom of humanity with a purpose, a meaning, that gave direction to his existence. Does it alter the essential balance that can be seen in that existence of his that its purpose, its meaning, would have seemed ridiculous, unreal, a delusion, to most other people? I interfered. The effect of my interference took that purpose, that meaning, from him. He became just another of those aimless drifting old nuisances who are barely tolerated and whose final passings, usually by one kind of accident or another, are regarded with suppressed relief by those about them.

Was my interference a mistake too? Should I have calculated the possible result instead of simply reacting according to the emotional and thinking-I-was-thinking composition of the individual atom that bears my name? Can the ancient problem of good and evil, of rightness and wrongness, be applied to my interference? I do not know, not with any certainty. But I do know that the impulse launched long ago by Johnny Yeager and a man named Mills still exists, communicated to me, and that it colors, if ever so slightly, my attitude towards and my relationship with all other atoms of humanity around me.

And it still radiates outward. If you have followed me this far, it has been communicated, if only in another brief wondering, a brief pondering, to you.

Enos Carr

*

HE WAS touched in the head all right.

Myers sent a man to meet us and we worked winding up the long snowy slopes in a jeep and pulled in by the log ranchhouse with its string of sleeping units beside it. The driver took our bags and Peyton and I were easing out the guncases from the gunnysack padding around them, when this character came along leading two tired horses down towards the barn. He had a long thin spraddle-legged carcass topped by a face like a blunted ax blade, the whole wrapped in a wide-brimmed hopeless old hat, a decrepit thick old jacket hunched high around his shoulders and neck, pipestem dungarees long ago shrunk to highwater mark, and heavy old boots. He stopped and looked us over. He turned away and couldn't have been talking to anyone but those two horses.

"Another batch of predators," he said. He patted the near horse on the neck. "Don't worry any, boy. They're not after your kind." He started on.

Peyton couldn't take that. "Hey, you!" he said. "What the devil do you mean?"

This character stopped again, looking back. "Up here after deer, aren't you?" he said. His voice was mild, even friendly. "Never shy away from the truth, boy." He moved on, setting down those boots in easy spraddled stride.

Myers himself was coming out to greet us. Peyton wasn't waiting for any greeting. He pointed a finger down-slope. "Who or maybe what is that?"

Myers turned it on, a grin, the one developed through years of operating the place in the hunting season, keeping everyone happy, smoothing away frictions. "That's old Enos Carr," he said. "Didn't you run into him when you were up here last year? No, maybe not. Has a ranch over beyond that first high ridge."

"What the devil," Peyton said, responding to the grin, trying to keep this light. "What the devil is he doing here?"

"Shucks, man," Myers said. "When we're full up like now, have to borrow some of his horses. Damn good horses. He won't let anyone else take care of them. We have his horses, we have him too."

"He called us a couple of predators."

Myers put more power into the grin. "One thing you learn up here is not to let old Enos bother you any. He's touched a bit in the head." Then Myers was himself, serious, the man you got to know behind the grin. "But don't go getting old Enos wrong. A damn good rancher. A damn good neighbor too." Myers grinned again, hearty, strong. "Shucks, man, the thing to do is take him as part of the natural scenery around. Kind of interesting, viewed that way."

A lot of things happened while we were up there. But I'm not writing about them now. Peyton got his deer, a fine big buck. I was his partner this trip so he was out another day with me till I got mine. Peyton's a good man.

Matter of fact, about the best I know. He writes about guns for the sports magazines and what he knows about guns, what he can do with a gun, any gun, makes you proud to know him. He's a real sportsman. Clean. Decent. He writes about that too and always acts straight on what he writes. It wouldn't even cross his mind to take a shot at anything out of season or bag a single bird above the limit. He tosses a coin with his partner for first try at whatever they're after and sticks to that toss no matter what. He never pulls trigger till he knows absolutely what he has sights on. I've known him to pass up a fine elk because he'd got separated from his partner and wasn't certain that partner wasn't somewhere between him and that elk. I've known him to push on alone in nasty weather and be out all night in bitter cold tracking down a wounded deer to put it out of its misery. But I'm not writing this about him. I'm writing about this Enos Carr character. Not a story, not anything like that, because it doesn't have any form and hasn't any action and doesn't get anywhere. Just an account of what we saw of him and learned about him. I'm writing it because I collect odd characters, like to get them down on paper. They're quaint, interesting. They're not important because a world made up of odd characters would be a weird one to live in and probably couldn't even function at all. Matter of fact, studying odd characters can help you appreciate the normal everyday capable people who keep the world wagging on a fairly even keel, a place where most of us can earn a decent living and get some enjoyment out of life.

And I'm writing this because this Carr character was one of the oddest I've encountered, because Peyton can get along with anybody and most people naturally take to him and this character is still the only one I know anything about he couldn't get along with. No trouble, no real arguing, nothing like that. But this Enos Carr rubbed him the wrong way, seemed to irritate him by just being around. I guess Peyton just couldn't take him the way I could, the way Myers said, as an interesting local oddity.

It was late afternoon when we arrived and we'd be out riding higher in those mountains before daylight next morning so we stayed in and after an early dinner were in the big main room cozy and comfortable by the big stone fireplace. Quite a few there, more arrivals and others who had already been around a day or two. We were feeling good, all of us, passing a couple of flasks around and staking out in talk the general territories each pair or more of us would be trying next morning so we wouldn't be getting in each other's way and run much risk of a shooting accident. It was pleasant in that room. Heat and light mean a lot when you're way up in the cold and the mountains. The fire in that big fireplace that could take four-foot logs without crowding was mighty reassuring. And from a shed outside you could hear the steady chugging of the mounted truck motor that ran the generator supplying electric current.

The outside door opened and in came this Carr character, stomping snow off those heavy old boots, lugging another big chunk of log. He went over to the fireplace and reached in with one of those boots and kicked a place for that log and dropped it in and hopped back from the bouncing sparks and then squatted off to one side on the raised stone hearth. He was limp and relaxed there, that long thin carcass doubled up, and he took off that hopeless old hat and set it on one bent-up knee and he was about bald, just a fringe of scraggly hair over his ears and dipping in back. That slant-sided head beveled smooth on top looked even more like a blunted ax blade than before. He was in shadow to the side there, just a queer-shaped bump against the fireplace stones, and quiet, and it was easy to forget he was there at all.

Peyton couldn't forget. He kept looking at the old character and looking away. Finally he gave up looking away and when there was a break in the talk spoke right at him. He was just trying to get something straight, friendly, just one man by a fire talking friendly to another. "Carr," he said. "You called me a predator this afternoon."

That was Peyton. He tied that remark strictly to himself. He left me out of it. If he was going to raise an issue that might lead to a little arguing, he wasn't going to presume on friendship and pull anyone else into it.

This Carr character didn't even move. He just said, mild: "Likely I did."

"Yes, siree, you certainly did," Peyton said. "And that makes me curious. People I pal around with generally reserve that particular label for things like wolves and mountain lions. Just how do you mean it?"

This Carr uncoupled a bit. It was like Peyton had pulled a cork out of him and a big supply of words had just been waiting to pop out, not fast, just steady, in that mild voice of his, patient, like he was explaining a lesson to some kid. "I'm a dictionary man," he said. "There's more real sense in a dictionary, providing you read it right and fit things together, than in about all other books boggled into one big heap. I read my dictionary the way some folks read — well, read sports magazines. It says a predator is an animal that preys on other animals. That's prey spelled with an e not an a and a mighty lot of difference that one letter makes. Now a man is an animal.

Maybe something more too, but an animal all the same. Mammal variety. You're a man. You prey on other animals. That makes you a predator."

"Because I shoot deer?" Peyton said. He had a good hold on himself. You had to know him as well as I did to sort of feel the little sharp underneath edge to his tone.

"That's part of it," Carr said. "But you have to look at — " He stopped talking because someone else was talking. That was one thing about him, he was willing to let another man, any other man, have his own say too. That someone else this time was a youngish fellow up there for his first hunting season and all excited about it. "Fooey!" he said, sudden and sharp. He seemed surprised at himself for being so sharp but went right on anyway. "That's no way to talk. That type of thinking puts men right beside wolves and coyotes and cougars and such and anybody with any sense knows those are slinky sneaky cowardly things."

"Well, now, yes," this Carr character said. "They do slink around and they do sneak around, especially when after a meal off a fat deer, and they are cowardly in the meaning that a man comes along, especially a man with a gun, they scat out of his way fast as possible. But when you get out in these hills tomorrow hunting your deer too, you'll be slinking along and sneaking along just the same as they do and after a deer or two's got away from you you'll be wishing you could slink and sneak as efficient as they can. And anybody has a mind to bet'd have a certain thing betting if you were out there without a gun and some other man with a gun was roaming around right ready to pot you first chance you'd be scatting out of his way fast as you could. There's a point you missed too some folks make which is they say critters like wolves are cowards because sometimes they hunt in packs. Look at it right that's not being cowards. That's being efficient. Take any batch of men and let them get hungry enough and let game be the only food around and mighty scarce at that and they'd be pack-hunting too. I've read somewheres that's how they did it back before they had things like guns and hunting was a serious food-getting business not just a pleasuring. Fact is, they still do it anyway, even nowadays, like over at Skinner's place up the north creek where they're so all-fired anxious to guarantee a man his deer they put him in a good spot and some of the hands swing out around driving game his way. That's pack-hunting any way you look at it."

Old Carr had that young fellow stopped. It was Peyton who went after him again.

"I suppose you don't hunt deer?" Peyton said.

"That's right," Carr said. "Nor elk or turkey either. But I don't claim any special credit on that. I'm a predator too. I belong to the race of man and that's a race of predators. Always has been. Always will be. I don't shoot deer. But I raise cattle for market. That's the same thing only better organized. I eat beef mighty regular. Enjoy it too. When it comes to deer, though, I kind of figure — "

"Whoa, now," Myers said. I guess Myers had seen something like this happen before and was stepping in to shoo old Carr down a side track. "That's a new one, Enos. Never heard you spring that 'better organized' business before. Raising cattle the same as hunting deer, only better organized. What kind of addled egg you been hatching this time?"

"Certain they're the same," Carr said. "There's a lot of differences, but there's plenty of sameness too. What's raising cattle at bottom? Letting some critters breed and multiply and graze and put on weight. What for? So they can be killed and butchered and the meat tucked away in folks's bellies. What's this state government we're living under do with deer? Sets up laws to keep some deer around to breed and multiply and graze and put on weight. And what for? So hunters can go out kill and butcher them and bring in the meat to be tucked away in bellies. The pattern's the same. But look at it right the deer doing is kind of sloppy. Hit-or-miss all through. Breeding's not controlled. Slaughtering is just chance, which hunter stumbles into which deer and can he shoot straight. And he has to do his own messy butchering of the carcass. That's plain poor organization. The cattle business is almighty neat against it. Breeding's controlled for the best stock. The right animals, by age and weight, culled out for killing. Sent off to a place set up to do the killing and butchering quick and efficient. Look at it right that's plenty more civilized. My dictionary says civilization is a state of being well organized and refined. I notice one thing civilization tries to do is cover things up for people. Shut off things that aren't refined and maybe aren't pleasant to see or know. Like the fact some critter had to be killed and butchered for there to be meat to eat. Man goes into a store buys a piece of meat and that's all it is to him, a piece of something good to eat and he doesn't even think about the killing and butchering and pulling out of guts had to be done for that meat to be there. Civilization, being organized, shuts that off for him. Hunting, being sloppy, just plain rubs his nose in the messy part."

This Carr character had everybody stopped. Nobody was going to talk to an old head-touched oddity who rambled on like that, missing most of what hunting is all about. And he was stretching up to his feet anyway. I guess he always shut himself off in time and Myers knew that which was why Myers had been letting him run on.

His voice got almost plaintive. "You boys," he said. "You ought to know better'n get me to talking. I don't want to spoil your fun any. Just talking for myself. Maybe civilization shuts off too blamed much. Maybe rubbing noses in the messy part of living is a good thing now and again."

He jammed that hopeless old hat on that bald beveled head and went spraddle-stride to the door and on out.

It was morning. I mean it would be morning soon. There was the first faint graying of light creeping up behind the mountains. We'd had breakfast, Peyton and I, and shrugged into our coats and caps and picked up our packed lunches and got our gear and when we went down towards the barn there were our horses saddled and waiting. Not just the horses. Old Carr was there too. He had his back to us and didn't see us coming. He was talking. To those horses.

Peyton took me by the arm and stopped me. We stood there, listening.

"No tricks now," old Carr was saying. "Not a one. Understand? Especially you, Joe. This is business. For your own good. Understand? You're earning money and we'll be needing that money to buy feed for your greedy belly before the winter's done. You know well as I do it's going to be a tough one. What'd you grow that longer thicker coat for if it isn't? No tricks. Your men get lost today you bring them back. Not to our place. Back right here. Understand?"

I guess he noticed the horses looking past him at us because he turned around.

"Quit worrying, Carr," Peyton said. "Predators like me don't get lost."

"Don't talk foolish, boy," Carr said. "No skin off a man's pride to get lost. You know well as I do any man

can do it. Especially in winter. Snow changes things
plenty. You get caught in a bad storm, can't see ten feet,
then what? Your horse brings you in. Man's way ahead of
a horse on a lot of things. Not on that."

Peyton wasn't wanting any long palaver. Peyton was
starting on a hunt, already getting the way I knew he
would be as soon as we were really out, keen, alert, concentrating on the job in hand. We just swung into the
saddles and started off. But as I said old Carr seemed to
irritate Peyton just by being around. We hadn't gone
more than about twenty feet when Peyton reined back.
"Carr," he said. "Why the devil do you talk to your horses
like that?" He changed his voice, giving it that mild drony
tone Carr used. "You know well as I do they don't understand you."

This Carr character hesitated, the one time I saw him
seem to search around for what to say. "Maybe they don't
exactly understand the words I use," he said. "But they
understand me. Maybe better'n I understand them. And
they like it. Folks like Myers here wonder why my horses
are always good horses. Just scrub mountain ponies like
the others around. But good horses. Well, I give them
something. They work for me so I try to give something
back more'n just feed."

Peyton was reining away again and rightly too. We had
more important things to do than stall around listening to
odd talk like that.

Old Carr raised his voice a bit. "And it's not just for
them I do it. For myself too."

Peyton was the one who was right on that as I knew he
would be. We didn't get lost. We didn't have to depend
on those horses to bring us in. We worked all the way up

Hart Mountain and along the top ridge some and even down the rough breaks on the other side and tied the horses and went plenty more miles in and about on foot and we knew where we were every minute. We made it straight back to the horses without any wandering around. It was working back down Hart that Peyton got his buck, a shot from the saddle off through thick timber that dropped that deer after one jump. Peyton dressed it out quick and neat and not the least bit messy. Then we didn't just hang it and ride on in and send someone the long way out with a packhorse for that deer. We tied it tight over the saddle on my horse and we took turns the long way in, one hiking and one riding Peyton's horse and switch about. I'll say this: those were good horses. We didn't have any trouble with them at all.

Peyton felt good that evening and rightly too. This Carr character was in his place on the hearth, just a quiet odd-shaped and odd-thinking bump there, and I guess Peyton couldn't help going after him again.

"Carr," Peyton said. "Speaking as one kind of predator by your definition which I'm not sure I accept to another kind of predator which you admit being, I'm curious. Last night you started to tell how you figure about deer and I take it about elk and turkey and no doubt any other kind of game and then you got steered off sideways. I'm curious about that figuring."

"Nothing much," old Carr said. Maybe Myers had got hold of him and told him to take these things easy. "I just don't figure on adding to the general competition is all."

"Competition?" Peyton said. "Do you mean competition with hunters like me? Do you mean you've kidded yourself into thinking you ought to be what you regard as noble enough to stand aside so there'll be more chance for me and other hunters? That's ridiculous. The law allows you one deer. One deer isn't going to make much difference."

"It makes one deer difference," old Carr said.

"So it does," Peyton said. I could feel that little underneath edge slipping into his tone and I knew by the way his eyes tightened a bit at the corners he was trying to hold it down. "But don't expect me to be grateful. A dyed-in-the-wool predator like me, again by your definition which I don't accept, is ready to take his chance in any competition. He's not asking for any nobility from you."

That did it. That pulled out the cork again. "Being noble," old Carr said, mild, patient, explaining a lesson again. "That's your word. I didn't use it. Just being a bit fair is all I mean. Fair from my way of thinking. I said general competition and I meant general. Including other predators like wolves and coyotes and mountain lions and such, in this country mostly lions I expect, who don't have much else of anything to turn to the way men have when deer and other game get scarce. Look at it from their side they've been pushed around plenty. Men get so blamed greedy, want all the deer for themselves, they hire rangers and such to go around shooting lions to cut down the competition. Get to like talking like those lions, just because they want to keep on eating and living, are mean slinking cruel sneaking cowardly critters for doing only what those men are doing too. Men make laws about hunting. What for? To protect deer and other game, so they say. Protect them enough so they can keep on making a few more to be killed. And protect them against what? Mostly against men themselves. Lions been killing deer a long time and always more deer around. Men get to killing them and without those laws a year or two and there'd

be no more deer. Lions been in these mountains long before any men. Look at it right you can call deer their cattle. They don't organize their cattle business because they
don't need to. Don't put up fences, go around knocking
off competition, making laws how many deer can be killed
and such. Don't need to. Nature keeps a balance and they
leave it at that. Along come men strutting and thinking
the whole dadburned universe was made just for them to
kick around. Times are I get to kind of dozing and thinking and half dreaming, silly maybe but some sense in it,
and I see those lions up on a mountain top somewhere
holding a meeting. Those dadburned two-legged predators, they say, are getting too thick around here with their
slinky sneaky cowardly ways, killing off our cattle. Don't
even go up and wrassle the things down and do nice clean
brave killing. Have some kind of cowardly contraption
that messes up a deer while still a long ways off. So they,
that's those lions, pick a few of themselves that have good
claws and husky jaws and say to those, we'll keep you supplied with meat which'd be their way of giving pay and
you put in all your time hunting down and knocking off all
you can find of those dadburned two-legged predators that
are killing our cattle. Don't go getting queasy about it,
they say. Those things are outlaws, taking what's ours and
been ours long as there's been any of our race around, and
being hoggish about it too, wanting to take all."

This Carr character had Peyton stopped. Peyton's eye
corners were mighty tight and I knew there were plenty
of things he wanted to say. A man like Peyton could see
right away talk like that was just silly sentimental at bottom and about so full of holes a sieve would be watertight
by comparison. I guess Peyton was realizing there was no
sense trying to get anywhere with an old oddity like that.

Carr was stretching up to his feet anyway. "They don't do that, of course," he said. "Those lions. They don't think that way. Can't think that way. Not civilized enough. But I get to thinking that way for them and got plenty beef in my belly I just figure I'll stay away from the competition."

He jammed that hopeless old hat on his head and the only way you could tell he had worked himself up some was that he jammed it on backwards and he went spraddle-toed to the door and on out. But he left a funny feeling in the air. Nothing definite, just a little uncomfortableness around the edges of the big room. I guess Myers felt that. He grinned. "Old Enos tells that one mighty well," he said. "But there's a wrinkle that occurs to me he ought to add. Ought to have those lions of his round up a passel of wolves or coyotes to use as a hunting pack getting after the two-legged predators. Reckon I'll have to try that on Enos next time."

There were chuckles around the room and I guess it was worth listening to an old oddity ramble on just to have the following, a chance to see a man like Myers operating, big and solid and sensible, big enough and not just in size to tolerate and joke along with and even stand up for a touched-head old neighbor like that.

Next morning when we went out the horses were there and this Carr with them. But he saw us coming and he just waved at us and pointed to the horses and went off towards the barn. I got my deer that day and we packed it in the same as before. And that evening he wasn't squatting there on the hearth and didn't come in to squat there. Peyton kept looking at the spot and finally Myers said: "Enos went back over to his place for the night. Likes to check every few days to see everything's all right."

The talk drifted around the way it does and then Peyton said: "What's the story, Myers? Did he just grow that way or did something happen?"

Myers knew who he meant all right. Myers settled back some and stretched out his legs and put one booted foot on top the other, heel on toe, and looked at the top toe-point. "Both," he said. "Enos grew that way though I don't know too much about that and then something happened. Leastways I think what happened had plenty to do with it. He was already up in these hills when my dad came in here homesteading. Already known as a character when I was a sprout and first noticing things. Couldn't have been much more'n in his thirties then but looked about exact as now. He'd had a wife though likely that's hard to believe and maybe her dying with a still birth did something to him. Talks plenty about damn near anything but not a word all the years about that which likely means it cut clear down to the quick. Took to making pets of all kinds of animals. You can figure how that'd appeal to a kid so I was over at his place a lot. Got to know him mighty well. Best man with a gun I ever knew though mostly just peppering at marks. I wouldn't be surprised, Peyton, if he could still take that old Enfield hanging over his fireplace and get you mighty worried slapping slugs right alongside yours from the fanciest latest custom-made you have. But even then he was just hunting in the lean years when he really needed the meat. Said he didn't see much sense in showing anybody even himself what he could do when he knew already damn well what he could do. But that's getting off the mark. It was those pets, one of them, that made what happened happen. And damn it, I've never quit damning it, it was me had to be the one to do it. Had my size then and my dad was dead and I was running this ranch and likely biggity about it and we had sheep as well as cattle up in here in those days and we formed a sort of stockmen's association and I was a big talker forming it and the neighbors made me president of it that year."

Myers raised his top foot carefully and set it down beside the other. He wouldn't look at anybody, just into the fire. "Well," he said, "it was a coyote. A damned little coyote. Enos got it when a squirming little pup, I never knew just how, and a part-collie sheepdog bitch he had suckled it for him. Cute little critter, no doubt about that. And smart. Got to be fair-sized, big as any collie, and with the good food he was giving it regular furred out mighty nice. Yes, as nice-looking a doglike critter as you could find anywhere. Trouble was Enos treated it like one. Like a dog. Trained it like one. Gave it the run of his place like that collie. Maybe you think I'm stretching this but wasn't long before he had that coyote bringing in his one old milk cow morning and evening. You'll be thinking I'm stretching it more when I say he had that coyote helping him handle his sheep. It had that collie to kind of copy but it caught on fast and before long that collie was loafing with that damn coyote doing the work."

Myers was quiet a minute or two, looking at the fire. Nobody else said a word. That's one thing about sitting around a fire up in the mountains in hunting season. A man starts telling a story, you let him tell it and in his own way.

"Well, now," Myers said, "there's no need explaining what came of that. Coyote's a coyote, not a dog. Even at that there's dogs get to acting like coyotes now and again. First notice was when deSilva down the valley, he's not around any more, lost some chickens. Coyote sign around. Then Skinner found a dead lamb and a few days later an-

other. Things like that scattered along over a month or
two and talk was passing around. Folks came to me because I was president of the association. Knew how they
felt because I'd lost a calf myself. Weren't thinking much
of Enos's pet at first because it was so damned dog-like and
there were still wild ones roaming through here. Still a
few even now. Maybe always will be. Anyhow, folks were
saying I ought to be doing something, putting out poison,
getting a ranger up in here, something like that. Then
deSilva, he was raising some turkeys, tipped it. Was worried about those turkeys. Put some traps about. Came to
me one morning collecting neighbors along the way.
Had found a trap sprung and a couple of toes, claw pads
that is, in it. Coyote. Had followed the trail a ways by
blood drips and seen where it was heading."

Myers lifted the same foot again and set it on top the
other and looked down along his legs at it. "No need explaining what had to be done. Three of us went over to
Enos's place. Told him we figured his coyote was one of
them, maybe the one. He wouldn't believe it. Hard as
hell for a man, any man, to believe that about one of his
own. Asked him had that pet come home limping, shy a
couple of toes. Not that he knew of. Where was it? He
whistled and called and there was a shuffling under the
porch on his place and that damned coyote crawled out,
limping. It was like someone had hit old Enos on the
head with a club. He knew, just like that. And that
damned coyote knew too. It slunk right back, snaking on
its belly under that porch again. No sense letting a situation like that go on getting sour and bitter so I asked Enos
was he going to shoot it or did he want us to do that for
him. He just looked at me kind of blank and went inside
his place and came out with the old snap-top purse he kept

hid in there somewhere. Wanted to know what damage we figured had been done so he could make it good."

Myers reached up one hand and ran it fingers-spread through the thick shock of hair he had and let it drop. He still wouldn't look at any of us, just at that boot toe. "No need explaining why that wouldn't do," he said. "Money damages don't come into a thing like that. Not with neighbors that know each other and pull each other out of holes now and again when pulling's needed. Wasn't a one of us would've touched a cent of old Enos's money on a thing like that. But when a dog takes to killing stock there's only one recipe for it and that's killing the dog. That's been the rule long as men have had dogs which I expect goes way back to when they were living in caves and first learning to fuss some with sheep and cattle. And this thing wasn't even a dog. Just a damned coyote hc'd been trying to make act like a dog. Tried to make him see it that way. And that's when he got excited. Hard to believe now I expect but Enos could get excited in those days. Not just talk but get going like a blamed preacher at a revival. Kept saying that damned coyote wasn't to blame, it was all his fault. Kept saying he'd taught it not to touch anything around his place but'd been too stupid to realize it wouldn't know that applied to other people's places too. Kept saying it oughtn't have to pay for his stupidity."

Myers raised his head a bit and looked around at all of us, then back at that boot toe. "Yes," he said. "You all know how it is. A man has to do something he has to do it. Letting that thing live wouldn't be fair to the association I was president of. Wouldn't be fair to old Enos himself. People'd be getting bitter about him. Anybody lose anything and right or wrong he'd be getting the blame.

Way he was carrying on I wasn't sure what he might do so I motioned the other two with me to grab hold. Which they did, one on each arm. I took my rifle out of the saddle scabbard and looked under that porch. Couldn't see much except the eyes and the teeth showing in a kind of snarl. Aimed smack between those eyes and that was that."

Myers stopped talking. Nobody said anything. It was Peyton who finally spoke, just two words. "And Carr?" he said.

"Oh, he didn't do anything," Myers said. "When the others let go just stood there a while. Acted like we weren't even around. Went over to a shed he had and got a shovel. He was digging a hole out in the little orchard he had when we rode off. I hung on the ridge top a while where I could see his place. When he finished his burying he just went inside and shut the door. That was the last I saw of him, anybody saw of him, for quite a stretch. Just stayed to himself and nobody figured on pushing in. Then we had a big rain on up in the hills and the creek rose clean up in my meadows out the side here and carried away some fence and some of my best steers I was grain feeding took off. Figured to fix that fence before I went scouting. Was working on it when along came Enos on one of those ponies of his bringing in my stock. Swung down and helped finish that fence. Same old Enos. Only quiet, talking the way he has ever since, you know how, mild, kind of patient, like a teacher explaining things to kids. Aggravating, I expect, till you get used to it. Never said a word about what happened. Never has."

Myers straightened up some and looked around. "I've shot that damned coyote a hundred times," he said. "Lying awake at night and thinking. I did right. I'd do it again today. And tomorrow. And the day after. All the same, anytime old Enos gets to blowing his offside notions around my place he's going to blow and nobody's going to stop him. Except maybe me. And I don't have to. He stops himself."

Next morning Peyton and I were pulling out. Myers let us have the jeep to take our deer down to the little town where we'd left our car. We could tote them on the fenders from there. He had someone coming in later who would bring the jeep back. We were packed and ready to leave when we saw this Carr character back again and down by the barn. He could stay there as far as I was concerned. We had heard him talk and odd as it was once you caught the hang of it, if you wanted, you could spin out that kind of stuff by the yard yourself. We had his story, what there was of it, and it was interesting enough as stories about oddities can be but it was also really about Myers as much as old Carr and Myers had put a nice finish to it and there wasn't much sense in adding any more. But Peyton wasn't satisfied. That character rubbed him wrong just by being in sight. Peyton was driving and he swung the jeep down by the barn and stopped it.

"Carr," he said. "What the devil are you aiming at in your talk? Where the devil does that cockeyed thinking of yours lead you?" He was keeping this light the way he would, even taking Carr's own label for him to hold it friendly. "To the notion that all we two-legged predators ought to resign from the competition and let the lions take over?"

You couldn't catch this character off balance. He always had words ready. I guess he spent his time at his own place, when he wasn't reading his dictionary, just sitting around thinking up answers to anything anyone might ask him. "No," he said, mild, patient, aggravating the way Myers had mentioned. "I don't go laying down rules for other people. Just for myself. Anyway, men and lions been competing as long as both have been around this old world. Just plain natural for both." He stopped, hunching that decrepit old jacket up around his neck against the morning cold.

"Go on," Peyton said. "I know damn well you don't stop there."

"Well," this Carr said. "Look at it this way. We're men. Me, you, everybody. All tarred with the same stick. It's our brand and we wear it. Mighty nice too, in a way, being men. Top dogs of creation or so it seems. Being predators is our nature just like with about all living things. It's the way things are. Even deer eat grass and leaves and such and those have life too. It's the way things are. No sense trying not to be predators because that'd be unnatural and about impossible anyway. We're animals like I say. But we're thinking animals and that makes a mite of difference. We can think about what we do. Don't often, but can. Lions and the others can't. Not in the same way. And that kind of puts an obligation on us. Seems to me we, all of us, myself anyway, ought to realize other animals have living problems too, have their places too in the over-all mixed-up scheme of things we're sitting on top of. Seems to me it makes things a mite better if we just mix a little something more than just being proud to be men and taking for granted the whole dadburned universe is made special for us in with our thinking."

He stopped again. I could see Peyton's eye corners tightening and I was hoping Peyton would slip the clutch and we'd be rolling.

"Go on," Peyton said. "What the devil would you want to mix in?"

"That's hard to put," Carr said. "Maybe the right word's not been thought up yet. I've looked through my dictionary plenty times and can't find it. Best one there comes close but still misses some."

"All right," Peyton said but I knew by his tone this wasn't right with him at all. "What's that word?"

"Humility," Carr said. "Seems to me it makes things better to put a bit of that in with being a man."

I was afraid there for a moment that Peyton was going to let his irritation at a sermonizing platitude like that bust right out. But he didn't. Not Peyton. He just let the clutch out with a snap and swung the wheel and we sliced around and over to the road. We headed down the long curving slopes with the jeep slugging hard in low in the deeper snow ruts and I noticed he was gripping the wheel hard and his eye corners were crinkled tight. I tried a couple of times to start him talking and he wouldn't say a word. I was beginning to get peeved at this Carr character for irritating a man like Peyton and maybe spoiling the finish of our hunting trip together.

We worked on down. Then Peyton kind of shook himself. "There's plenty of time," he said. "After we get the car let's swing around by the turnpike. There's a fellow along there I know who has a new rifle Fanzoi made for him over in Austria he wants me to see."

He sat up straighter behind the wheel. "There's a man for you. Josef Fanzoi. Lives in a little village called Ferlach. Did you ever hear about that place? More gunsmiths and the best there are than any place else in the world. They start them in as kids. Even have a damn fine school just for that . . ."

I sat back listening to Peyton talk about what he knew as well as any man alive, about guns and those who make them, and watching him drive that jeep the way he did whatever he ever tackled, easy and sure and efficient. Everything was all right again.

The Coup of Long Lance

*

THIS WAS a large camp, a late-spring hunting camp, more than forty lodges, set in a broad bottom by a river. The lodges stood in a wide circle with a gap, an entrance-way into the central open area, at the east to face the rising sun. They were arranged, clockwise around the circle from the entranceway, in the customary order of the ten divisions or clans of the tribe. Always a Cheyenne camp of any size was made thus, even the great bustling camp of the midsummer Medicine Lodge ceremony when all the people of all the villages and camps within traveling distance gathered for eight days of feasting and dancing and careful ritual in honor of the annual rebirth of the spring now accomplished again, the re-creation of the earth and of life upon it.

This was a large camp. It slept, close to the earth in its hollow, under the moonless star-touched night of the high plains of the heartland of North America. And out across the rolling plains, scattered in small herds across the endless plains, the buffalo too were bedded down for the night in their own vast slow migration northwestward into the late-spring winds bringing their subtle sensed message of the renewing grasses.

The first faint glow of dawn crept up the eastern sky.

Across from it, in the western arc of the camp circle where stood the lodges of the *Hev-a-tan-iu,* the Rope Men who used ropes of twisted hair instead of the usual rawhide, the aging warrior Strong Left Hand stirred on his couch. He turned his head. The door flap of the lodge had been swung wide, letting in the rising light. In the center of the lodge by the hollowed-out fireplace his wife, Straight Willow, knelt by a small pile of twigs with her fire sticks in her hands. There was a woman. A true Cheyenne woman. The mother of tall grown sons, with work-gnarled hands and deepening lines in her face, yet still strong and supple and independent, firm mistress of the lodge and its place in the camp. Always he woke with the first light of dawn and always she was awake before him, tending to her woman's duty, her woman's privilege, of lighting the lodge fire. It was no longer crowded in the lodge now that the three sons, the two real sons and the foster son, were married and living with their wives' clans as was proper, because descent and clan always passed to children through the mothers. But it was never lonely, would never be lonely, in a lodge shared with Straight Willow.

He spoke to her, using one of the silly names out of their long-ago early years together, and without looking up she called him a lazy lie-abed as she always did. He chuckled, filling the lodge with good feeling, and rose with the couch robe held about him and stepped past her and out into the morning air. Ah, it was good, fresh and clean the air, and rich color was climbing the eastern sky. Already smoke was coming from other lodges too. Men and boys were emerging from them and heading for the river for the morning plunge that all male Cheyennes took when near water, the hardiest all through the year, even when thick ice had to be broken.

Behind him Straight Willow put larger twigs on the fire and picked up her two buckets of bullhide. She brushed past him and joined other women on their way upstream, above the swimmers, where they would dip fresh water. No Cheyenne woman, when she could avoid it, used dead water, water that had stood all night.

That was Bull Hump beckoning to him, a wide grin on his face. Bull Hump's middle daughter had been married yesterday. He was coming from her new husband's new lodge and she was in front of it, waving him on. Bull Hump spoke quickly. The young men who had visited his new son-in-law last night and feasted late and stayed in the lodge all night, according to custom, to be there to eat the new bride's first breakfast as a wife, were still asleep. They were true lazy lie-abeds. Here was a chance for some sport in the old way. But it must be a man who had counted many coups. A man like Strong Left Hand.

Strong Left Hand stepped into his lodge and dropped the robe on his couch. He came out, clad only in his manhood string around his waist with the breechclout suspended from it. He hurried towards the new lodge of Bull Hump's new son-in-law, picking up a long stout stick. He stood just outside the entrance and his voice rolled out, deep and strong, telling a coup, short and quick so the young men would not have time to get past him.

"It is Strong Left Hand who speaks. Traveling by the yellow river I met a man of the Crows on a good horse. He fled. I came up by him and pushed aside his lance and knocked him to the ground and took his horse."

The young men were awake now. They knew what to expect. Like rabbits out of a burrow they ran headlong through the entrance and Strong Left Hand thwacked each a stinging blow with the stick. They ran, scattering, towards the river and he ran after them, thwacking those he could reach until they plunged into the water, shouting and pretending to be hurt mightily. Strong Left Hand stood on the bank laughing. It was not all pretending on their part. He was not so old after all. He had given them some good thwacks and kept up with them in the running. He tossed the stick aside and waded into the water and dived under and came up spouting. The young men splashed water at him and called out cheerful morning greetings to him and moved out of the way in the instinctive Cheyenne custom, invincible through life, of deference to one older.

When he returned to his lodge to put on his leggings and shirt and get fresh pine gum to hold his hair in a dozen bunches hanging down his back, Straight Willow had food cooking over the fire. There was no need to tell her of the thwacking. He knew by the way she looked up at him sidewise, her eyes bright, that she knew. It was amazing how every woman in the camp always seemed to know almost everything as soon as it happened. And he knew she liked him to be doing things like that. She was strong on the old customs, stronger on them, as women usually were, than he was. She was of the *Suhtai* clan and even now she wore her dress longer than most women and dipping on the right side and still wore her hair in braids with little deerskin and sweet sage ornaments bunched on the back of her head, not in the new fashion of doubling them up in two humps, one on each side.

He left her with her cooking and went out beyond the camp circle where the other men were gathering, waiting for the boys who had gone to round up the horses. Only a few horses, the most valuable, were kept in the camp at night, tied by their owners' lodges. The rest were out over the rolling ridges where the grass was good.

The horses came trotting over the last rise before the camp, the boys behind them. Strong Left Hand's eyes swept over them with the keen almost unthinking glance of the Plains Indian who, once having seen a horse clearly, could know it unerringly any time, any place. There were his six horses. Yesterday morning he had had eight horses. But Bull Hump was his cousin and yesterday Bull Hump's daughter had been married and it had simply been right that Strong Left Hand should add two horses to the presents Bull Hump was giving to the bridegroom's family. There too were his wife's twelve horses. She was very proud of them, perhaps too proud. She was the richest woman in horses in the camp. She was also the best robe maker. But that was different. She made them to give as presents. She liked to think that newly married couples slept under her robes. She was not like that with her horses.

Strong Left Hand caught the horses with the one glance but he did not say so to the boy coming towards him, his nephew, the son of his brother, Owl Friend. This was the boy who herded for him now that his own sons were grown. It was good for the boy to feel important.

"Are they all here, little one?"

"Every one, my uncle."

"Is any one of them lame?"

"The black one with the two white spots limped a little. It was only a stone in the hoof. I took it out."

"You took it out? He stood for you?"

"Yes, my uncle."

"You will be a brave man with horses, little stone picker."

A meadow lark, startled by the many hoofs disturbing the grasses, rose out of them to the left and swooped, trilling, up into the glowing color of the rising sun, and the heart of Strong Left Hand leaped within him. So it had been long ago, in his youth, in the time of his starving on a hill for his dreaming, and in the dawn of the third day a meadow lark had risen trilling into the rising sun and he had a vision, a vision of himself with hair thin and gray, and he had known that he would live to be an old man and count many coups. And always, after that, when a meadow lark had risen thus from near his feet, trilling for him and the morning, the day had been a good day for him. The clean sweet air of this morning was like a strong drink.

"Little lifter of horses' feet, listen to your uncle. You will tie the gray horse that is quick and fast and the spotted one that is thick and strong by my lodge. We hunt today. The others go back with the herd. You will take good care of the black one because from this moment forward he is yours. Remember what I say. You will do with him as your father tells you. Now run."

The boy ran, leaping like a grasshopper, frantic in his hurry to tell the other boys, and Strong Left Hand turned back towards his lodge remembering when his uncle, who had given him his name, had also given him his first horse and he, too, had run leaping like a grasshopper. And now he was a man and a warrior with tall grown sons and he was a giver of horses to eager young nephews and the life cycle, endlessly repeating, moved on and it was all good, all of it, the youngness and the manhood and the drawing on towards old age, for still the meadow lark rose trilling into the sun of the morning to tell him it was good.

Back at the lodge the food was ready. Straight Willow took a small piece from the kettle of boiled Indian turnips and a small piece from the other kettle of stewed meat and each in turn she held high towards the sky, an offering to *Heammawihio,* the Wise One Above, then laid it on the ground by the fire. There the pieces would remain until she swept out the lodge. Once offered, they were as consumed, no longer really there. She scooped more of the food into two wooden bowls. She and Strong Left Hand sat cross-legged by the fire, eating with the ornamented spoons he had made of the horns of the first buffalo he had killed after their marriage. They talked quietly and between talkings they listened. The old crier was making his round, riding along the inside of the camp circle, calling out the news.

The chiefs (one of the tribe's four head chiefs and three of the forty council chiefs, four from each of the ten clans, were with this hunting camp) had said the camp would not be moved for many days . . . The Kit Fox Soldiers would have a social dance that night . . . All men should remember what had been told yesterday, that there would be a hunt today . . . Word had come from Yellow Moon's camp, two days eastward, that Big Knee, chief of the Red Shields, the Bull Soldiers, had pledged to be this year's Medicine Lodge maker and the celebration would be in the first days of the *Hivi-uts-i-i-shi* moon (July, the buffalo bull rutting month) when the grasses would be long and the leaves of the cottonwoods in full growth . . .

Big Knee? Ah, there was a man. He and Strong Left Hand had been boys together. They were both Bull Soldiers now, Red Shield carriers. Not many men could say that. A man could not just join the Bull Soldier band; he had to be mature and seasoned and be chosen for it. Strong Left Hand had helped persuade Big Knee to take the present term of leadership. Did Straight Willow recall the time that he and Big Knee . . .

What was the old crier saying? The Dog Soldiers in

the camp had challenged the Bull Soldiers to a coup-telling competition that night. They were foolish; good young men, but foolish. Perhaps they thought they could win because there were more of them in the camp. They would find out. The Bull Soldiers were fewer but they were real warriors, with age and experience on them. Anyone could know that from the many red coup stripes on their wives' arms at the ceremonial dances.

Ah, this competition would be a fine thing. Strong Left Hand was full of talk. Their youngest son, Long Lance, would have a chance to tell his first coup. He was a Dog Soldier. Four days ago he had returned with the others who had gone with Many Feathers, chief of the Dog Soldiers, raiding the Crows to the north. They had gone on foot, as they had pledged to do, and they returned on horses, herding others, and they carried two scalps — but there had been no scalp dance and telling of coups, because one of them had been killed by the Crows. Long Lance could claim a coup, but he had not spoken of it, because a true Cheyenne did not go about speaking big words about his deeds; only in telling a coup did he speak of them and then he simply stated the facts. It was for others to tell what he had done in many fine words. And the others had told what Long Lance had done.

They had found a Crow camp. In the first light of morning they had crept close and started the herd of Crow horses moving away and each caught a horse and mounted and they were slipping away fast when someone, perhaps a guard hidden where they had not seen, gave an alarm and many Crow warriors, on horses kept in the camp, came after them. The chase was long and the Crows were gaining and the young Cheyennes turned, few against many and proud it was so, and charged in the swift sweeping charge their enemies knew so well, and the Crows, close now, slowed and wavered, and the Cheyennes were among them, striking and scattering them. Many Feathers was in the lead, as was right, and an arrow struck him in the shoulder and he fell from his horse, and a Crow, a brave one that Crow, swung down from his own horse and ran towards Many Feathers swinging his war club. And Long Lance, rushing up from behind Many Feathers in the charge, almost past, too far past to turn his horse in time, leaped from its back and struck bodily against the Crow and sent him sprawling. The Crow scrambled to his feet and ran and another Crow swung back and took him up behind on his horse and all the Crows were scattering and riding off except two who would ride no more. Many Feathers, not minding his wound, was on his feet and shouting to his men to come back from the chasing because the horses were stampeding. It was when the horses, most of them, were gathered and quieted and moving along together again that they saw that one of their own men was missing. Many Feathers chose Long Lance to ride back with him and they found the body. They laid it in a low hidden place with head towards the east so that the spirit, hovering near, would find the spirit trail where all footprints point the same way. They left it there because it was right that the body of a man killed in battle far from his home village should become food for the birds and the animals of the plains who would scatter his bones across the earth from which all that he now was, with the spirit gone, had originally come. Then they saw the Crows, gathered together again, coming again, and they hurried to join the others and all chose fresh horses from the herd and pushed on fast. The Crows, with no fresh horses, not eager for another Cheyenne charge, followed until late afternoon, dropping back more all the time, and then were seen no more.

Strong Left Hand was full of words, talking about their son. Straight Willow said little and then she stopped him, raising her hand. "We are happy for him. Why is he not happy too? Look."

Strong Left Hand looked out through the lodge doorway. Over in the eastern arc of the camp circle where were the lodges of the *O-missis*, the Eaters, so known because they were always good hunters and well supplied with food, his youngest son sat on the ground before his still new lodge. His hunting weapons were beside him and his hunting horses were close by and he sat with his arms resting on his knees and his head sunk low. A sadness was on him.

Strong Left Hand set aside his bowl and rose. At sight of his son in sadness a shadow seemed to be over him fighting with the clean light of the morning. He spoke to Straight Willow. "Perhaps there is trouble with him and his wife. They are still new together. Perhaps you can be close to her today and she will speak to you." He drove the shadowing away from his mind. It was time for the hunting. He took his stout bow made of the horns of the mountain sheep, the bow that few other men could bend, and his quiver with twenty good arrows, arrows he had made from well-grained red willow shoots tipped with edged bone heads and firmly feathered. He took his hair-rope hackamore and the single pad he used for a hunting saddle and went out to his horses.

The whole camp was abustle now. The hunters were gathering. Women and older girls were starting off with digging sticks to find the white potato roots that grew on some of the slopesides. Other women were following the path downstream where a stand of cottonwoods beckoned them to gather wood. Already small children were assembling around two of the old men who would teach them stories of the old days and of the old ways of the tribe. Older boys were splashing across the river at the ford, holding their small bows above the water, bound for the marshy land beyond where they would practice shooting wild fowl and perhaps bring in food.

Straight Willow came out of the lodge, her sewing things in her hand, the bone awl for punching holes in tanned hides and a handful of threads, separate strands plucked from the big sinew that follows along the spine of the buffalo. Her sewing guild was meeting to help one of the women make a new lodge. She saw Strong Left Hand swinging up on the spotted horse in the Indian way, from the off side. "Perhaps you will bring me an untorn bull's hide. It is in my mind to make a heavy robe." He looked at her and he knew that she meant that his arrows should sing true and that he should come back to her unharmed, and in his mind he pledged to her the biggest bull of the day's hunting. He rode off, leading the gray horse, and was one with the hunters, all the able-bodied men of the camp, moving out across the plains.

They talked and laughed as they rode, for they were Cheyennes, a gay and talkative people, but not too much now because this was not sport, like fighting, this was the most important work of men, the obtaining of food and of materials for clothes and lodges and the necessary articles of daily life. On the success of the hunting during these good days would depend the welfare of the tribe during the long snowbound months of winter.

Strong Left Hand rode up close by his youngest son, should he wish to speak. He would not press him, for a grown Cheyenne did not interfere with the thoughts and visions of another. He spoke of such things only when that other wished to speak of them and seek counsel. But now his son rode straight ahead, silent and stern.

The hunters rode on, far out across the plains, and then Many Feathers, in charge for this day, stopped and gave his orders. Scouts had reported a herd of buffalo over the next rolling rise. Quietly they changed to their hunting horses and left the heavier burden bearers in the keeping of a young man. In small groups, as Many Feathers directed, they slipped away to come on the herd from all sides.

Silence held over the plain under the climbing sun and the endlessly moving wind, broken only by the rustling of the buffalo in the grasses and their occasional small snorts and belchings. Suddenly from the far side a shouting rose and Many Feathers and his group rushed over the last rise between them and the buffalo, and the buffalo snorted loud, facing towards this disturbance, heads up, and then they turned and ran, slow at first, then galloping in their seemingly awkward gait that could outdistance all but the best horses. Ahead of them, shouting and waving, rose another group of mounted men, pounding towards them, and they swerved to the side, and ahead was another group. The buffalo snorted and galloped, tails stiffening upright in terror, and always a group of shouting men on horses was in front of them. And now they were running in a big circle, milling around it in the frantic feeling that because they were running they were escaping.

Many Feathers raised his bow high and waved it and the hunters began swooping in close to the milling buffalo, superb horsemen the equal of any the world had known, and their arrows sang death and mortal-wound songs in the dust-driven air. Buffalo staggered and fell and others stumbled over them and now and again a stricken animal would dash outward from the milling circle at the pounding horses, and the horses, quick and fast, would dodge and twist until an arrow struck true and the buffalo went down.

Strong Left Hand swept in close, wasting no arrows, searching always for the biggest bull. He would like to kill that one himself. Two cows and a young bull had gone down under his arrows, stopped almost in their tracks by the power of the big horn bow that few men could bend. Ah, there was strength still in his left arm, his bow-string arm, that had given him his name.

Ahead of him, hazy through the dust, he saw a horse step into an animal ground hole and its rider thrown towards the milling buffalo, and a huge old bull, bloody-frothed at the nostrils, come charging out towards the man. Another horse swooped in, its rider leaning down to pick up the fallen man, and the bull swerved and its great head drove under this horse's belly and its short thick horns ripped upward and its great neck strained and horse and rider rose into the air, the horse screaming, its legs flailing, and now two men were scrambling on the ground. Other men came swooping in, Strong Left Hand foremost among them. There was no time for full bow-draw and certain aim. His arrow struck too far forward, close by the shaggy neck, and drove in only a short way, slowed by the matted hair and thicker hide there. Yet it stopped the bull, made it pause, pawing the ground, shaking its great head. But the circle of hunters was now broken. The bull rushed through the opening, bellowing, and other buffalo followed, streaming across the plain.

Now it was the chase, the hard riding, the pounding after the fleeing buffalo, the riding alongside them and in among them. But the chase did not go far because the hunters had killed enough for one day's hunting and their arrows were nearly all gone. And back along the trail of the chase lay the huge old bull with another of Strong Left Hand's arrows driven deep into its side.

Now there was no more wild excitement, only hard drudgery, bloody work that would take much of the next day too, skinning and butchering and loading the meat on the slower, stronger horses, and the patient searching for arrows to use again. Only once was there an interruption when a warrior gave warning that he had seen a man peering over a nearby rise and Many Feathers sent two men to circle around while the rest stood ready by their horses, weapons in hand. Then the two men came back, straight over the rise, and a boy was with them leading a black horse with two white spots.

Strong Left Hand smiled to himself when he saw his nephew approaching. But Owl Friend, his brother, father of the boy, stepped forward, stern of face. "What are you doing here?"

"To see the hunt, my father."

"And to ride your new horse. I did not say you could come."

The boy looked down at the ground and suddenly Owl Friend smiled at him. "You are not much bigger than a badger, but you will be a brave hunter one day." He took the boy by the hand and led him to Many Feathers. "Here is a small man who thinks he is a hunter."

Many Feathers, too, was stern. "Is this the first hunt you have seen?"

"Yes, my chief."

"Do you know what must happen the first time?"

The boy stared at him and then Many Feathers smiled. He bent down by the carcass of a buffalo and dipped his right hand in a pool of blood there and lifted it, dripping, and smeared the blood over the boy's face. "Now you know how it feels, still warm from the life that was in it, how it smells, how it tastes. You must not wipe it from your face until you are home. Now the time is for work. Take this knife that is yours from this day forward and do as I show you, freeing the hide from the good meat."

The sun was low in the west, sending long shadows into the hollows, when the hunters returned to the camp, leading the loaded horses. As they neared it they passed many boys out on the plain playing games with sliding sticks and hoops and the boys, seeing them, ran up to race about and follow them. As they came nearer a group of older girls too was approaching the camp. They had been out digging bear roots and turnips and they carried tied bunches of them. They shouted at the hunters and raised the war cry, daring the young men to try to take their roots. Some of the young men called to boys to hold their horses and they ran towards the girls and the girls quickly dropped their roots and began gathering sticks and buffalo chips and clumps of sod and one of them took her root digger and drew a line in the ground all around them. Such a line was their fort and it could be passed only by a man who had counted a coup within enemy breastworks. The young men dashed around the line-circle, leaping and laughing and teasing and dodging the missiles thrown at them. One stepped inside and told his coup and the girls had to stand aside and let him take what roots he wanted. He scooped up several bunches and tossed them to the other young men and they all went towards their horses munching on the roots and throwing back teasing remarks at the girls. They were good young men, not too tired after the day's work for leaping and laughing. But Long Lance was not with them. He sat on his horse, stern and silent, and his head drooped.

Inside the camp circle the hunters separated to their lodges. Strong Left Hand stood his tired horses in front of his lodge and went down to the river for a thorough washing. Straight Willow came hurrying from woman-talk with a neighbor and unloaded the spotted horse. Most of the meat she put away under covering. She would be busy now, beginning tomorrow, for many weeks, cutting this meat and that from other huntings into strips and flaking it into chips to be sun-dried and smoke-cured for winter saving and the other women would be doing the same and all of them gossiping endlessly around the drying racks. Three hides were there too, Strong Left Hand's share of the day's taking, and she put these where she would peg them on the ground for scraping. Then she led the spotted horse to the river to wash away the buffalo blood and fat clinging to its short hair. She rolled up her skirt and waded into the water with the horse and then, only then, her work well in hand, she looked over the horse's back at Strong Left Hand, who was sitting for a few moments' quiet and rest in the late sun.

"It is a good, big, very big bull's hide," she said and he knew she was saying more than that. The meadow lark had trilled true, for it was a good day. And then the shadow was over him again, for he saw his youngest son, Long Lance, walking on down by the lower river, slow and with a sadness on him.

Straight Willow saw too. "His wife does not know. He has been like that since they came back with the horses. But she does not know."

Strong Left Hand went back to the lodge and took a bunch of his stored willow shoots and sat on the edge of his couch and began smoothing and shaping them for arrows while Straight Willow rebuilt the fire and began her cooking. This was one of the times he liked, the two of them together in the quiet companionship built through the long years, the good years and the bad years and all part of living. This would be one of the best of days but for that shadow in his mind.

It was a fine meal as the evening meal of a successful hunting day should be. There was much meat, and there was feasting all around the camp. Soon darkness dropped over the land and the mystic living light of the many fires lit the camp. A huge fire began to glow out in the circle where the Kit Fox Soldiers would soon be having their social dance.

Strong Left Hand took out his pipe and filled it with tobacco mixed with dried bark of the red willow. He held it by the bowl and pointed with the stem to the sky and to the earth, making his offering to the father spirit above and to the mother earth below. He pointed the stem to the four cardinal points of the compass around, making his offering to the spirits that dwell in those quarters. He took a burning stick from the fire and lit the pipe and drew in the smoke with slow satisfaction. Straight Willow sat by the fire and watched him in quiet content, for no one should move about in a lodge when the pipe was being smoked.

Music began to sound through the camp. Drumming and songs were beginning by the dance-fire. The quick lively beat of a gambling song came from a nearby lodge where some were playing the hand-hiding game. Strong Left Hand put aside his pipe and took his big red shield, his Bull Soldier shield with the buffalo head painted on it, made of the thickest bullhide with deerskin stretched over it and raven feathers around the edge. He went out and as he moved away he saw several women coming towards his lodge. He smiled to himself. Straight Willow would be having company. He went on to the big temporary lodge that had been put up during the day well out into the camp circle by the wives of the Dog Soldiers. Most of the other men were already there.

To the left inside, in a line, were the Dog Soldiers, his son, Long Lance, among them. They would give a brave account of themselves this night. There were staunch old veterans among them and two of them were men who wore black-dog ropes into battle, leather loops that passed over their shoulders and under their other arms and had ropes fastened to them with picket pins at the ends. Such a man, dismounting to fight the enemy hand to hand, must stick his pin into the ground and in the doing pledge himself not to retreat from that spot. He himself, no matter how hard-pressed, must not pull the pin loose or be dishonored forever after. Only another of his band could free him by pulling up the pin and striking him to drive him back. Such a man counted coups or died on the spot.

To the right were the Bull Soldiers, fewer in number but the same as many in experience and honors. And at the back of the lodge, behind the central fire, sat the man who would preside, as always an old man belonging to neither of the two competing bands. He was well chosen. He was Standing Elk, twice chief of the Elk Soldiers in his younger years, now one of the most honored men of the tribe. He was wise and just and he knew well how to keep a competition close and exciting in his calling for coups. And he wore the scalp shirt.

Only three men in the entire tribe wore scalp shirts.

Such a shirt could be made only by a man who had worn one. It could be worn only by a very brave man, a man who dedicated himself to his people. When he wore it, he must be the first to advance in battle, the last to retreat. If a comrade were dismounted or fell, he must dare all dangers to pick him up. He must act always as a chief should act, be above personal angers and quarrelings, not become angry even if his wife should run away or be carried away or his horses be stolen, never seek a personal vengeance. He must take care of widows and orphans, feed the hungry, help the helpless. Some men had worn the scalp shirt and given it up. Standing Elk had worn it many years and always with honor.

Strong Left Hand waited according to custom until Standing Elk pointed to the place kept for him. He went to it, passing behind the others, careful not to be so discourteous as to pass between anyone and the fire. He placed his big shield against the lodge wall behind his place and sat down before it. Two more men arrived and they were ready to begin. Standing Elk asked one of the young men to close off the entrance. He had beside him a pile of small sharpened sticks. His pipe lay on the ground before him with the bowl towards the south, the symbol of truth-telling. No true Cheyenne would speak false in its presence.

Standing Elk passed one of the pointed sticks to the first of the Dog Soldiers. "Which one of you has counted a coup on foot against an enemy on horseback?" The Dog Soldier passed the stick to the next man and it went down the line until it reached a man who could claim it. He told his coup. The stick went back to Standing Elk and he stuck it in the ground on the Dog Soldiers' side. He started another stick down the Dog Soldier line and it came back unclaimed. He passed it to the Bull Soldiers and he passed yet another before they were through with that question and they had two sticks in the ground on their side.

Standing Elk asked his questions. He was a wise old man. He knew the history of every man there and he framed his questions to give everyone a chance to speak and to keep the score close. Good feelings and memories of brave deeds done, always good in the retelling, filled the big lodge. And yet young Long Lance, in his place in the Dog Soldier line, sat silent, his head sinking lower and lower. Now everyone else had spoken at least once and much time had passed and the sticks were even on the two sides. Standing Elk looked at young Long Lance and then he looked at Strong Left Hand and his old eyes twinkled in the firelight. He looked straight ahead. "This is the last. Which one of you has leaped from a horse to count a coup against a Crow warrior by striking him with your whole body to save the life of your soldier chief?"

There was a stirring among the Dog Soldiers and a chuckling and they passed the stick quickly and the one beside Long Lance thrust it into his hand. Long Lance held it, but he could not speak. And suddenly he raised his head high and spoke with the strongest truth-telling pledge a Cheyenne could give. "I say this to the Medicine Arrows. I did not do it. I did not know Many Feathers was down. I did not see the Crow warrior. The thong in my horse's mouth had broken and I was leaning forward to grasp his nose and guide him. He stumbled and threw me and I struck against the Crow. It was not my doing." And Long Lance tossed the stick into the fire and his head dropped again.

The heart of Strong Left Hand was big within him.

There was no shadow over him even in the dim darkness of the big lodge above him. His son was a brave man, brave enough not to grasp a false bravery. But it was not for him to speak. That was for Standing Elk. The silence in the lodge held, waiting.

And Standing Elk, his old eyes twinkling even more than before, picked up another stick. "Which one of you has counted a coup because he had a horse that knew when to stumble and throw him against an enemy?" And the laughter in the lodge, the good feeling sweeping through it, seemed enough to lift it into the air. The stick passed down the line and young Long Lance held it and he raised his head, his face shining in the firelight, and spoke: "I claim it as a coup only for this night so that the Red Shields must provide a feast for my brother soldiers. From this time forward I give it to Many Feathers as a laughing story to tell."

The camp was quieting, most of the lodges were dark, only embers remained of the dance-fire, when Strong Left Hand entered his own lodge again. In the dark he heard the soft regular breathing of Straight Willow on her couch. He put away his shield and squatted on his heels by her couch to tell her of their son, and because he wanted to and she wanted him to, he told it to her again.

He rose and stood tall. There was no sleeping in him yet a while. Quietly he left the lodge and walked through the outer star-touched darkness, out of the camp circle, up to the top of the first rolling rise. Behind him, in the camp, the only firelight remaining shone faintly through the entrance of the lodge where the gambling game was still being played. Always there were a few men who would keep at that until they had nothing left to stake on the next chance. They played with whispers now that would not disurb other lodges. The only sound drifting to him from the camp except the occasional muffled shifting of horses' hoofs or stirring of a dog in its sleep was the faint trembling flute song of a lover serenading his sweetheart somewhere on the far side of the circle. And even this was not a real sound but a sweet lingering pulsing of the silence.

He stood on the rise and stretched his arms upward and from him flowed a wordless prayer of thanking to the meadow lark of the morning of a good day and through this to the Great Mystery of which it was for him his personal symbol. He sat on the ground and the small night breezes moved through the grasses and the clean sweet dark was around him and in him and he was a part of the earth beneath and the sky above and the web of life they nurtured and it was good.

Why should the thought of old Standing Elk come into his mind at this moment? Ah, there was a man. A tribe needed men like that. They were an example to the young men, even to older men who had grown sons. Strong Left Hand rose and walked quietly back to his lodge. He took off his shirt and leggings and moccasins and lay on his couch. He spoke softly: "O my wife."

He heard her shift a little on her couch. "What is it, my husband?"

"In the morning I will carry the pipe to Standing Elk. I will keep my gray horse and my spotted horse for the hunting and take my other three horses and a quiver of arrows to him as an offering. I will ask him to make me a scalp shirt."

There was silence in the lodge. Strong Left Hand sighed gently to himself. It would be hard on her, it would mean more work and a harder time for her, too, when he wore the shirt. He heard her shifting on her couch again. "O my husband. Standing Elk is a great one of the tribe. There should be more. You will take half of my horses too. We will have need of the others when you wear the shirt."

Strong Left Hand breathed in so deeply that he felt as if his lungs would burst. A meadow lark sang in his heart. "O my wife. You are far away from me there on your couch. I feel young again tonight."

He heard her moving to throw off her robe covering and come to him. Her voice was low with a small chuckle in it. "When her man feels young towards her, a woman is young again too."

Salt of the Earth

*

OLD CLYDE FOSKINS finished milking the one old cow and turned her out into the poled pasture behind the barn where a few clumps of winter-cured grass remained. He tilted the milk from the pail through a strainer into another pail. He carried this out and to the well and pulled on a cord hanging down into the shadowy depth until a large glass mason jar rose dripping from the water. Carefully he unscrewed the top and filled the jar from the pail. Carefully he screwed the top tight again and lowered the jar into the water. He stared down after it, sniffling some through his limp mustache. "Beats any icebox," he said. "Keeps it cold in summer. Keeps it from freezing in winter."

He picked up the pail and went to the pigpen beside the barn and poured the rest of the milk into the tin-lined trough there. He watched the old boar and two unwieldy sows jostle each other for position. "Funny way of doing," he said. "Take it out of one critter and put it right back into some others." He carried the empty pail into the barn and hung it with the other on their regular nails in an overhead beam. He stood peering about the dim interior wrinkling his nose. "Kind of sour. Needs an airing." He pushed and heaved at the wide old main doors and the hangers squealed on the track above and the doors moved and the morning sunlight streamed through the opening.

Old Clyde Foskins stood in the wide doorway and looked across the rutted barnyard at the brown field beyond long since stripped of the last grass tufts and at the horse close behind the rails, still, motionless, a part of the brown country stretching on to the broken gullies that led to the far hills. Gaunt with age, big bones pushing against shrunken hide, the horse stood as if propped on four stiff legs and the big head hung low with its weight, almost touching the ground. Old Clyde whistled through his mustache, sharp and shrill. The big ears of the horse twitched and the head rose a few inches and stopped and sank slowly again. He turned back into the barn and reached with a fork to pull hay from the low loft. He gathered an armful and went out and across the barnyard and dropped it over the rails close by the big head. "Cri-ma-nently!" he said. "Get some interest in life. At least you can still eat." The head moved and the neck stretched and the horse took a mouthful of hay, not in hunger but in old instinctive obedience to do what was wanted. The big jaws ground in slow rhythm working the hay back over worn gums and the nubs of the few remaining teeth.

Old Clyde slapped his hands on the top rail and surveyed the horse from scraggly burr-locked tail to graying bearded muzzle. "You certainly aint very pretty," he said. "Crowbait, that's about all. Maybe even they'd pass you by." The horse rolled its eyes towards him till the white of the near one showed plain and he slapped his hands on the top rail again. "Don't go getting worried. It's near to plowing time, certain enough, but I'll not be making you do that. I'll be getting me another one. Maybe two. It'll take two to match what you were." He rubbed his hands along the rail and stared at them and for a moment had trouble seeing them through the mistiness clouding his eyes. "You've done enough for a dozen," he said. He pushed against the rail and straightened his old shoulders. "Company. That'll perk you some." He snorted at himself and at the horse in exasperation. "No. You don't need company. Not at your age." He turned and started across the barnyard ruts towards the small back porch of the silent three-room house. "Like me," he said.

Sunlight through the kitchen window had reached the crack in the floorboards that meant the general neighborhood of two o'clock. Old Clyde sat at the kitchen table turning and returning the pages of last week's newspaper and worked with slow sips at the last cup of coffee, reheated, half milk the way he liked it, from the pot made for lunch. Old dishes on the shelf above the corner cupboard rattled gently and he looked up and out the window and heard the hoofs first then saw the team of small quickstepping trotters and then the buggy sagging with the weight of his two stout sons as it slid to a stop in the lane beside the house. He started up in sudden eagerness and put his face close to the glass and dropped back into the chair. "Cri-ma-nently," he said. "Both at once. That means something." He pushed up again, slowly, and went to the door and opened it for them. "Afternoon, Ed. Same, Mert. Find yourselves chairs. Won't take a moment for a fresh pot of coffee."

"Not now, Father." Ed Foskins, owner of the trotters, owner of a smooth fresh face, ruddy with good living, watched his younger brother hurry to the nearest chair and sink his wide shape on it with a sigh. "What's the matter, Mert? That road get you? You're softer than me already." He closed the door and stood with his back against it facing old Clyde. "No time for coffee, Father. I have to be back at the bank by closing. Mert here oughtn't be away from the store. But Lord knows when we'd have another chance to get out here. We want to talk to you."

Old Clyde backed across the room until he felt the sustaining solidity of the table behind him. He was painfully aware of his unshaven face, of his crusted heavy work shoes and stained dungarees and patched flannel shirt. He looked from one to the other of his sons, neat and respectable in their town clothes, and as always pride and regret matched themselves in him. "Go ahead, talk," he said.

Mert shifted for more comfort on his chair. "Ed'll do it. But I agree with him. Absolutely. It's logical. It's right."

"Well, now." Ed Foskins, the glib one, the good talker, swung into stride. "We didn't want to rush you right after the funeral and all. But it's been six months now since Mother was buried — "

"Six months," old Clyde said. "And four days."

"Right. And four days. But you can't go on living way out here alone. It isn't natural. It doesn't make sense. On an old rundown farm that — "

"It aint rundown!" Old Clyde's voice shook with indignation. "I had a good corn crop last year, didn't I? Wheat did good too. Paid off my seed loan and some over. You ought to know, you being in the bank."

"Well, yes, sure you did. But you don't need to. That's it. That's the point. No sense a man working when he doesn't need to. You've done your share. All Mert and me can remember when we were boys is you working. All the time. Never any end to it. And you don't need to any more. I checked your account again this morning. You've got better than two thousand. With what you can get for this place, which won't be too much but I can help you get what it's worth, you'd have enough to take it easy in town for — well, for — for as long as — "

"Go ahead, say it!" Old Clyde's voice shook again. "For the little time I've got left you mean. I know that ain't much. I'm your father but I'm old enough to be your grandfather, I got married so damn late." The words were coming and he could not stop them. "Maybe that's why we didn't get along so good, you had to hurry out of here into town soon as you could. Both of you. Maybe I was too old already to be the kind of father you wanted. Well, you wasn't exactly the kind of sons I wanted either. Had to keep after you getting things done around here. Had to do most of it myself. Well, I did it, didn't I? And, well, I'm older now. But I aint afraid of it." He shifted along the table and around the corner and sank into the chair there and pushed with a shaking finger at his half-empty coffee cup. "Cri-ma-nently! I aint meaning to get mad. What d'you have to keep worrying about me now for? Whyn't you just let me worry about myself?"

Mert Foskins teetered his bulk forward on his chair. "See, Ed? Still the old rooster. That's what I keep telling Flossie. I want him to move in with us. Pay a little board to help out but that's all. Be good for the kids, the way she keeps spoiling — "

"Shut up, Mert." Ed Foskins, the elder, the leader from boyhood, was in command. He took a deep breath. "Father, you don't understand. We aren't trying to push you into anything. We're just thinking what's good for you. These days people take things easier. There's no sense doing the way you do, rest some in winter and then be at it every daylight hour soon as the ground is soft enough for plowing. Maybe that made sense when it was the only way to get along. These days things are different. How do you think you make Mert and me feel, us doing well in town and you living out here like you didn't have a nickel?" Ed Foskins saw the muscles of old Clyde's face tightening. "Now wait a minute, Father. This is hard to say, to you anyway, but I'm saying it. Maybe now Mert and me are older too and we're realizing a few things we didn't before. We wouldn't be where we are now if you hadn't worked like that. Not many men could do what you did, past fifty already and with a wife and two little kids and having to start all over again with nothing on a piece of poor government land. You raised us and you squawked when we pulled out but all the same you helped us get started in town with what you could and, well, your job's done and it's about time you quit working and took life easy. Mert and me, we — "

Old Clyde was no longer listening. His head was high. He was thinking back twenty-some years. "I had a horse," he said.

He looked out the window past the buggy and the shining young trotters, beyond the fence, at the big gaunt figure propped on four stiff legs, head low, motionless. "I've still got him."

Mert's chair squealed as he straightened on it. "You mean that rack of bones out there is old Mark? I thought he was gone years ago. Must be more'n thirty."

"Twenty-eight," old Clyde said. "Twenty-five years I've had him and twenty-five years he's been doing anything I ever asked of him." Old Clyde's head dropped and he stared down at his coffee cup. "Nearly twenty-five anyway."

"You mean," Ed Foskins was surprised, "you mean you've been thinking of going right on farming and with that old horse?"

"No!" Old Clyde pushed his coffee cup clattering on its saucer. He looked up at Ed half apologetic, half defiant. "Not that horse. He's done his share. Gave out on me one day last fall and more'n about time the way I see it. I been figuring to get another one. Maybe a team. Herb Calloway towards town has a few for sale." He grabbed the cup and gulped the cold remainder of his coffee and wiped his mustache. "No siree bob, that horse aint going to do another day's work. He's earned his rest. He's going to get plenty to eat and loaf around and take it easy and — " Old Clyde stopped, startled at his own words.

"That's right!" Ed Foskins jumped at the chance. "That's exactly what we mean. You've earned your rest too. You're going to loaf around and take it easy and let somebody else, me and Marilyn or Mert and Flossie or likely both of us in turn, take care of you and see you get decent meals. You're going to quit working and do just what you feel like doing and not a damn thing else. You said it yourself. You've earned it."

Old Clyde felt trapped and by his own reasoning and this time he felt no answering urge to pull free. He was suddenly aware of what he had kept hidden, even from himself, the tiredness deep in him, the desire to be still, like the big gaunt figure out by the fence, head low, doing nothing. "I don't know," he said. "I been getting muddled, off and on, lately. Never could figure things quick like you, Ed." He slumped lower on the chair and felt the tiredness taking him. "But I'd just be a nuisance around."

"Sure you would. But so what?" Ed Foskins, the first

rebel, the sound at heart, grinned in remembrance. "Me and Mert were nuisances to you. Turn-about's fair enough."

"No," old Clyde said. "I can't do it. There's that horse — "

Mert's chair squealed again. "Old Mark? Him too. There's a field back of my place. Won't cost much to rent it."

"Well, then," Ed said, quickly. "That's settled. That's the way to do things, make up your mind and do them. Suppose you move in with Mert first. My new place isn't finished yet and he has more room right now. You'll be wanting a little time to get used to the idea. Suppose we make it week after next. Monday. I'll send a wagon . . ."

Old Clyde Foskins stood on his little back porch and watched the buggy back and swing and move out of the lane into the road. There was an ache in his throat, a tightness no gulping could ease. "I didn't know they felt that way," he said. He watched the buggy dwindle into the distance and drop out of sight beyond the first rolling ridge. "Maybe Ed's right. Maybe Ed's been right all along. Certainly doing well." He saw the buggy, small, a moving dot in the distance, top the second and higher rolling ridge and disappear beyond towards town. He turned slowly and looked at his old outbuildings and the leaning fences in ragged lines between his fields. "It is kind of rundown. Needs a lot of fixing. No sense doing that now."

The water was hot on the stove, steaming in the bucket and making it wobble on the rusty burner. Old

Clyde sloshed some into the dishpan and did up his breakfast dishes with a minimum of soap and effort. He rubbed
one hand around his chin and felt the stubble there. "Cri-
ma-nently," he said. "Must be a week, ten days, since I
shaved last. Time's coming and they'll be wanting to slick
me some. Might as well get in practice." He sloshed more
water into a basin and set this on the chest-high shelf by
the window. He rooted around in the corner cupboard
until he found his nubbin of a brush and his old straight-
edge. He put these with a small square mirror on the shelf
beside the basin and went to work on his whiskers. He
pulled at the loose skin under his chin to stretch out the
wrinkles and let the blade catch the bristles. "Kind of a
silly business," he said. "Most natural thing in the world
for a man to have hair on his face. Wouldn't feel a man
without it. Yet right away they have to come off." He
rooted in the cupboard again and found a pair of old
scissors and went back by the shelf and started trimming
his mustache. "Got to be more particular. Bird could
build a nest in this thing." Suddenly he pulled back and
stared at himself hard in the mirror. "Talking to myself.
How long've I been doing that?" He shrugged his old
shoulders and grabbed the flour sacking that served for a
towel and rubbed his face vigorously. "Aint nobody's
business but my own anyway." He tossed the flour sacking
on the table. "But it will be. Have to quit it come next
Monday."

He was reaching to gather the things on the shelf when
he caught a glimpse of movement through the window. He
shifted to see more clearly. Out in the field, just beyond
the fence, the big gaunt figure was moving. Head up,
sniffing the air, stiff and awkward with age, the old horse
was walking along the fence line. It reached the gate op-

posite the barn and stopped and looked over. It turned and came back to the familiar resting spot opposite the house and turned and started up along the fence line again.

Old Clyde watched, his eyebrows twitching upward. "Well, now," he said, "look at him perking some. Must be a touch of spring." He went out on his little back porch and sniffed the air himself. The unending wind was strong and chill but faint along its edges was the old eternal promise. He drew in a deep breath. "It's there. Snow's been gone about three weeks. Dampness going. A man figuring on some planting would be getting the ground ready." He sighed softly. "Not me. Mighty nice not to have that hanging over me any more. Sit all day if I feel like it."

Inside, by the stove, old Clyde soaked up warmth and began to leaf through his pile of farm journals for the articles he had always intended to read but never got around to. He read slowly, sometimes following the lines with a blunt forefinger, mumbling the words to himself, agreeing and disagreeing with what he read. The sun inched across the kitchen floor and he hitched his chair along to follow it. And outside the wind blew and carried its ancient message and the sun shone and the old horse stood in its resting place opposite the house, head low, motionless, and now and again raised its head and sniffed and walked, slow and ungainly with the wind ruffling its long winter hair, up along the fence line to look over the gate opposite the barn and swing around and return.

Old Clyde fidgeted on his chair. Suddenly he dropped the journal he was holding. "Got things to do. Might as well get at them." He went to the dusty telephone on the front room wall and took down the earpiece and cranked the handle on the side. He gave his number and waited a moment and then, as always, put his mouth close and shouted. "Mrs. Calloway? Clyde Foskins down the road. You tell Herb I've got a cow and some pigs to sell him. You tell him to be here right after lunch or I'll sell 'em to somebody else."

Herb Calloway finished fastening the tail gate of his big stock wagon. He climbed to the driving seat and waved a cheery farewell. He clucked to his team of plump young workhorses and they surged willingly into the traces. Old Clyde watched the wagon turn into the road and start its steady rolling into the distance. The sun was so warm on his bare head and old jacket that he settled himself on the edge of the back porch to enjoy it. He chuckled softly to himself. "These younger ones don't know how to bargain any more. Got eleven dollars more'n the top I figured on getting."

Out in the field, just beyond the fence, the old horse had turned, head up, to watch the young team go past. It swung around and started up along the fence line and broke into a lumbering trot. It stopped by the gate opposite the barn and looked over. Old Clyde studied it, eyebrows twitching. "What you so all-fired interested in that barn for? There's hay out there if you want it." He moved a bit to look at the old barn straight on and saw that the wind was swaying one of the big main doors and that the wood at the top was rotten and the hangers were tearing loose. "Well, now, aint that too bad," he said. "Can't argue I'll be sorry to leave this rundown old place, everything falling apart." He let his breath out in a long sigh. "Mighty nice not to have to be doing things all the time. Just what I feel like doing. Right now I feel like sitting."

He sat in the sun and watched the old horse go back down the fence line, wait a moment, turn and go up again and stop by the gate, and swing yet again and repeat the maneuver, over and over. "Cri-ma-nently!" He stood up. "If you want some exercise, why keep following that fence? You've got a whole damn field to move around in." He walked towards the barn and stood staring up at the creaking door. "Shucks. Might as well fix that anyway. Can't get a good price, things falling apart."

The wind blew, steady and chill but with a softness blunting its bite, and fiddled with the edges of the loosened worn shingles old Clyde was renailing on the barn roof. The morning sun was warm on his back. He fastened the last shingle and inched, crablike, down the slope to the ladder. Rung by rung he descended, moving slowly, calculating each step like a man who knows his muscles have lost their snap and he must use what strength he has carefully, spread out over a job. On the ground, he straightened himself, wincing a little at the twinges in his back. He looked up the ladder. "Well, now," he said, "that ought to be worth fifty dollars more on the price."

He went around and through the wide open doorway and hung his old hammer on the wall between its two nails. He stood in the doorway and saw the big gaunt figure in the field moving, moving, slowly, steadily, up the fence line and stop and down and return, wearing ever deeper into the pathway already worn. Suddenly an anger, out of nowhere, forced his voice into a shout. "Stop it! What's got into you?"

The old horse had reached the gate opposite the barn again. It looked over and across the barnyard at him. One big forefoot rose and pawed at the lowest rail. There was a small crackling sound and little splinters broke from the wood. Old Clyde stared and as he stared the anger dwindled in him.

He went towards the gate and the old horse raised its head higher and whiffled softly at him and pressed its chest forward against the top rail. "Mark," he said. "Mark boy. You want out? What in hell for?" He felt a strange lightheadedness, a deliberate emptiness of thought. He stepped forward, hardly aware what he was doing, and the horse stepped back and he tugged at the rails till they fell at his feet. Head high, breathing deeply, the old horse stepped over them and past him. Straight to the barn it went and in through the wide doorway. He followed. He stood in the doorway and saw it standing, waiting, motionless, patient, by the harness rack, and seeing he felt the anger flare and fill him, strong and bitter. "So you think you've still got it in you! I'll show you! You couldn't drag it ten feet!" With trembling, hurrying fingers he snatched the old bridle with its long driving reins from its peg and jammed the rusty bit between the big old waiting jaws. He grabbed the harness and threw it over the big bony frame. He fought with the buckles to fasten them and cursed at the clumsiness of haste. He took the reins and slapped with the loose ends hard at the horse's rump and swung it around and backed it to where the old plow lay on the barn floor. He fastened the tugs with sharp jerks, muttering steadily under his breath. He took the reins again and slapped again with the loose ends. "All right, get moving! I'll show you! I'll show you good!"

Head high, ears forward, the old horse moved and the old plow clattered on its side along the rough floor planks and old Clyde walked beside it. Out of the barn, around the pigpen, past the empty back pasture, to the wide spreading rear field where the corn stubble marked its old rows with withered tufted weeds and grass between.

Old Clyde's voice rose, still in anger but with a note of frantic appeal. "Cri-ma-nently! Aint I been telling you? You're too old! There aint any sense to it! Wait'll you hit the dirt! Wait'll the 'share digs in! That'll show you!"

He yanked on the reins and the old horse stopped, leaning its weight slightly forward into the harness to hold the tugs tight. Quickly, with the sureness of old habit, he knotted the rein ends together and flipped the loop over his head and around his shoulders. He leaned and took hold of the plow handles and struggled with them until the plow was upright, ready. "Giddap!" he yelled. "Yank your goddamn heart out! That'll learn you!" The old horse surged forward and as it moved old Clyde heaved up on the handles so that the blade pointed into the ground. Smoothly, surely, the blade sank in and leveled for the straight pull and stopped against the hard mass of the subsoil. He heard the breath of the old horse wheeze in its throat and saw the ribs straining through the shaggy hide and the old cracked hoofs digging into the dirt — and the plow moved, slow, hesitating, forward and stop and forward again and not stopping and the clean earth rolled from the moldboard and lay in a darkened ribbon by the fresh furrow beside his plodding feet.

Slowly, unsteadily, but always forward, concentrating with an intense earnestness, the horse and the man with the plow biting into the earth between them crawled along the length of the wide spreading field.

They stopped at the far end and old Clyde turned his head to look back along the furrow. "Cri-ma-nently," he said softly. "Straight as a string." He jerked his head around and pulled quickly on the plow to free the blade from the ground, for the old horse, breathing heavily, was moving again, was starting to swing in the arc that would bring them around for the return trip back along the field. He fought with the plow to get it turned in time and pulled it upright and heaved quickly on the handles so they would not lose the forward momentum and the blade sank into the ground and leveled and the new furrow began to unroll. And suddenly he was no longer an old man plodding along, plowing often-plowed ground behind an old gaunt horse that struggled with each forward step, whose big old bones thrust out against shrunken hide. He was a man with snap still in his knees, striding along, striding behind a huge young horse, filled out, great-muscled, sleek with sweat, big head slogging forward into the terrific strain as the plow sliced deep through the tangled matted roots of virgin prairie sod. "Yippee!" he yelled. "Smash into it, Mark boy! I know what people are saying. That Foskins is a damn fool. He'll never make it. Have to have oxen or a four-horse span to break that ground. I aint got those. But I've got you, boy! We'll show 'em!" He was striding along, feet striking firm beside the furrow, striding along behind huge young Mark, the tireless, the indomitable, great heart driving great muscles, plowing forward through unending resistant sod, through the days and the weeks and the months, and the sweat of their work salted the earth of the years.

Old Clyde Foskins realized he was standing still, gripping the plow handles so hard that his fingers hurt. The plow had stopped. Ahead of him the old horse wavered on four stiff legs and shudders ran through its body and its breath whistled shrill in its throat. The big head sank lower and lower and the big gaunt frame crumpled and toppled forward and sideways and to the ground and the weight dragging on the harness pulled the plow over on its side.

Carefully old Clyde lifted the knotted reins over his head and dropped them. He went around by the still figure and looked down. The eyes were open, staring, and there was no life in them. He stood quietly, looking down, for a long time. "It'll take a mighty big hole," he said. He raised his head and looked out along the fresh furrows. "I expect a corner of this field'll be about right. It's as much his as mine." He stood quietly, staring into the distance. He raised one calloused old hand and brushed it across his eyes to clear the mistiness from them. "Yes," he said. "Yes. He was right. That's the way to do it."

He walked, slowly and steadily, out of the field, past the empty back pasture, around the empty pigpen, across the barnyard, up on his little back porch and into the house. He went straight to the dusty telephone on the front room wall and took down the earpiece and cranked the handle. He gave his number and waited. He put his mouth close and shouted. "Marilyn? You tell Ed when he gets home I don't want any wagon on Monday. Or any time." Quickly he pushed down the receiver hook with a finger and waited again. After a moment he released the hook and cranked the handle once more and gave his number. He put his mouth close and shouted. "Mrs. Calloway? You tell Herb I'll be there to see him shortly. Want to dicker for a couple of horses."

He pulled his old jacket closer about him and went out on his little back porch. He heard the telephone ringing behind him, three rings, his call. "Let 'em keep that thing buzzing all day," he said. "I aint got time to argue. Got my spring plowing to do." He went around the house and along the lane. "That team Herb had here yesterday. The two of them together might do. Maybe buy back that cow too. She always gave down good for me." Walking slowly and steadily, he headed up the road.

One Man's Honor

✳

T HIS HAPPENED out where distance ran past vision
and only clumped silver-green of sagebrush and blunt
bare rising ridges of rock broke the red-brown reaches of
sand and sun-baked silt. No highways or railroads sliced
it into measurable stretches. Only a lone rutted trace
snaked through, following the lower levels, worn by
freighters who crawled at long intervals with their clumsy
wagons from the last meager town far southward on the
river to the rolling cattle ranges far northward on the more
fertile uplands. Yet here and there, off the trace, widely
separated and hidden between the ridges where slow
short-season streams made narrow areas of green before
dying in the sand, the first settlers had come. They would
increase and windmills would rise to draw upon the sub-
surface water and in time a network of roads would fan
out and wheels would grind dust for hot winds to whirl.
Now they were few and far, lost in the immensity of distance and red-brown desolation under the limitless depth
of sky.

Late afternoon sun slanted over one of the higher ridges
and shone on the sparse beginnings of a homestead claim.
Clear and hot in the clean air, it shone on a long strip of

shallow-plowed ground that followed the gradual curve of an almost-dry stream bed where a few brackish pools lingered and on a sagging pole corral where an old milk cow and two stocky ungainly draft horses drooped in motionless rest and beside this on the shelter, half dugout cut into the rise of a small ground swell, half timbered with scrub logs from the stunted cottonwoods that straggled along the other side of the stream bed. Trimmed branches corded together and plastered over with clay formed the roof and a rusting stovepipe rose from it. On the split-log doorstep sat a little girl. Her short scratched sunburned legs barely reached the ground. Her light brown hair, sun-bleached in lighter streaks, curled softly down to frame a round stub-nosed face whose dark eyes, unmasked by the light lashes, were wide and bright. A twenty-foot length of rope was tied around her waist and fastened to a staple driven into the doorjamb. She was small and serious and very quiet and she smoothed the skirt of her small flour-sacking dress down over her bare knees and poked, earnest and intent, one small moccasined foot at an ant scurrying in the dooryard dust.

Behind her, in the dim recess of the one-windowed shelter, a tall flat-bodied man stooped over a rumpled bed against the rear wall and laid a moistened cloth across the forehead of a woman lying there. His voice was low and harsh with irritation but the touch of his hand was gentle. "What's got into ye?" he said.

The woman stared up at him, apology plain on her thin flushed face. "I don't know," she whispered. "It just came on me sudden-like." Her thin body under the patched gingham of dress shook with slight tremors as with a chill yet drops of sweat streaked her cheeks. Her voice came faint and wavering. "You'll have to do the food. There's soup in the kettle."

The man brushed one hand impatiently at the flies hovering over the bed. "Ye'll be better in the morning," he said. Abruptly he turned and went to the stove set against the right wall. The woman watched him. She tried to speak and could not. She lay still a moment and summoned strength to rise on her elbows and send her voice across the room to him. "Wait," she said. "Wait. You'll have to do the game with her. It's her fun. It helps her learn."

The man swung his head to look at the doorway. The little girl sat still, her back to him, her head bent forward as she peered at something by her feet. The last sun slanting over the ridge filtered through the tangled curls along her neck. Slowly the lines of worry and irritation faded from the man's face and the tightness around his mouth eased. He went to the doorway and leaned low to untie the rope around her waist. She stood up, small and soft beside his hard height, and stretched back her head to look up at him. She raised one small hand and reached to put it in one of his big calloused hands. Together they went along the front of the shelter towards the corral.

Near the corner the man stopped. He slapped his free hand on the side of the shelter. "This," he said.

Gravely the little girl regarded the shelter. A triumphant smile crinkled her small face. "Hello, house," she said.

"Right," the man said. They moved on and stopped by an old wagon pulled in close alongside the shelter. The man reached under and pulled out an empty milk pail and held it up. Gravely the little girl regarded it. Her small eyebrows drew down in a frown. She looked up at the man in doubt and back at the object in his hand. "Hello," she said slowly, "hello, buck-et."

"That's it!" The man grinned down at her and reached

to put the pail back under the wagon. They moved on to the sagging poles of the corral. The man pointed over the poles at the cow and the little girl peered through them beside him. She spoke at once, quick and proud. "Hello, cow."

"What's the cow's name?"

"Bess-ie."

"Mighty smart ye're getting to be," the man said. He pointed over the poles at the draft horses standing together in a corner.

The little girl tossed her head. "Hello, horse."

"No," the man said. "There's two of them. More than one. Hor-ses."

The little girl looked up at him, small and earnest and intent. She looked back through the poles across the corral. "Hello, hor-ses."

Forty-three miles to the south and five miles west of the meager town on the river, where the ground dipped in a hollow some ten feet below the level expanse around, a saddled horse stood alone, ground-reined, patiently waiting. A wide-brimmed weather-worn hat hung on the saddle horn. Several hundred yards away the river road followed the bank, a dust track running west into fading distance and east towards the low hills hiding the town. Close by the roadside two small rocks jutted out of the ground, butted against each other. Together they were little more than three feet wide, irregular in shape, no more than eighteen inches high at the highest point. The late afternoon sun slanted down on them and they made a small lengthening patch of shade. Beside them, stretched out, head and shoulders into the shade, a man lay flat, belly down, pressed against the ground. Beside him lay a rifle. Its barrel had been rubbed with dirt to remove all shine. He was a short man, short and thick, with a head that seemed small, out of proportion to the thick body, set too close into the hunched shoulders. His hair was a dirty black, close-cropped with the rough scissor slashes of his own cutting plainly marked, and it merged with no visible break into the dark unshaven stubble down his cheeks and around his narrow tight-lipped mouth.

He raised his head higher to sight along the road to the west through the cleft where the tops of the two rocks joined. Pushing with his toes in beaten scarred old knee-length boots, he hitched his body a few inches to the left so that it lay almost exactly parallel to the road, invisible to anyone approaching in the distance from the west. As he moved, the hammer of the revolver in a holster at his side made a tiny groove in the ground and he reached to test the firmness of its seat in the holster and free it of any clinging dirt. His voice was a low murmur lost in the vast empty reaches of space, the flat inflectionless voice of a man accustomed to being alone and to talking to himself. "Last place they'd be expecting trouble," he said.

He lay flat, his head relaxed on its side with one ear against the ground, and the sun dropped slowly down the sky and the patch of shade of the rocks spread down his back and reached the brass-studded cartridge belt around his waist and far out along the road to the west a tiny puff of dust appeared and crept closer, barely seeming to move only to grow imperceptibly larger in the angled foreshortening of distance. Faint tremors in the ground came to the man's ear. He raised his head and sighted through the rock cleft. He rolled on his side and pulled the tattered old bandanna tied loosely around his neck up over his face, up to the bridge of his nose so that only his eyes and forehead showed over it. He rolled back into position and took the rifle and eased the barrel forward through the cleft. Propped on his elbows with the curved butt of the rifle against his right shoulder and his right cheek under the bandanna against the stock, he watched the puff of dust far out along the road.

It was no longer just a puff of dust. Emerging from it yet never escaping and always emerging as the dust rose under the hoofs was a light fast freight wagon drawn by two stout horses at a steady trot. Two men sat on the board-backed seat, the driver and another man with a shotgun between his knees, the butt on the floorboard, the barrel pointing at the sky.

The man behind the rocks waited. He waited until the wagon was little more than one hundred feet away and in a few seconds he would begin to be visible over the top of the rocks and his finger tightened on the trigger of the rifle and with the crash of the shot the man with the shotgun jolted hard against the back of the wagon seat and the horses reared, beating upward with their front hoofs and trying to swing away, and the man with the shotgun dropped it clattering on the floorboard and struggled to stand on the swaying platform and toppled sideways into the road dust and lay still.

The man behind the rocks let the rifle stock fall to the ground and leaped up and in the leaping took the revolver from the holster at his side. He moved out and around the rocks and closer to the wagon and watched the driver fighting with the horses to quiet them. He watched the driver pull them to quivering stillness and become aware of him and the gun in his hand and stiffen in a tight silence. "That's right," he said. "Keep your hands on those reins where I can see them." He moved closer and to the right side of the wagon and with his left hand took the shotgun from the floorboard and tossed it back from the road. He moved out and around the horses to the left side of the wagon and took the driver's revolver from its holster and threw it towards the river. He stepped back, away from the wagon. "Now," he said. "Take it slow. Wrap the reins around that brake. Put your hands up behind your head." The driver hesitated. His lips were pale, pressed tight together, and a slow flush crept up his cheeks. He reached slowly and looped the reins over the brake handle and raised his hands and clasped them together at the back of his head.

The man with the gun stepped up by the body of the wagon. He was careful to stand facing part way forward so that the driver was always within his angle of vision. With his left hand he unfastened the rope lashed over the wagon and pulled away the light canvas dust cover. Four square boxes and several small crates and a half-dozen sacks of potatoes were exposed to view. He chuckled, a strange harsh sound in the wide silence. "Mighty little load to be packing a guard," he said. He swung his head for a quick check of the load and back to look straight at the driver. His voice was suddenly sharp and biting. "Where is it? I know you're carrying it." The driver had pivoted his body at the hips to watch him and stared at him and said nothing.

The man with the gun grunted and reached with his left hand to yank aside one of the sacks of potatoes. He reached again and heaved to move aside the one that had been beneath the first. He plunged the hand into the hole opened to the bed of the wagon and felt around and pulled out a small metal box. He stepped back and again his strange harsh chuckle sounded in the silence.

The voice of the driver broke through the tight line of his lips. "You'll never get away with it, Kemp. I'd know that gunbelt anywhere."

The man with the gun let the metal box fall from his left hand and lifted the hand and pulled the bandanna down from his face. "Too bad," he said. He raised his right hand and the gun in it bucked with the shot and the driver rose upright off the seat arching his back in sudden agony and fell sideways over the footboard to strike on the wagon tongue and bounce to the ground between the harness tugs and with the roar of the shot the horses were rearing and they plunged ahead and the wheels crunched over the driver's body as they rolled forward along the road.

The man with the gun took one leap after the wagon and stopped. He raised the gun again and in almost aimless haste fired the four remaining bullets in it at the plunging horses. The horses drove forward, goaded by several flesh wounds, and the reins ripped off the brake handle and the wagon careened after them and swerved to the left and the left front wheel struck against the rocks behind which the man had been hiding. The wagon bounced upward as the wheel cracked and the harness tugs snapped and the horses, freed of the weight, surged in frantic gallop along the road.

The man threw the empty revolver to the ground. He raced to the wagon and around it to the rocks and leaped over them and grabbed the rifle. He dropped to his right knee and braced his left elbow on his left knee to steady his aim and fired and one of the horses staggered and fell and the other, pulled sideways by the falling weight, lashed frantically with its hoofs and the harness parted and the horse galloped ahead alone along the road. Already it was a far shape, dwindling into distance, and the man fired again and again until the magazine of the rifle was emptied and the bullets kicked small spurts of dust and the horse galloped on unhit into the low hills. The man threw down the rifle and stood erect. He was shaking with a tense fury. He stood still, forcing himself to quiet, driving the shaking out of his body. He drew a long breath. "That'll tell 'em too damn soon," he said. Quickly he took up the rifle and opened the breech and blew through the barrel and loaded the magazine with bullets from the pocket of his faded old shirt. He hurried back where he had dropped the metal box. The two bodies lay near in the road dust and already the flies were gathering and he paid no attention to them. He picked up the revolver and loaded it with bullets from the brass-studded belt around his waist. He reached down and blasted the lock of the metal box with a single shot and ripped the top open and took out two small plump leather bags and a sheaf of bills and jammed these into the pockets of his old patched pants. At a steady run he moved away from the road, across the level expanse, to the hollow several hundred yards away and the waiting horse. With swift sure gestures he slapped the hat on his head and pushed the rifle into its saddle scabbard and transferred the two small bags and the bills to the saddlebag. He swung up and yanked the horse around, lifting it into a fast lope, and headed north through the red-brown reaches of distance.

Early morning sun slanted in from the east on the homestead shelter. It made a narrow triangular patch of brightness on the packed dirt floor through the open doorway and pushed a soft glow further into the room. On the edge of a low short trundle cot against the back wall by the foot of the big bed the little girl sat, her body bent forward, her small face puckered in a frown as she concentrated on the problem of putting the right little moccasin on the right foot. On the bed itself the woman lay thin and motionless. Her eyes were closed. At intervals the eyelids twitched and flickered and were still. Her mouth was partly open and her breath drew through it in long slow straining gasps. On the floor beside the bed, stretched on an old quilt folded over, the man lay asleep, fully dressed except for his short thick boots.

The little girl finished with the moccasins. She slid to the floor and turned and tried to smooth the old blanket on her cot. She took hold of the cot and tugged at it to pull it a few inches out from the wall. She went to the end of it away from the bed and turned her small back to it and against it and pushed with her feet to move it along the floor and slide it under the bed.

The scratching sound of the cot runners scraping on the hard dirt floor roused the man. He bent his body at the waist to sit up and wavered and fell back. He pushed against the floor with both hands and was up to sitting position. He looked around, his eyes glassy and staring, and saw the boots and his attention focused on them and he reached for them and struggled to get them on. He heaved himself over on one hip and pushed against the floor and stood swaying on his feet. Sweat streamed down his face and his body shook as with a chill. He took a step and staggered and fell towards the wall and clutched at it for support. He moved along it to the head of the bed. Leaning his weight on one hand on the bed, he reached with the other to the woman's shoulder and gently shook her. Her head wobbled limply at the pressure and her eyes remained closed. He straightened against the wall. Slowly he wiped one hand down over his damp face and let it fall to his side.

The little girl stood by the foot of the bed and looked up at him. Slowly his attention focused on her. He stared at her for a long moment and she looked up at him and a small smile of greeting touched her face and was gone. He drew a long slow sobbing breath and by sheer effort of will pushed out from the wall. His feet dragged and he moved in a strange lurching walk. He took the old quilt from the floor and reached under the bed to take the old blanket from the cot and pulled a pile of empty flour sacks down from a shelf. With these in his arms he staggered to the doorway and out and along the front of the shelter to the old wagon beside it. He heaved his load into the body of the wagon and leaned panting on the side to reach in and spread out the sacks and put the blanket and quilt over them. Weakness took him and he swayed against one of the wagon wheels and hung over it while sweat dripped in tiny glistening beads from his chin to the ground below. He pushed out from the wheel and veered to the shelter wall and hitched his way along towards the door. The little girl was in the doorway and she backed away inside and he held to the doorjamb and pulled himself around and in and a short way along the inside wall and reached for the team harness hanging on two wooden pegs and in the reaching suddenly sagged in a limp helplessness and collapsed doubling forward to bump against the wall and slide to the floor. His body stretched out and rolled over and his unseeing eyes stared upward a few seconds and the lids dropped and no motion stirred in him except the long slow heaving of his chest.

The little girl stared at the man lying still and silent

and her eyebrows drew together in a frown. She looked at
the woman on the bed and back at the man on the floor.
She turned away and went to the table under the one window in the right wall and climbed on the chair beside it
and then onto the table. Standing on tiptoe and leaning
out she reached one hand into an earthenware jar on the
shelf by the window and took it out with a cracker
clutched in her fingers. She climbed down to the chair
and sat on it with her short sunburned legs swinging over
the edge. Gravely she regarded the object in her hand.
"Hello, crack-er," she said in a soft hushed voice. Gravely
she bit off a corner and began to chew it.

A mile and a half to the southeast the early morning
sun sent long shadows streaming out from a man and a
horse climbing the rough slope of a twisting boulder-
strewn ridge. The man rode with his short thick body
hunched forward and the sun glinted on the brass stud-
dings of the cartridge belt around his waist. The horse
was sweat-streaked, tired, taking the slope in short spurts
as the man kicked it forward.

They topped the ridge and dropped a short way down
the near side and stopped. The man swung to the ground.
He took off his weather-worn hat and slapped at himself
with it to knock some of the dust off his clothes and hung
it on the saddle horn. He turned back to the top of the
ridge and lay flat on the blunt bare rock to peer over. No
motion anywhere disturbed the empty distance. He
turned his head to look at the horse standing with braced
legs apart, head hanging, grateful for the rest. He settled
himself more comfortably on the rock and watched over
the ridge top. The shadows of the boulders down the
slope shrank slightly as the sun crept upward and far out
along his back trail around a swelling shoulder of wind-

piled sand a straggling line of seven tiny figures crawled into view. "Damn funny," he said in a flat inflectionless voice. "Can't shake 'em."

The seven tiny figures crawled closer, increasing in size, seeming to increase in pace as the distance dwindled, and they were seven men on horseback, six in a ragged relatively compact group and one alone in the lead.

The man on the ridge top shaded his eyes against the slant sun and studied the figure in the lead, distinguishable now across the dwindling distance, a lean long-armed figure wearing a buckskin shirt, slim and straight in the saddle on a tall gray horse. He wore no hat and his hair, iron-gray and long, caught the sun clearly in the bobbing rhythm of riding. He rode at a fast trot and at intervals pulled his horse to a brief walk and leaned in the saddle to check the ground beside and ahead.

The man on the ridge top smacked a clenched fist on the rock. "That's it," he said. "Thought he'd left for the mines." He licked his dry lips and spat out the dust-dirty saliva. "Can't just keep running," he said. "Not with him after." He crawled down from the ridge top a few feet and turned squatting on his heels to look down the near slope. Down where it slipped into level expanse of red-brown ground and sparse silver-green of sagebrush, a few-score feet out from the base, a stony dry stream bed followed the twisting formation of the ridge. To the right, swinging in along the level from around a curving twist of the ridge and cutting across the dry stream bed to push in a long arc towards a far break in the next ridge, ran the wagon trace. Plain in the sand dust of the trace, visible from the height, were the day-old unending ribbon ruts of wheel tracks and the hoofprints of many horses heading north.

The man's eyes brightened. He leaped down the slope

to his horse and took the rifle from the saddle scabbard
and was back on his belly at the ridge top. The seven figures, suddenly larger, made grotesque in the clear clean
brightness of sun by the long shadows streaming sideways
from them, were little more than half a mile away. Deliberately, in slow succession, careless of exact aim at the
range, he fired once at the figure in the lead and twice at
the group behind and a strange harsh chuckle came from
him as he saw them scatter and swing their horses and
gallop back and cluster again in a jumble around the lean
man on the gray horse. "That'll do it," he said. "They'll
take time working up this hill." He pulled back from the
ridge top and ran to the horse and jammed the rifle into
the scabbard and slammed the hat on his head and swung
into the saddle. At a hard run he drove the horse angling
down the slope, across the first few-score feet of level
stretch, across the dry stream bed and angling on across
the level to the wagon trace.

He rode along the trace thirty feet, forty, and eased the
horse to a slow stop. Holding it steady, headed north, he
backed it along the trace, back to where he had angled in
and past, back to the crossing of the dry stream bed. Gripping the reins short and pulling up hard on the horse's
head so that it rose on its hind legs, front hoofs pawing the
air, he yanked its head savagely to the left and slammed
the heels of his heavy old boots into its flanks and it leaped,
twisting sideways, and was off the trace on the dry stones
of the stream bed and he clamped down hard on the reins
to hold it from breaking into a surging gallop. Head bent
to one side, peering down in steady concentration, he
walked the horse along the stream bed, picking his way,
holding to the side where the rolled loose stone lay thickest.

He turned his head to look back and up at the ridge top where he had been. Faintly, over the high rock, came the sound of a shot and then another. He looked ahead where the stream bed, following the ridge, curved left with it and disappeared from sight. He urged the horse into a trot and he was around the bend, out of sight of the wagon trace behind. He pulled the horse to the right and out of the stream bed and on the easier sand-silt ground he pushed it into a lope, moving west as the ground rose and swinging northwestward as it dropped again.

The morning sun, higher now, shone clear and hot on the homestead shelter and beat slanting against the high ridge behind and beyond. A quarter of a mile away, up past the long shallow-plowed strip by the almost dry stream bed, close in by the base of the ridge, a man sat, short and thick and hunched in the saddle, on a tired sweat-streaked horse. He held the wide brim of his weather-worn hat low over his eyes with one hand as he studied the whole scene before him. Not a sound that he could hear disturbed the empty silence. Not a living thing moved anywhere in sight except the two horses and the old cow in the corral twitching in patient endurance at the flies. He dropped the hand from his hat and reached to take the rifle from its scabbard and hold it ready across the saddle in front of him. He urged the horse into a slow walk, along the base of the ridge and swinging to come to the shelter from the rear.

Fifty feet from the low blank rear wall of the shelter he stopped the horse and dismounted. Quietly he slipped the rifle back into the scabbard and took off his hat and hung it on the saddle horn and in the same gesture flowing onward took the revolver from the holster at his side.

Quietly he walked to the rear wall of the shelter. He moved along the rear wall to the right corner and leaned to peer around and then to look across the short space at the corral. He saw that the horses were heavy draft animals and he shook his head in disgust and he saw the swelling udders of the cow, and a puzzled frown showed through the dark stubble on his face and the cow, sighting him, pressed against the poles of the corral and lowed with a soft sighing moan. At the sound he leaped back, close against the rear wall, and the empty silence regained and held and he relaxed and moved again, forward and around the corner.

He was moving past the wagon drawn in by the side of the shelter when he stopped and dropped below the wagon level and listened. Faint, from inside the shelter, he heard a slow creaking sound, then again and yet again and continuing in slow steady rhythm. He waited. The sound stopped and in the silence there was another sound, not heard, below hearing, sensed or felt, and the slow creaking began again and continued, deliberate, unhurried. Cautiously he moved, forward, around the front corner, along the blank wall towards the open doorway. Half crouched, gun raised and ready, he swung swiftly around the doorjamb and into the doorway and there, halfway across the room and confronting him, perched on the seat edge of an old rocking chair and swinging her small body to make the chair roll on its rockers, was a little girl. Caught, rigid in a kind of frantic immobility, he stared at her and her eyes widened at the sight of him and her small body stiffened, swaying gently to the dying motion of the chair. Gravely she regarded him. Her lips lifted slightly in a suggestion of a smile. "Hello, man," she said.

Slowly he straightened. He turned his head and saw

the woman motionless on the bed and the man limp on the floor and heard the other sound, audible now inside the room, the long slow unconscious gaspings for breath. He looked back at the little girl and suddenly he was aware of the gun in his hand and he turned his body side-wise to her and as he turned, his head remained towards her swiveling on his short thick neck and with a quick fur-tive motion he slid the gun into its holster. He stood still a long moment, his head fixed in its sidelong tipped slant over his shoulder, and looked down at her and gravely she watched him and he seemed unable to look away. Abruptly he jerked his head around straight, swinging his eyes to inspect the room. He went to the shelf by the one window and took a nearly empty flour sack from the floor beneath and laid this on the table. He reached to the shelf and snatched the few cans there and dropped them into the sack.

He stopped, silent and tense, his jaws clenched together, the cords in his neck standing out in strain. He swung around and leaned against the table and jutted his head forward and down at her. His voice struck at her with an angry intensity. "There'll be people coming! They'll un-tangle my trail! They'll get here sometime!" She stared at him, understanding or not understanding unknown on her face, and he pulled himself around and scooped the bag off the table. He strode to the doorway and out and along the front wall of the shelter and around and back to his horse. He jammed the old hat on his head and fumbled in the saddlebag until he found a short piece of cord and with this tied the flour sack close up to the sad-dle horn. He mounted and the horse, stronger for the rest, responded as he pulled it around and headed off northwestward, angling towards the high ridge.

He rode slowly, head down, hunched in the saddle, letting the horse find its own pace. There was no urging along the reins, no drumming of heels on its flanks, and the horse stopped. The man sat still in the saddle. He drew a long breath and let it out with a sighing sound. His voice came, flat, inflectionless. "Maybe they won't," he said. Suddenly an explosive fury seemed to burst inside him and strike outward into action. Viciously he yanked the horse around to the right and kicked it into headlong gallop, heading northeastward towards a far lowering of the ridge.

The fury in him dwindled with the wind of movement and a quietness came over him. He was aware of the horse straining under him, of its heavy breathing. He pulled it to a steady jogging.

He rode on, a short thick man on a tired horse, dirty, unshaven, dingy in old stained clothes except for the glintings of brass on the cartridge belt around his waist. He rode on, a small moving blot in the vast red-brown reaches of distance, and he passed over the far lowering of the ridge and down the long gradual slope beyond and up a wide ground swell of shifting sand and before him, stretching out of distance into distance, was the wagon trace and a third of a mile away, headed north along it, moving away from him, were seven men on horseback. The lean man on the gray horse and another man were in the lead, one on each side of the trace, bent in their saddles, studying the ground as they moved ahead, and the other five followed.

The man on the ground swell of shifting sand stopped his horse and took the rifle from its scabbard. A strange harsh chuckle sounded in the sun-hot silence and was cut short by the shot and he saw the spurt of dust beside the lean man's horse and all of them halt with sudden startled jerks and swing in their saddles to look towards him. He jammed the rifle back into its scabbard and lifted his horse rearing to wheel it around and drove it at a fast gallop back down the ground swell of sand the way he had come. He was well up the long gradual slope towards the lowering of the ridge when he looked back and saw them coming over the ground swell and lining out in full gallop behind him. Savagely he beat at the horse and it surged up and over the lowering of the ridge and as it raced down the other side towards the long level stretch to the homestead shelter he felt the first falterings in its stride, the slight warning stumblings and recoveries, and he took hold of the sack tied to the saddle horn and snapped the cord with a lurch of his weight in the saddle and let the sack fall. The horse drove on, frantic in lessening rushes of strength, and again he looked back. They were coming steadily, no closer than before, coming with steady intensity of purpose. He saw them pull sliding to a bunched brief stop by the sack and one swing down and grab it and shake out the contents in a flurry of flour and in the stopping he increased his lead. The shelter was just ahead now and he yanked the horse to a skidding stop in front of it and whipped the revolver from the holster at his side and fired two shots towards the doorway, low, into the doorstep. He caught a flashing glimpse of the little girl inside shrinking back from the roar of the shots and he was beating the horse forward again, past the corral, across the shallow-plowed strip, angling back towards the high ridge.

He reached the base and started up and the horse, faltering often now, labored into the climb. It stopped, legs braced and quivering, ribs heaving, a bloody froth bub-

bling in its nostrils. He pivoted to the right in the saddle
and looked back. Riderless horses stood in front of the
shelter and the lean man in the buckskin shirt near them
directing the others. One man ran towards the closest
brackish pool in the almost dry stream bed with a bucket
in his hand. Another strode towards the corral with the
team harness over his shoulder. Another heaved at the
tongue of the old wagon to swing it out from the side wall
of the shelter. And yet another mounted one of the saddled horses and swung off southeastward.

The man on the ridge slope checked each in the one
swift sliding glance and stared intently at the blank walls
of the shelter as if trying to force vision through them.
Suddenly, as thought and bodily awareness coincided, he
pivoted around and to the left in the saddle. Two of them
had not stopped by the shelter, had galloped on past and
swept in a wide arc towards him. They were little more
than three hundred yards away. One of them was still approaching and the other had stopped and was raising a
rifle to his shoulder. The man on the ridge yanked upward on his reins trying to lift the horse into motion and
even before he heard the shot he felt the horse leap shud-
dering and its forelegs doubled under and he jumped
free as it collapsed forward and sideways on the slope. He
leaned down and jerked the rifle free and crouched behind the still quivering body of the horse and sent a single
shot crashing down towards the level and saw the two
men circle back to a safer distance and turn their horses
sideways towards him and dismount to stand behind them
with the barrels of rifles resting over the saddles.

He reached with one hand into the pocket of his old
shirt and with fumbling fingers counted the rifle bullets
there. He turned his head to study the slope rising be-

hind him. Bare rock climbed with scant crevices and small pockets of dirt where a few scraggly bushes clung. Fifty feet higher the slope leveled in a small ledge that had caught several large stones in age-gone descent. At intervals above were other small ledges. He looked back over the body of the horse and sent another shot crashing down and leaped up crouching and scrambled towards the first ledge above and a barrage of shots battered from the two men below and out and a bullet smashed into his left shoulder and spun him falling and he rolled back behind the body of the horse and hitched himself around to hold the rifle with his right hand over it. The sun beat clean and hot upon him and the two men below and out watched over their saddles and he lay quiet watching them.

Down and across the level expanse the lean man in the buckskin shirt stepped out from the doorway of the shelter and around the corner for a clear view of the ridge and the body of the horse, small at the distance yet distinct against the rock. His eyes narrowed as he peered intently and he made out the dull dirtied deadliness of the rifle barrel pointing over the body. He walked to the tall gray horse ground-reined in front of the shelter and took his rifle from its saddle scabbard. Quietly, paying no attention to the harnessing of the draft horses to the old wagon, he walked around the other side of the shelter and started back towards the ridge directly behind. He came on tracks, hoofprints in the loose dirt heading southwestward into distance towards the far lowering of the ridge. He stopped and looked down at these a long moment and moved on and came to the base of the ridge and climbed until he was almost parallel on it to the man behind the body of the horse not quite a half mile away. He lay flat on a slight leveling of the slope and adjusted the sights on his rifle and pushed the barrel out in front of him and settled into position and waited. Several shots came from the two men out on the level expanse and the man behind the body of the horse hunched himself forward and up to reply to them and the man in the buckskin shirt tightened his finger on his trigger in a slow steady squeeze. He saw the man behind the body of the horse jerk convulsively and try to rise and fall forward over the body of the horse and lie still. He saw the two men out on the level mount and start towards the ridge. Quietly he stood up and walked back towards the shelter.

The wagon was ready. Two of the saddled horses were tied behind it and a blanket had been rigged over the wagon body for shade. Under it lay the still forms of the man and the woman from inside the shelter. The little girl, small and shrinking and silent, sat on the seat between two of the other men.

"Take it easy but aimin' for time," the man in the buckskin shirt said. "Hit for the trace then towards town. Maybe the doc'll meet you part way."

The draft team, fresh and strong, leaned into the harness and the tugs tightened and the wagon moved away. The man in the buckskin shirt turned to watch the two men who had ridden to the ridge approach leading their horses. An old battered saddle and a bridle hung bouncing from the saddle horn of one of the horses. The body of a man, short and thick with a brass-studded cartridge belt around its waist, hung limply over the saddle of the other horse.

"Did you get it?" said the man in the buckskin shirt.

"Yes," said one of the men. "In the saddle bag there."

The man in the buckskin shirt stepped forward and

bent to slip a shoulder close against the saddle up under the body of the man in the brass-studded belt and lifted it away and went and heaved it over the saddle of the tall gray horse. He stepped into the shelter and came out carrying a spade in one hand. He took the reins of the tall gray horse with the other hand and led it away. Head low, staring at the ground before him, he led it, past the corral, across the almost dry stream bed, and stopped at last by the straggling row of stunted cottonwoods. He looked up. The other men had followed him.

"Don't be a fool," one of the other men said. "Drag him out somewheres and let the buzzards and coyotes have him. He wasn't no more'n an animal himself."

"No," the man in the buckskin shirt said. He looked back past the shelter, on into the vast empty distance where the trail of a tired horse led northeastward towards the far lowering of the ridge and returned. "He was a murderin' thievin' son-of-a-bitch. But he was a man." Quietly, bending to the hot task in the clean sun, the man in the buckskin shirt struck the spade into the red-brown earth.